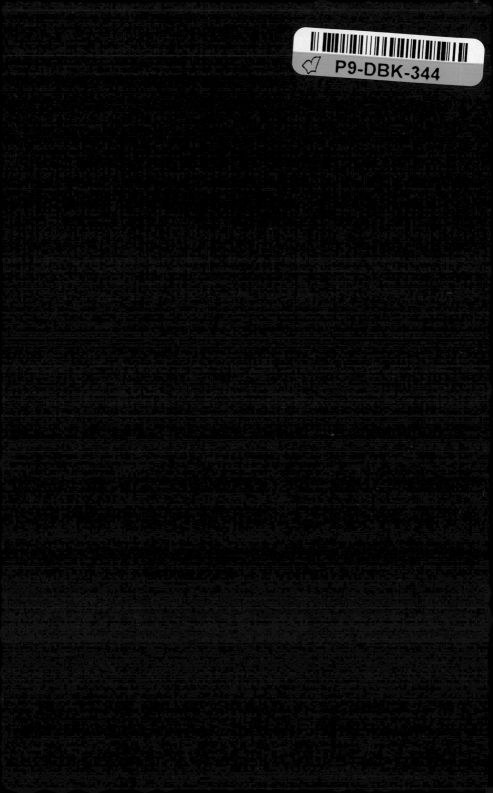

BRIAR GIRLS

Also by Rebecca Kim Wells

Shatter the Sky

Storm the Earth

BRIAR GIRLS

REBECCA KIM WELLS

SIMON & SCHUSTER BFYR

NEW YORK · LONDON · TORONTO · SYDNEY · NEW DELHI

SIMON & SCHUSTER BFYR

An imprint of Simon & Schuster Children's Publishing Division
1230 Avenue of the Americas, New York, New York 10020

This book is a work of fiction. Any references to historical events, real people,
or real places are used fictitiously. Other names, characters, places, and events
are products of the author's imagination, and any resemblance to actual
events or places or persons, living or dead, is entirely coincidental.

SIMON & SCHUSTER BOOKS FOR YOUNG READERS
and related marks are trademarks of Simon & Schuster, Inc.
For information about special discounts for bulk purchases, please contact
Simon & Schuster Special Sales at 1-866-506-1949 or business@simonandschuster.com.
The Simon & Schuster Speakers Bureau can bring authors to your live event.
For more information or to book an event, contact the Simon & Schuster Speakers Bureau
at 1-866-248-3049 or
visit our website at www.simonspeakers.com.
Interior design by Hilary Zarycky
The text for this book was set in Adobe Jensen Pro.
Manufactured in the United States of America
First Edition
2 4 6 8 10 9 7 5 3 1
CIP data for this book is available from the Library of Congress.
ISBN 9781534488427
ISBN 9781534488441 (ebook)

For myself, because I believed first—and longest

CHAPTER ONE

Cold wind bit at my cheeks, bearing the scent of fallen leaves in decay. I ducked my head and hunched my shoulders as I trudged along a path overgrown with wild grass, my feet aching with each step. My skin was chafing where my pack rested against the small of my back, and my boots pinched. We'd been walking for weeks—long enough for my resolve to wear thin, for my stomach to clench into an angry pit of hunger. Though we'd rationed the little food we'd brought with us, our provisions had run out yesterday morning.

Father looked over his shoulder, as if he sensed my dour mood. "We're almost there," he said.

I didn't bother to reply. Instead, I pulled my scarf up over my chin as he turned and strode ahead of me through an empty field, his walking stick striking a steady beat upon the ground. He had been promising *almost there* for days now, as though our destination were something to look forward to. As though we hadn't been forced to flee our last home because of what I'd done.

I supposed that an end to our journey *was* something to celebrate. We'd managed to outrun any rumors chasing us and avoid the notice of keepers of the peace. And most importantly, there were no signs that the witch had caught our scent. Still, part of me had welcomed the discomfort I'd endured during this flight. I deserved this pain. And at least my aching feet and empty stomach kept my thoughts from other, darker things. I didn't know what I would do when the distraction went away.

In front of me, Father stopped walking. "Look, Lena."

I lifted my gaze from the ground. We'd crested a small hill, and a valley lush with greenery lay before us, a huddle of houses at its base. There was a lake to the north that fed a stream running south through the village. And to the east, on the other side of the houses, was the Silence—a forest of trees so dense and dark they looked almost blue.

A prickling sensation skittered down my spine as I stared out at the trees. Even from a distance there was something unsettling about them. I couldn't shake the feeling that somehow they were watching me, too.

"What do you think is in there?" I asked.

Father shook his head. "We're to keep people from going into the Silence. It's not our duty to speculate on what might reside within."

"But shouldn't someone investigate—"

"No," he said sharply. "The Onwey council sent very clear instructions. The Silence is deadly. No one who walks into those trees ever comes out again. You're not to go near it, Lena."

He started down the hill without waiting for my reply, leaving me no choice but to fall in line. It didn't matter that I thought there had to be more to the Silence than what we'd been told. My father wouldn't listen to me, and I had long ago learned it wasn't worth challenging him—not on things like this.

The wind picked up, and I shivered, stuffing my gloved hands into my pockets. Maybe Father was right—maybe it didn't matter what was in the Silence. He would have taken the job no matter what risks it entailed. Anything to get us away from—*screams, the stench of blackened, burning skin*—

Don't think about that. I shook my head, as if I could shake the memory away. It was over. I was safe. I took a deep breath and followed my father down the hill.

The village houses were arranged in rough curves that gathered around a central square. It would have seemed quaint, were it not for the gloom that permeated the air. The streets were silent and empty, despite it being only midafternoon. Doors and windows were shuttered. The only sign of life was a thin plume of smoke rising from the chimney of a large building on the south side of the square, so we headed in that direction. The faded sign hanging above one window told us it was a tavern—the Midnight Song.

"Gloves?" Father asked, pausing on the stoop.

I held up my hands in answer. We were lucky to be traveling in autumn—no one would look askance at someone wearing gloves, even indoors.

He nodded curtly and pushed open the door.

My shoulders tensed as I stepped over the threshold, and I tucked my elbows in, trying to make myself as small as possible. But there were no drunken patrons veering clumsily in our direction, nor jovial groups brushing past us on their way out. In fact, it seemed unusually quiet. Only a few people bothered to look up from their glasses to take note of Father and me. I tried to force myself to relax.

As we moved farther into the tavern, my gaze fell on a small cluster of people on the other side of the room. At the center of the cluster was a single chair, which held a man with flushed cheeks and disheveled hair. His limbs were restrained by leather straps even though he was perfectly motionless, his head lolling to one side as though unsupported by his spine.

A charred corpse on the ground, unmoving—

Suddenly the man thrashed against his restraints, dragging me back to the present.

I drew a great, shuddering breath. *That's all in the past. This man is different. He's alive.* As if he could hear my thoughts, the man opened his mouth and began to sing in an eerie cadence that raised the hairs on the back of my neck and clawed against my skin.

"Down below the briars and the vines, let me down, until roses come to claim me, set me free, let me down . . ."

What was wrong with him? I glanced over at Father. His face was grim as he watched the man sing.

"Can I help you?" a woman's voice called out, cutting through the song like a knife.

Father and I turned to see an older woman with neat gray hair standing behind the bar, eyeing us suspiciously.

Father cleared his throat. "Yes. I'm Joren, the new watcher. This is my daughter, Lena." He nudged me with an elbow. I raised my hand in greeting, trying to avoid meeting the woman's eyes. "But it seems we've arrived at an inopportune moment."

She sighed, her expression turning resigned. "We were expecting you tomorrow, but you may as well stay. I'm Olinta, one of the council members."

The man in the chair thrashed harder, catching my attention once more. His song had dissolved into incoherent mutters, and as I watched, he began to weep.

"What's wrong with him?" The words burst out of me, unbidden and louder than I'd intended.

All eyes turned toward me. I felt my cheeks grow warm and saw Father's jaw tighten before I looked down at my feet. I shouldn't have said anything—Father would have the answers soon enough. There was no need to call attention to myself.

"Melor has been infected by the Silence, child. There's no hope for him now," Olinta replied.

I dared another glance at the man—Melor. A slight woman approached him now, a bowl of water in her hand. She dabbed at his brow with a cloth, then looked up at the others in the room. "It's time," she said.

The men standing next to her moved woodenly as they loosened the straps that held Melor down, then grabbed his arms and pulled him upright. He struggled and began to scream, and I stepped quickly aside as the men wrestled him toward the tavern door.

The unnerving cries cut through the air even after the door closed behind them. But those who remained in the tavern made no move to follow Melor and his escorts. Instead, a quiet hum of conversation picked up as they returned to their tables and plates of food. I looked around the room, surprised. Was it so easy for the residents of Onwey to ignore the sounds of such suffering?

"I'm sorry you had to see that, but it *is* the reason you are here," Olinta said, addressing Father as she came out from behind the bar. "Would you mind stepping outside with me?"

Father moved to follow her but put out a hand to stop me as I started after him. He leaned in, whispering in my ear. "Go talk to someone."

"What?" All my life he'd taught me to avoid close contact with others—why was he reversing course now?

"You're new here. It's only natural that you would be curious. That's what they expect. Be careful and you'll be fine."

And then he followed Olinta outside, leaving me standing by myself.

I wanted to press my back against the wall and will myself into invisibility. My palms were sweating inside my gloves. But Father was right—it was imperative that I appear as normal as possible. The illusion of normalcy might be the only thing that would save me if anyone ever came searching for us here.

Most of the people in the tavern looked at least as old as my father, but there was a group of three around my age sitting at a table in the corner. I took a deep breath, steeling myself. Then I walked over to them, stopping a safe distance away.

It was a few moments before they noticed me. "Come closer," said a girl with kind brown eyes and long dark hair. "We don't bite."

Ah, but I did.

I took a tiny step forward. "Hello," I said, trying not to let my voice quiver.

The dark-haired girl smiled at me. "That's quite a cloak you have."

I couldn't tell whether she was teasing or sincere. Years ago the cloak had belonged to my mother, and as such it was too long on me, falling almost to the ground. It had been mended over so many times that it was difficult to tell it had once been brown; now it was a patchwork of colors snatched from whatever scraps of cloth were handy.

"Thank you," I said uncertainly.

"You must be with the new watcher," said one of the others, a boy with a contemplative air about him.

They must have seen us arrive. "He's my father," I said. "I'm Lena."

"I'm Wren," said the first girl. She nodded to her companions in turn. "That's Jasper, and this is my sibling Corina."

Corina had the same dark hair as Wren, though it was cut shorter. They looked a little younger than their sister—or maybe that was because of the way they were nervously interlacing their fingers again and again.

"So, Lena," Jasper said, "where are you from?"

I shrugged. "Lots of places. Minos, for a few years." It wasn't quite a lie. We had lived in Minos, though not recently. But I couldn't risk naming a city tainted by my curse.

"*Minos*," Wren said, her eyes gleaming with interest. "What's it like, living in a city like that? You must know so many people!"

"Fewer than you'd think," I replied. I'd spent most of my time indoors or in our garden, hidden away. But there had still been things to love about the cities I'd seen only from a safe distance— the different foods Father had brought home, the books from the city libraries, the people from so many places I'd made a habit of watching from my window . . .

Now all that was gone, traded away for this beleaguered village and its wan and weary inhabitants.

I blinked and realized they were watching me—waiting for me to say something more. "It was fine," I said. "Crowded. Too noisy sometimes."

Wren sighed. "Sounds wonderful."

"I . . . suppose you don't get many visitors here?"

Jasper snorted with contemptuous laughter. "Do you think anyone's yearning to visit Onwey when we have *that* hanging over our heads every day?" He tipped his head in the direction of the door.

I smoothed the edges of my gloves, making sure my skin was completely covered. "I thought the Silence took people. But he's . . ."

"Still here?" Wren said.

I nodded.

"People don't just walk into the forest by accident. Something calls to them if they get too close. *Bewitches* them."

"And they just go?"

Wren and Jasper nodded in unison.

"You saw Melor. They caught him before he crossed the border into the forest, but he's not *there* anymore," Jasper said, tapping a finger to his temple for emphasis.

I glanced back at the chair that Melor had been strapped to. "Will he recover?"

Corina shook their head. "He's gone," they said, their voice cracking. They stood up from the table without another word. I shied away as they ran past me and out of the tavern.

I looked at Wren, who bit her lip. "Corina was sweet on him," she said.

"Well, there's no cure for what ails him now," Jasper said. "Once a person's bewitched, they rave about the Silence until they can't speak anymore. They stop eating and drinking—eventually they die. That, or find their way into the forest, never to be seen again."

Jasper's flat tone took me aback almost as much as his words. Dead? And these would be his last days, strapped down and delirious as his loved ones watched him waste away?

"So where did the men take him?" I said.

Jasper and Wren glanced at each other. "Sometimes the families elect to let them go into the Silence," Wren offered. "But Melor's family has chosen to . . ."

"Put him out of his misery," Jasper finished.

"You mean *kill* him?" My voice cracked. If this was what happened to *victims* of ensorcellment, what might they do to me, if they found out what I was capable of?

"He's already as good as dead," Jasper said. "It's better this way."

Wren grimaced but didn't argue.

A shiver ran down my spine. It was a horrific choice. Now that I was beginning to understand the extent to which the Silence preyed upon this village, it was shocking to me that anyone still lived here. "Has it always been like this?"

Wren shook her head. "The Silence has always been unearthly, but my grandmother said people used to go inside safely. She doesn't remember exactly when it changed, but I think something happened—turned it vicious."

"The *forest* itself does this?" What could a forest possibly want with befuddled humans? How could a forest possibly want *anything*?

Jasper shrugged. "No one who goes in ever comes out, so who knows?"

I took a breath to ask another question but was stopped by an inconsolable wail that rattled me to the core. That sound—*his piercing scream*—

"I—I have to go," I stammered, backing away from the table.

"Don't," Wren said. "It's better not to see."

But the roaring in my ears told me I had to flee—for anything

9

was better than letting my legs fold beneath me here, where they might jump up to help. Might reach out and—

I turned and ran.

I yanked the tavern door open and stumbled outside. The sudden light was blinding, and I threw up a hand to block it as I crossed the square and saw the men from the tavern, solemn and still; my father, his hands clasped behind his back; a wailing woman, on her knees beside—the body.

From this vantage point I couldn't tell how they had killed him, only that it had been bloody. It was everywhere, on the stones, on their shirts, their hands. And I could smell it now, the warm, metallic tang causing my throat to seize. They'd killed him, they'd truly killed him, it had been a *slaughter*, and they would do the same to me—

The roaring in my ears returned, and I sank to the ground. I was sweating despite the cold, and my heart raced—there was the stench of burning skin again, the stench I'd tried so hard to wash off—

"Lena!" Father's voice came from far away as my vision blurred.

Flames crawling up the boy's skin but I cannot help him. The falling rain does nothing, he is already dead—

Hands under my arms lifted me up. I leaned against Father as he put an arm around my waist, taking my weight and leading me away from the grisly scene.

"You're all right," he murmured under his breath. "You're all right, it's going to be all right."

But I didn't see how it could. Not here and not anywhere, not after what I had done. And there was nothing he could say that would make it so.

CHAPTER TWO

The watcher's outpost was a rickety two-story house that sat right up against the edge of the field between Onwey and the Silence, a lone sentry facing the darkness. It had stood vacant since the last watcher had departed, though Olinta had not said whether they'd moved on to a better opportunity, or whether they, too, had fallen victim to the forest.

I waited numbly as Father turned the key in the lock and shouldered open the door, revealing a cramped hallway with dark rooms and a staircase beyond. We shuffled inside and set down our packs. Father walked quickly through the first floor, lighting the lamps. I lingered in the hallway, my feet as heavy as lead. Having reached our destination, it suddenly felt impossible to take another step.

"Come here," Father called.

I dragged myself after his voice and found him in the kitchen.

"Sit," he said, nodding to a chair. I sank down upon it as he turned to light the fire. Some minutes of rummaging later, he pressed a steaming mug of tea into my hands. I clasped it like a lifeline, letting the heat sink into my skin.

Father unpacked a basket of provisions Olinta had given him. The villagers had provided a veritable feast—there was a cut of venison and a jar of pickled cabbage, along with a mess of carrots, potatoes, and onions. Wrapped in a dishcloth was a fresh loaf of crusty bread with two small pots of butter and jam. Without saying a word, he cut and buttered three slices, and passed them to me.

I ate mechanically, swallowing the food without tasting it. Before arriving in Onwey I had been famished, I remembered. But now all I could think of was how these people had chosen to *kill* a man because of something out of his control.

"Why did we come here?" I said at last.

Father looked at me somberly. "You know why."

His words stung—but my fear won out over my guilt. "We could have gone somewhere else. *Anywhere* else. But you chose this place. These people will always be on the lookout for anything out of the ordinary. What if someone discovers what I am?"

"I know it's not ideal—"

"I don't see how it could be any *less* ideal!"

"What's done is done," he said sharply. "I have always kept you safe, and I will continue to do so."

"But Melor—"

"*Enough*," Father barked. "I won't be harangued about this when *your* carelessness is the reason we're here at all."

I rocked back in my seat, stunned. For a moment I stared at him. Then, to my horror, I burst into tears.

His face fell. "Lena, I didn't mean—" he began.

I didn't wait for him to finish. I jumped up and ran from the kitchen to the hallway and up the stairs.

An open door at the top of the staircase led me into a small bedroom. I closed the door and leaned back against it, clenching my fists.

Your carelessness is the reason we're here. Did he truly think I didn't know that? That what had happened did not haunt me every hour of every day?

The worst part—the worst part was that he was right. If I'd only been more careful, perhaps we *would* still be in that little house with its garden of flowers I'd loved so much.

I took a deep breath, trying to reach for composure. I *would* be more careful. And perhaps we could make a new home here, too. The house was rickety, yes—but if we swept the floors clean, threw open the windows, turned up the lamps . . .

And yet, the image of Melor's lifeless body flashed before my eyes, raising more doubts about how long this new refuge would last.

A soft meow broke the silence, and I looked up to see a small gray cat poke its head out from under the bed.

I peeled off my gloves and knelt down. "Hello," I said softly, holding out a hand.

The cat studied me, unblinking. Then, after a moment, it sauntered out from under the bed and butted its head against my fingers.

I swallowed down my tears as I scratched behind the cat's ears. I'd begged for a pet when I was younger, as animals were unaffected by my curse. I'd even gone as far as feeding a stray dog in Minos for several weeks before Father found out. But he'd insisted that keeping an animal would make us more identifiable, not to mention being a liability every time we moved. Never mind that a pet would have offered me some small companionship—he'd made up his mind, and that was that.

"Where did you come from?" I asked. The cat didn't answer, only lay down on the floor and presented its belly for further petting, purring as it did so.

I heard the creak of footsteps on the stairs, followed by a soft knock at the door. "I'm sorry for snapping at you," Father said, his voice slightly muffled. "Will you come downstairs? Supper's ready."

After a moment I heard him retreat down the stairs. I briefly entertained the idea of staying put. But my stomach was growling again. And besides, I couldn't keep this anger burning forever. Father and I—we only had each other.

I sighed and stood—against the cat's protests—and opened the door.

We sat with our plates on the stoop of our new house, watching the sun set over the Silence.

"Do you think what they did to Melor was right?" I asked after a while. "Can it be so much better to die than to go into the forest?"

Father sighed. "I think . . . that some things are worse than death. And that they are doing the best they can under terrible circumstances."

I stared out at the trees. Though there was still light in the sky, the forest was a deep well of darkness. What was it like for the villagers, to live so close to something that might easily be their doom?

"Why hasn't the village done something more? One of the girls at the tavern said the Silence wasn't always this way. So maybe it could be fixed?"

"Some things are too powerful to be changed by human means. This is one of them."

I wondered at his certainty. Until we'd come to the Silence, we'd never before encountered anything to rival my own uncanniness. So how could he know there was nothing to be done but walk the border of the forest and try to save those who would fall into its trap?

Before I could organize my thoughts into a coherent question, Father rested a hand lightly on my shoulder. "You'll stay here tomorrow while I take a look at the forest boundary. I need you to be careful and keep to the house. Perhaps you can make it presentable while I'm out." He paused, and then added, "Good night, my girl."

He rose to his feet and took the plates in, leaving me alone on the stoop.

I pulled my legs up against my chest and rested my chin upon my knees. I'd always known that I was different. I still remembered the first time I had cried to my mother, asking why I couldn't play with the other children, why my parents discouraged me from going outside at all. And then there was the night they had sat down with me and, for the first time, explained the curse. I'd been six years old, and Father had told it like a fairy tale—like it was something happening to the heroine of some grand story. For a while I thought that the curse made me special, somehow. That I only needed to figure out how to break it, and my life would become marvelous.

I hadn't believed that in a long, long time.

Still, even with the curse, it hadn't always been so grim between Father and me. Back when we'd had Mother, we'd at least been happy. I remembered Father laughing, even playful. But it was like the life and mirth had drained from him when she'd left us. The transformation had taken place almost overnight—he'd turned dour and humorless, his only prerogative keeping me safe.

If only safety didn't feel quite so much like captivity.

I tried not to resent my father. I knew he regretted his role in my being cursed. But regret changed nothing about the outcome. We'd managed to evade the witch for many years, but deep down,

I knew that one day she would find me. Until then, my curse was an unceasing reminder of what I owed—what my parents had bargained away.

I barely slept that night, the memory of Melor's screams echoing through my dreams. I tossed and turned in the unfamiliar bed, waking to find my cheeks wet with tears. I was glad Father wasn't much of a conversationalist at breakfast the next morning, as it was all I could do to keep my eyes open.

Once Father left to meet with the council, I opened every door and swept out every room, hanging dried sprigs of lavender I'd found in the pantry. For lunch I heated the remains of last night's supper over the fire, and although it filled my belly, nothing could alleviate the chill that had settled in my bones the moment I'd seen Melor in the tavern.

Father had said there was nothing to be done about the Silence—that there was no escape from the trap in which Onwey was caught. But what the villagers had chosen instead was horrific in its own right. Could the Silence truly be more evil than that?

I was supposed to stay inside. But there wasn't much else for me to do indoors. Besides, this was no bustling city with people around every street corner. Before I could second-guess myself, I grabbed my cloak and boots and pulled on my gloves. I let myself out of the house and walked toward the Silence, scuffing my boots through the grass.

Up close, the Silence was no less foreboding. Its trees were so tall I had to crane my neck to see their tops. Their branches tangled and interlocked, blocking out the light. I felt an all-encompassing sense of stillness. The Silence was not dead—it was waiting. Watching.

The villagers believed the Silence so terrible that they would rather kill their own than allow them to be taken. But I, too, was dangerous. I, too, was deadly. And that made the two of us alike, in a strange, misshapen way. Was the Silence like me—cursed, somehow?

I stared into its darkness . . . and the darkness within me unfurled, pulling me forward.

I took a step—then caught myself, trembling.

Was this what is was like, to be called?

No. Yesterday Jasper had described something like delirium. And I was not delirious.

But there was *something* about this forest that called to me nevertheless.

"Lena!"

I gasped. Could it be—?

"Lena!" I turned to see Wren running toward me. I suddenly felt foolish. Of course the Silence hadn't called my name.

Wren slowed to a stop, then bent over, gasping for air. I didn't know what to do with my hands. I settled for clasping them behind my back. "Hello," I said cautiously.

She straightened. "You're all right," she said, her cheeks flushed. "The Silence hasn't gotten you."

My brow furrowed. "Of course not, why would you—" *Oh.* No one would choose to come so close to the forest, so naturally she had thought I'd been infected when she saw me standing almost below the trees. And now I had to give a reasonable explanation for what I had been doing. "No. I was just helping my father."

An uncomfortable silence stretched between us. "Thank you for your concern," I continued belatedly.

Wren smiled nervously. "You're welcome. But come away from

there, won't you?" We walked back toward the village as Wren went on. "I was coming to call on you anyway. I saw you with your father yesterday, after . . . Well, it must have been quite a shock. I wanted to make sure you were all right."

Warmth bloomed in my chest. She'd been concerned for me? "Thank you. You're right—it was a shock."

She nodded. "I know. I'm sorry."

"Why do people still live here?" I asked, unable to contain the question. "This all just seems . . . horrible."

"It is," Wren agreed. "And many people do leave. But Onwey is still home. And some of us still have hope that someday things will change." Her face brightened a little. "I'm meeting a few friends in the tavern. Join us?"

She reached toward me—*no, wait*—and I flinched, stepping back. Hurt flashed across her face.

"I—I'm sorry," I stammered. "I can't."

I turned and walked—almost ran—back to the house. Father had been right, after all. No matter how careful I was, it wouldn't be careful enough. The only way to keep everyone completely safe was to keep myself away from them.

Three days passed as Father set himself to planning a strategy for guarding the Silence. Parchment papers covered in sketches piled up on the kitchen table, depicting everything from some sort of trip wire hidden in the field to a scribble that might have been a bonfire, though now that I'd caught a glimpse of what we were facing, I had my doubts that anything he came up with would be enough.

In the meantime I cooked and cleaned—anything to keep my mind occupied. The gray cat came and went, and I was grateful for its company. But nothing could save me from my thoughts when I lay down to sleep. Even after everything that had happened, I'd been incautious. I'd put Wren in danger. I had to be better—but was this to be the entirety of my future? Constantly vigilant, constantly afraid?

What would I even say, when I saw Wren again? I didn't know how to answer her if she asked why I had run.

Because I'm a monster. Because I've killed. Twice.

The first time it had happened my mother had clasped my hands tightly between her own and whispered, *No. The curse killed that boy. The* witch *killed him, not you.*

But I'd been cursed my entire life. Sometimes I felt that the curse and I were one and the same. And my mother? She must secretly have thought me monstrous—why else had she finally chosen to abandon us?

I sat up and went to the window, looking out at the stars hanging low over the Silence. My life had always been bound by constraints—*don't go outside, Lena, don't touch them, don't forget your gloves, don't, don't, don't*—and I'd learned to live with them. Learned to make myself small. Shut away any desire for anything beyond the cage of my own body, and resigned myself to a life spent always looking over my shoulder.

But being here, seeing the Silence—something had broken open within me. It frightened me . . . but also, it made me feel alive. And I hadn't felt like that in a very long time.

I still wanted, I realized. To touch, to kiss, to love, to simply move freely through the world without fear of hurting someone. But I knew there was no hope of such a life for me. So what was worse? To shrivel into a husk of a person waiting for a witch, or to seek out the darkness myself? Even if on the other side lay things more dangerous than me, even if the forest never gave me back, at least I would have had one reckless taste of freedom.

My resolve strengthening, I dressed quietly and slipped out of the house, then made my way across the field to the Silence.

At night the Silence was as black as the open jaws of a beast, ready to snap shut on any who took a wrong step. And oh, tonight I wouldn't have minded being devoured.

There was no sign of a path into the forest. There were only the trees that flowed on and on until I could see no farther, and their impossible stillness.

I took a defiant step forward. My father's warnings echoed through my mind. But the earth on the other side of this tree looked no different from that beneath my own feet.

I took off a glove, my heart pounding. The cold nipped at my skin, and I welcomed it. I flexed my fingers and reached forward, pressing my palm against the cool, rough bark.

There. I'd done it. And I was still here.

Feverish energy flooded my limbs, whispering that I could do more, go further. I grinned and looked out into the forest.

There was movement, a change so slight it could have been the rustle of wind through the trees. I froze, waiting, listening. In the darkness it was difficult to see. Panic clawed at my throat as I stepped back slowly, searching my surroundings. *Tree. Grass. Rock—*

Human.

CHAPTER THREE

I screamed and jumped back, jamming my hand hastily into my glove. The figure leaned against a tree not fifteen paces away—and then stepped toward me, their movements sluggish and shaky. Had they been wounded? Or was this a symptom of the Silence bewitching them?

"Stay back!" I cried, but the figure kept coming. Terror ran quick through my veins as the stranger moved into the moonlight and was revealed to be a tall girl, her tangled hair dark in the night.

"Please—help me," she said desperately, stumbling forward.

I reined in the urge to flee, though fear still leapt at me like a vicious dog. This girl had come from within the depths of the Silence—something the villagers claimed had never happened.

"Who are you? How did you get out?" I said.

Instead of answering, the girl staggered and dropped to her knees mere steps from where I stood.

All this could be a trap, a ruse to make me let down my guard. If the girl was an agent of the witch, I should run. If she was truly injured, if whatever had hurt her was still out there in the dark . . . I looked up, but the Silence was as still as it had ever been. Except for the girl, who was listing to one side. My skin was clammy with sweat. Run. I should run *now*.

"Please," the girl begged again, and I knew I couldn't leave her. I was the only one here.

But what if I touched her and—*his scream*—

The girl moaned with pain and began to pitch toward the ground. Without thinking, I darted forward and caught her under the arms as she fell unconscious.

She was heavier than I would have guessed, and my breath grew short as I strained to pull her away from the forest. Looking back, I saw a dark smear on the ground where she had fallen. Blood.

I swallowed hard. Someone *had* hurt her, and that someone, or some*thing*, was still out there.

Suddenly even the air I breathed felt sinister, but I could do nothing except try to move faster. The muscles in my arms ached as I dragged the girl out of the Silence. When her boots were clear of the last grasping tree root, I flopped to the ground, gulping in deep breaths.

A lantern loomed out of the night, and I scrambled to my feet, raising a hand against the glare. Who—

"*Lena!*"

Father. Relief flooded me—Father would know what to do.

He lowered the lantern, and as my eyes adjusted I saw that he was still wearing his nightclothes. He'd run out of the house without even grabbing his coat.

"What happened? Are you all right?" he said urgently, searching my face.

"I'm fine," I said. "But this girl came out of the Silence!"

"What?" Whatever he'd been expecting me to say, this wasn't it. He looked down and seemed to notice her for the first time. "She came out of the Silence? You're certain?"

I nodded. "And she's hurt." I hugged my arms to my sides, waiting for him to take charge. But he did not. Instead he just stood there, expression impassive, and made no move to touch the girl.

"Father, she needs help!" I said impatiently.

"Quiet," he said harshly. I closed my mouth.

Finally he stepped toward her, cautiously using his foot to nudge her shoulder. There was no response—but her chest still rose and fell. She was alive.

In the lantern light, I noticed that a trickle of blood had dried into a thin line beneath the girl's nose. Her garb was plain and muddied, but as I looked closer, I realized that beneath the dirt, the fabric of her shirt was finer than any I'd ever seen. Father passed me the lantern, then knelt down and rifled through her clothing. He soon uncovered something else I'd been too hurried to notice—a tear in the leg of the girl's trousers, through which I could see a bloody mess of a wound. He whistled one low, sharp note, and sat back on his heels.

"All right. I'll carry her—you run ahead. Put water on to boil and find some clean rags. And, Lena—keep your gloves on."

He gathered the girl in his arms, then pushed himself to his feet, grunting with the effort. I wavered for a moment.

"Lena—go!"

I ran.

By the time Father came through the door I'd added wood to the fire and poured water into a pot to heat. Rags were harder to come by—I rummaged through the kitchen cabinets and an upstairs closet before surfacing with a few old towels.

Father went to the spare room on the first floor, which must have been a study for a previous inhabitant, as there was a desk and chair, as well as a couch. He set the girl down on the couch and removed her boots, his movements ruthlessly efficient. I hovered uncertainly in the doorway, towels in hand.

"Is the water ready?" he said, turning toward me.

"Almost."

"Good. Go get the sewing kit—and see if there's any edrik's leaf in the kitchen."

I left the towels on the desk and hurried out again. When added to food, edrik's leaf gave a light citrusy taste, but it was also used for warding off infection in open wounds. We were in luck—there was a small jar of it on a shelf in the pantry. I shook several leaves into a bowl of cold water, then ran upstairs to retrieve the sewing kit. The pot was boiling when I came back down, so I took it off the fire. I brought the edrik's leaf, the water, and the kit back into the study and set them down next to the couch. Father had lit the lamps while I was gone, and the room was cast in a yellow glow.

"Stand back," Father warned.

He took the sewing scissors and cut a slit up the side of the girl's trousers. The fabric stuck, and he had to tease it gently away from her skin. He took one of the towels and dipped it into the hot water, then pressed it gently against her leg, blotting it clean. The girl shifted but did not wake. And as the blood came away, I saw bite marks.

"What could have done that?"

"A wolf, perhaps," Father said, studying the wound. "I'll have to stitch this shut. Lena, come hold up a lamp."

I did as he said as he threaded a needle and began stitching the deepest of the girl's wounds shut.

My stomach began to roil at the sight, so I tried to focus on her face rather than what Father was doing. Her skin was pale in the lamplight, and her features were delicate, with a thin nose and full, dark lashes. Her hair—a deep, dark wine red—spread wildly across the cushions. She was *beautiful*. The sort of beautiful that people painted into portraits.

Having finished with the stitches, Father packed the wound with edrik's leaf and wrapped a towel around the girl's leg. When he was done, he got a blanket from one of the bedrooms and laid it over her. Then he gathered our supplies and ushered me out into the hall, closing the door behind him.

"What now?" I asked.

He let out his breath in a sigh. "We wait and see if she wakes up. And in the meantime, you are not to go into that room."

"What about the council? What if she's a villager?"

"She's not."

"But shouldn't they be notified? They must know things about the Silence that we don't. And if there's a wolf out there—"

"Lena, let it *be*. This girl is not a villager, and it would be unwise to tell the council about this before we have a handle on what is going on."

I stared at him. "How do you know that?"

"Know what?" he said, exasperated.

"That she's not a villager."

"Her clothing. It's not from these parts. Maybe she's just passing through. She's lost a lot of blood. No use in alarming them about her presence if she . . ."

The word *dies* hung in the air, unsaid, as his gaze slid away from mine. I stared at him, my chest tightening. Had he just lied to me?

Father cleared his throat. "It's late. You should get some rest.

But don't think I've forgotten that you were out of the house when you weren't supposed to be. We'll discuss it tomorrow."

His tone made it clear that the conversation was over. So I turned reluctantly and went upstairs.

If the girl wasn't from Onwey, then where had she come from? Father had suggested she might be a traveler, passing through—but I had seen her emerge from *within* the Silence. And unlike Melor, she hadn't seemed bewitched.

Once again I found myself unable to sleep, though now all of my previous worries had been pushed aside by the mystery of this girl, and the Silence—and what my father could possibly be hiding.

I thought I was the first to rise in the morning, my curiosity making me restless and impatient. But when I dressed and went downstairs, I heard muffled voices coming from the other side of the study door.

I put my hand on the doorknob, then hesitated. If I went in, Father would surely find a reason to send me out again. So instead I pressed my ear to the door, holding my breath as I strained to make out their conversation.

Father was speaking. "But you must know—" I couldn't catch the rest of his words.

"I don't," replied a firm voice, pitched low. "If that's the only reason you helped me, then I'm afraid I must disappoint you. And I'll take my leave as soon as I'm able."

"At least tell me this: Who rules the Gather?"

What was the Gather? I'd never heard of a place by that name before, nor seen it on any of Father's maps.

There was a pause. "If you know of the Gather, you know I should not say his name."

"We are in the Mundane," Father said impatiently. "Shale's magic does not stretch so far."

I drew in a sharp, surprised breath. Had he just said *magic*? So he *was* keeping secrets from me.

"And what do *you* know that makes you so certain of that?" the girl replied.

I held still, waiting for Father to answer. Instead he asked, "What about his daughter?"

"She rules by his side, as always," she said. "There, I've answered your questions. Do we have an accord?"

"Yes. Two days," Father replied. "Then you must go. I cannot have you raising suspicions. And do not speak with my daughter while you are here."

There was a slight, musical peal of laughter that danced across my skin. "Do not worry, Watcher. I am as eager to be rid of you as you are of me."

A floorboard creaked, and I realized too late that Father was moving. I stumbled back as the door opened. Alarm flashed across his face. "Lena, what are you doing?"

"I heard voices," I said. "She's awake?"

I tried to look past him, but the curtains were closed and the lamps unlit—I could see nothing.

Father stepped out into the hall and shut the door firmly behind him. To my surprise, I watched him produce a key and turn it in the lock before looking back at me. "She's improving, but still needs rest," he said, his expression more composed. "She will stay here for two days, and then she will be on her way."

"That's all?" I looked up at him. I'd known him all my life, but in this instant, he seemed almost like a stranger.

"That's all," he said, drawing me toward the kitchen.

I pulled away from him. "What is the Gather? And who is Shale?" I asked.

His face darkened. "That has nothing to do with you. You should not have been listening. And you're to stay away from this room until that girl leaves."

"Why can't I help? I helped you care for her last night."

His jaw tightened. "And last night you also showed that you cannot be trusted. You were out of the house when I specifically told you to stay here."

"But—"

"Do you think these rules are for my own amusement, Lena? Need I remind you why we are here in the first place? What you risk every time you disobey me?"

I flinched.

"You will not go into that room. You will not speak to the girl. You will not speak of anything that you overheard again. That is final."

His mouth in a thin line, he turned and walked away, leaving me shaking in the hallway.

My own anger rose up within me, overwhelming the sting of his words. He'd been needlessly cruel, and I was sure he'd done it to avoid answering me. And the lies he'd just told me—my father was strict, but he'd always been honest with me . . . hadn't he?

I wasn't a child anymore. I deserved the truth. And if he wouldn't tell me, perhaps there was someone who would.

CHAPTER FOUR

I wasted precious minutes searching for the key once Father left the house for his rounds, before realizing that of course he would have taken it with him. For a brief moment, I considered giving up. Even if I could get in, the girl might not talk to me. And even if she did, whatever I learned from her might only serve to torture me in the endless days to come, gloves over hands, alone except for Father, little more than a captive in this house—

No. The Silence had woken something in me. I would no longer be held down, boxed in, told *no*, and *don't*, and *you can't*. There was a larger world out there that my father had been keeping from me. I would not rest until I knew it.

If the door was locked . . . then I would go in through the window. I tugged my gloves up before going outside and around the house. I took a deep breath, bolstering my resolve. Then I exhaled as I prized open the window, pulled myself up over the sill, and tumbled into the room, landing with a thump on the floor.

"Who are you?"

I looked up. The girl was still lying on the couch, but she'd propped herself up on one elbow to study me. In the morning light, her hair was even more striking. I would never have mistaken her as a villager by day. Aside from her garb, her coloring was much closer to the people of the Northern Isles than anyone I had met in Onwey.

"I'm—I'm not here to hurt you," I stammered, pushing myself to my feet. "I just wanted to meet you."

"You must be the daughter," she said, looking me up and down with quizzical gray eyes. Having seemingly determined that I was not an imminent threat, she relaxed, leaning back upon a pillow set against the arm of the couch. "Your father is very protective of you."

I couldn't disagree with that.

"In fact," she continued, "he told me that if I valued my life, we must not speak. And that got me to wondering, what is so special about you? Is he frightened that I might seduce an innocent girl?" She quirked an eyebrow at me.

Nervous laughter rippled from my throat. I was shocked that she would be so blunt—although I couldn't deny that I was drawn to her, and not only because of the answers she might hold.

Even so, I didn't know how to respond. Instead I pressed on. "I want to know about the Gather."

She snorted. "Then talk to your father. He's been there before."

"That's not true." My counter was automatic, but even as I spoke, I doubted myself.

"Oh? He certainly isn't from the Mundane. He was born on the other side of the Silence. Like me."

I leaned back against the wall, trying to steady myself. Trying not to show how much her words had shaken me. "What do you mean? What's the Mundane?"

She shook her head. "Ask him yourself. *I'm* trying to keep out of trouble." But there was still a glimmer of mischief in her eyes . . . as though she was daring me to keep going.

"He won't tell me," I said.

"Then he certainly doesn't want *me* to."

But she was speaking to me nonetheless. If she really meant to hold to my father's decree, she would have shut her mouth the moment I confirmed my identity. I smiled, feeling emboldened. "He doesn't need to know."

A smile tugged at the corner of her mouth. She pushed herself up into a seated position. "You want answers? I'll tell you—but only if you tell me why your father went to such lengths to keep us apart."

I bit my lip. *Don't ever tell.* That was what my parents had instilled in me from the moment I could understand what the curse was.

But this was different. Wasn't it? This girl was no keeper of the peace, trying to coax a confession out of me. No avenging sister, come to kill me for what I'd done. Still, I wavered.

"You first," I said.

"Very well," the girl replied, her eyes sparkling with amusement. "Ask me a question."

There were so many. But the one that bubbled up first to my lips surprised me. "What were you running from, when we met? What attacked you?"

She pressed her lips together, suddenly serious. "The Gather is ruled by a tyrant. I displeased him, so he sent his Wolves after me."

"What's the Gather?"

"What's your name?" she countered.

I could feel my cheeks flush and resisted the urge to touch my face. "Lena," I said. "And you?"

"Miranda."

Miranda. It fit her perfectly.

She leaned forward, her hair falling over her shoulder as she gazed at me intently. "I'll tell you what the Gather is, but you'll have to make good on your bargain."

I had no doubt that she meant it, though I wasn't certain how she might ensure my cooperation.

Miranda cleared her throat. "The Gather is a city within the forest of the Silence."

I stared at her. "But I thought no one lived in the Silence. No one who has ever gone in has come out again."

She held up a hand. "A bargain is a bargain. Tell me what makes you special."

I could leave. Slip away out the window with Father none the wiser. I didn't believe Miranda would tell him we had spoken. I could still return to exactly the life I'd had yesterday, and the day before, and the day before that.

But I didn't want to. Now that I'd tasted the truth, I'd do whatever it took to know more.

"I'm cursed," I said, the words rushing out of me like a river. "Ever since I was born."

I felt light-headed, almost dizzy. I'd done the thing my parents had told me never, ever to do. And I was still here, still standing. Nothing had changed. *Everything* had changed.

"Ah," Miranda said, a curious gleam in her eyes. "What's the curse?"

"Why do you want to know?"

"You want to know about the Gather; I want to know about your curse. Why can't we both be merely curious?"

I supposed it didn't matter if I told her. Not when she said she'd come from a place I wasn't even sure existed, and would return there in a matter of days. "I'm dangerous," I said finally. "To others around me."

Her gaze slipped down to my hands. "Something to do with

your gloves, perhaps? And the fact that you've kept yourself all the way on the other side of the room from me?"

I inhaled sharply. She noticed too much. And yet she was looking at me so *kindly*. I'd told her this much, and she hadn't even flinched.

I suddenly wanted to tell her . . . everything. I'd never told the story to anyone. I'd never had the opportunity.

"My parents cheated a witch before I was born," I said softly. "My mother was very ill, and the only person that could help was a witch who lived nearby. She saved my mother's life, but the price she demanded was *me*. She said that my parents would have a child, and that when the child was born, she would claim it. At the time, they agreed. But when I came, they fled rather than fulfill the bargain. For that, the witch cursed me. And we've been running from her ever since."

My parents had never told me exactly what they thought the witch would do to me. My imagination had filled in the gaps a thousandfold. I looked down at my hands, properly gloved. "I can't touch *anyone* with my bare skin. If I do, they—" My voice broke. "Two people have already died because of my mistakes."

When I glanced back up, I saw Miranda was studying me intently. I wondered what she saw. Sometimes I thought of myself as absolutely nothing but this curse, this blight. A monstrosity wearing the shape of a girl.

"You must be very lonely," she said at last.

I couldn't speak past the sudden lump in my throat. Instead I just nodded jerkily.

"You know, there may not be much magic here, but that's not the case on the other side of the Silence."

"What do you mean?"

"I mean there's magic there—inside the forest, and the rest of the world on the other side. Perhaps there's a way to break the curse."

"There isn't," I said harshly. "There is no remedy. Only death."

"And who told you that?" she asked, her voice silky. "Your father?"

"It's true," I insisted, even as my certainty began to crumble away.

"Then perhaps your father isn't as protective as I thought. Because if my daughter were so afflicted, I would walk the whole world to break the curse. And like I said, he *has* been to the Gather." Miranda leaned back. "Look, Lena. I have my own problems. I don't need to take on yours. But there *are* mages in the Gather who might know what to do. I could help you get there. . . ."

She trailed off, and I understood that such help would not come free. Nothing did. I tried not to betray my inner turmoil as I raised an eyebrow.

"In exchange for what?"

"There is a legend about the Silence—about a castle hidden somewhere in the forest, and within the castle, a princess under a sleeping spell. She's rumored to hold the key to liberating the forest from its rulers. That's the real reason the Wolves of the Gather were chasing me—because I tried to wake her. I intend to try again . . . and perhaps, if I had you with me—"

"You think I could help you with *that?*" I said, cutting her off. Princesses and tyrants and deadly wolves? I was no intrepid adventurer. I'd spent most of my life alone, indoors. Poor qualifications indeed for such a quest.

She shrugged. "Your curse could come in handy, don't you think?"

"No!" I cried, horrified. "You're suggesting that I *kill* people for you?"

"Not *people*, just Wolves," Miranda insisted.

"But my curse doesn't work on animals," I protested.

"These Wolves were human once, before the tyrant twisted their bodies and souls with magic. And I'm not suggesting that we would go about looking for trouble! I only meant that you could offer . . . certain defensive advantages. If we *were* to be attacked."

"If *you* were to be attacked, you mean."

Miranda shrugged one shoulder, not denying it. I continued. "You've spun this wondrous story, but you haven't given me a shred of proof that what you're saying is true. About the curse or the magic or the Silence."

"You want proof of magic?" Miranda said.

She reached down and pressed her fingers under the edge of the bandage covering the wound on her leg. When she lifted her hand, I saw blood on her fingertips. She turned her palm up and began to murmur under her breath.

At first there was nothing. And then something that looked like silvery thread rose from her fingers, weaving together in the air. I gasped. Miranda kept murmuring as the weave thickened and stretched, forming a shimmering net about the size of my hand. It hovered in the air, and then fell into her lap. She slouched back against the couch cushions, clearly fatigued by her efforts.

"Is that magic enough for you?" she said.

I could scarcely speak. "What is that?"

"Nothing—a trinket. Magic is much harder to do in the Mundane. This would be the work of an instant in the Silence."

"Is it real?"

She laughed. "Here, hold out your hand."

I hesitated. Then, slowly, I stepped forward and did as she asked. She dropped the net into my palm.

It was small, but it was *real*. She had created this out of nothing. Well, not out of nothing. Out of magic.

"Impressive," I acknowledged, trying to conceal my astonishment. "But this would not help me break the curse."

"Look," Miranda said, her voice strained with exhaustion. "As I said, I have my own problems. I just thought—you seemed like someone in need. And I thought maybe we could help each other."

There were so many emotions roiling inside me that I could not untangle them. It was terrible, what she had suggested I might do with my power—but holding this net spun by magic . . . it gave me *hope* again. In this moment I actually believed that there was a chance, even the slightest, that I could change my stars.

"My father would never let me go," I said.

She nodded in agreement. "Respectfully, I invite you to consider the idea that perhaps your father hasn't told you the entire truth about the curse. Or the Silence. Or himself, for that matter. And regardless of what he told you in the past—it's *your* future." She closed her eyes. "I won't press you further. In two days I return to the Silence. If you decide you are ready to take your life into your own hands, meet me at the border."

CHAPTER FIVE

I was waiting at the kitchen table when Father returned to the house.

"I need to talk to you," I said.

He paused in the hallway, distracted. "Can this wait?"

"No, it can't." My heart thundered with nerves.

His attention snapped to me. "What is it?" he said, alarmed. "Are you all right? Tell me you haven't touched—"

"No!" I said, louder than I intended. "Of course not."

"Oh." He came into the kitchen, shrugging off his coat. "Well?"

I searched his face, seeing only impatience. Had he truly been lying to me my entire life?

"What is the Mundane?" I asked.

His jaw tightened. "You spoke with the girl? I told you not to—"

"And why not?" I interrupted, noting that he hadn't contradicted me. "Don't I deserve to know about it?"

I waited, expecting him to snap at me again. Instead he was silent for a long time. Finally, he sat down across from me and let out a heavy, exhausted sigh. "You're asking about dangerous things, Lena."

"I don't care. Tell me the truth."

He looked down. "The Mundane is the world we live in. A place without magic."

"But there's another place," I said. "Someplace *with* magic. Inside the Silence . . . and on the other side?"

He shot me a sharp look. "What exactly did she tell you?"

I was sure he would gauge what to say based on my answer, and it made me furious. For so long I had thought myself an aberration in a world where magic didn't exist. Now he was admitting to me that wasn't true—that all this time, he had known there was more to the world. Someplace where perhaps my curse could be lifted. And he had kept it from me.

My hands clenched into fists. "What does it matter what I heard? Why can't you just tell me the *truth?*" I spat.

"You are a *child*, Lena. I am trying to *protect* you."

"I'm nearly eighteen," I shot back. "And it's been a long time since I was a child."

"That is irrelevant. You may know the world is a hard place, but you've never seen beasts like those that inhabit the Silence."

"But if there's magic there, maybe there's someone who could help me!"

He slammed his hand down on the table, and I jumped. "That is impossible!"

"How do you know?" I said. I stared down at my hands. "You've suffered being my father, I know that. But not the way that *I* have suffered. How could you know about such a place and not at least *try?*"

"Because I know the Silence, and the people who live there."

"How?"

"Because *I* lived there. Is that what you want to hear? I was born on the other side of the Silence, and yes, magic can be wondrous. But you've never seen what it can do when put in the hands of evil people."

"Like the witch?"

"*Worse.*"

What could be worse than what I already knew of magic? "But if there's a chance to break the curse—"

"There isn't," Father said. "And this conversation is over."

No. No, this couldn't be it. Not when I felt as though a door had opened for the very first time. I grabbed his arm as he started to stand. "Father, please!"

He shook me off. "Believe me, I wish there was a way to break the curse just as much as you do. But there isn't."

"So you would just have us live this way forever? Father, I—I *can't.*" As soon as I said it, I knew it was true. I couldn't go on like this. Not anymore.

"You *can.* Because this is what keeps you *safe.*"

I was crying now, and I couldn't stop. "Safe? I'm only safe until the next mistake. I'm only safe until the witch finds us—and what then?"

Father's expression turned stricken. "I love you, Lena," he said, speaking softer than before. "And it's because I love you that I forbid you from going to the Gather or anywhere else in the Silence. You will not go there, not so long as I am alive."

I pushed back from the table and ran—out of the house and across the field, until I came to the lake that marked the village's northern border. I stood there, shivering as the wind blew up off the water. In my haste I'd forgotten my cloak.

Miranda's net was in my pocket. I took it out and held it up to the light, studying the way it shimmered. Everything that Miranda had said was true. I didn't know my father at all. He'd lied to me about everything. And now, was he lying about what I might find in the Silence?

Rain began to fall, pattering against the surface of the lake. Soon I would be soaked through. I closed my eyes, dreading the thought of returning to that house and pretending to my father that everything had settled back into its place. My father had tried to keep me safe, but that safety was an illusion. It always had been. For most of my life I'd been consumed by the terror of dying at the hands of the witch. I'd despaired over what my curse made me, and tasted bitter guilt over the lives I'd taken and destroyed. I could not bear it any longer. I might die within the Silence—but if I stayed here, I would surely die standing still.

What do you want?

Something snapped within me. I closed my fingers tightly around the net and opened my eyes, turning my gaze toward the Silence. Miranda was right—it was *my* future at stake. I had made my decision. Whatever the dangers, I would survive them. Whatever my destiny was, I would meet it head on.

The scent of warm cinnamon greeted me as I opened the door, and I knew immediately what my father was making: queen's cakes. Our family had little in the way of yearly traditions, but Father had made these airy cinnamon-sugar cakes on birthdays for as long as I could remember. I'd burned my tongue more times than I could count, snatching cakes off the skillet before they'd fully risen. My mother had clucked her tongue at my impatience. She'd preferred to wait until the cakes had cooled and Father had drizzled orange-honey glaze over their tops. The glaze was delicious, of course, and queen's cake was unfinished without it. But to me there had always been something irresistible about biting down on a fresh cake and puffing too-hot air out of my mouth. That Father had made them now, without occasion, meant he was trying to make peace. To apologize, without saying the words.

I hesitated. I didn't want to go into the kitchen. I could hold on to my resolve as long as I was alone, but I was afraid that the moment I saw him, the truth of what I'd decided would come pouring out.

Before I could make up my mind, Father came out of the kitchen with a plate. On the plate were six fresh cakes and a sliced apple, arranged to look like a flower.

I couldn't look at it without tearing up. But I couldn't look at him, either.

"Here," he said gruffly. He pressed the plate into my hands. "I know you think I'm being unfair. I'm sorry."

I only nodded.

I took the plate up to my room and changed into dry clothes. The rain was coming down harder, pounding against the window until the field outside was just a blur of green through the wet glass. For a while I sat in silence and wept.

When I could cry no longer, I wiped my cheeks with my sleeve and ate the queen's cakes one by one. When I was done, I packed a small bag and hid it under my bed. It was easy to do. Years of practice enabled me to go through the motions almost without thinking. And I needed that now, because if I stopped to think, I might never leave.

I spent the next two days in fear of giving myself away. The enormity of the decision I'd made was so overwhelming that at any moment, it felt as though I was mere seconds from flying apart completely. So I did my best to stay out of Father's way, jumping at every shadow and shift of the house. For his part, he made sure to keep me away from Miranda's door, though I was glad to see that he brought her regular meals and fresh bandages.

On the morning Miranda was due to leave, I heard Father unlock the door. I stood at the top of the stairs and watched her walk out of the room with a slight limp, her red hair shining in the lamplight. She looked up at me, and my heart thumped painfully in my chest at her impassive expression. Had she changed her mind? Had I dreamed everything that had passed between us?

She nodded almost imperceptibly, and relief flooded through me. I raised a hand in acknowledgment. Then she turned and was gone.

As soon as the door closed behind them, I ran to the window and watched their progress toward the Silence. They walked slowly. I wondered if they were talking, and if so, what they were talking about.

But as soon as they parted ways and Father turned around, I realized I'd been so preoccupied by my nerves that I'd failed to anticipate the obvious: once he came back in the house, he wouldn't let me out of his sight.

I locked the bedroom door behind me. With luck, he would assume I was sulking, at least for a few hours. I opened the window facing the back of the house and threw my bag out onto the damp grass. Then I swung a leg over the windowsill and turned, lowering myself down until I hung by my fingers. My feet dangled over the hedges planted against the side of the house. I wasn't *too* high above them . . . I hoped.

But it was too late to haul myself back inside. I held my breath—and let go.

I hit the hedges and tumbled to the ground, jarring my back painfully. I lay still, my ears ringing, as the shock of impact dissipated. Then I pushed myself to my feet. I scooped up my bag and pressed myself against the side of the house, listening intently.

Soon enough I heard the front door open and close. It was time to run, but I couldn't make myself move.

All the thoughts I'd held at bay suddenly flooded me. What if this was a mistake? I knew nothing about being on my own. I knew nothing about the Silence, or the world that lay on the other side. I was putting my life in Miranda's hands. *And my own*, I reminded myself. If this was a mistake, it was mine to make. My life to take.

I put one foot firmly in front of the other—and then another, and another. And then I was running, my breath shallow and fast, my heart thumping in my chest until I had made it across the field and found Miranda waiting for me just before the trees.

"I wasn't sure you were going to come," she said. She had a small bag slung over one shoulder—my father must have given it to her.

"Me either," I replied truthfully.

"Are you ready?"

I snorted. "As ready as I'll ever be, I suppose."

She smiled, and that smile was like sunshine. "No one is ever truly prepared for the Silence."

I looked past her, staring into the dark trees. "What will we find inside?"

"To enumerate the dangers would take days, and I don't even know them all," she admitted. "Once we're inside, we make for shelter. Hopefully the Wolves are long gone, but in the event they aren't . . . we may have to run. Or fight."

I swallowed, hard. "What makes you think the Wolves *won't* be waiting for us?" Not to mention whatever else was lurking beneath the branches of the Silence.

"Magic doesn't work the same way in the Mundane. The Wolves can't cross the border, so they don't like to linger here. And it's been two days—they probably grew tired of waiting. We should be all right."

I wanted to trust her confidence. But still . . .

"Come with me," she said, as if she could see my resolve wavering. She held out a hand.

I hesitated. Even though I was wearing my gloves, there was always a risk. And yet here she was, offering a hand to hold while knowing exactly what would happen if our skin touched.

I held my breath as I lifted my hand. She reached out, matching her fingertips to the fingers of my glove. Her featherlight touch, when it came, shot sparks through my body. She folded her hand carefully around mine and I tensed, afraid to move, and—

There was nothing. Nothing but the feel of her hand in mine as we faced the Silence together.

"Lena!"

No. I flinched and dropped Miranda's hand, turning to see Father sprinting across the field toward us.

I looked back at Miranda. Her expression was eerily calm. "Do you still want to come?" she asked.

"Yes," I said.

"*Lena!*"

The desperation in Father's voice pierced through me, but I forced myself not to look back again. I grabbed hold of Miranda's hand once more. "Let's go!"

We ran forward, into the Silence. A sudden wind rushed by, whipping my hair about my face. The trees swayed, branches lashing through the air. Miranda's hand tightened around mine.

The sounds of crashing reached my ears, as though something heavy was breaking through the underbrush. I chanced a glance back and stumbled to a halt in shock. The forest—it was *moving.* The trees behind us shifted before my eyes, snapping together like a gate slamming shut. The field disappeared from view.

The Silence had swallowed us whole.

CHAPTER SIX

W hat was *that?*" My voice came out cracked, panicked.

"Sometimes the Silence moves," Miranda said, as calmly as if she were commenting on the weather.

I had no words to come to terms with what I had just seen. If the forest could move, perhaps it *had* devoured all those villagers who had been drawn into its depths. I gaped at our surroundings, waiting for the Silence to move again. Instead, all was quiet once more.

The forest had cut us off from any path of retreat. Gone was Father, the field, the watcher's house, Onwey . . . My chest tightened as I remembered Father's anguished shouts. I fought hard to push my feelings aside. It was done. There was no going back now.

We were completely enveloped by the trees. Branches spread over us like dark cracks in the sky. As we went farther in, I was sure the trees would block the sky out entirely. Already I could feel cold emanating toward us. And in this strange, eternal twilight, it felt like we were the only two people in the world.

Miranda squeezed my hand, sending warmth through me. "We should get going."

"And just pretend that was normal?" I said helplessly.

"That *is* normal for the Silence," Miranda said. "If you can, I'd recommend doing exactly that: pretending. Because believe me, it's better not to be known as a newcomer when it comes to the Gather."

With that she let go of my hand and walked ahead. I gathered my courage and followed. This was what I had chosen. I could be brave enough. I had to be.

The forest was thick with creeping vines and ferns, and tree roots sprawled across the ground, slowing our progress. From the outside, the Silence had appeared utterly still. But now the soft chitters and chirps of small creatures disturbed the quiet. I saw movement out of the corner of my eye, but when I turned my head, there was nothing there.

"Don't worry," Miranda said. "They won't trouble you if you don't trouble them."

"But what are they?"

"Creatures of the Silence. There are more strange beasts here than I know how to identify. It's better if you just ignore them."

"And what about the Wolves?"

"Trust me—Wolves would make a lot more noise. Besides, I already told you. They don't like it here. The Mundane affects their magic."

I shifted my bag, remembering how difficult it had been for her to create the magical net. At the time, she'd said it was because we were in the Mundane.

"The other day, when you made the net—there was blood on your hand," I said hesitantly. "Is that the source of your magic?"

"Yes. I'm a blood mage." Miranda shrugged. "But most mages living in the Silence are like me. I'm nothing special."

So she claimed, but she'd still worked more magic on a whim than I had seen in my lifetime.

"Then why weren't you concerned about coming through to the Mundane? Didn't you think you might lose your power?"

She smiled wryly. "I wasn't really thinking about that at the time. Mostly I was thinking about not dying."

Her foot caught on a root, and she stumbled. Without thinking, I reached out to steady her, catching myself only at the last moment. I grimaced. *What are you doing?* I'd long ago been trained not to give in to the impulse to touch others. What was it about Miranda that made me forget? I bit my lip and looked down at my gloves.

Miranda straightened and continued walking, oblivious to what I had almost done.

"Anyway, we need to be careful now," she said. "It's a long way to shelter, and it's best to avoid unnecessary encounters."

A fern unfurled toward me, its fronds glowing gently, and I stepped out of its path. A tiny blue light flickered in the darkness to my right, only to wink out when I turned my head. "What's that?" I said, my heartbeat quickening.

Miranda smiled as she followed my gaze. "Just ghost lights. They're not so bad—if you get tangled up with one, you'll find yourself talking to a dead relative for a few hours. But there are other things in here that are much worse. That's why it's important to keep to a safe path. Spend too long away from one, you might never find your way back."

I looked at the ground. Though Miranda had been leading confidently, there was no path beneath our feet. "But we're not on one . . . are we?"

"No," she said, sighing. "We're still too close to the Mundane. We just need to get a little farther in so that I can call a guide."

"Will you use blood magic?"

"No," she said shortly. "Using blood magic in the depths of the Silence is a risk best avoided unless absolutely necessary."

"Because . . . ?"

Miranda looked back at me. "Do you always ask this many questions?"

"The Silence is new to me," I said, a little defensive. "*Magic* is new to me. Can you blame me for wanting to know more?"

She laughed a little, but I could tell it was forced. "Fair enough. All right. But we—"

A piercing howl interrupted her reply, making my skin crawl. Even in the dim light I could see the blood drain from Miranda's face.

"What is that?"

"Wolves. We need to run. Now!"

She sprinted away through the intertwined trees. Adrenaline coursed through me as I ran after her, stumbling over the uneven ground. Branches whipped across my arms. Even with her injured leg, Miranda was close to leaving me behind as she maneuvered over tree roots and through thick shrubbery. I fought to keep her in sight.

I'd seen wolves in the Mundane, but I had no doubt that the Wolves of the Silence were different creatures entirely. Images of bloody dismemberment flashed through my mind.

"Can't you do something?" I shouted, my words coming in gasps. "Magic?"

Miranda's limp was becoming more pronounced. "Bloodletting would just draw them faster!" she called over her shoulder. "Keep running!"

So we kept going, and I dared not look back. I imagined yellow eyes fixed on me and heard the beating of paws on the ground as they loped behind us. I imagined their tongues out, tasting the wind for our scent. I imagined I smelled like fear.

Ahead of me, Miranda was slowing. Another howl rang out, so close it raised the hair on my arms. I ran faster—but Miranda had stopped short, and I skidded to a halt just in time to avoid running straight into her. We had come to the edge of a cliff. I whirled around to see four hulking figures emerge from the trees. *Wolves.* They stalked toward us, blocking off any hope of escape.

Miranda drew her knife, though it seemed a futile gesture. She peered over the edge of the cliff as I took off one of my gloves and stuffed it into my pocket. My fingers were trembling.

Miranda glanced back at me, her eyes widening as she saw my hand. "No!" she cried. "Lena, come on!" She sheathed her knife, then turned and leapt right over the edge of the cliff. No time for hesitation—I flung myself after her.

For an instant I was airborne. Then something yanked me backward. I fell heavily to the ground, the impact forcing the air from my lungs. A Wolf was above me in an instant, their fangs bared as they planted elongated paws on either side of my face, pinning me to the ground. The others gathered around me. I froze, staring up into their glinting eyes.

Up close, I could see their fur was dark and thick. Their limbs seemed too long for their torsos, and their facial features were strangely discordant—though their long snouts and sharp fangs were unmistakably lupine, their yellow eyes were frighteningly human. Their ears, though long and slightly pointed at the top, lacked fur. It was as if some macabre transformation had been caught somewhere in between human and wolf, and the result was horrendous. Blood magic had wrought *this*?

The Wolf standing over me dug their paws into the ground next to my ears, their claws almost fingerlike in their precision. I shuddered, and the creature growled a warning in response.

"She's not the one," rumbled the largest of them, a gravelly human voice ripping from its wolfish throat.

"Then we've no use for her," said another.

The others bared their fangs as if in agreement. The Wolf above me lowered their head, and I began to shake as I felt their hot breath hit my face. The Wolf struck, their claw ripping through my cloak and into my arm. I screamed as pain shot through my body.

Suddenly the Wolf reared back, smoke rising from their bloody claw—and then it glowed a hot, bright orange as the paw caught fire and began to melt like candle wax. Flames licked up their leg, charring it black. The Wolf fell, their agonized howl piercing the air. The rest of their body caught fire as the acrid scent of burning flesh hit my nose.

A boy's face in agony, skin melting away—the air filled with his screams—the street scorched black by flames—Father pulling me away as I sob—

I came back into myself to see what was left of the Wolf's body twitching on the ground beside me. As I watched, it collapsed in on itself like a dying fire, then lay still.

A wave of nausea hit me. What Miranda had said must be true—somehow, the Wolves had once been human. And I had killed one of them. I waited for guilt to wash over me as it had in the past, but it didn't come. I felt . . . nothing. No, not nothing. A pang of relief . . . and a small, sharp shard of satisfaction.

The other three Wolves had retreated from the burning body, but now they looked at me with murderous intent in their eyes. I scrambled to my feet, holding my bare hand out before me.

"Stay back!" I shouted.

The Wolves hesitated. I took one step back, then another. Then I turned and launched myself over the cliff, tumbling heavily down a steep rocky incline. I scrabbled unsuccessfully for a root or vine to slow my fall—and then the cliff gave way and I plummeted into an icy river.

Water filled my nose and mouth, and I choked as the current buffeted me about. My lungs burned, and I realized I was sinking, dragged down by the weight of my bag. I flailed underwater, trying to untangle my arms from the straps, but they were trapped. I couldn't reach the riverbed nor find the sky. I was going to drown.

Lena.

My eyes opened. For a moment I thought I saw a face in the water, staring at me—and then I felt a sharp *tug*, and suddenly my arms were free. I kicked hard, propelling myself to the surface, and came up sputtering as the river bore me away from the cliff.

I blinked water out of my eyes as I searched frantically for Miranda. Where was she? I didn't dare risk drawing the Wolves' attention by calling out. There! Miranda's head broke the surface downriver as she made for the shore. I swam in the same direction, struggling to keep myself afloat in the swift current. Just as I thought I was out of strength, my boots finally touched the silty bottom. I dragged myself up onto the muddy bank and collapsed on the ground, coughing. There was water in my ears and up my nose. My body was trembling, and not just from the frigid river or my exhaustion. Only a month ago I had killed a boy. Now I had killed again. This time, though, I felt . . . hollow. And somehow *fierce*. For the first time, I felt the power of how the curse had turned the tables on my enemies. How *I* had turned them.

I pushed myself to my feet. As soon as I stood, nausea hit me, my ears ringing and my vision doubling. I bent over and retched until I was blinded by tears and completely emptied.

"Lena!"

Somehow my glove was still in my pocket. I pulled it out and forced my fingers into the wet fabric as Miranda walked toward me. I wiped the back of my glove against my mouth and managed a smile, surprised by how relieved I was to see her alive. Of course I didn't want her to die. She was my only guide in the Silence. But it was more than that. I was coming to *like* her. I felt immediately sheepish at the thought—and embarrassed that she was seeing me like this.

"Are you all right?" she said. She'd managed to hold on to her bag—now she pulled out a flask and offered it to me.

I took a swig of water and swished it around in my mouth before spitting it out. The sour taste on my tongue lessened. "No," I replied. "I don't know." The memory of the river swept through me again, and I realized—I had almost drowned. I would have, had it not been for that tug as I was pulled free of my bag. A face in the water . . . and that *voice*. Had I imagined it all?

"I lost my bag," I said slowly.

"Better the bag than you." Miranda's gaze fell to my arm. "You're hurt!"

The fabric of my cloak stung as it pulled across my skin, and I winced. "One of the Wolves clawed me. But it's nothing, really," I said quickly.

53

"Show me."

She hissed in sympathy as I rolled up my sleeve, revealing the bloody scores the Wolf had clawed into my skin. Seeing them for the first time, I was grateful that my cloak had protected me from worse.

"They had you," Miranda said softly. "How did you get away?"

Her expression darkened as I explained what had happened. "We need to get away from here." She was angry, I realized. But I didn't quite understand why.

"But—isn't it a good thing that the Wolves were frightened of me?" I said uncertainly.

Miranda pressed her lips together. "You don't understand. The Wolves serve the ruler of the Gather. The ones who got away will report back to their master. And *he* will certainly be interested in newcomers with dangerous abilities."

Shale, I remembered Father saying. In Onwey, Miranda had been frightened even to say his name aloud.

"I'm sorry," I said, the apology coming out automatically.

She let out an exasperated huff, then collected herself. "No, I'm sorry. I'm glad you're safe—I'm just worried about you. Are you all right to keep moving? I don't know if I have the strength left to heal you now. And we need to get to a path."

"And that will keep the Wolves away?"

She shook her head. "No. Wolves are part of the Gather—their power comes from the blood magic of its ruler. But a path will keep us safe from the Silence."

I didn't have the energy to ask what other terrors the Silence had in store. I just nodded.

She knelt down and sorted through her bag, and then pulled

out an acorn. As I watched, she popped off its cap and cupped it in her palm. Then she brought her hand to her mouth and whispered, "I seek a guide to the nearest safe path. In payment I offer this token only." The rest of the acorn she pocketed.

"What now?" I said.

"We wait."

An unsettling answer. I tried to keep still, but water squelched uncomfortably in my boots every time I wiggled my toes. And I couldn't stop thinking about what had just happened. Why did this death feel different? Why didn't I feel as guilty? Was the curse turning me a little more monstrous every time I used it? Or was it something to do with these strange new surroundings? When I'd been outside the Silence, I'd had the sense that the forest was watching me. Now that I was in it, I felt the weight of its gaze a hundredfold.

A skittering sound caught my attention, and I looked up to see a tail vanish behind a tree trunk. Glittering eyes blinked at me, then disappeared. I shivered and looked away.

Soon there was a rustle in the bushes, and then a squirrel broke out from the branches and bounded toward Miranda. It bobbed up on its hind legs and sniffed the air. Miranda crouched down and offered it the acorn. To my surprise, the squirrel took the nut delicately between its paws and popped it into its mouth. It began to chew noisily.

Once finished, the squirrel chittered softly.

"Now that you have accepted my offer, please guide us to the nearest safe path," Miranda said formally.

The squirrel flicked its tail. Then it turned and ran off into the gloom.

"Come on!" said Miranda, running after it.

I, feeling quite ridiculous, followed. Considering the gravity of the situation—that our lives had just been threatened by Wolves, that I'd just used my curse with little remorse—it seemed wrong that we were now entrusting ourselves to the care of a squirrel. An ordinary squirrel. The sort that I had seen in fields and gardens almost every day.

Eventually the squirrel stopped and waited for us to catch up, twitching its tail. Miranda bowed to it and gave her thanks for the guidance. The squirrel scampered away again, vanishing into the forest.

"Look here," Miranda said, pointing at the ground. I followed her gaze and saw pale stones dotting the path at irregular intervals. They glimmered, despite the dimness of the forest. "You can tell it's a safe path by the markers."

"This is it?" I said. When Miranda had said the paths would keep us safe from the dangers of the Silence, I'd thought there would be walls or towers or guards. Instead this looked like any other path through any other forest.

"Yes," Miranda said simply.

"And only squirrels can find the paths?"

"Guides are not always squirrels. Many creatures of the Silence will guide us, if we offer them the right currency."

"Acorns," I said flatly.

"And other things," she said, distracted. She knelt down on the path and put her hand to the dirt, then rubbed the particles between her fingers. "I think this is the right way. But let's get moving before someone else comes along."

CHAPTER SEVEN

W here exactly are we going?" I said after a while. It seemed a safe time to inquire—we were walking rather than running, and Miranda had even pulled a few apples out of her bag to eat. They hadn't taken too much of a knocking during our flight, and were still sweet and crisp. For the moment, the danger had passed.

"The Gather."

"But I thought the rulers of the Gather were the ones after you?" I said, confused.

"It's a large city. And we'll need supplies before we embark on any sort of rescue operation. I know some people who will help us."

"What sort of supplies do we need?" It occurred to me suddenly that when I'd met Miranda, she hadn't had anything with her.

"The usual," Miranda said. "Food, weapons. A few magical trinkets."

Magic. Despite everything I had just witnessed, I still had difficulty wrapping my mind around its existence.

I thought of my father. Of how long he had denied this knowledge to me—*lied* to me. And then I thought of my last glimpse of him, sprinting after me as I stepped into the Silence. The forest had kept him out. I wondered if he had waited there at the border, if he had tried to find another way in.

What if I never see him again? The thought caught me by surprise, ripping into my anger and exposing something else underneath—something rough and sorrowful.

I did my best to shove those feelings back down. I didn't want to feel them. I couldn't. If I allowed it, they might drown me.

Ahead of me, Miranda slowed, then stopped. She stared down at the ground, frowning.

"What's wrong?" As I caught up to her, I saw a line that looked as though it had been drawn in charcoal cutting across the path.

She shook her head. "We're not on the right path."

"It's not safe?"

"No, it's safe. It's just leading somewhere I'd rather not go."

"Where?"

She bit her lip. "There's a community of people who have left the Gather—they are no friend to the tyrant. This path leads to their camp. But . . . I'm not well liked there."

If these people were enemies of the tyrant, and Miranda was trying to wake the princess who would liberate the forest from the Gather's rule, then what reason could they have for not liking her?

"Is there somewhere else we can go?" I asked.

Miranda looked up at the sky—what little of it we could see through the trees. "It's getting late," she said, clearly torn. "We shouldn't be out in the Silence after dark. There's no telling what might show up."

"Then we should go to this place. Even if the people aren't the most welcoming."

She nodded. "You're right. But you need to be prepared. The Gather is a complicated place, and so is this camp. You'll see some terrible things here."

"It can't be more terrible than what we've already seen," I said, trying to convince myself.

A smile tugged at the corner of her mouth. "You're very brave," she said, and the strangest thing was, she seemed to mean it.

Brave? I wasn't so certain of that. I'd spent most of my life being afraid. But Miranda made me believe that perhaps there was room in the Silence for a new Lena. A braver Lena.

"Anyway," she continued. "What I'm trying to say is that nothing here is exactly as it seems. So stick close to me and don't listen to what anyone else might try to tell you. You can't trust that they're telling the truth."

I nodded. She'd led me this far.

So we stepped over the line and followed the path through the dimming light.

It wasn't more than half an hour before we came to another line in the path, this one deeper and darker, as though it had been burned straight into the earth. Here Miranda hesitated once more. "This is it," she said. "Are you ready?"

I checked my gloves and nodded. Miranda stepped carefully over the line.

"Halt!"

I peered into the darkness, but there was no one there. Miranda held up her hands to show they were empty. I did the same.

"I come to seek shelter," she called.

"What shelter?" came the voice again.

"The shelter of those foresworn, for I have traveled more than seven days and nights to find this place," Miranda said, her words lilting like an incantation.

There was a pause. I wondered how many were watching us,

unheard and unseen. And whether they might have weapons. My fingers twitched with nerves.

"Come," said the disembodied voice.

Miranda walked forward. The air shimmered around her—and then she disappeared.

What?

"Come on." Miranda's voice floated back to me.

I braced myself and took a step. The air suddenly felt solid and impenetrable, as though I'd dropped into a vat of mud. I leaned forward, straining to move my arms, legs, anything—and then I was falling.

I scarcely had time to be afraid before my body jerked to a halt, my head snapping back. Something had caught me—something that felt unnervingly alive.

The darkness lifted, and I gasped.

I'd fallen into a wide pit so deep I couldn't see the bottom. The only things saving me from the fall were *hands*—disembodied hands that appeared to be made of clay. They grasped me by the arms and legs, suspending my body in midair. I recoiled, but the hands held me fast.

"Be still," Miranda said. I turned my head and saw her suspended on the other side of the trench, though she looked significantly more at ease than I felt. "Don't worry. They won't leave us down here for long."

"*Who* won't?" I said, fighting to control my breathing. The sides of the trench were closing in around me. No matter that these hands were made of clay—the sensation of being restrained like this was unbearable. But if they let me go, I would fall. Falling would be worse.

As if on cue, there came a sharp whistle from above. The hands rotated our bodies slowly until we were upright, though that was little comfort. I looked up to see someone lean over the top of the pit and peer down at us—a man with close-cropped white hair.

"What's your business?" he said. So he had been the one speaking to us.

"We ask for shelter for one night," Miranda said, sounding shockingly calm. "And some travel rations."

"Shelter?" A new voice spoke, and an older woman's head appeared next to the man's. "What needs has Miranda, pet of the Gather, that she must seek them here among the outcasts?"

Miranda's face fell. "Rin," she said flatly. "I didn't know you had come here."

Rin raised her voice. "This girl is a liar and a thief. I don't know who shared with her the words to gain admission to Haven, but she should not have been allowed within these walls. She is *working* for the king."

What? I looked at Miranda, alarmed.

"I have been cast out," Miranda said. "Surely even *you* are aware of that."

"Only because of Calanthe."

Miranda flinched at the name, then collected herself. "I displeased them. The Wolves almost caught me only a few days ago. You can inspect my wounds yourself, if you don't believe me. They would have killed me if I hadn't escaped. Would they have done so, if I were still a loyal servant of the Gather?"

Rin turned to the gatekeeper. "Cast her out now, Tadrik," she said. "She'll only bring harm upon us."

The hands tightened their grips, and I hissed in pain.

"I swear to you I mean no harm to Haven's inhabitants," Miranda said quickly. "We only need a place to stay for one night. What can I say to convince you that I'm telling the truth?"

Rin's gaze slid over me. "Nothing," she said.

Nothing? The hands loosened their grips, and I felt my arms begin to slip. "There must be something!" I cried, sweat dripping down the back of my shirt. "We are not servants of the Gather—I swear it!"

Tadrik turned to Rin and murmured something to her. At last she nodded. He turned back to us. "A blood oath has served us before in such circumstances."

"Fine," I said. Whatever would get us out of this pit, I would do it.

"No!" Miranda said sharply. "She cannot take the oath."

"Why not?" Tadrik said.

"She has a blood condition," Miranda replied. "I will take the oath for both of us."

"Ah." His expression softened. "Very well, then."

Their heads disappeared from view, leaving only gray sky above us.

"Are they coming back?" I asked uncertainly.

"Yes," Miranda said, though I got the feeling she was less than confident in her answer.

And then the hands moved, lifting our bodies toward the sky. They spilled us out of the trench onto solid ground, then released their grips. I pushed myself to my feet and staggered away, shuddering.

From the path I had seen only a veil of darkness. Now, on the other side, I could see a number of squat houses sitting in the shadow of a small hill.

Miranda clambered up beside me. In front of us stood the gate-keeper, leaning on a staff. Next to him stood Rin, who had one arm in a sling. She glared at Miranda, but the man waved us forward.

"Fine," Rin said to him. "If you're so set on accepting a viper into our midst, who am I to stop you?" She stalked angrily away.

Tadrik produced a needle from his pocket. "Come forward."

Miranda stepped in front of me and knelt before him, holding out her hand, and I suddenly realized why she had offered to take the oath instead of me.

The gatekeeper pricked her finger with a needle, drawing one drop of blood that rose and floated in the air. "Do you swear on behalf of yourself and your companion that you do not intend to harm Haven or its inhabitants?"

"I do."

"And do you swear not to harm Haven or any of its inhabitants for the duration of your stay or thereafter?"

"I do . . . so long as they do not harm me first. You cannot expect me not to defend myself if attacked."

Tadrik frowned. "No qualifications."

Miranda sighed. "Fine. I do."

The gatekeeper gestured with his hand, and the blood turned silvery, flowing around Miranda's wrist and settling against her skin. Now it looked like a bracelet. "Then be bound, by your own word and blood. May your blood be devoured if you break this oath, if you betray the location of this place to any servants of the Gather, now or forevermore."

Miranda jerked her hand back as if stung. "That wasn't part of the deal!"

He looked at her impassively. "If you truly mean us no harm, if you are who you say you are, it will be no great trial to you."

For a moment I thought Miranda might strike him. Instead she schooled her face into a neutral expression. "Very well."

"Then you may stay here until noon tomorrow, but no longer."

"How *generous* of you," Miranda said bitingly. She stood up and turned to me. "Let's go."

She led the way past the houses. As we approached the hill, I realized that there was a tunnel carved into its side. Next to the entrance was a stack of lanterns. When we reached the opening, Miranda picked one up and lit it. Together we entered the tunnel.

For a while the only sounds were our footsteps. At first the walls were dry, but over time, they turned mossy and damp. From somewhere in the distance came the sound of water trickling. Once the light from outside had completely faded, I turned to Miranda.

"Why did the gatekeeper react like that when you said I had a blood condition?"

Miranda laughed, though it wasn't a happy sound. "I forget how much you don't know." She paused, seemingly struggling to find the right words. "The Gather was founded by blood mages because they are looked down upon elsewhere."

"Why? Is there something wrong with being a blood mage?"

"No, it's just that . . . Look, a blood mage is someone born with magic in their blood—like me. When we draw blood, we're able to access our magic. But every use of magic is draining. Once our natural stores are spent, we must wait for them to regenerate. In order to get around that, some mages choose to store their magic in other humans—even humans with no magic of their own."

"Which means a blood mage could access more power than they'd be able to alone," I said slowly.

"Exactly. It's an extra reservoir of power. The trouble is, when someone is forced to carry more magic than their bodies are naturally meant to hold, the magic starts to . . . erode them. They become very sick. Eventually, they die."

"That's horrible!"

"I agree. It's called blood plague, but some think it's more polite to say 'blood condition.' It's why those who rule the Gather are so evil—they use those below them just to store their power. Suck them dry, then throw them away once they break."

"So you just told the gatekeeper that I have blood plague?"

She shrugged. "It's common enough. And there aren't many visible signs at the beginning."

"I see," I said, everything she'd told me swirling through my mind. Miranda had said the rulers of the Gather were tyrants— now I understood why one might go to considerable lengths to take them down. Though I couldn't ignore what Rin had said, about Miranda being the pet of the Gather. And I wanted to know who Calanthe was and what had happened to her. But I wasn't sure how to ask Miranda about any of these things.

I wished I had her confidence. Even after our encounter with the Wolves, she hadn't been shaken. She'd known how to find a path and taken us to Haven even though she knew she might not be welcome. She had a plan, and the strength to see it through. And here I was, unable to form a simple question.

So instead we walked in silence. My clothes were more damp than fully wet now, though that didn't make them any more comfortable. Slowly my mind began to drift to thoughts of a warm bed and hot food.

◆　◆　◆

I heard Haven before I saw it. The trickling sounds grew into a steady stream and then a dull roar. Soon the tunnel widened, and then finally opened into a cavern so large I couldn't take in its full expanse in one look. At its far end, almost directly opposite us, a waterfall fed a pool at its base. Makeshift shelters hugged the cavern walls closer to us, lit by lanterns set on roughly cut ledges. A fire pit commanded the center of the chamber. It seemed we'd arrived at mealtime, as dozens of people milled around a cauldron suspended over the fire.

"Stay close to me, and be careful," Miranda said.

As we approached, I saw that many of these people walked with their shoulders hunched as if against a strong wind. Bone-rattling coughs reverberated throughout the crowd. More than a few of them limped, and there were strange marks on their faces, as though someone had spilled black ink upon their skin. As I looked closer, I realized that the marks *moved*, swirling across their cheeks like living creatures.

"Is that the blood plague?" I whispered, mindful of the fact that someone familiar with the Gather would likely not need to ask such a question.

"Yes," Miranda said shortly. "Try not to stare if you can help it. Like I said, it's common here."

We made our way to an unoccupied shelter made of canvas stretched over mismatched wooden poles that leaned against the cavern wall. It was dry enough, but that was the best that could be said for it. There was nothing inside except a small stack of musty-smelling blankets in the corner, neatly folded.

"Stay here," Miranda said, setting down her bag. "I'll get us some food."

I waited as Miranda cut through the crowd to the cauldron. She retrieved two bowls and walked back to me, her limp more pronounced than before.

I accepted the bowl carefully—it was full of clear broth with doughy dumplings floating on top.

Miranda sat down gingerly and started eating.

"Is your leg all right?" I asked.

She grimaced. "Not really."

"Could a healer help?" I myself had never been to a healer. Not when I'd gotten an angry rash from playing in the weeds, nor when I'd broken my leg falling out of a tree. My parents had always patched me up as best they could—and I'd survived, as best I could. But Miranda didn't have such restrictions.

"Not necessary," she said, her face pinched.

"Do you think they would refuse to help you? Because of . . . Calanthe?" I said cautiously.

"What about Calanthe?" she snapped.

I was surprised by the bite in her tone. "Rin mentioned her when we arrived. Were you lying, about being against the rulers of the Gather? Because Rin seemed to think you were a loyal servant to the king," I said, finally giving voice to my questions.

Miranda leaned forward, letting her hair fall over her face. "I wish you hadn't heard that," she said softly.

"Why?" I asked, my suspicions growing.

"Because I don't want to talk about it," she said fiercely. "Because I don't owe you details about my life."

"I—I'm sorry," I said. "I just don't know what to believe. I thought—"

"You don't think that being chased by Wolves is enough to

prove that I'm not on their side?" she said, cutting me off.

If this had been any other day, a conversation with any other person, I would have ducked my head and made my excuses, made myself as small as I could, hoping to disappear.

But this was today, and I had ventured into the Silence and killed a Wolf. Much as I was drawn to Miranda, it was dawning on me that I didn't know her very well at all.

"What I am saying," I said carefully, "is that perhaps there is another explanation for what happened with the Wolves. It could have been a ruse, to make it seem like you were on my side, not theirs."

Miranda scoffed. "Oh really, lady of suspicion?" She threw her spoon into her bowl and crossed her arms, glaring at me. "Then answer me this: If that was the plan, how did the Wolves know it? I was in your house from the time we met until the time we left. And need I remind you that they attacked me *before* we met? Do you truly believe you are so special that I'd go to such lengths, just to snatch you away?"

Put like that, my doubts seemed ludicrous.

But Miranda *had* gotten to the edge of the Silence before me.

And there had been no witnesses to the first attack.

"I only have your word to trust," I said, pushing back. "Nothing else."

Slowly Miranda's expression softened. "Look. I hate talking about Calanthe, but I'll tell you. If that's the only way you'll believe me."

CHAPTER EIGHT

iranda picked up a twig from the ground and twirled it between her fingers. She sighed heavily, looking away.

"The truth is, I grew up a forgettable child in a crowded house far from the Silence. My father was a fisher, and it was understood that we would all follow in his footsteps. I did my best, and the business did well enough. But I was never happy there. I was always . . . wanting more."

Such familiar words, but I would never have expected them to come from her mouth.

"I only had one true friend, growing up. Callie—Calanthe. She—she understood me." From her hesitation, I understood that there were countless other ways Miranda might have described her friend.

"There are mermaids in the ocean where I grew up," Miranda said flatly. "I suppose you don't have them in the Mundane, but mermaids . . . you hear their songs, and suddenly you want nothing more than to walk into the water and sink down when the land falls away from your feet. To let them take you."

I swallowed hard, a lump in my throat.

"The village caught me before I got too far out. But their song never really leaves you. It stays with you forever, ready to lure you back in. So they sent me away from the ocean. Callie was the only person who went with me. For a while our wanderings were aimless. . . . Then she heard about the Gather."

Miranda spread her hands out in front of her. "Callie's not a mage like me, but she thought we could find a place there. And once we arrived . . . The Gather isn't like other places. You'll see. It shimmers and changes when you least expect it. She was seduced by it all, especially the magic. She became a blood carrier—just like everyone else you've seen here with the blood plague. I knew it would kill her eventually, but she wouldn't hear of stopping."

"I don't understand," I said. "Why—"

"Why would anyone willingly do it? Because that's the only way to rise up in the king's court, if you're not a mage. To become one of the exalted ones, you must serve." Her lips twisted. "I agreed to serve the king in order to stay close to her. In time, I thought I could convince her to leave. I thought our friendship could free her. I even tried to bargain with the king to release her from his service." Her voice turned harsh. "But I was wrong. She died."

My breath caught in my throat. "I'm so sorry."

"Why should you care? You didn't know her."

But I would have liked to. Like I want to know you.

"That was when I left," Miranda added. "That was when I made up my mind to wake the sleeping princess and bring the Gather down."

I believed her, about Callie. I could hear the pain in her voice as she'd told her story. But I couldn't shake the feeling that she was still holding something back from me.

She sat up straight, wiping her hands on her trousers, and I could see her shake off the memories she'd just conjured. "But that's enough about that. Hand me my bag, will you?"

She'd dropped it on the other side of the shelter. I retrieved it and passed it to her. She pulled off her boots, revealing thick woolen socks, then stripped off her trousers, leaving her legs exposed aside from her undergarments. Her legs were strong, but the bandage around her calf was grimy and askew. Small spits of blood dotted the fabric covering her wound.

She was just a girl, and legs were just legs. But the sight of them still brought heat to my cheeks. *Stop staring!*

"What are you going to do?" I said, trying hard to keep my eyes above her waistline.

"Something I couldn't do in the Mundane." She pulled her knife from her coat pocket, then cut through the bandage and peeled the layers away, uncovering the wound.

It appeared to have scabbed over since I'd seen it last, but sprinting through the Silence had torn it open again. It was oozing blood once more. At least it didn't seem to be infected—the edrik's leaf had done its job.

"Don't worry. It isn't as bad as it looks," Miranda said.

"It seems pretty bad to me."

"I've had worse."

I watched as she rolled up her left sleeve and drew the blade across the back of her arm, cutting shallowly into her skin. She touched two fingers to the blood that welled to the surface and brushed them over the length of the open wound.

At first nothing happened. Then the flesh began to shift, mending itself before my eyes until the skin was smooth and unbroken. Miranda flexed her leg with an air of satisfaction, then wriggled back into her trousers.

"How did you *do* that?" I asked.

"Magic," she said simply.

"I know that, but *how?*"

For a moment she looked at me as though she'd never seen me before. "It's difficult to explain to someone who doesn't have it," she said. She blew air out of the side of her mouth, fluffing up a tuft of hair. "It's a matter of knowing exactly what you are asking of your magic. I couldn't create a stained glass window, for example, because I don't know the craft. But I apprenticed as a healer in the Gather. I can visualize the impurities being drawn from the wound, the muscle knitting back together, the skin becoming whole . . . and so I can use my blood to do the same."

"So you can do anything, if only you can visualize it."

"Well, not quite anything. There's the matter of how much power you can access at a time. And besides that, workings can go wrong in any number of ways: fatigue, inexperience, simple bad luck. . . . But you're right, in a manner of speaking. The boundaries of blood magic are carved by one's knowledge and imagination."

"But you do need to spill blood to access the power?"

"Yes. But enough about that. Let me see your arm."

I'd been distracted by the events of this afternoon, but the pain returned as I eased my arm free of my cloak and pulled back my sleeve.

"They would have had you," Miranda said softly as she studied the gash. "If you hadn't been able to use the curse, you would be dead."

It was true, but hearing her say it felt too much like justification. I shrugged uncomfortably.

Miranda leaned toward me, holding my gaze. "You never told me what using the curse is like, but I imagine it must be difficult."

Despite my apprehension, I looked back into her eyes. It *was* difficult.

There was a wound deep inside me that was close to tearing apart. It had cracked open the day I'd met Miranda—the yearning to share my story. To say *This is what happened to me. This is what I am.* As though by telling it, I could be less alone in my monstrousness. But I'd only told her part of the story—I wanted to tell her the rest. To show the same trust she had shown, in confiding to me about Callie.

My hands wanted to fidget—I held them still as I opened my mouth. "I used the curse a month ago. I killed someone. That's the only reason my father and I came to Onwey—the reason you and I met.

"We lived in a port city before. It was . . . pleasant. We had a house there, and a garden, and my room had windows that opened onto a view of the water. I spent hours there, sitting, watching. Dreaming.

"There was a house across the way where two elderly sisters lived. And then one day there was a boy there too—a nephew, I think. He was about my age."

I swallowed, hard. "His room was opposite mine. He played the violin, and sometimes he opened his window so I could hear. We didn't even speak. But we somehow—we became friends."

Memory swam through me, of him leaving sweets wrapped in a handkerchief at my bedroom window. The way I had washed the cloth and folded pressed flowers into it before running across the street in the dead of night to leave it at his doorstep. The way he had waved to me in the market, on one rare occasion when I had visited with Father.

"And then one day there was a storm," I said, my voice choked with emotion. "Father was out. I had to close all the shutters myself, and one of them stuck. I wasn't thinking about anything except the rain getting in and ruining our books, so I ran outside without putting on my gloves. But a tree branch had fallen across our stoop. I tripped over it and fell, and he saw from his window and tried—" My voice broke. "He came out and tried to help me."

This was too much. I couldn't go on.

I couldn't describe the way his hand had felt against mine, or the way his eyes had widened—how his expression had shifted from concern to pain to fear. The way his skin had glowed, and then ignited with a fire that could not be put out by the rain, his body collapsing in the street, his screams—*his screams*—

"Oh, *Lena*," Miranda breathed. "I'm so sorry."

"You shouldn't be sorry for me," I said gruffly. "*I* was the monster. Just like today. I was ready—*willing*—to use my curse against those Wolves."

"Lena, that boy's death was not your fault," she said fiercely. "And wanting to protect yourself is not wrong." She reached out to me before catching herself, realizing.

I turned away. It *was* my fault—for not being careful, for believing that I could get close to someone without everything turning to ash around me. And the telling of this story reminded me exactly why I needed to break the curse. It didn't matter that I'd felt almost empowered in that one moment, facing the Wolves. The longer it took to break the curse, the more likely it was that I might hurt someone else innocent and undeserving of such a fate. I could not waste any more time.

"What do we need in order to wake the princess?" I said, turning back to her.

For a moment it seemed Miranda wouldn't let the subject drop. Then she nodded. "First, we need to find a way past the Wolves. That's the easy part."

The easy part? She had to be joking. Getting around the Wolves seemed near impossible, if there were as many of them as Miranda had said.

"Then there's the castle itself. People have died on the briars, trying to claw their way through to the wall. There's a powerful magic that protects the castle, too. And after that, who knows? I've never heard of someone actually making it that far."

"How far did you get?" I asked.

Miranda bit her lip. "I couldn't get past the briars. And then the Wolves caught up to me."

"If that's the case, how do you expect us to do any better?"

"Now that I've been there, I'm more prepared. I have a few ideas."

I was still skeptical. "Say that we do make it into the castle, and find the princess, and wake her. What will she do? How will she save the forest?"

Miranda's gaze slid away from mine. "I'm . . . I'm not sure, actually. Legend has it that when the princess wakes, so will the Silence. And that she will help it tear down the Gather, and all of its rulers."

My father's face flashed through my mind. He'd told me the people of the Gather were not to be trusted. And Miranda had told me much the same—but only about the people who mistrusted *her*. Even I had to admit that this legend sounded far-fetched. Did that mean that Miranda was the one who was untrustworthy? And yet, I knew she'd been telling the truth about Callie. You couldn't fake pain like that . . . could you?

I picked at a stray thread coming off the cuff of my glove. I didn't know how to do this—parsing what people said, knowing what to believe. Growing up so isolated, I'd had no opportunity to learn what a lie looked like, felt like, when put up next to the truth. All I could do now was trust my instincts, faulty though they might be.

"Here, let me see that arm again," Miranda said.

I held very still as she bent over to inspect the wound. I could feel her breath on my skin, and it took everything I had within me not to flinch away. She was so close. Too close. My heart pounded as she brushed her fingers with blood and held them in the air above my arm. A few drops fell onto my skin as her eyes closed. I watched, fascinated, as the skin on my arm knitted itself back together. In a matter of moments the claw marks disappeared, leaving only a smear of my blood—and hers—behind.

Miranda opened her eyes and sat back, smiling in satisfaction. "It's late. We should sleep. It will be another long day tomorrow."

I *was* weary—the effects of using the curse, perhaps. Or every other exertion I'd put myself through since entering the Silence. Miranda tossed me a blanket. I spread it on the ground and lay down. No need to seek a comfortable position—I suspected there was none to be found. I left the lantern lit, to chase away whatever might lurk in the shadows.

On the other side of the shelter, Miranda shifted and murmured something indistinct, already fast asleep.

I closed my eyes. When I slept, I dreamed of a wall of black briars.

CHAPTER NINE

M y eyes opened into darkness. I didn't know where I was. There was no bed, no breeze tapping tree branches against my window. No light from the moon cutting across my room. Just the dark, and the steady roar of falling water.

Haven, I remembered. I was in Haven, with Miranda.

I propped myself up on an elbow and looked around, bleary-eyed. Our lantern had gone out, but elsewhere in the cavern there were lights. A small group of people stood together near the tunnel that led back out to the forest.

Curiosity sparked within me. I looked over at Miranda, who was still fast asleep. Then I got to my feet and straightened my clothing, pulling my gloves up and adjusting my collar. I stepped carefully around Miranda and made my way across the cavern.

As I approached, I saw that there was someone lying on a cot at the center of the group—a woman moaning weakly. The sound sent shivers down my spine, bringing back memories of Melor at the tavern. For a moment I thought about turning around, but then the group shifted, and I saw her clearly for the first time.

She wasn't so old, I thought. But it was difficult to tell because of the black marks shifting across her face, obscuring her features. They swirled and pulsed as I watched, strangely mesmerized. With every pulse, it seemed that the marks grew larger, and the woman's moans grew fainter. She batted the air with her arms as though fighting against an invisible assailant. But those motions too were weakening.

Those standing around her began to back away, forcing me to retreat to avoid them. They were murmuring, humming a tune that raised the hair on the back of my neck. But they made no move to help the woman. Was she beyond that now?

If I could touch her, I would cradle her head and press a damp cloth to her brow and tell her that she was not alone. But I couldn't.

I could only stand by and watch as the marks grew larger, engulfing her cheeks, spilling down her throat and below her shirt. They bled into her mouth and her eyes, turning her pupils black. She began to choke and thrash . . . and soon she lay still.

I pressed a fist against my mouth, stifling a sob. This death was quieter than Melor's, but it was still violent in its own way. This woman had been devoured by shadows, and we'd all simply stood here and watched it happen.

A few people returned and drew a shroud over the woman's body. The marks on her face were still visible. The rest of the group began to disperse.

I looked away. So this was what the end was for those people who became blood carriers. This woman must have served a blood mage of the Gather. I doubted they even remembered her now.

"You handled that well," said a voice nearby.

I jumped in surprise and turned to see Rin, holding a lit pipe.

"I'm sorry?" I said.

"Your first plague death," she replied. "Most people don't have the stomach to watch."

"It's not my first—"

Rin held up a hand. "Save it for someone you have a chance of convincing." She looked me up and down. "So you're Miranda's new girl."

My cheeks grew warm. "I'm not Miranda's anything," I said.

"If you say so," Rin said sardonically. The end of her pipe glowed orange as she inhaled.

I tried to remind myself that Rin's ire wasn't meant for me—it was for Miranda. But that did nothing to ease the anger that flared within me at her pointed words.

"You have her all wrong," I said. "She left the Gather."

"*Has* she," Rin said. "Then riddle me this, girl. Shale has great protections spelled into his palace walls. The only people who do not need permission to enter are those who carry his crest—a silver medallion stamped with the image of a wolf. It's something only granted to those *loyal* to him. Miranda was granted one. If she's loyal—and I know she is—she still has it."

"You're wrong," I said instinctively. But her cold certainty chipped away at me.

"Trust me, I take no pleasure in being right. I only seek to save you a world of hurt. What you do is entirely up to you."

She looked down at the dead woman's body once more. Then she turned on her heel and walked away, leaving me shaken.

She's wrong, I told myself. *She was speaking only out of spite.*

But there *had* been reason to doubt. The story Miranda had told me hadn't been completely convincing. Could this be why?

I had to know.

I went back to the shelter. Though Miranda was still asleep, my heart raced as I picked up her bag and brought it out into the light. For a moment I hesitated. This was wrong, an invasion. But I had to know.

I undid the straps and took off my gloves before reaching into the bag. My hand touched cloth, then the sack that contained what was left of our food. A sheathed knife, a small book, and . . . my fingers brushed against a coin.

I pulled it from the bag, keeping my fist closed. I looked down at my hand for two—three breaths. And then I forced my fingers to uncurl.

Silver glinted up at me. Though the light was low, the outline of the wolf was clear.

My heart plummeted. Rin had been right. Miranda was lying to me. She wasn't working against the Gather—she was working *for* them. I couldn't trust anything she said . . . and I couldn't stay with her now.

But without her, where would I go?

I looked at my hands in the lantern light. The Silence was deadly, yes. But I had already proven to be a match for the Wolves.

The Gather was full of mages, Miranda had said. If I made my way there, I could surely find someone with real knowledge of how to break the curse. I only needed to find a way to get there. . . .

The acorns.

I reached back into the bag, exploring by touch until I came across one acorn, then another. I pulled them out and pocketed them. Guilt twinged through me, but I ignored it. If Miranda was loyal to the Gather, she could navigate the Silence without these. I needed them more.

I repacked the bag and placed it back in the shelter. Miranda turned over, and I froze, holding my breath.

Her eyes stayed closed. I let out my breath and crept as quietly as I could out of the shelter.

Small bags had been set out for us sometime in the night—the provisions Miranda had requested. I picked one up, still debating myself. Was this wise? What if I was wrong about all of this? What if walking out of Haven without Miranda was a mistake?

No. The Silence had turned me upside down and taken away my balance, but there had to be something I could hold on to, and it was this: I couldn't trust her. And if I couldn't trust her, I had to leave her.

Slinging the bag over my shoulder, I took a lantern to light my way and walked toward the tunnel.

It was nearing morning when I stepped out into the open air. A bird sang somewhere nearby, and my steps lightened as I left the cavern and Miranda far behind.

I made my way past the houses without seeing another human, but as I reached the border between Haven and the rest of the Silence, I saw Tadrik standing guard.

I stopped. Entering Haven had been difficult enough. I wondered what it would take to leave.

"Good morning," I said.

The gatekeeper leaned on his staff and nodded back. I waited, but he did not speak.

"I would like to leave now," I said after some time had passed. "Will you tell me how?"

He looked me up and down. Though I felt the urge to cower, I stood tall and raised my chin.

"You are new to the Silence, I think. Despite what your friend said," he said finally.

I looked at him sharply. "I don't know why you would think

that." What had he seen that drew him to that conclusion? Miranda had said not to tell anyone I was new here—but might that have been for her own reasons?

"It's obvious to those who know how to look, child," he said.

I studied the gatekeeper. Rin had guessed anyway. Soon everyone in Haven might know. And Tadrik had a kindly look about him, if stern. I nodded hesitantly.

"And you know where you are going?"

Truthfully, I did not. But I had two acorns in my pocket and a growing determination not to trust anyone.

"I have a plan," I said. "If you'll just allow me to cross the trench, and tell me where this path leads."

He let out a sharp whistle, and out of the trench rose the hands. In the gray morning light, they looked even more unsettling than I remembered.

"What are they?" I asked. "Is this done by blood magic?"

"Travelers are not privy to the secrets of Haven. But they will carry you across."

As he spoke, the hands pooled together to create a sort of carpet, which floated toward me and came to rest on the ground before my feet. I held my breath and set one careful foot on the carpet, then the other. The hands shifted, and I stretched out my arms, trying to keep my balance. I looked back over my shoulder at the gatekeeper.

"Going alone is a difficult path. I wish you good fortune of it," Tadrik said.

The carpet lifted off the ground and I lost my balance, falling forward onto my hands and knees. My breath caught in my throat, and I resisted the urge to recoil as we slowly crossed the trench. The tension in my body began to ease only when we touched down on the other side and I staggered onto solid ground once more.

"There is a fork in the road, some ways ahead," the gatekeeper called. "To the left will lead you out of the Silence. The right will take you to the Gather."

I wanted to ask him where, specifically, the path out of the Silence led. Would I simply end up back where I had started, a few days dirtier? Or would it spit me out on the other side—the side where there was magic?

But I didn't dare ask. I didn't want him to be more aware of my ignorance than he already was. So instead I waved to him in thanks, turned around, and pushed my way back through the veil separating Haven from the rest of the forest.

Alone.

In some ways I'd always been alone, but I had never been alone like this—in a deadly place, with no one to protect me but myself. I should have been terrified. But my fear had receded, at least for this moment. I had survived my first night in the Silence. And I had the curse on my side for a change.

It was strange to think of the curse helping me. I had spent so long counting it only as a burden, the thing that made me a monster. But now I was beginning to realize that monstrosity could be power.

I thought of the Wolves, and the fear their appearance engendered in their prey. I thought of the Silence itself, and how the villagers of Onwey had spoken of it.

There is power in love—that was what my father had always said. But that love had been stifling. He and my mother had tried to protect me, and where had that gotten them?

For the very first time, I considered whether they had been wrong all of those years. Maybe they had even been wrong to keep me from using my curse.

Because there was power in fear, as well. When I had struck one Wolf down, the rest had looked at me with that fear. Not because I was good or kind. But because I could kill them.

My parents had taught me that it was important to be good, and that a good person was defined by their actions.

But what did it mean, when being good necessitated harming yourself in the process? I'd done all I could to protect those around me from myself. But how much had I lost? How much had I sacrificed? *Everything.*

Maybe it was my turn to walk freely. Maybe it was everyone else's turn to cower away from me, rather than I from them.

From somewhere nearby came the sound of running water, and all around me was the steady hum of insects singing to each other. A breeze shifted through the trees, rustling leaves. I kept careful watch, half expecting the forest to move the way it had when Miranda and I had entered yesterday morning. But the Silence stayed put.

Not so the other beings to either side of the path. Iridescent beetles as large as my hand buzzed through the air. Dark vines of ivy slithered along the ground like snakes, making my heart jump and stutter. Vibrant purple and yellow flowers chittered to each other, only to fall silent as I drew near. Ghost lights glimmered in the distance, though they winked out as soon as I turned my head to look. And farther away I heard the movements of larger creatures—but I was more curious than frightened. I wanted to know more, see more.

I looked down at the path, the marker stones clear and glimmering. What would happen if I stepped off it? What wonders might I find?

Come in.

I jumped. What *was* that? It had felt almost as though something—or someone—had spoken *inside* my head.

I looked around, but there was no one there. "Hello?" I said, feeling foolish.

Come in.

There they were again, those words that were not my own. Their tone was soft and dark—like night given voice. And there, in front of me, a glimmering path unfolded, bordered by glowing ferns and brightly colored mushrooms. It was inviting—alluring. I took one step forward before I caught myself and stopped. The memory of Melor came rushing back again. And here I was in the Silence, about to step off the path.

"Who are you?" I asked. "What do you want?"

Wind rushed through the forest, shaking the trees around me.

A friend, I heard eventually. **I am a friend.**

A shiver ran down my spine. A friend? A friend that wanted me to leave the safe path . . . and go where?

"If you are a friend, then show yourself. Come out where I can see you."

I fingered the edges of my gloves, ready to tear them off.

But there was nothing. And the voice said nothing further.

Heart pounding, I lowered my hands. Casting one more glance at the path that had appeared, I hurried on.

I kept to the safe path as morning waned into day. At the edge of the Silence the trees had been so dense they blocked out the sky. But here I could look up and catch an occasional glimpse of the sun. The only things that marked the distance I had traveled were my tired legs and my hunger. I wanted to curl up and rest, but I couldn't. I had to reach the Gather. I grabbed a bun from my bag and ate it as I walked.

Eventually I came to a fork in the road and remembered what the gatekeeper had told me. Left led out of the Silence. Right, toward the Gather.

I paused and ate a handful of roasted chestnuts while considering.

Everyone had told me the Gather was dangerous. But I wasn't powerless. I could protect myself.

Besides, I hadn't come all this way to lose my nerve now.

I took a deep breath, mustering up my courage, and turned right.

I made it only a few steps past the turnoff when I heard footsteps approaching from behind me. I thought about jumping from the path to hide—but that seemed foolish. What if I couldn't find my way back to it later?

I stripped off my gloves and shoved them into my pocket, preparing for whatever was coming around the bend. I counted to three before whirling around to face—

Miranda.

Her face was flushed from running. She stopped a few feet away, bending over to catch her breath.

"What are you doing here?" I said. I lowered my hands but did not put my gloves back on.

"What are *you* doing here? I woke up and you were gone! I

thought that someone had taken you! I couldn't believe it when the gatekeeper said you left on your own. What were you thinking?"

I took a step back as she came closer to me. She stopped moving, her expression twisting with hurt. I felt a pang of guilt but brushed it away. She could very well be pretending, just to win my sympathy and trick me.

"There are parts of your story that don't add up," I said. "I decided that perhaps I made a mistake, trusting you."

Miranda frowned, exasperated. "You still don't trust me? I'm trying to *help* you."

"Why was it so important to keep the curse a secret back there? Why didn't you tell the people at Haven that you're trying to wake the sleeping princess? Isn't that something they support?"

Miranda rolled her eyes and sighed loudly. "The rulers of the Gather do not allow challenges to their power. And your curse is an exceptional challenge. I couldn't allow you to risk yourself in that way, or let any spies in Haven learn of your curse."

"Really? You're not just trying to keep me dependent, so I can be of use only to you?"

Miranda laughed harshly. "Of course I want you with me. Because you *are* useful. But that is irrelevant. We made a bargain, and I'm holding up my end."

"And what about the medallion?" I said.

She stilled. "What?"

"You heard me. The medallion that shows your loyalty to the Gather. To Shale. If you have left them behind, then why do you still have it?"

She scowled at me. "Who told you about that? Was it Rin?"

"It doesn't matter," I said, keeping my voice steady. "Why do you have it, if you're no longer working for them?"

Miranda bit her lip. "It's more complicated than you think. I—" She looked past me, her eyes suddenly wide with fear.

"What is it?"

"Alaric," she said, the name almost as soft as a whisper.

I turned around.

CHAPTER TEN

The boy who had appeared behind me looked about my age, tall and all sharp angles. His dark, shaggy hair fell nearly into his eyes, and he was cloaked entirely in black. He wasn't carrying any visible weapons . . . but Miranda had still paled when she saw him.

"What are you doing here?" Miranda said.

He ignored her, instead staring straight at me. His eyes were pools of midnight—so dark and magnetic that I almost felt I might fall into them if I looked too long.

"Lena," he said, his voice musical and low.

I stepped back, shaken. "How do you know my name?"

"I have been hunting you for a very long time," he said.

The witch. He was working for her—he had to be.

"You can't take her," Miranda said. She turned to me, pleading. "Come with me, Lena. He's *dangerous*."

Alaric laughed. "As are all who walk willingly through the Silence. You trust this girl, Lena? She is a liar, and a cheat." He looked at Miranda. "Tell me, Miranda. Is this all part of some grand scheme to win Calanthe back to your side? Because it won't work."

My lips parted in surprise. Callie was alive?

That was impossible. Miranda had been mourning in Haven—

her grief had been so palpable I could almost taste it. Callie was dead—wasn't she? I turned to Miranda.

"Is that true?" I hissed. "You lied to me?"

She looked at me, stricken. "Callie is dead to me. She is forsaken, beyond saving. What I told you is true in the way that *matters*."

Was it, though?

Miranda continued, "But you cannot trust *him*. He serves *Katen*, the princess of the Gather. The daughter of the king. You don't know them, not like I do. If he takes you to her, you will die."

But what if that, too, was just another attempt to manipulate me back into trusting her? I was caught—between the girl who had charmed me and a stranger who knew my name.

I chanced a glance at the trees at the edge of the path. How far could I flee before they caught me? Miranda was just a human girl, regardless of her magic. And though Alaric was frightening, I'd seen nothing to convince me he was anything more than a boy.

A line of ferns unfurled into the forest, a smaller version of those that had appeared to me before. **Run, Lena.**

"Don't run, Lena," Alaric said softly, and my gaze jerked back to him. His eyes were still focused on Miranda, but somehow he seemed to have read my thoughts. "It would behoove you to come with me willingly, both for your own sake and for Miranda's."

"Lena, don't—"

But I had already made up my mind. I darted off the path.

I'd only gone a few steps when a hard shove against my back sent me sprawling. I hit the ground hard and rolled to see Alaric standing over me. He turned around as Miranda rushed forward, knife in hand. He easily sidestepped her attack, then grabbed her by the collar and lifted her effortlessly off her feet. I gasped as he threw her through the air. Her body collided with a tree before collapsing to the ground.

"Miranda!" I cried out. She didn't move, and my chest tightened at the possibility that she was seriously wounded—or dead.

Alaric turned his attention back to me. I scrambled to my feet, raising my hands. "Don't come near me," I warned. "Or I will kill you."

He smiled a cruel smile. "It's adorable that you think you can."

I was rigid with fear as he stalked toward me, heedless of my threat. I tried to rally myself, tried to remember how powerful I'd felt after the Wolf had burned. But this was different. This was a boy, just like the last one. *The scent of burning flesh dampened by rain*— My stomach roiled as I pushed the memory away. I had to do this. I had to be strong.

Alaric closed the distance between us quickly, and then he was standing only inches from me. If he worked for the witch, he must know of the curse, but he made no move to defend himself as I lashed out, striking his cheek with my bare hand.

Nothing happened.

Alaric's grin widened. He reached out and grabbed my wrist, the warmth of his fingers a shock against my skin—*that boy's hair shriveling into smoke*—I gaped up at him. I could hear the rush of my own blood in my ears. This was impossible—how—

"I don't understand. You're supposed to be dead," I whispered.

"Come, Lena. It's time for us to go." He yanked me by the wrist, and I stumbled forward, colliding with his chest. Dazed, I tried to pull away, but his arms enveloped me in an embrace, holding me tightly. Wind lifted my hair and tore at my clothes as branches whipped around us. I ducked my head down as the forest whirled and fell away from our feet.

Somehow, incomprehensibly, we were flying.

Shadows spread out from Alaric's shoulders, creating the ghostly impression of wings. I looked down. We were higher than the trees now, soaring over the Silence's canopy. Freed of the forest's eternal twilight, I could tell that it was still afternoon. Trees stretched out in all directions, as far as I could see. If I fell, I might simply disappear. My stomach lurched at the thought, and I squeezed my eyes shut.

Soon we began to descend. My feet touched the earth, and suddenly the world righted itself again. Alaric let me go. My knees buckled, and I pitched forward onto the ground.

Alaric knelt at my side, his hand resting on my shoulder. I threw it off and pushed myself to my feet. "What did you just do? Where are we?"

"We're still in the Silence. This is just a place where we're less likely to be interrupted. I wanted to speak to you privately before I deliver you to my mistress. And I know you have questions of your own. I promise we'll get to them in due time." His tone was infinitely patient, and it infuriated me.

"Don't talk to me like that. I'm not a child."

He raised an eyebrow and rose gracefully to his feet.

My hand itched to slap him. But I was afraid to touch him again. I was afraid of what it meant that my curse had failed me *now*, when I needed it most.

"How long?" I said, my words clipped.

"What?"

"How long have you been hunting me?"

"Seventeen years."

I gasped. "That can't be possible. You look—"

"Dashingly handsome?" he said, smirking.

"*Young.* You can't be more than a year or two older than me."

Alaric visibly deflated. "Appearances can be deceiving," he said, sounding suddenly exhausted. "I've been this way for a very long time."

I rolled my eyes.

"You don't believe me."

"No, I don't." For some inexplicable reason, I could believe that a boy who could fly had abducted me—but accepting that he was also some unearthly ageless being was a step too far.

"Strange, that. But I understand why. You just found out that you've been lied to for your entire life."

I frowned. "But I've only known Miranda a few days."

"I'm not speaking of Miranda. I am speaking of your parents."

"What could you know of my parents?" I spat.

"I knew them before you were born. Their names are Joren and Edina. And, if I'm not mistaken, that's your mother's handiwork on that cloak." He reached for my hood, rubbing the fabric between his fingers. "Clever of her."

I could have explained away so much. But I could not explain how he knew my parents' names. Unless he *was* telling the truth.

I swallowed, hard. I was afraid of what he might tell me next. But I had to know. "Why didn't you die when I touched you?"

"Because your curse is not what you think it is."

"How—"

"I was there when Katen placed the curse on you," Alaric interrupted me.

Katen . . . the princess of the Gather. "Katen is the witch?"

"A witch . . . is one name for what she is. There are others."

Katen. The name rang through me like a bell. Katen was the

witch who had cursed me. And Alaric was the lackey who would take me to her, to my death.

"Lena, we are short on time."

I looked up at him, feeling numb. "What does that matter, when all you're going to do is drag me back to your mistress? Because I don't really care if I inconvenience *her*."

"Not her," said Alaric. He looked away, running a hand through his hair in frustration. "*Us*."

"What are you talking about?" I shot back. "There is no *us*."

"If you wish to break the curse and foil my mistress, then I am your best chance. It is true that I am bound to carry out Katen's commands. But I do not serve her willingly. If I deliver you to Katen, she will kill you. So I have an offer for you instead. If you help me win my freedom, I will kill her for you. And your curse will be broken."

"And you don't think I can do that myself?" I said, scoffing.

"No," he said simply. "Because the power inside of you is not your own. It is hers."

That made no sense. "What do you mean, it's not mine?"

"I see you carry a bag from Haven. If you were there, you must have seen some of the blood carriers. Katen is a blood mage. She put her magic in you to keep it a secret from her enemies. And then she placed a curse on you—the Hand of Mora. Anyone who touches you without being told the name of the person who placed the curse will die. So you could not kill her with it if you tried. It is her curse, her power."

I raised my hands before my eyes, feeling as though they had betrayed me. My own body was monstrous, but it had always been mine. I thought we understood each other. But if this was true . . .

"I don't know you," I said slowly. My voice sounded faint even to my own ears. "How do I know if any of this is true? How do I know you're not simply toying with me?"

Alaric scoffed at me. "Such games are human conceits. I don't play them."

"And you aren't human?"

"No," he said somberly. "No, I'm not."

Strangely, I found that I believed him. "Then what are you?"

He leaned back against a tree. "Once, I was a raven of the Silence," he said, a note of sadness creeping into his voice. "Before there was a Gather, Shale and Katen were just ordinary people who came here, fleeing their troubles elsewhere." His words turned bitter. "Katen tricked me out of my wings and bound me into her service. I have served her for more years than I can count."

He looked at me, his black eyes unblinking. "You ask whether I am telling the truth. If I were truly loyal to Katen, I would take you to her immediately. There is no reason for me to tell you all of this, except that I need your help."

Miranda had also asked for my help.

But of the two of them, Alaric's story was more convincing . . . and his plan more achievable.

"You said that you've been hunting me for a long time," I said slowly. "If Katen is so powerful, then why didn't you find me until now?"

"Because of your cloak. Your mother wove a spell into it that conceals you from magical scrying when you're close enough to it. So Katen could only find you by the curse—when it's used, the power is strong enough for her to sense. You've used the curse three times—most recently yesterday, when you killed that Wolf. Katen has felt it every time."

They'd felt me *every time*, including the first—

I'm seven again, clinging to my mother's hand as she walks through the market. I'm bundled up as though we are in the dead of winter instead of early summer. It's hot, and my throat is parched. I pretend I am a flower, waiting for rain.

A soap bubble floats across the sky, and I giggle, watching it.

"Stay right here," Mother says, and she turns to haggle with a merchant. I know the rules: stay where you're told, don't talk to anyone, don't touch anything, don't touch anyone—

But two children run past me as fast as they can, and the girl smiles at me, hair tangled and feet bare, and she is everything I want to be, and a wildness rises within me that calls back—I want, I want, I want. I don't even understand what I want, not really, but I want it so desperately—my toes wiggle in my shoes, neatly buckled, and when the children run by once more, shrieking with delight, I follow.

It is so easy to follow them, to melt into this gaggle of children and their games. Though I don't understand all the rules, I understand the freedom that unfolds in front of me.

The girl takes my hand through my glove, and I let her. We run together, and I am laughing—until I'm grabbed by the other wrist, tagged, and I hear a shriek of pain.

The boy who touched me is on fire. He is running as flames lick up his arms to his neck, his face. His hair catching light, curling up into smoke—

There are so many people screaming, and the girl has long since let go of my other hand. I close my eyes, put my hands over my ears, but I can't block it out.

My mother is there suddenly, lifting me into her arms, running with me, and when we are safe inside again she slaps my face and tells me never, never break the rules again.

And I am crying, saying "I'm sorry, I'm sorry, is it my fault?"

"Yes. Yes, it's your fault. And you must never do it again."

And all the while Father is hurrying around us in a blur, packing our bags like so many other times before.

"Lena." I was wrenched back into the present by the sound of Alaric's voice as he shook me by the shoulders. I refocused, taking in the concern on his face. Then I looked past him into the trees, digging my fingernails into the earth as if to anchor myself. There was a metallic taste in my mouth—I'd bitten the inside of my cheek. My entire body was shaking.

I suddenly thought of my father standing in the kitchen, drizzling glaze over the queen's cakes. He had gone to such pains to protect me—and yet he and my mother had lied about our history. They had lied to me about my own curse. My very nature. How could they? How *could* they?

This was too much. A sob rose up in my throat, and I could not swallow it down—not after this. In the middle of the Silence, before the stranger who had just shattered my understanding of my entire world, I wept.

"Lena, whatever pain you've suffered in the past—we can make Katen pay for it now." Alaric's voice was soothing, almost seductive.

Like Miranda's had been.

"Don't pretend that you care about my pain," I said. "You want this for yourself."

"That is true," he replied, his face like stone. "I want nothing more than to bleed the life out of my mistress. But when I do that, both you and I will be free. And that, I would think, is something worth fighting for."

Of course I should not trust him. He wanted to use me, just

as Miranda had. But something about him spoke to me. We were both bound by things outside our control.

"Then answer me one more question," I said, wiping away my tears. "One question and I'll agree to join you." Not that I had much of a choice—it was either join him or be delivered to the witch.

"If it is within my power to answer," Alaric said.

"Why did Katen do this to me?"

Alaric smiled—a small, sad smile. "We are all bound in our own way. She is a princess, but her father is a tyrant. He will allow no one to challenge his rule, and she is powerful enough to be a threat. If he'd learned how much magic she truly possesses, he would have killed her long ago. Katen knew this, so she hid her power far away, where it would never be stumbled upon, or turned against her."

"In the Mundane. Inside of me."

Alaric nodded and held out his hand. "As I said before, the hour grows late. Shall we?"

What was I doing? Jumping from one terrible situation into the next. And yet Alaric was right—Katen *should* pay for the anguish she'd caused me. My fury at my parents' deceit might never find its target. But I could help bring down the witch and finally break this awful curse. How extraordinary that I was thinking such mercenary thoughts. A week ago I would have been horrified by the prospect—I would have been sick at the idea of using the curse on purpose.

But I was done with running away. This was how I would win my freedom.

I took his hand.

The shadows of wings spread around us, and he spirited me away.

CHAPTER ELEVEN

O ur second flight was shorter than the first. Now that I
was somewhat more composed, I could appreciate the
grace with which Alaric navigated the sky, catching different air currents and riding them smoothly. Still, I couldn't see
myself ever growing accustomed to the experience of being held so
closely to someone else without burning them alive.

Before long, Alaric took us down again, this time landing in
front of the hollow of an enormous tree.

"We're not on a path," I said, almost without thinking. I'd been
too distraught earlier to realize how deep we were in the wilds of
the Silence.

"I'm a creature of the Silence," Alaric said, barely glancing at
me. "I don't need a path."

I gritted my teeth at his arrogance, then realized that the hollow was actually a shelter, with supplies tucked into its nooks and
crannies. As I watched, Alaric picked up a stick and drew a rough
circle in the earth around us. "As long as you stay within the circle,
my magic will protect you."

"From what?"

He raised an eyebrow. "From detection by the Wolves. Creatures of the Silence. Other things." He snapped his fingers, and
a cook fire sprang to life before me. Then he pulled out a small

cast-iron pan and some vegetables from his supplies and settled down to cook. It was so incongruous a scene that I felt a sensation oddly like whiplash.

"What, no magic food?" I couldn't stop myself from laughing.

"No," Alaric said shortly. "Food conjured by magic is always lacking. If you have a choice, do not take it." He refocused his attention on the pan.

I sat down near the fire, crossing my legs. It still made my shoulders tense to sit so close to Alaric, even though I knew I didn't have to worry about what would happen if he shifted unexpectedly. I wondered how it would feel to be this way around everyone, once the curse was broken. Try as I might, I couldn't imagine it.

"Here." The vegetables were done—Alaric pulled a bowl from somewhere and passed it over. Our fingers brushed, and the touch sparked heat within me. I looked away, hoping he wouldn't notice if I was blushing.

After we had eaten, I set my bowl aside and looked at Alaric. "All right," I said. "What is your plan?"

He stared into the fire. "Katen stole my wings and hid them. That is the source of her power over me. When they are in my possession once more, I will be free to strike against her."

"Does she know that you're looking?"

He shrugged. "I'm not sure. She knows I'm not as besotted with her as I once was. But whether she believes I would ever betray her on purpose . . . I don't know. Regardless, we must retrieve them before I can strike her down."

I nodded. At least on the face of it, the task seemed simple enough. "So where do we start?"

"That's the trick," Alaric said. "I've scoured the Silence over the years. I've found no trace of them."

"So you have no leads," I said, my heart sinking.

"Not exactly. There is a woman who used to work for Katen who might know where they are. She fashioned locks and keys around the palace, that sort of thing."

"But then this woman must be loyal to Katen, correct? Or she wouldn't still be alive."

He raised an eyebrow at me. "I see you're catching on to the way Katen works. And you are correct—except that Katen doesn't know she's still alive." And there was something about the smug way he said it. . . .

"You were supposed to kill her," I said slowly. "But you didn't."

He smiled wryly. "I thought I might have need of her someday. But it was difficult. I was ordered to wipe her from the face of the earth—so I erased her existence . . . but only from Katen and myself. I placed a charm over her so that I cannot find her, cannot see her, cannot interact with her, not by word or action or deed, so long as she does not betray me to Katen."

I thought this through. "That would mean you need someone else. Someone you trust. To find her and speak to her."

"Exactly," Alaric said, the approval in his voice sending warmth through my body. "That's where you come in. I have reason to believe she is still in the Gather—you should be able to find her there. Then I'll tell you what to say on my behalf, and you'll get the information from her."

"What makes you think she's still there?"

"I can't sense her . . . but what I do sense, sometimes, is an absence. At times, there are places within the Gather that seem to disappear entirely from my sight. I can think of no other explanation than that the spell is working to keep me from seeing her."

He'd crafted himself a loophole. Clever of him. This also suggested that he'd been planning this for some time.

"What would you have done, if I hadn't come along? Who would you have asked for help?"

"No one, perhaps," Alaric said, his eyes gleaming. "I've waited a very long time to find someone with as much at stake as me."

There were many ways to reckon time . . . but I had a feeling that Alaric was talking in decades, not years.

"How long have you been in Katen's service, exactly?" I said.

He shrugged. "Time passes differently in the Silence. But to the outside, to the Mundane? One hundred years—perhaps longer."

I gasped. That was a lifetime. I'd thought my almost eighteen years of solitude unbearable. But he'd been waiting five times as long.

He picked up a twig from the ground and twirled it between his fingers, then tossed it into the fire. "Do not feel sorry for me, Lena," he said tightly. "I deserved much of what I have suffered. But I am ready to be free."

I believed him. Foolish and dangerous of me, perhaps. But I did. And more than that, I wanted to help him.

"All right," I said. "Let's go to the Gather."

Alaric smiled at me, and for a moment I could see what he must have been like all those years ago—carefree, trusting.

Then he turned, as though he'd heard something that I could not. "Get behind that tree," he said, his voice strained. "Quickly. And do not move, no matter what you hear."

He sounded worried enough that I scrambled to obey. I

crouched down, leaves crackling under my boots, but couldn't keep myself from peering around the tree trunk.

The air above the fire shimmered, and then somehow parted, as though someone had cut through it with a knife. Through the gap I saw a woman's face framed by long, red-gold curls, and a wall of stone behind her.

"How goes the hunt?" she said impatiently.

Katen. I pulled myself back behind the tree, my heart racing.

"The girl was not where I expected to find her," Alaric said. He sounded disinterested.

"But you killed a pack of Wolves. Why?"

"They saw the girl just before I arrived. I could not take the chance that they would report back to Shale. Besides, it amused me," he replied, his voice frighteningly cold.

The woman laughed cruelly. "See that you restrain yourself next time—I am running out of excuses to make to my father."

"As you command," Alaric said.

"And do not let the trail go cold. We cannot risk someone else finding her first."

There was unnerving silence—and then a heavy sigh. "You can come out now, Lena," Alaric said.

I stood up, my shoulders tight. "That was her? Katen?"

He nodded. "She was checking up on me. Since I haven't *found* you yet."

I swallowed. "Did you really kill those Wolves?" I said, my voice tiny.

Alaric looked away. "I had to."

"When you spoke with her, you sounded so . . . different," I said.

"It is an act, Lena. My entire life is a charade." He stalked to the edge of the shelter and put one hand against the tree trunk. "It's unbearable," he said, almost too low for me to hear. "That is why I need you, and why we must not fail."

I slept fitfully that night, nerves fluttering under my skin. I thought I'd made the right decision in aligning myself with Alaric, but the stakes were so, so high. I dreamed about Miranda as I'd last seen her, crumpled on the ground in the Silence. I didn't even know if she was alive. I hoped she was. Even though she'd lied to me, I didn't want to consider a world without her in it. And that thought alone scared me.

Lena.

My eyes sprang open. It was the same voice that had called my name in the river, that had tried to call me from the path.

I sat up. Alaric was asleep on the other side of the shelter, his chest rising and falling evenly as he breathed. The fire had burned down to embers.

"Who are you?" I whispered.

Come see.

Ferns unfurled, lighting a path that led outside the circle Alaric had drawn.

I hesitated. Alaric had said to stay put. And I now knew there were dangers in the Silence that I was unequipped to handle.

"No," I said. "If you want something from me, then show yourself. I won't play games."

A breeze rippled through the trees. Something snapped in the underbrush, and a deer crossed in front of me, its antlers wreathed in luminous pink flowers. I stared, captivated—and then I saw the figure standing behind it. It was tall and slight, its features indistinct, and as I watched, it beckoned to me.

I got to my feet.

"Lena?" Alaric was instantly awake. "What are you doing?"

The figure vanished.

"I thought I saw something," I said sheepishly.

I couldn't see his face in the darkness, but I could feel the weight of his attention. "The Silence will try to trick you," he said finally. "Try not to let it. Go back to sleep." I heard him snap his fingers, and just like that, the fire sprang back to life, chasing away any lingering shadows.

In the morning Alaric flew us most of the way to the Gather and let us down on a path before we arrived. We were still deep in the Silence, but in the distance, I could hear the rumblings of people. Lots of them.

"It's important that we are not seen together," Alaric said. "You'll follow the path and enter the city alone. You'll blend in better without me by your side. Once you're in, go to the tailors' quarter. I've felt a strong absence there."

"I don't suppose you'd like to provide more specific directions?"

"Ah. Yes," Alaric said, looking just a little sheepish. "The Gather is divided into two districts, high and low. The low district is where you'll enter—you'll see mostly markets and tradesfolk. The tailors' quarter is there."

"And the high district?"

"That's where Shale built his palace. Most blood mages live there as well. But you needn't worry too much about it. You won't be going anywhere near it, and besides, you wouldn't be allowed admittance anyway." He cleared his throat. "The woman you're looking for is named Cyn. When I knew her, she was tall with green eyes—and she wore her hair long. She had a dog; I remember that, too. I don't know how much of that is still true."

That was it? Not much more than a name and a description that was who knows how many years out of date. The task felt impossible before I'd even begun.

"And what shall I say to her, if by some miracle I actually find her?" I said.

"Tell her that the raven has come to call in her debt. She won't fight you on it."

"What should I ask her?"

"I will tell you what to say."

"Very well," I said. Alaric nodded once before dissolving into thin air, leaving me standing alone.

A cold wind blew across my face, and I pulled my cloak around me. I hadn't put on my gloves this morning—now I fished them out of my pocket and drew them up over my hands. I had to be careful. The Gather would be rife with mages—and people. It would be so easy to trip up, to get caught—to hurt someone.

I steeled myself and started down the path. Soon I rounded a curve, and there before me lay the Gather.

The city's silhouette was as sharp as broken, jagged blades against the sky. It was beautiful, spread out in glittering black stone and a sea of lights that dazzled against the eternally twilit backdrop of the Silence. And somewhere within waited the mage who had cursed me—and her more dangerous father.

I was seized by an urge to run.

Instead I pulled my hood over my head and made my way toward it.

As I got closer, I saw the buildings reached high, narrowing into pointed spires at the top. There were no gates at the city entrance, but it didn't take long for me to notice that there were still defenses at play. Certain stones glowed underfoot as people stepped over them, and there were guards standing watch.

What did the stones do? I knew so little about the extents and limits of blood magic. What if the stones were somehow able to sense criminal intent? Or . . . what if they sensed the amount of power within each passerby? For the first time, I wondered just how much of Katen's magic was flowing through my veins. Why hadn't I succumbed to blood plague, like so many others? I decided to ask Alaric about it later—for now I had to focus on the task at hand. I walked forward, keeping my head low and holding my breath as I passed over the stones.

Nothing happened. I let out my breath, but my pulse jumped as the flow of traffic pushed me farther into the city. I hunched my shoulders and kept my elbows tucked in, taking short steps to avoid bumping into anyone.

The crowd emptied out into a market with stalls lining the street. The aromas of all manner of food filled the air. Despite my caution, I had to stop myself from staring. Sparks of light danced along a young girl's knuckles; as she clapped, the light coalesced into lightning between her palms. A brightly colored cart displayed a sign advertising THE SECRETS TO ALL MANNER OF WONDERS, and the pages of books on display fluttered as I passed. Musicians on one corner played instruments that I did not recognize, but my feet felt an unsettling urge to speed up and step in time with the tune. There were stalls filled with baubles that moved without being touched, glowing potions in bottles that emitted colored smoke when unstoppered . . . There was even one shop proprietor boasting that her hats brought good luck to their wearers.

I was enchanted. For a split second I imagined what it would have felt like if Miranda had been standing beside me. How she would have taken my hand and led me through, showing me this wondrous place in a world where, for the first time, I could picture myself belonging.

But then I caught a glimpse of the blood plague dancing across a face, and I shuddered. There was darkness here, too, now that I remembered to look for it. Uniformed guards jostling through the crowds, leaving glowering faces in their wake. Side alleys harboring people huddling together against the cold. An ever-present sense of wariness.

I looked around, hoping to see Alaric nearby, but he was nowhere to be found. I was on my own.

I couldn't find a sign pointing the way to the tailors' quarter so I took a deep breath and approached a woman wearing a blue kerchief who was manning a clothing stall at the edge of the street. "Excuse me," I said. "I'm looking for the tailors' quarter. Can you tell me how to get there?"

She peered at me. "New here, are you?"

I flushed and tensed, readying myself to run or to pull off my gloves and defend myself.

Her lips pursed as she took in my reaction, and she lowered her voice. "You've nothing to fear from me, dearie. But take care to guard yourself—it's not safe to ask just anyone for help around here. As for the tailors' quarter, you're close. Go to the end of the street and turn right," she said, pointing.

I nodded my thanks and tried to walk with purpose, like I

knew where I was going, as the clouds above burst and a sheet of rain descended upon the city.

I was shivering with cold and my breath was misting by the time I passed below the sign signifying my arrival at the tailors' quarter. Someone fell into step with me—Alaric. He wore a hat drawn low over his face, and a shabby brown cloak. It was a good disguise, for something improvised. I wondered how recognizable he was in the Gather—although in the rain, there were few about to notice him.

"Here," he said suddenly, stopping in the middle of the street.

We were in an open square. There were easily fifteen businesses with signs swinging in the wind, and far more places to look if one counted all the residences I suspected to be set above the shops.

"That's most helpful," I said dryly. "I don't suppose you have anything more specific to share?"

I took Alaric's silence to mean that he did not.

With nothing else to go on, I knew of only one way to find Cyn. I walked to the nearest door and knocked. Loudly.

No one answered at the first or second door I tried. The third opened upon an elderly man who looked me up and down, then shut the door in my face before I'd even gotten a question out. I was about to knock at the fourth storefront when I looked across the square and saw a small spotted dog sitting on the stoop outside a door, waiting to be let in.

As I watched, the door opened. A woman wearing a red scarf over long blond hair bent over and picked up the dog in a towel, then went back inside. The door closed behind her.

Alaric had said that Cyn had once had a dog.

"Did you see that?" I asked.

"What?" Alaric said, frowning.

That was all the confirmation I needed. I crossed the square and knocked on the door.

CHAPTER TWELVE

To my surprise, a short, dark-haired woman answered the door. She looked at me suspiciously. "Yes?"

"I'm looking for Cyn," I said.

"Are you with *him?*" she asked, pointing at Alaric.

I nodded. "Yes. Tell her the raven has come to call in her debt."

The woman rocked back in shock. For a moment I thought she would slam the door in our faces. Finally, she pressed her lips together unhappily but stood aside. Alaric and I stepped into the house.

"I'll get her," the woman said. "Just . . . stay here."

She climbed the stairs that ran along the right side of the room, leaving us alone. Alaric turned around, studying our surroundings. Somehow, despite the rain, he'd stayed maddeningly dry.

"I'm surprised she's not running," I said under my breath.

He smiled. "I bound her with a true vow. She would not be able to turn away my representative."

I wasn't sure how I felt about being someone else's representative. It sounded like being in someone else's service.

I looked around. A couch with faded blue cushions sat against the far wall. There was a small table with two chairs near the fireplace. A mending basket sat on one of the chairs. This was a comfortable home, if a little shabby.

The woman I'd seen with the dog came down the stairs, her steps slowing as she saw me. She scanned the room, but her gaze passed right over Alaric without pausing. So it really was true that she couldn't see him—just as Alaric couldn't see her. He was looking only at me.

"Who are you?" she asked.

"No one," I said. Only a few days ago I might have given my name—I had thought myself anonymous when I entered the Silence. But I knew better now—if Alaric had known my name, others might know me as well.

"Is she here?" Alaric asked.

I nodded slightly.

"Then say this: 'I come on Alaric's behalf, for what is his by right and vow.'"

I repeated the message.

She nodded. "I thought that might be the case. Is he here?"

"Yes."

She blanched and drew herself upright. "Let's make this quick, then. What does he want?"

I looked at Alaric. "What do you want to ask?"

"Ask exactly this—no more and no less," he said.

I listened carefully, then turned back to Cyn. "He asks, what exactly did his mistress ask you to make after he left the room that day? And he asks where it is hidden."

She lifted her chin. "So he's going to try to free himself," she said. I didn't like the tone of her voice—she reminded me of the magistrate who'd lived down the street from Father and me in the town of Savin, always sniffing for information he could use for leverage.

"That's none of your concern," I said, trying to sound threatening. "He found you once, he can do it again if necessary."

She looked at me appraisingly. "And who would he send? You? You look like a half-drowned cat."

My cheeks flushed, but I swallowed down my outrage. It might behoove me to appear less dangerous than I actually was.

"Lena," Alaric said impatiently.

I looked at him. "She refuses to answer."

Cyn's eyes widened with fear. "Now see here, I didn't say *that*—"

I ignored her, listening as Alaric gave me his response, his voice devoid of emotion.

I turned back to Cyn. "He says that you are bound to tell us what you know, or suffer the consequences."

"Fine," she snapped, though she was clearly shaken. "Tell him that his mistress had me make a box. She wanted it entirely made of wood, with wings carved down the sides." Her voice softened as she spoke—she clearly took pride in her work. "But she requested one unusual specification. The box had to be waterproof. As to where she hid it . . ." Her gaze went inward as she concentrated. "The princess said she would hide it where the raven would never be able to find it, not by foot, nor by wing."

Alaric's expression darkened as I repeated Cyn's words. So this meant something to him.

"Do you want to ask anything else?"

Alaric shook his head. "This is the information we came for. Let's go."

"We will leave now," I told Cyn.

"Wait," she said. "Does this discharge the debt? I don't want to be looking over my shoulder for the next twenty years of my life."

I didn't like this woman—in fact, I didn't mind the idea of her looking over her shoulder for years to come. I spoke without looking to Alaric for guidance. "If the information proves useful, perhaps," I said.

And then we were walking out of the house, the door slammed shut behind us.

"You scared her," Alaric said.

"How would you know?" I replied. "You couldn't even see her."

"Because you looked . . ."

I waited for him to finish. "Well?"

"Dangerous," he said finally. Though there was something in his tone that made me wonder whether he thought that was a good thing.

"We got what we needed, didn't we?" I said. "So what now? I don't want to be standing in this rain longer than we have to."

"We can't discuss anything here," Alaric said. He glanced around, and I realized that he was afraid we might be overheard. "Let's get out of the Gather first. Stay behind me."

The rain was clearing up as we made our way out of the tailors' quarter and back toward the edge of the city. People who had gone into shops to escape the downpour were now returning to the streets. Alaric led the way through the crowd, keeping a few paces ahead of me so no one would know we were together—disguise or not. But as we approached the black stones that marked the city border, he stopped abruptly.

I craned my neck, trying to figure out what he'd seen. The people around us were stopping too, their murmurs growing louder, and then I saw them—the black stones in front of us were glowing a bright, sickly green.

The stones beneath my own feet changed color. Suddenly the ground shifted under me, and I stumbled. I dove for the nearest building, pressing myself against a sturdy doorframe. When I looked back for Alaric, he was gone.

The stones shifted again. This time they cracked upward, and enormous roots erupted into the air, breaking the street apart. The entire city seemed to be rocking and swaying. Animals brayed in fear, and stalls collapsed. Cracks ran up the side of one house across the way, and I squeezed my eyes shut, hoping it wouldn't fall. People screamed.

And then everything went still once more.

Was it over? I tentatively tested my footing. Then I realized that no one else had moved. The street was entirely silent.

In the distance I heard hooves echo upon the stone.

All around me, people prostrated themselves on the ground. I followed their lead as an opulently gilded carriage appeared at the end of the street, pulled by enormous gray horses.

The carriage rolled past me, staying to one side of the split street. It halted near where the roots had first broken through the stone. I glanced up to see the carriage door open.

Two Wolves disembarked from the carriage, followed by a dark-haired man who looked to be in his forties. Last came a younger woman with red-gold curls in a simple brown dress.

Katen. My body went rigid with fear. What if she sensed me, somehow? But I could not run. If I stood now, I would only draw their attention.

I held my breath as the group walked to the broken stones closest to the edge of the city. The man stared down at the stones, then turned to face the people on the street. I quickly averted my gaze.

"Who has dared to call the Silence into my city?" he said. *Shale.* I shivered at the fury in his voice. "Tell me, who?"

No one dared look up at him.

"Captain, are your guards good for nothing? Who was it?" Shale called.

I chanced another glance in time to see a guard raise his arm and point at an older woman on the ground next to a baker's stall.

Shale's mouth curled into a cruel smile. "Come here," he said, beckoning to the woman.

No, no, don't go.

But the woman stood and walked over, her shoes scuffing against the stone. She stopped before Shale. In the silence, I could hear her weeping.

"Rise, my subjects, and bear witness to my justice," Shale said. All around me, people rose to their feet. I did the same.

There was a knife suddenly in Shale's hand. "Turn around," he commanded the woman.

Slowly she turned so she faced the crowd, trembling.

"Though the Silence desires to crush us, I keep the Gather safe for *all* who live here," Shale cried. "But I cannot do this when there are those who would invite the enemy inside."

He grabbed one of the woman's arms, yanking it back. Then he raised the knife high and brought it down, slicing her hand clean off.

I flinched. The woman screamed, collapsing to the ground as blood spurted from the stump of her wrist. At first she writhed in agony, but her movements soon slowed—and then she lay still.

Shale knelt by her side, pressing his palms into the pool of her blood. As I watched, he raised his hands and drew a pattern through the air. Then he lowered them once more, placing them upon the broken stone.

The roots that had torn through the streets began to burn. They hissed and curled, releasing black smoke into the air, until nothing was left except piles of ash. The broken stones rippled underfoot, as though they were ice melting into water, before resolidifying back into place. One by one, the stones up and down the street followed suit.

Shale rose to his feet. "There. Behold how I have restored our city."

One person began to clap, then another. The street was filled with applause as Shale stalked back to the carriage and climbed inside.

Katen knelt by the body and raised her hand, calling for a Wolf. "Find this woman's family," she said, her voice pitched to carry. "See that her body is returned to them."

The Wolf nodded, and Katen returned to the carriage, her shoulders slumped. Of all the people in Shale's escort, she was the only one who looked even slightly remorseful.

The carriage door slammed, leaving the Wolves to deal with the body. Then it rolled away. The street was silent and still.

"Lena." I jumped as Alaric reappeared next to me, his face hard. He grabbed my hand. "We have to go."

He pulled me toward the forest, abandoning all pretense that we were strangers. Not that it mattered—after what had just happened, I doubted anyone was watching us. I looked down as we passed by the spot where Shale had stood, expecting to see pools of blood. But there was nothing below my boots but glassy black stone.

I turned back to see the bustle of the market resuming. Unease crawled down my spine. How could they go on just as though nothing had happened?

My gaze caught on a man in the distance who I could have sworn looked like my father. Then I blinked, and he was gone.

"What *was* that?" I asked as soon as we were clear of the city.

"*That* was Shale and Katen," Alaric said grimly. "I'm sorry I left you. I couldn't take the risk of being seen. Not when I'm supposed to be out in the forest hunting you."

I absorbed this new information. I was beginning to understand why everyone was so frightened of Shale. But Katen had seemed . . . surprisingly compassionate?

"Katen was not what I expected," I said.

"She hides her true nature. It's easy for her to do, next to him."

"And what about the stones? Did someone really invite the Silence in?"

Alaric shook his head. "No. Disturbances like that have been happening more frequently, and he needs someone to blame each time, to show the people that the city is under his control. But he's a fool if he thinks anyone here is convinced."

"Why do you think these disturbances are happening?"

He weighed his words before speaking. "The Gather—Shale and Katen and the rest—were never meant to exist here. They encroached on the Silence. And sometimes . . . sometimes the Silence fights back. That is why humans must stay on safe paths. In truth, none of your kind should be here."

"In the Mundane, the Silence bewitched humans. It dragged them into the forest, and they were never seen again," I said. "Does this have anything to do with that?"

Alaric pressed his lips together. "There are some things I am forbidden to speak of," he said. "I'm sorry."

So someone—Katen, I supposed—had bound his tongue. It was disappointing, but neither here nor there. Regardless of this tangle with Shale and Katen, we had gotten the information we came for.

Alaric looked behind us. "We've put enough space between us and the Gather. Let's get going." He put his arms around me, and we flew once more.

CHAPTER THIRTEEN

B ack at the shelter, Alaric tossed me a slightly stale roll of bread to eat. Then he began to rummage through his supplies, packing a small bag. He unearthed a sword from somewhere and buckled it around his waist. I tried not to watch him and failed.

"Where are we going?" I said. The rain had settled into a cool mist, and the trees blocked most of it from reaching us.

Alaric shook his head, as if ridding himself of an unwanted thought. "There is a place on the other side of the Silence where I believe she hid the box."

"Why outside the Silence?"

He frowned. "I cannot leave the forest unless she allows me to."

Of course. "But there are so many places she could have hidden it. What makes you think you know where it is?"

Now Alaric smiled. "Katen trusts almost no one—but those she does, she trusts completely. She befriended a family of dragons many years ago. I'm almost certain they're the ones guarding the box. And I know where they live. But we won't be able to fly there. We'll have to walk."

"Why?" I asked.

His face blanched, and I realized that whatever it was, he didn't want to say.

"Tell me."

"We need to take the canyon path. And those that rule the canyons are no friends of mine. If we fly, they will attack."

Now I was confused. "The canyons aren't ruled by Shale?"

Alaric hesitated before answering. "There are limits to what I can speak of," he reminded me. "But there are powers in the Silence other than blood mages. And the ones that reside in the canyons would not be happy to see me there."

He is lying to you.

I jumped. The voice was back.

"Are you all right?" Alaric said, looking concerned. "You look as though you've been stung."

"It's nothing," I said quickly. "Let's go."

The voice went quiet again as Alaric and I made our way through the Silence. We were on no path that I could see, but Alaric walked sure-footedly, slowing only when the landscape began to change around us. Though there was no break in the trees, scrubby grass appeared underfoot. The soil grew looser, then redder. Our steps quickly fell into a comfortable rhythm, leaving my mind to wander elsewhere.

Why did the voice care about Alaric? It seemed to be connected to the Silence somehow. . . . Perhaps Alaric would know what it was, if I asked. But if I were going to ask him about anything, it wouldn't be the strange voice I was half-convinced was a figment of my imagination. . . .

My parents. It suddenly occurred to me that he knew my parents—or had known them. While I knew my father better than anyone else, my mother was an enigma. Those hazy days before she'd disappeared blurred together in my memory. But she'd been so angry the day that boy had died. And I remembered the sound of her sobs behind closed doors that night, when she thought I wouldn't hear. Until one day she was gone.

I didn't remember much else about her. But perhaps Alaric did.

I watched Alaric's back as he led the way. It surprised me, how much I wanted to ask him. I'd kept my feelings about my mother locked away so tightly, I often didn't think of her at all. It was too painful otherwise. And then Father never spoke of her—it was easier, this way. No sense dwelling on what was long gone. But I'd never thought I'd have such a chance.

Before I could actually open my mouth, Alaric stopped walking. He held up his hand, and I froze. We'd arrived at the mouth of a vast canyon of red rock.

After a moment he put his hand down and squinted up at the sky. "It's getting late. If you can bear it, it would be better to cross at night. They don't come out as much after the sun sets."

I could feel fatigue pulling at my limbs, but I nodded. "I can do it."

We settled down against a tree trunk to wait.

I must have dozed off, because when Alaric nudged me, the sun had disappeared below the horizon and the moon had risen.

In the moonlight, the canyon rock was cool grays and blues. Alaric was tense as he walked, his shoulders hunched. I tried to stay alert as I wondered just what powers he had spoken of, the creatures that would be displeased to find us trespassing on their land. At least it was easy to follow the trail—a scar upon the ground carved by a river that had long since gone dry.

The trail dipped and swelled, widening in places before shrinking back down to a crevice barely wide enough for two people to walk abreast.

The night was silent around us. The sounds that we made were amplified in my ears. My breathing. Small stones skittering out of our way as our boots hit the ground.

And then there was another noise—something I couldn't identify. I stumbled and almost fell. Alaric whirled, catching my elbow. "Careful!" he whispered harshly.

"*Careful! Careful! Careful!*" The word came back at us, shrill and mocking.

Alaric winced, and I realized too late that these weren't mere echoes off the canyon walls. There was something out there.

Alaric's fingers dug painfully into my arm. "Leave your gloves on and let me do the talking," he said. He put himself in front of me, his hand resting on the hilt of his sword as the eerie voice grew louder, coming closer.

There was a fluttering in the night, and a dark shape flew down from the sky, landing on a naked tree branch in front of us. Two other birds followed the first. I was certain there were more out there that I couldn't see.

The first bird spoke. "We made it clear you are unwelcome here, false feather. And yet here you are."

"Bekit," Alaric said carefully.

The bird's voice bristled. "You are no raven to address me by such a name. Do not do so now, traitor."

So these must be the ravens of the Silence.

"Your memory is short, old friend."

"And yours appears to be nonexistent. You were warned about what would happen if you crossed this way again."

Alaric's jaw clenched. "I had no choice."

"And whose fault is that?"

"Will you let us pass?" Alaric said. "We will not disturb you or the canyon."

"You have already disturbed us!" cried another of the ravens. In a flash they flew forward and struck Alaric across the face with a claw. He stumbled back, cursing as he put his hand to his face. When he took it away, I saw blood running down his cheek.

I stripped off my gloves, readying myself for an attack, as Alaric drew his sword. The third raven lifted off the branch, flying toward us. I ran forward, hands out—

Bekit, who had remained on the tree, let out a raucous caw. The other ravens pulled up, circling above us. I held my breath, feeling the tension in the air. How many more were out there, waiting for the signal to strike?

Bekit cocked his head as if seeing me for the first time. "Who is this girl?"

"No one," I said. "No one important."

I felt pinned beneath his gaze. After a moment he croaked in a way that sounded like a cough—or a laugh—and hopped backward along the branch. If he had been a human, I would have thought he was surprised. "Alaric . . . ," he said slowly. "What games are you playing?"

"Bekit—please," Alaric said. "I am trying to make things right."

The ravens in the air muttered among themselves, then quieted.

Finally Bekit said, "Begone, then. It matters not to me which path you take—only that you are gone before daybreak, for there will be no one to save you then."

Alaric nodded sharply, took me by the elbow, and escorted me past the tree. I was surprised—I'd thought the ravens meant to detain us.

Once we were well away, I turned to him. "What just happened?"

"You were there, you heard."

He was being evasive again. I shook my head. "They attacked you, and then that raven saw me, and—"

"Do not read so much into nothing," Alaric said.

"They called you a *traitor*."

"Because I work for the humans, no matter how unwillingly."

You know he is hiding something. The voice in my head spoke, startling me into silence—just as Alaric wanted—as we made our way through the canyon, leaving the ravens behind.

I'd been able to ignore the voice's taunts before. But now it was clear that the voice wanted something from me, and that I would not be able to ignore it much longer. I glanced over at Alaric. I would have to speak with it. Not here, though. This would have to wait until I was alone.

We reached the end of the canyon as the sky was beginning to lighten with the colors of day. On this side of the Silence, the forest was sparser, a landscape of rolling hills. Alaric led the way down another path through the trees.

"Those ravens knew you before Katen," I said. "You were one of them."

Alaric nodded in acknowledgment but said nothing.

One hundred years. That was how long he had said he'd been

bound to Katen and the Gather. And for that he must have been cast out. Not only that, those ravens had held a grudge against him for all this time.

I couldn't imagine what it would feel like, to be threatened by the very ones who used to be family. I wondered what exactly Alaric had done, to bring such animosity down upon himself. Was it such a crime, to be tricked? To fall into a trap?

"Would they ever take you back?" I asked.

Alaric laughed. "Impossible."

"Then what will you do after you win your freedom?"

"I don't know. Where I go, what I do—it will not matter to me, as long as I am free. The life I live now is no life at all."

I believed him. And more than that—I was drawn to him. Hearing my own thoughts spoken aloud made my heart ache. Here was someone who understood the pain I'd felt my entire life.

But what is freedom without power?

I blinked, unable to push the question away. Alaric did not have to choose between the two. I'd already seen some of what he could do.

But as for myself . . .

Only recently had I begun to realize that as much as the curse had been a blight upon my life, it also afforded me a certain sort of power. Once it was broken, that power would be gone.

Perhaps it was wrong of me to admit it, but I had enjoyed the wary look on Cyn's face as I had threatened her. I'd been taught to think of myself as a victim, to paint myself into smaller and smaller corners for the safety of the world. But when I'd wielded the curse like a weapon, I had felt powerful. Untouchable, but on my own terms.

I never wanted to be beholden to anyone ever again—no controlling parents, no sinister mages. But what if the voice was right? What if freedom on its own wasn't enough? Without power, freedom could be wrenched away in an instant. If I wanted to keep it, I had to be ready to defend it. And without the curse, I wasn't sure I could.

CHAPTER FOURTEEN

The sun was high in the sky as the trees around us faded to shrubs, then grasses. Alaric stopped just as we reached the end of the shrubbery.

"I can't go any farther. This is the end of the Silence." He looked at me. "If I'm correct, my wings aren't far. But you will have to go alone."

Alone, again. *Wonderful.*

"What do I have to do?"

"If you follow this path for, say, half an hour on foot, you'll come to a house. It is set back from the path but clearly visible. The last time I was there the walkway to the door was made entirely of white stone. Anyway, there is only one house in these parts. It should be impossible to miss."

"Then what?"

"You go up to the door and knock. Although it's anyone's guess as to whether the dragons will let you in."

Dragons. Like most in the Mundane, I'd always thought dragons were simply a myth. I swallowed. "What if they . . . attack?"

"Humans are not their preferred meals," Alaric said impatiently. "Dragons also love to play games. Though some of their games can be deadly. They don't really understand the frailty of other creatures."

"So I should offer to play a game with a house of dragons in exchange for an enchanted box containing your wings," I said, incredulous.

"Yes," Alaric replied. "But not right now. They sleep during the day. If you go now, they'll be cranky and unlikely to be cooperative. We should get some rest. You can go closer to sunset."

The moment he said it, I realized that I was exhausted. Adrenaline had kept me going through the night as we had navigated the canyons and encountered the ravens. But now my lack of sleep was catching up with me.

Alaric found a copse of trees standing close enough together to provide some shade, and we settled down to wait out the afternoon.

Yet I found it difficult to sleep, despite my exhaustion. After several minutes of trying unsuccessfully to keep my eyes closed, I looked over at Alaric. He was also awake, staring up at the sky.

There was a chance I would not come back from the house of the dragons. The time to ask questions was now. Even though the prospect of getting answers still terrified me. I clasped my hands together, drawing a deep breath. "Why did they do it?" I asked.

Now Alaric did look at me. "Do what?" he said.

"Why did my parents make the bargain with Katen? Why did they risk *me*?"

"Humans make terrible mistakes sometimes. They made the bargain to save your mother's life before they knew she was pregnant. I imagine it was easier to give away something that was still . . . hypothetical. They didn't realize Katen would put so much magic in you that she'd have to kill you to reclaim it. They never knew about the curse until it was too late."

So it was true, what my father had told me about the curse.

They had done their best. But that didn't stop me from being angry—furious, even—that they had made that bargain in the first place. No matter what they had been told.

"My mother left us," I said. "She couldn't cope with having a cursed daughter."

Alaric was silent for a long time. "I would be gentler to your parents, if you can find a way to do so," he said after a while. "Katen did not offer a fair bargain."

How could I forgive them, after hearing what he'd said? I wanted to scream at them both—to slam doors and stomp my feet and hurt them the way they had hurt me. I had spent my whole life being gentle, being small. But I didn't want to be gentle anymore. I wanted to be fierce.

"No," I said. "I suppose I understand why they felt they had no other choice, with Katen. But the lying and the leaving—how can I forgive that?" I let out a soft, mirthless laugh. "Sometimes I wonder whether my parents regretted having me at all. If not for me, there would have been no bargain. No curse."

My words hung in the air between us. Then Alaric spoke. "For what it's worth, I do not regret them having you."

I turned on my side and propped my head up on my elbow to look at him. He turned his head and looked back at me. For a long moment we stared at each other.

In repose, his world-weariness fell away, and his eyes softened. I could imagine the carefree creature he must have been all those years ago. But I was drawn to him as he was now. His anger and desperation mirrored my own. He was the only one in the world who could even come close to understanding how I felt.

He was also the only one who I could touch—and not kill.

My gaze fell to Alaric's lips, and I wondered what it would feel like to kiss him. Would he kiss me back? Would he thread his fingers through my hair and— Warmth rushed through me at the thought, but I resisted the urge to look away. Before I could second-guess myself, I pushed myself up and closed the gap between us.

I planted my hands on the ground on either side of his face and leaned down, my hair falling over one shoulder. Our breathing fell into sync as we gazed at each other, and I watched color rise on his face. Ever so slowly, I bent my head lower—and kissed him.

For one eternal instant the world stood still. Then Alaric's arms wrapped around me, drawing me against him as he deepened the kiss, and I felt both lost and safe at once, consumed by heat. This was too much—and yet this was not enough—

He broke away suddenly, scrambling to his feet as I fell back against the ground.

"I'm sorry," he said. "I'm sorry, that shouldn't have happened. I—it was my mistake." He gestured at the forest behind him. "I'm going to—to take a walk. I'll be back soon."

Embarrassment churned in my stomach as he walked quickly away. Had I done it wrong? I'd seen people kiss before, but perhaps I had made a mistake. What if I had misread him completely?

Only a few days ago the greatest gift that could ever have been given to me was the ability to touch another person. I'd never considered that someone else could call that gift a mistake. And yet, I could still feel the hot flush of my own cheeks, the feel of his lips on mine. If the kiss had been a mistake, it hadn't been his. *I* had kissed him. Because I could. Because I had wanted to. And I was almost certain that he had wanted it too. Why else would he have kissed me back like that?

I didn't care what excuse he had made—I wanted that closeness again. It was as if that one kiss had awakened something powerful and wild within me, and I thought I might fly apart if I didn't release it. It was a selfish thing perhaps, to want this. But didn't I deserve a little selfishness? I'd spent my entire life putting other people's safety before my own. And I didn't know what was waiting around the next bend, or if I'd ever have another chance to be with someone in this way.

Besides, I wasn't a child. I knew what went on between people of consenting age and inclination. I just had never dreamed of it for myself. And now that it was possible, truly within my reach . . .

I got to my feet and ran after Alaric.

I found him sitting in a clearing not too far away, his head in his hands. He looked up as I approached, his expression unreadable.

"Lena . . ."

"Let me speak," I said, still a bit breathless. "It wasn't a mistake. I want you."

Alaric looked down. When he looked at me again, his eyes were dark with desire. But there was caution there too. "You don't know what you're asking," he said.

"I'm not *asking* anything," I replied. "I'm stating a fact. You kissed me back—I know you're attracted to me just as I am to you. This doesn't have to mean anything. It can just be—*this*."

"It would complicate things," he said softly. "You might find yourself . . . attached."

"I don't care," I said. "If I'm going to die facing the dragons or when I meet Katen—something you've admitted is possible, even likely—then this is what I want. I want you. In my"—I paused and waved a hand sheepishly—"bed," I finished.

His lips twisted into a wry smile—and then he leaned back and laughed, a full-throated, melodic laugh. "Wouldn't that be an exceptional mess," he said, almost to himself. "I want to, gods help me. But Lena—it's a terrible idea."

"You're only saying that because you didn't think of it," I countered. I walked toward him, trying to look alluring. Undeniable. "There is so little I have control over right now. But I have control over this. I want this. If you will have me."

"I would," Alaric whispered. In a flash he was standing before me, his hands framing my cheeks, speaking so, so softly. "I would, Lena. But I fear you won't forgive me for it later."

"I don't care about later," I said. I stood on tiptoe and leaned into him, meeting his lips with my own.

He needed no further encouragement. He pulled my shirt over my head, leaving me shivering as he stumbled out of his own clothing. I had never *fathomed* I would ever be unclothed in front of someone else. I felt oddly exposed, fighting the urge to cross my arms in front of my chest until he put his arms around me once more. I glanced down at him and a new rush of heat filled my body. Suddenly I was very aware of the difference between reading about something in books and actually experiencing it.

Alaric's fingertips grazed the top of my trousers, then tugged them down along with my undergarments, and we were finally naked before each other. Our fingers laced together as he pulled me down with him into the grass.

We rolled over so that I lay half on top of him, stretched out across his body. After a lifetime without touch, now I was drowning in it. Every place our bodies met was on fire, and I couldn't bear to stop.

Alaric's lips met my neck as his hands wandered lower, and then—

I closed my eyes, and stars danced behind my lids. I'd never felt so seen, or so *wanted*. In this moment, everything felt possible.

Wetness pricked the corners of my eyes, and I realized I was crying.

"Lena," Alaric said softly. "Are you all right?"

He reached up, tucking a strand of hair behind my ear. I opened my eyes and saw an immense tenderness reflected back in his—so different from the sharpness that had characterized him since the moment we met. I realized I didn't know him at all, not really. That there was so much more to him than I understood. But in this moment, I didn't care.

"I'm happy," I whispered.

He smiled at me, and that smile was like a lightning strike.

"Come here," he said, and I did.

CHAPTER FIFTEEN

❦

A breeze whispered along my skin as I opened my eyes. My cloak was draped over my body, but I was still cold—and *naked*, I realized. What—

Memory washed through me, and I was suddenly uncomfortably warm. I sat up, clutching my cloak to my chest as I looked around.

Alaric was already awake. He stood facing away from me, clothed, his hands clasped behind his back. He looked as though he was waiting.

I searched for my shirt and pulled it over my head. Had I truly said those things? *Done* those things?

Yes, my body sighed. Every part of me glowed with the aftermath of being touched. The memory of what had passed between us felt blurry, almost feverish. And *wonderful*. Even the few moments that had been awkward and even a little uncomfortable had been glorious. Everything was different—not because the act itself had so changed me, but because I'd never thought I would be able to have it. And now I had. It felt as though my entire being was brimming with possibility.

I stood up and went to Alaric's side. I wanted to touch him again, but all my courage had fled. Strange, that we had been so intimate with each other, and I still felt unsure of how to approach him now. "What are you doing?" I asked.

"Waiting for all of this to come crashing down." He stepped closer and put a tentative arm around my shoulder. I hesitated before leaning into him, his presence solid and reassuring. He turned to face me, and I could see the apprehension on his face.

"I'm sorry," Alaric said. "I—"

"Don't," I said, cutting him off. "Don't take it back." I had made this choice. I couldn't think it was a mistake. Not when I had spent my entire life robbed of the freedom to connect with those around me in even the most insignificant of ways. The memory of what had passed between us was mine to shape and to keep. As was the rest of me.

He nodded soberly. "I wish we had more time."

I smiled. "I do too."

He sighed. "We should get going."

I nodded and squeezed his hand. He bent forward and pressed a kiss to the top of my head. My breathing hitched, and I pulled back, my emotions threatening to undo me. I walked quickly away.

The directions that Alaric had given me were simple enough to follow. One moment I was walking upon a path, solitary and accompanied only by the sounds of the natural world around me—and then there was a path of white stones to my right leading to a house painted in uneven bright colors. It looked like a child's drawing, and I imagined the story that would go along with it. *Once upon a time, there was a family of dragons that lived in a house with no windows. . . .*

And I was about to go inside.

You need not help him. The voice was back, and I couldn't ignore it any longer.

"I'm sick of this," I snapped. "Who are you, and what do you want from me?"

You needn't speak so loudly. The voice sounded amused. **I can hear your thoughts well enough.**

I swallowed, hard. This thing, whatever it was, could listen to my *thoughts?* I tried to muster my courage. "I don't care. I've had enough of your pestering. If you want something, then tell me. Otherwise, leave me alone."

I want to help you.

Help? If there was one thing I had learned since entering the Silence, it was that no one offered help unconditionally.

"How could you possibly help me?" I said.

I've watched your struggle. You are human, weak. And even if you manage to break your curse, you will have nothing. I can offer you the power you seek.

The voice was echoing my own fears, and that terrified me more than anything else. I took a breath, trying to steady myself.

"And who are you to offer such things?" I asked.

For a moment the voice was silent. **You would have drowned without my intervention. Is that not enough to merit consideration?**

The memory of the face I'd seen underwater flashed through my mind. At the time it had been easy to dismiss it as my imagination.

That wasn't enough, though. The voice might have saved my life somehow, true—but now it was using that to justify keeping its identity secret from me. And I'd had enough of secret keeping to last my entire life. I clung to that certainty as I turned once more toward the dragons' house.

"No," I said shortly. "I am helping Alaric, as I promised. And until you are ready to tell me the truth, I want nothing more from you."

The voice was mercifully silent as I marched up to the front door and knocked three times. *I can do this, I can do this, I can do this.*

There was no answer. Perhaps the dragons were not at home? I knocked again.

This time there was a rattling sound. The door swung slowly open, but there was no one standing behind it. I couldn't see much farther than the hallway—there were no lights. I hesitated.

"Well? We are waiting."

I jumped, but the speaker remained hidden. Did I dare?

I did. I stepped over the threshold and entered the house.

The door swung shut behind me, and my shoulders tensed. I didn't think the curse would work on dragons, since they could be considered a sort of animal, I supposed, but I took off my gloves regardless and tucked them into my pocket. Strange, that baring my skin had so recently made me feel completely vulnerable. Now it made me feel strong.

I walked slowly, waiting for my eyes to adjust to the dim setting. At the end of the hallway was an open space so large that I could hear my footsteps echo. I stopped at its edge.

"Hello?" I said.

Hello, hello, hello echoed back at me.

It was much warmer in here than outside—as though a furnace were heating the room, though I didn't see the glow of flames. But there was movement, a soft, persistent shifting of air that told me there was something living in the shadows.

"A human girl," someone said, their voice gravelly and rumbling. "How novel."

A chorus of murmurs sprang up around me. How many *were* there? I wished for light, though I wasn't certain I was ready for what it might reveal.

"Shall we eat her?" one asked.

My heartbeat quickened at the suggestion. "I was told on good authority that you find humans unappetizing," I said more confidently than I felt.

"We do not recognize the authority of those on the outside," said one.

I swallowed. "Ah. Then I won't trouble you for longer than I have to. You have something that belongs to a friend of mine. I am here to reclaim it."

"Treasure? You seek to steal from us?"

Their tone was so affronted that I was tempted to roll my eyes—then realized that I didn't know how well *they* could see in the dark either. "Not treasure," I said. "A box. Its contents are insignificant to beings so mighty as you, but they carry . . . personal value for my friend."

"A box, a box . . ." More murmurs scattered through the room. "We may have something of the sort. But you will have to convince us that you are worthy of seeking it."

"How?" I asked.

A light flared to life, and I put a hand up to shield my eyes, blinking at the sudden glare. When I lowered my hand, I saw that I was standing in a cave with roughly hewn platforms made of rocks and little else in the way of furnishings. And on those rocks reclined the dragons.

They were smaller than I'd thought—but then, the stories always spoke about dragons as great fearsome beasts the size of houses. These weren't any larger than horses. I quickly counted seven. Their limbs were unnaturally long, and the way they were coiled upon the rocks reminded me of snakes sunning themselves. Their bodies were covered with glittering scales and something softer—feathers, I thought, or fur—that shimmered in the light. Long whiskers hung from their narrow snouts, and sharp fangs glinted as they turned their heads toward me.

"How?" The dragon in front cocked their head curiously. "You have the audacity to enter our domain and make demands of us, and you have no idea how to pay us?"

A strange sort of chuffing sound filled the room. For a moment I was worried—then I realized that the dragons were laughing.

Suddenly I was angry with Alaric—he was far more familiar with dragons than I was, and he'd neglected to say *anything* about what they valued. What I could offer them.

"I have nothing," I confessed. "I'm really no one."

"No, but there is still something about you," said another dragon, inhaling deeply. "There is power locked within you. We would be interested to know where you came by such power, little human."

Katen's magic. My hands clenched. Why did they want to know? Did they have a way to steal it?

The first dragon yawned. "I'm bored. This human is not nearly as diverting as the last one."

The *last* one? "What did the last one do?" I said, not sure that I wanted to hear the answer.

"Offered us a much more interesting bargain," they snapped. "Kept us entertained for *hours*."

I swallowed, hard. "I'll tell you about the power, if that's what you want," I said quickly.

One of the dragons that had not yet spoken slid down their rock and splayed on the floor before me, their teeth gleaming as they grinned. "Yes, yes, tell us a story."

The demand chorused through the room. A line of sweat trickled down my back. It was easy to guess what would happen to me if the dragons weren't satisfied with my story. The tales of dragons roasting humans to a crisp couldn't have sprung from nowhere.

Did I dare tell them the truth about myself? What if they were closer allies with Katen than Alaric realized?

Well, if that was the case, I was done for anyway.

"It is true that I am no one," I said. "But it is also true I am cursed to carry power that is not mine." I held up my hands in front of them. "I can kill with a touch, but I cannot harm the witch that cursed me. I am entirely beholden to her."

Interested murmurs swept through the room. "You're a riddle," said one of the dragons.

"If you say so," I said. "I call it someone's idea of a cruel trick."

The chuffing swept through the room again—for some reason they found this funny.

"And if you are beholden to the witch, what are you doing here?" a dragon asked.

What purpose was there in lying to these creatures? They could kill me with a breath.

"To free myself," I said simply.

"How marvelous!" said one in between chuffs.

"How stupendous!"

"It isn't funny," I said, my temper rising. "I understand that dragons are above such—such human affairs. But this is all that I want in the world."

Now the dragon on the ground was rolling back and forth, seized by peals of laughter. "And she talks just like a human on a quest!"

"What do you want from me?" I barked. "I won't stand here and be laughed at."

The dragons' laughter stopped abruptly. Without warning, the lights went out. The room went cold, and I shivered. Something slithered behind me, brushing against my calves, and I flinched.

"Humans should not make demands," said a voice that raised the hairs on the back of my neck. "Humans should understand they are here only as long as they amuse us. That was *not* amusing."

"I—I'm sorry," I stammered.

"Sorry is not good enough."

"What shall we do with her?"

"Break her bones, watch her cry."

"This one is no fun."

"*I* want to burn her."

I was acutely aware that there was no way out of this mess. I was entirely at the dragons' mercy.

"I did not mean to offend," I said desperately. "I'll tell you a story."

"A story? That is too small a price for the prize you seek. And for the offense you have given, we require something more. You say you seek something of personal value. Your payment must be personal too."

"Anything," I said, before realizing how foolish such an offer might be.

"Anything?"

Something—a tail, I thought—coiled around me and tightened, squeezing my body like a vise. I tried not to panic.

"Even your happiest memory? Your dearest dream? Your keenest pain? How much of yourself are you willing to give?"

I kept my mouth shut. Could dragons truly take such things as currency?

I thought of all the pain I had experienced and what I would have given to be rid of it, at certain times in my life. Then I thought of all the things I would give anything to hold on to now.

The light returned, just enough for me to see the murky figures of the dragons. One of them still had their tail wrapped around me, holding me in place. This close, I could confirm that this dragon had fur on the areas of their body not covered with scales.

"Or," one dragon practically purred, "you can give us a piece of your future."

"What does that mean?" I asked shakily.

The dragon holding me—the same one who had lain at my feet earlier—looked delighted. "Same thing as the past," they said cheerfully. I got the sense that they were younger than the others. "You will owe us a memory. But if it's from the future, you don't get to pick which one. One day it will simply . . ."

"Vanish."

"Poof."

"As though it was never there."

I closed my eyes. The thought of giving up one of my memories was close to unbearable. But if the alternative was to have no control over what I lost . . .

"All right," I said. "In payment I offer a memory from my past."

"Very well."

The dragon released me from their hold, and I felt an unnerving presence touch my mind. My head twinged with pain, and my thoughts turned back in time, falling into memory.

They weren't all bad, I realized. There were memories of happiness, too. I felt years fly by as my mother taught me how to swim, my father baked queen's cakes—I lingered on the riotous scent of a flower garden in bloom, the feeling of reading a book by the fire—and then there was the curse, the deaths, the Wolf. Miranda's smile blurred before me, Alaric's arms around me were there and gone in an instant. And then—

"Here," said one dragon. A flicker of sunlight behind my eyes, the scent of rich earth. "Give us this one. Do you agree?"

Whatever I'd expected, it hadn't been this. I'd thought they would ask for my happiness. It hadn't occurred to me that they would savor the taste of my pain. Now I was surprised to realize how much I valued it too. My pain had forged me into what I was today. How might I be changed, once it was taken from me? Could I bear to lose it?

"Are we agreed?"

"If I give this memory to you, will you give me what I seek?" I said. "It is a wooden box, with wings carved on its sides. And it has never been opened."

The dragons sobered, and they glanced at each other. They knew exactly what box I was speaking about, I realized.

"We agree," said one dragon. "We'll allow you to take the box. Now, tell us the story of that day."

I closed my eyes. Part of me was disappointed that they'd accepted. But this was the only way.

"I was seven," I said slowly. "That's ten years ago—I don't know if dragons mark time in the same way that humans do."

The colors of that day brightened in my memory as I spoke, and an odd sensation overtook me. It felt as though someone were looking *through* me, using my mind as a lens.

"After the first death, we moved to a new city—Minos. It was spring, and my mother was planting a garden. The plot was small enough that she could turn it by hand, the way she preferred."

The presence sharpened, focused, as I continued. "I was still having nightmares about the boy. Sometimes I dreamed the ground melted into liquid fire beneath my feet. I woke shaking, convinced I was burning alive. I don't remember why I went to the door that day—maybe to call her in for supper. But she was coming in at the same time, and we nearly collided."

My voice wavered. "She hadn't looked at me since the boy died, not really. But she did on that day. She stared down at me and then she knelt down to my level. She hugged me. Her arms around me were so delicate, as though she thought I might break." I'd burrowed into the embrace, nestling my head in the comfort of her warmth and inhaling the scent of fresh earth underneath her fingernails. I'd squeezed my eyes shut to keep from crying. Something had fractured, broken between us, and I was so frightened that I'd done it. A lump formed in my throat at the memory. "That night she and my father talked for hours, their voices too low for me to hear. And the next morning, she was gone."

There was intense pressure behind my eyes. I couldn't move as the presence bore down upon my memory, slowly leeching each emotion and sensation—the way I had clung to her while trying to hold back my sobs, the bright morning light streaming through the window and across our table as my father told me she wasn't coming back, my voice cracking as I shouted at him and ran outside into the garden. Everything I'd tried to bury, the dragons' magic dug out of me. The pressure turned into a searing pain, and I screamed, trapped in that memory, second by second of anguish—

And then I fell forward onto the cold stone, gasping for air. Tears had tracked down my cheeks, and sweat coated my neck. I could taste salt at the corners of my mouth. But the pain was gone.

I looked up.

The dragons stared back at me with equanimity. My heart was racing, but as I breathed, it slowed. My body calmed. Was it over? Had it worked? I tried to conjure the memory they had requested—the day my mother abandoned us. My chest went cold. Whatever had been was just . . . gone.

There was quiet as the dragons muttered among themselves. Then the largest of the group spoke. "We accept your pain as payment, but we have one more request."

I braced myself to hear the dragons' last demand.

"If you should succeed in your quest, you must return here one day and tell us how you managed it," they proclaimed.

It was so preposterous that I almost laughed—but I managed to keep myself in check, for fear that I might offend them again and they'd demand something more. "Yes," I said. "I can do that."

"Then go on. The little one will take you to the box."

The dragon who had held me immobile jumped up and trotted toward the back of the room. I followed warily and found that this room led into a tunnel lit by rocks that glowed a faint blue.

"I like you," the dragon said, practically prancing ahead of me. "Your memory was delicious. Very sad."

"Oh?" I said, trying not to panic that I could not remember it.

"Yes. Grandmother says I must cultivate a liking for happiness as well, but it's not to my taste." They made a disgusted sound that almost brought a smile to my face. Almost.

"Do you dragons ever . . . go outside?" I asked.

"Yes. But I'm not allowed yet." The dragon's doleful tone was surprising—and familiar.

"Why not?" I asked.

The dragon turned their head and smiled at me, their fangs glinting. "Too dangerous." A shiver ran down my spine. I had a feeling they weren't referring to danger to themself.

We walked a ways before the dragon turned around. "We are here," they said. Then they raised one leg and extended a claw to me.

I looked down. Nestled in their open claw was a scale.

"I see more pain in your future. Should you ever wish to share it, break the scale."

I picked it up quickly and tucked it into my pocket. The dragon frightened me, but this seemed as close to a favor as one of their kind might ever offer. I would be a fool not to accept it. "Thank you," I said.

"Go forward. There is the place with the box. But be careful. There are more things with teeth down there."

I nodded and walked forward. The tunnel sloped sharply

down, and my foot slipped on something slick. I fell, and then slid, scrabbling for purchase. My fingers raked through wet moss—or what I hoped was moss—to no avail.

The dragon called to me from somewhere above. "The weakness is its eyes!"

The words echoed after me as I slid at an ever increasing speed, my heart in my throat.

CHAPTER SIXTEEN

t last the tunnel gave way, and I splashed down into a swampy pool. The water closed over my head, and I flailed—then my feet hit the bottom. I stood and found that the pool only came up to my chest. Looking up, I saw that I was in a cave dimly lit by more of the same glowing rocks I'd seen in the tunnel.

Piled high in corners of the cave were gold coins, jewels, crowns, and swords—a veritable hoard. The box must be somewhere in here—but where?

You're in danger.

The voice again—just when I thought that I'd banished it.

"Go away," I said. "I don't have time to argue with you."

Take cover! the voice shouted. I ducked automatically, and something whooshed over my head, landing with a splash in the shallows on the far side of the pool. As I watched, a creature rose from the water and turned toward me. It was lizardlike, about the size of a large dog, and I saw the glint of fangs and claws. The beast roared, the sound reverberating throughout the cave.

Trying not to panic, I waded as fast as I could toward a treasure pile. I could hear the creature's breathing as I climbed out of the water and up onto damp ground, the suck of mud slowing me down. There was a sword lying half-covered by coins—I lifted it with both hands, surprised by how heavy it was.

I heard the sound of water splashing and turned just in time to see the beast leap at me. I swung the sword wildly and managed to make contact, sending painful vibrations up my arm. The beast yowled as it lost its footing and slipped back into the water.

You won't win this way. Its hide is impenetrable.

How helpful. I backed away from the water's edge. *Think.* What had the dragon said to me? Something about eyes?

The beast came out of the water more cautiously this time. I picked up a jewel the size of my fist. I had to be ready to strike— but as the beast stalked toward me, I realized something. It had eye sockets on its face, at least four of them. But it had no eyes.

Of course it has eyes! But they are sensitive to water—it must have set them on higher ground!

I threw the jewel as hard as I could at the beast and followed that with another swing of the sword. It hissed at me, baring its fangs. Higher ground—which high ground? I glanced past the beast, looking wildly around the cave.

The mounds of treasures all stood taller than my head, but there was one markedly taller than the rest. Its peak didn't glitter with treasure—rather, it was dark and almost flat, forming a sort of platform.

The beast stood with its claws planted in the mud, growling. I took a step back and almost tripped into the mound behind me. Treasure shifted, spilling down . . . and I had an idea.

I scrambled up the mound, my knees bruising against the shifting piles of coins. Once I reached the top, I turned to see the creature climbing, closing the gap between us. I sat down, digging my boots into the treasure and kicking an avalanche of gold and jewels directly upon it.

Overpowered, the beast lost its footing and fell, sliding back into the water.

I slid quickly down the other side of the mound and ran around the edge of the pool. The weight of the sword hindered me, but I didn't dare drop it as I began to climb.

Behind you!

I kicked my leg back without looking and felt something catch and bite down on my ankle. I yelped in pain and twisted, swinging the sword and striking the beast's head. The beast released my ankle and fell halfway down the mound. I gritted my teeth and kept climbing.

My fingers hurt from digging into the treasure, and I wished I'd thought to put on my gloves again. By the time I reached the platform, my hands were scraped and bruised, and my injured ankle ached.

There was a rank animal smell so strong here it made my eyes water. My foot caught and I stumbled, shuddering as I realized what I'd tripped over. Bones. Gnawed-upon bones, scattered all around me. I scrambled past them, trying not to think of their origin. And there in the center of the platform sat the creature's eyes—a cluster of glittering red orbs that narrowed angrily as I approached. I set down the sword and picked them up. There were seven altogether, and they squirmed wetly in my hands, trying to wriggle free. I tightened my grip. Behind me, the beast howled.

I fought the urge to vomit as I turned to face the pool. The beast crawled onto the platform. Though it was clearly in pain, it charged toward me, its fangs bared in a snarl. I was out of time.

Taking one step forward, I threw the eyes as hard as I could over the side of the platform and into the pool below.

There was a splash as the eyes hit the surface of the water and sank. The beast stiffened, its back arching in agony, and then it began to scream. I grabbed the sword and prepared to defend myself, but there was no need. The beast turned and dived into the pool, disappearing below the surface.

I let out a relieved breath.

It will be occupied only until it finds the eyes. You must go.

"I'm not leaving without the wings," I said. Now that the beast was gone, the cave was eerily quiet. The only sound was my breathing as it slowly returned to normal. I wiped my palms on my trousers, trying to get rid of the slimy residue the eyes had left. Then I went to the edge of the platform and surveyed the cave.

The perimeter was broken by dark tunnel mouths, so at least I wasn't trapped here. But it would take days to search through so much treasure, if not longer. I shook my head and cursed the dragons—but even I had to admit this was as much my fault as theirs. Assuming that the box *was* somewhere in this cave, they had held to their end of the bargain. It was I who should have been more specific in terms of how I wanted the box given to me.

My shoulders slumped. Finding the box was an impossible task.

Not so.

"Oh? And here I thought you didn't want me to help Alaric."

But I would help you. I wish to be your friend.

Again with the vague promises, with no mention of the price to be paid.

"No," I said.

I made my way back down to the ground and set the sword to the side. It *was* an impossible task, but refusing to begin wouldn't make it any less so. I put on my gloves and began to sift through the coins and jewels.

You won't succeed that way.

"How helpful of you to say that," I replied.

The box isn't there. You must look elsewhere. This I offer freely.

I sat back on my heels, taking the time to carefully study my surroundings. There was treasure everywhere, glinting and eye-catching. Even the pool of water reflected its shimmer.

Cyn had said that Katen had requested the box be waterproof. Everything in this cave was at risk of falling into the pool if disturbed . . . but what if the box had always been meant for the water?

I walked to the edge of the pool and crouched down, trying to see past the reflections of gold into its depths.

After a while, the bottom of the pool resolved in my sight. There were loose coins and other detritus scattered across its bed, but most of what I could see were smooth stones and the occasional stick, all covered in dark algae. I imagined that most of the pool had gone undisturbed for a very long time. I kept scanning— and suddenly my gaze snagged on something that looked oddly out of place. I peered closer. It was wood, but unlike other sticks in various states of decay, this piece had sharp angles. It was half-buried under some stones, but its surface was completely untouched by algae.

I hesitated. The beast was surely still nearby. If this was the box, there was no way to get it except by getting back into the water.

I steeled myself, and then jumped in. Debris clouded the water as my feet touched down, and I forced myself to wait for it to clear, holding my breath at the thought of the beast springing up at me. Finally I could see again. I reached down and tugged at the edge of the box.

It moved, but only slightly. I ducked under the water and grabbed the box with both hands, pulling harder until it popped free of the stones. Then I retreated as quickly as I could out of the water and back onto dry land.

I wiped away the water dripping into my eyes. The box was much smaller than I'd expected—it would fit easily into my pocket. I ran my fingers over its sides, searching for a seam. There was none. But I did feel an undulating curve etched into the side of the box, almost like a wave. *Or wings.* I shook the box, and there was the distinct feeling of something shifting within.

I thought of Alaric, waiting in the Silence. All of his hopes were locked up in this box—if indeed it was the right one.

You cannot trust the raven. He is bound to Katen.

"Of course I know that," I said. "But I have no better options."

You have me.

"Ah yes. A friend who invades my head and won't tell me who they are. Who promises power but won't tell me its price."

I thought the voice would disappear again. Instead it spoke. **Come away from this place, and I will tell you.**

I bit my lip. Engaging with this voice any further was dangerous. But it had also helped me—saved my life, even. Would it have done that if its only intentions for me were nefarious?

"All right. If you want to talk, help me get out of here. Do you know which tunnel leads to the surface?"

The one on your right, the voice said promptly.

I put the box in my pocket next to the dragon scale and picked up the sword before entering the tunnel.

There were no glowing rocks to light my way, and soon I was walking in complete darkness. I hesitated, listening. There was nothing but the sound of my breathing, my beating heart.

For a moment I considered whether to keep the sword. One never knew what one might encounter along the way. But if I tripped, or if there was a sudden drop—I might very well impale myself by accident. I reluctantly set down the sword and continued without it, putting my hand on the tunnel wall as a guide. As long as I was touching something, I felt that I was still anchored, still in the world.

"Are you certain this is the right way?" I asked, far too late.

There was only silence in reply. Silence from the voice that had, up until now, been so eager to help.

I could go back to the cave, I supposed. But there was nothing waiting for me there except the beast. I had fallen so far down that I doubted the dragons would hear me if I shouted—and in any case, they seemed unlikely to help me. So there was no way out but through.

After a while I felt the tunnel change, angling upward, and all of a sudden there was a burst of light. The coil of panic that had been winding tighter and tighter in my chest snapped. I ran for the light, bursting out onto a grassy hillside. It was morning—I'd been gone for an entire night.

I bent over, gulping for air. My hands were scraped and stinging. I was disheveled and wet and slimy from the pool water, but I was alive. In the distance I could see the path leading back to the Silence. And the box was still in my pocket.

I took out the box and looked at it in the light. It had dried perfectly, without warping or water stains. The grooves that I had felt carved into the sides were in fact wings, doubled and repeating across the box. Alaric's wings. I had them.

I wondered if Alaric was concerned that I had been gone so long. Whether he was making a plan to try to rescue me. How long he might wait before deciding that I was never returning.

You should not trust the raven, the voice hissed in my mind. **He would abandon you if it ever served him.**

"Then give me another option," I said.

I tucked the box back into my pocket and started down the hill. But when I reached the path, I stopped in surprise.

There on the ground lay a traveler's bag. It was dirty and damp, and small trailing vines twined around its straps, but it was undeniably *mine*—the bag I had lost in the river.

"Did you do this?" I was almost afraid to touch it.

It is yours.

I undid the straps, my hands shaking. The food was ruined, but my clothes were still there, as was my knife and—and the net Miranda had made. I pulled it out and watched it shimmer in the sun. So much had changed in a few short days. Had Alaric killed her, or was she all right? Despite the lies she'd told me, I truly hoped she was. Remembering now how Alaric had thrown her, I was reminded that he was more powerful—and dangerous—than he seemed. Perhaps the voice had a point about not trusting him completely.

The forest has power. And it could be yours.

The forest? I thought of the things I'd seen since entering the Silence—the way the trees had moved, the vines that had ripped up the streets of the Gather. It had been impressive. Frightening.

The vines on the bag suddenly shifted, unfurling toward me. I froze, a suspicion dawning on me. Could this voice somehow belong to . . . the Silence itself? The thought was so terrifying, I couldn't bring myself to ask the question outright. Instead I asked, "Is the power enough to kill Katen? Because I believe the Silence has power, but I've seen nothing to convince me it could slay a powerful blood mage."

You doubt this? the voice said incredulously.

I could feel the weight of its anger, but I held firm. "You did not answer the question," I replied.

Without your cooperation, the power has limits. But together . . .

Cooperation. Yet another of those words that sounded suspiciously like coercion. "And what does that cooperation entail?"

Just a few drops of blood, the voice said reluctantly.

If there was one thing I was getting better at, it was spotting a lie. Perhaps the voice was telling the truth about the blood, but I was certain there was more to the bargain than that. I picked up my bag and slung it over one shoulder.

"I don't believe you," I said. And then I walked away.

CHAPTER SEVENTEEN

A laric was waiting as I came around the bend in the path. I saw relief break across his face as he saw me.

"Lena!" he called. "What happened?"

"You didn't mention a flesh-eating beast," I said flatly. "Or that the dragons would enjoy feeding me to it."

"A beast? How did you escape? Did you get the box?"

I was stung that he still managed to inquire about the box, as though that was what mattered most. He hadn't even asked if I was all right.

"The beast was in with the dragons' hoard. I was able to defend myself, and then I escaped through the tunnels," I said.

"But the wings," Alaric said impatiently. "Did you get them?"

I hesitated. The voice had said I shouldn't trust him, and the fact that he'd sent me into the dragons' lair without any preparation made me doubt his promises. What if I gave him the wings, and he decided that I had outlived my usefulness to him? He might turn around and present me to Katen anyway. Before I could change my mind, I shook my head.

"I was too busy avoiding being killed. I didn't have time to search."

Alaric's jaw tightened. He wheeled around and stalked away from me, his entire demeanor rigid. After a while he shook his head. "There's no way around it. We'll have to try again."

"Try again?" I said. "I almost got killed, and you want me to go back? It doesn't seem likely that the dragons will simply let me in a second time."

"I know that!" Alaric said. "But what other choice do we have? In order to help you, I *need* my wings. You must understand that."

"What I understand is that I almost got killed, and you care more about your wings than about me," I snapped. "I've been up all night, threatened by dragons, almost eaten by some sort of amphibious monstrosity, and I'm covered in slime. I'll think about going back there *after* I've decided whether it's worth it to me to risk my life again on your behalf."

His expression softened. "Well," he said, more gently this time, "I cannot help most of that. But there is something we can do about that slime. Come on."

He held out his hand. I took it, rolling my eyes at his lack of apology. He led me to a large pool of water sheltered by a rocky outcropping. There was a small waterfall flowing over the top of the rocks that fed the pool.

"There are no monsters here," Alaric said. "You can wash up—I'll stand guard."

I didn't hesitate before yanking off my boots and splashing into the water, ecstatic over the prospect of finally being *clean*. I went in fully clothed and only after I had submerged myself did I strip off my clothing, rinsing it in the water. Once it had reached a modicum of cleanliness, I spread it out on a flat rock under the sun before diving back into the pool and luxuriating in the feeling of washing everything about that cave from my body.

The day was warm, for autumn. I stayed in the pool far longer than was necessary, but Alaric kept his back turned and said nothing to hurry me along.

Perhaps I had misjudged him. The box was in the pocket of my cloak—I could give it to him at any time. But what would I say, to explain my lie?

The voice's words came to me once more. *You should not trust the raven.* But was there truth in that claim, or had it only been trying to sow discord between us? I didn't think I had imagined the anger in its voice when it mentioned Alaric. For some reason, it seemed to have a personal quarrel with him.

"Alaric?"

He turned slightly as I called but did not look at me. "Yes?"

"You've been here a very long time. Since before the Gather was founded," I said.

He nodded.

"Have you ever heard . . ." It sounded silly in my head just trying to formulate the words. "Have you ever heard of there being a forest spirit? The spirit of the Silence?"

If I hadn't been watching him closely, I wouldn't have noticed him flinch—just barely—before regaining his composure. "Why do you ask?" he said tightly.

"I've been hearing . . . things." That a strange voice had been speaking to me, promising me power, was not something I was sure I wanted to tell him.

Alaric whirled around, his face pale. "That is not a road you want to go down," he said, his strangled tone betraying his fear. "Trust me on this."

So it was true—there *was* something here. The longer I thought on it the more I realized I might always have known. The moment I had seen the Silence, I had felt it was more than just trees, more than a plot of land and rocks and water. The forest itself had a pulse, a voice—and, it seemed, some sort of plan for me.

"Why not?" I asked. Alaric clearly knew about the spirit—perhaps he also had an idea of what a bargain with it would entail.

"I am bound not to speak of it."

For whose sake? I wanted to press him on it, but it seemed useless. If he couldn't even confirm the existence of a forest spirit, he certainly wouldn't be able to speak on the intricacies of its powers or motives.

Alaric peered at me with worry in his eyes. It didn't seem like a ruse—he was truly concerned. For me. He cleared his throat. "Just . . . be careful. I'll be back near the trees when you're ready."

He turned and walked quickly away, leaving me puzzling once more. The voice—the *Silence*. I'd been speaking to the spirit of the forest this whole time. But why had it chosen *me*?

Eventually my stomach began to rumble, and I knew that this respite had come to an end. I stood up in the shallows, wringing water from my hair, and went over to the rock where I had tossed my clothing.

Nothing was fully dry, but at least the slime had washed out, so I couldn't complain very much about the dampness. The ankle the beast had bitten was bruised, but my boot had protected me from serious injury. I dressed quickly and went to find Alaric.

Suddenly I heard a shout in the distance. My entire body tensed. I pulled off my gloves and hurried as fast as my hurt ankle would allow toward the voice, watching for any disturbance in the Silence. Even the sound of branches rustling was sinister as I made my way toward the copse of trees where we were to meet.

There was a sudden flash of light off to my right. Fear spiked through me. I slowed and crept toward it as quietly as I could.

Leave him.

I won't! I thought fiercely. I took cover behind a large tree, peeking out from behind the trunk.

Alaric sat cross-legged on the ground. The air in front of him shimmered, and then parted as it had done before to reveal Katen's impatient face. My heart began to pound, and I pulled myself back behind the tree.

"Where *are* you?" Katen said. "I expected your return yesterday!"

"Out near the canyons," Alaric replied. "The girl has gone farther than we thought."

Katen scoffed. "She's just one girl. Don't tell me you need assistance in dealing with her."

"No," he said haughtily. "It's only a matter of time."

"Well, she will have to wait. The king has called a revel. I need you back here immediately."

He paused. "It will take some time to get back to you."

"Tonight," Katen said. "Or else the others will notice."

"Very well."

I heard Alaric move, and then he came around the tree, his steps heavy.

"Alaric," I said.

He jumped in surprise, then caught himself as he saw me.

"Lena," he said, his voice soft once more. "Are you all right?"

He serves Katen. The voice's warning flashed through my mind once more.

"What did she want?" I asked.

He grimaced. "She is calling me back to the Gather. I cannot disobey. There is a revel coming."

"What does that mean?"

"Shale calls a revel every time he must strengthen the blood stones against the encroachment of the Silence. For those who live in the Gather, it is the only time the palace doors are open to any, regardless of their station." He rose to his feet. "We will have to go back. I'll leave you somewhere safe until I can return."

"But what about your wings?" I said, very aware of the box in my pocket.

Alaric's lips thinned. "We'll have to come back for them. If I'm not in the Gather tonight, Katen will send someone after me, or worse, come looking for me herself."

He took my hand between his. My body wanted to lean into him. Instead, I held myself back.

"I am sorry for how I acted, before. I have been on my own for so long. I wish I could say—could *do*—more. But we must fly."

"Back through the canyon?" I said.

"Unfortunately."

"But didn't Bekit say the ravens would come after us if they saw us again?"

His face was grim. "We have no other choice, not if I am to reach the Gather by nightfall. You will have to hold on tightly."

This time I stepped readily into his arms. The forest floor fell away from our feet. There was a sense of urgency as Alaric flew, darting between wind streams. It was only early afternoon, but he was clearly worried about returning to the Gather in time.

Then, as the ground beneath us changed to the red rocks of the canyon, something collided with us in midair.

My heart leapt into my throat as we were knocked out of flight. We plummeted, the earth rushing up to meet us.

"Hold on!" Alaric cried. I locked my arms around his torso as he flung his arms out wide. The shadow of his wings spread around us. We caught an air current and slowed—just as a dark shape streaked toward us, striking Alaric in the side.

He grunted in pain and recoiled. His wings vanished, and we fell faster. We hit the canyon wall hard, my teeth jarring against my skull as we tumbled down a steep slope until eventually we rolled to a stop in a ditch at the bottom.

For a moment I could do nothing more than lie still, stunned. Sunlight glared painfully against my eyes. I squinted, making out dozens of dark shapes circling in the sky above us—the ravens. Their guttural calls filled the air.

I sat up, gritting my teeth as my body protested. Alaric was already on his feet, his sword drawn.

The canyon walls were steep. I couldn't see past a bend in the path ahead of us. And there was what appeared to be an entire army of ravens overhead. We were trapped.

The ravens' caws grew louder. They circled down toward us, and then dove at Alaric. One raven darted at him, claws out—Alaric swung the sword wildly, catching the raven's wing. The bird careened to the ground and lay still. But Alaric was favoring his left leg, and I could see that his grip on the sword was weak.

I pushed myself up, wincing as I put weight on my right foot—the one that the beast had bitten. Black wings flapped, and I ducked as a raven flew just over my head. It dodged Alaric's sword and swiped its claws across his face. Alaric let out a shout of pain—when he turned, I could see blood streaming down his cheek.

I stifled a cry. The ravens were flying too fast for me to reach them with my knife. I had no other defenses, could do nothing to help him. I couldn't even open the box that held his wings. And I wasn't carrying anything else—

My fingers froze in my pocket. There *was* something else. The acorns I had taken from Miranda. We were in the Silence, which meant that this would work—wouldn't it? Safe passage, that was what she'd said. But would a guide be brave enough to come to us now?

I only had two acorns, but I couldn't think of another way out of this attack. I crouched down, trying not to draw attention to myself, and popped the cap off the acorn.

A raven dove toward me, shrieking. I stumbled back and fell, crying out as my ankle twisted beneath my body. Tears sprang from my eyes as the acorn skittered out of my hand. I lunged after it— only to find that something else had arrived there first.

A small lizard no larger than my hand stood next to the acorn, its skin a mottled gray green. Could this be the guide? I tried to remember the words that Miranda had used when she had called the squirrel.

"Please, guide us to a safe path away from here," I said. I picked up the acorn and offered it to the lizard. "In payment, I offer this."

An acorn was a strange item to offer a lizard, but I didn't know what else to do. The lizard studied me, unblinking. Then it turned around and ran. My heart sank.

The lizard stopped and let out a little croak, looking inquisitively over its shoulder.

I pocketed the acorn and waved, trying to get Alaric's attention. "Let's go!" I shouted, pointing to the lizard.

I expected resistance, but there was none. Alaric came toward me, limping as he fended off two other ravens. I grabbed his hand, and we hobbled after the lizard. Our injuries made us easy targets, and I hunched my shoulders, trying to protect my neck. We wove back and forth, but it was of little use. A bird hit my back, clawing at my cloak. I ducked as another dove toward me, and another. Claws scratched at my face, and my cheek burned.

I couldn't see the lizard anymore—I could only see black wings buffeting me on all sides, blocking out the sky. It was getting harder to put one foot in front of the other. I clutched Alaric's hand. When his grip loosened, I realized that he, too, must be fading.

And then someone shouted, "Here!"

I looked up, shielding my face with my free arm. There was a figure in the distance, their hands held high. As I watched, a silvery net shot into the air, wrapping itself around a raven. The bird fell to the ground, hopelessly tangled.

The attack lessened as some of the ravens peeled away, turning toward this new threat. I staggered forward, almost dragging Alaric. There was no time to lose—I caught sight of the lizard again, waiting near an outcropping of rock. Behind us I could hear the sounds of more ravens hitting the ground. We had to get away before they recovered.

"Come on!" I said, pulling Alaric forward.

As we approached the rock, I heard running footsteps. I turned back to see the person who had cast the nets coming toward us at full speed, red hair ablaze in the sunlight.

Miranda.

CHAPTER EIGHTEEN

I stopped, shocked.

"What are you doing?" Miranda shouted. "The nets won't last forever!"

I shook off my stupor. She was right; there was no time to waste. We ran as quickly as we could after the lizard, which led us toward the canyon wall. At first I saw nothing but stone. Then the lizard scuttled sideways and disappeared, and I realized that what I had taken for a shadow was in truth a small passage burrowed into the wall. We filed into the passage.

I heard movement in the darkness, and a moment later a blue light flared to life over Miranda's open palm. She ran ahead, and we followed her, not stopping until the passage widened and we came to a small cavern.

"Are you all right?" Alaric asked, his voice rough with pain.

"I'm fine," I said. Fine enough, anyway. "You?"

He shook his head, waving off the question.

I stared at Miranda in the dim light. A flash of relief rushed through me, followed quickly by anger. She had lied to me. But I was still glad to see her, and not only because she had just saved us from the ravens. She was *alive*. I hadn't realized how much that mattered to me until now, and I didn't know how to make sense of it.

She stared back at me. Then she turned her head and stared at Alaric. Her gaze fell to our clasped hands.

My cheeks flushed. I dropped Alaric's hand. "I—"

"We need to move," Alaric cut in. "As she said, the nets will not last forever. We need to be clear of the canyons when they disappear."

"Then let's go," Miranda said impatiently.

"I can't," I said. "I hurt my ankle."

Miranda pressed her lips together and looked at Alaric. "Can I trust you not to cut my head off if I heal her?"

Alaric rolled his eyes but stepped back.

I lowered myself to the ground, wincing. Miranda knelt next to me and gently removed my boot. Then she used her knife to make a small cut on the back of her arm. I held my sock away from my ankle as she let blood drip down onto the wound. A few seconds later the pain began to ease.

"It's not perfect. We don't have time for that," Miranda said, her voice fatigued.

"As long as I can walk," I said. "Thank you." I pushed myself up and shifted my weight tentatively. The pain had lessened to a dull ache—good enough for a while, at least.

We proceeded in silence. The air cooled, and I could hear the soft dripping of water somewhere in the dark. Miranda held her light high as we followed the lizard. I was hurting *everywhere*. Gods, I needed a hot bath. And a soft bed to fall into for days—I never wanted to see a raven again.

I peeked at Miranda out of the corner of my eye. "Were you following us all along?" I asked.

She shook her head. "I spent a few days recovering," she said. "He could have killed me." She glared at Alaric.

"So dramatic," Alaric scoffed. "If I'd intended to kill you, you would be dead."

Miranda ignored him and continued. "Then I had to get some help to track you. But I couldn't get past the ravens—I was waiting for you to come back."

I bit my lip. We likely wouldn't have made it out of the canyon without her. "Why?"

She glanced at Alaric again. "I'd rather not say in front of him."

"Then don't," Alaric said wearily. "You're still a liar. I doubt that has changed since we last saw you."

"You're one to talk," Miranda snapped.

Alaric's jaw set, and he reached for his sword. I raised my hands up, putting myself between them.

"Stop it! Can't we agree to let this go, at least until we get out of here? At the very least, you must admit that Miranda helped us back there, and she didn't have to," I said, addressing Alaric.

"Fine," he said.

I looked at Miranda, who scowled, but shrugged in acquiescence.

"Good," I said.

A while later, the passage brightened and we emerged, blinking, into the forest once more. And there before us were the glimmering white stones that marked a safe path.

The lizard waited on the path, unblinking.

"You must pay him," Alaric said.

Of course. I'd forgotten that I'd pocketed the acorn back in the canyon. I knelt down and offered it to the lizard. It came up to me, peered at my hand—and then sank sharp teeth into the meat of my palm.

I hissed in pain and jerked back, dropping the acorn. The lizard's teeth were clearly imprinted upon my skin. As I watched, pinprick drops of blood welled up from the wound and spilled to the ground.

The earth shifted below me—for a moment I thought it was just dizziness, but then Alaric and Miranda staggered as well. I fell back as a sapling shot up from the ground. In an instant it was higher than my waist, then my head, unfurling with a flourish. Bloodred flowers bloomed before my eyes, and unfamiliar fruit the color of rich cider burst into being.

I stared at it, dumbfounded.

This is but a taste of what could be, the voice of the Silence purred.

An intoxicating, sweet scent wafted toward me, and I took a step forward.

Alaric grabbed my arm. *"Don't,"* he said harshly. He pulled me back, leading us down the path until the tree was out of sight.

"What—what was that?" Miranda said.

"That is not for me to say, but no good would have come from it," Alaric said. He looked up at the sky, which was approaching sunset. "We cannot tarry."

"You need to get back," I said.

He shook his head. "I can't leave you here. You're not safe."

I drew him away from Miranda. Lowering my voice, I said, "Can you fly?"

He nodded slowly. "I can ... but I can't carry you. I'm too weak."

I swallowed. "Then you must go."

"I can't leave you with *her.*"

"You don't have a choice," I said, lacing my fingers through his. "I can take care of myself."

He sighed. "There is a woman you can stay with until I return. Fallyne. She has a house near the west entrance to the Gather. Take care with what you say to her, but she is as safe a person as you will meet in the Silence."

I looked at him doubtfully. "Is she a blood mage?"

"She's a . . ." Alaric searched for a word and seemed to come up short. "A hedgewife? The humans have different words for her. In truth, she is a healer. She cares for those who have fallen out of favor with the Gather—or anyone who needs her."

"How will I find her?"

Alaric turned to Miranda and raised his voice. "You know the way to Fallyne's house?"

Miranda glared back at him, but nodded.

"If you do not deliver her safely there tonight, I will kill you," he said. There was no malice in his voice. It was a simple statement of fact.

Miranda paled, and she nodded again.

Alaric looked back at me and bent to whisper in my ear. "Be careful with her. She will try to win you back. And . . . if I don't return, don't come looking for me."

He spared one last withering look for Miranda. Then he launched up in the air and left us behind.

"So . . . ," I said, after Alaric had gone.

"So," Miranda replied. "Do you want to explain what that was back there? Or what you've been doing with Alaric in the first place?"

I raised an eyebrow. "Why should I explain anything to you? You lied to me. I can't trust you."

She opened her mouth to reply, then paused. "I suppose that's fair," she said finally. For a moment we just looked at each other. Then she pointed. "The path that goes closest to Fallyne's house is that way. If you want to arrive tonight, we'd better get moving."

"All right," I said.

Her eyes fell on my hands once more, and I realized I wasn't wearing my gloves—that in fact, I hadn't thought about them in some time. Now I dug them out of my pocket and put them on.

We started down the path.

"Can I just explain—"

"What's there to explain?" I interrupted.

Miranda fidgeted. "Yes, I lied. But I worried when Alaric took you. I still tried to help you. Doesn't that count for something?"

"I don't know," I said truthfully. Being near her again, everything I had felt for her came rushing back to the surface. It confused me. I didn't trust myself.

She frowned, frustrated. "I'm on your side! How can I make you believe that?"

"Well," I said, crossing my arms. "You could start by telling me the truth. About Callie and about that medallion."

"Oh, Lena." Miranda sighed. "The truth is, I'm not . . . I'm not a good person. I tried to be, once. But the Gather, it rips it out of you, the instinct to do right by other people. I came here with my best friend, the only person to stand by my side. When she was taken from me, I became desperate enough to do anything. Anything at all, just to free her."

"So you said."

"But I didn't tell you everything," she said. "Alaric was right, and so were the people at Haven. I *was* a loyal member of the king's court. That's why I have the medallion. But Callie . . . she's very ill with blood plague, and she refuses to leave. I went to petition the king for her freedom. And he told me that all I had to do was go to the castle of briars . . . and kill the princess sleeping inside."

Kill the princess? She'd told me she meant to save her.

"But I thought you opposed Shale?" I said faintly. "Killing the princess would end all the hopes for an uprising, wouldn't it?"

"I know," she said, looking away from me. "It's a common punishment, actually, for people that displease him. Because the castle does not want anyone coming inside. It's protected by its own kind of magic. Countless people have tried to get through only to die on the briars. But the tyrant can't be disobeyed. So either you kill the princess or die trying."

"So you were lying to me from the very beginning. You must have known about the Hand of Mora," I said. "You knew from the start, when I told you about my curse."

She had the grace to look ashamed. "I did."

"And you were going to make *me* kill the princess?"

Her eyes slid away from mine, and I realized that the truth was far worse.

"No . . . ," I said, finally putting the pieces together. "You failed. You were as good as dead. You should have stayed in the Mundane; it was safer than the Silence. And yet you went back. With me. Because you knew I would be a good bargaining chip. You intended to sell me to Shale—or to Katen."

"I'm not going to ask for your forgiveness," Miranda said miserably. "I know I don't deserve it. I only wanted to explain. I failed. I couldn't save Callie. So yes, I thought that if I could deliver you to the Gather, the king might see his way to granting her freedom regardless."

"You really *were* using me," I said.

"And you were using me!" Miranda countered. "Admit it! You wanted to come into the Silence to break your curse, not because you wanted to help me."

She said it hotly, but the truth was, as much as I had entered the Silence to break the curse . . . I had walked into the forest because of *her*.

"That wasn't all there was to it," I said, looking away. "There was—you."

Her voice softened. "When Alaric took you, I realized I couldn't go through with it. I couldn't stand the thought of him handing you over to Katen. And then, when I realized he hadn't, I thought there was still a chance to make things right."

"And what about Callie?" I demanded.

She shook her head. "Callie will never leave the Gather. I should have accepted that a long time ago. I just—she was closer to me than my own sisters. I never thought I would have to say goodbye to her."

"How do I know you're not still telling tales?"

"Not everyone is an evil mastermind, Lena!" Miranda snapped. "If I still wanted to betray you, I would have returned to the Gather by now and told the king that you were with Alaric. But I didn't. I came after you instead. Because I am done with the Gather—done with all of them. Yes, I lied and took advantage of you, and there's no excuse for that. But there's nothing I can do but apologize and do better going forward."

I was surprised to see tears brimming at the corners of her eyes. "You should know," she said, her voice catching, "I felt the same way too. About you. It . . . it scared me."

A surprised tug of desire moved through me as she walked away, but my anger still nipped at me. She had betrayed me. She had intended to sell me. She didn't care about me at all.

And yet . . . would she have told me the truth or apologized, if that were the case?

I hated this tangle of conflicting emotions. With Alaric I felt I knew where I stood—we were caged creatures, offering each other what little comfort we could in the fleeting time we had. With Miranda . . . With Miranda I felt the urge to dream again. She could break my heart, if I let her. And I wasn't ready to let myself be vulnerable in that way.

Ahead of me, Miranda stopped. "We're here," she said as I caught up, pointing to a house standing in a cluster of trees. "Do you still want to go?"

I hesitated.

"It is safe," she added grudgingly. "He was right to direct us here."

"All right," I said.

The door of the house opened, and an older woman stepped outside, the last rays of the setting sun falling on her silvery hair. She raised a hand in greeting.

"I thought I heard someone causing a commotion," she said.

Miranda and I approached her cautiously.

"Are you Fallyne?" I asked. "I was told that you could help us."

She looked me over with a critical eye. "Have you left the Gather? I can sense there's blood magic in you."

I ducked my head. Alaric had said nothing about the hedge-wife being able to see inside me. I felt exposed under her scrutiny.

But then she laughed, and it was such a kind sound. "Not to worry, dearie. What's your name?"

I hesitated. "Edina," I said, after a moment.

Fallyne nodded and looked past me, addressing Miranda. "And you?"

"Miranda."

"Well, come in then," Fallyne said, gesturing for us to come inside. "We're all just sitting down to supper."

CHAPTER NINETEEN

Inside the house a homey, delicious smell wafted through the hall. Fallyne led us into a large room where over a dozen people were seated, waiting. I felt my shoulders hunch into a familiar position as I looked for the seat farthest away from the rest.

"Sit," Fallyne said. "Eat something, and then we'll talk."

What else could we do? I tugged my gloves up as high as they would go and was careful of my hands as I took a bowl and a spoon.

Containing myself like this was nothing new, but now that I'd finally tasted freedom, these familiar limitations infuriated me. I would do *anything* to rid myself of them. And yet . . . I did not want to lose the power that had made the Wolves turn around and run. Both desires warred within me.

You could have it all, the voice whispered.

I tried to ignore it. Here I had to concentrate. I couldn't allow myself to be distracted when the consequence could be death.

I gathered my food and went to a table in the corner where I could sit with my back to the wall. Miranda joined me.

The fare was simple—rice, spicy pickled cucumber, strips of marinated meat—and I wolfed down my meal. After we were done, the other diners scattered, leaving us alone with Fallyne.

"Come now, Edina," she said. "Let's go into my office and talk. Miranda, if you'll wait in the hall? We won't be long."

Her office was a room of modest size, cramped by towering stacks of books piled almost everywhere. I navigated the space carefully, trying not to overturn anything.

Fallyne sat behind her desk and invited me to take the empty chair on the other side.

"So," she said. "Where have you come from, and why have you landed here?"

What was she most likely to believe? "I was in the Gather," I started. "But I don't wish to serve my blood mage anymore. I was told that you could help."

She sat back, steepling her fingers as she looked at me quizzically. "Well, I *could* help. If you were telling the truth."

I felt my cheeks flush. "I *am* telling the truth!"

"You are not such a good liar, actually," she said. "I know you're under the Hand of Mora."

She smiled at my alarm. "The spell is not so common that everyone remembers. It's old, very old. But it's obvious to those who know how to look for the signs: you wear gloves and long garb, even indoors, and you shied away from those serving the meal today and everyone else. I sense that you carry an immense amount of power, but there is no sign of blood plague on your face—that's very interesting. Most people who have the Hand of Mora placed on them do eventually succumb to it."

My palms were sweating. She had sussed out so much about me—and yet I had to remind myself that while she might know about the spell, she did not know Katen was responsible. I could still kill her, if need be.

"Ah, I see the wheels turning in your head, trying to figure out if I might somehow betray you," Fallyne said. "There is nothing that

I can say that would ease your fears. So let's turn to another topic. What I do here."

"I heard that you were a hedgewife, though I've little idea what that means," I confessed.

"Oh, nothing, and everything," Fallyne said, waving a hand dismissively. "I do a little of this and that. I don't trouble the Gather, and so the Gather doesn't trouble me. Although I generally do not harbor people carrying so much power."

There had to be more than that. I had a difficult time imagining that the Gather would willingly allow any power to slip through their grasp, no matter how small.

"Those who come here are suffering. I heal them of the plague, if they are not too far gone."

I heard myself gasp. "But I thought that was impossible."

"Not impossible . . . just not a process that everyone wants to submit to. It is dangerous. Not all survive."

"And what is it?" I asked.

"In short, I bleed them of the magic and use it for other things. Sometimes I just let it flow back into the world where it came from, and then there is balance once more. But again, I am not so certain that will work for you." She eyed me critically. "If someone cursed you with the Hand of Mora, they'll surely want their power back. You've stolen a lot of magic, girl."

"I didn't choose this," I snapped, before remembering that this was just the sort of thing Alaric would have warned me not to say. I backpedaled quickly. "I'm sorry. I'm just looking for a place to stay for a few days. I won't be any trouble to you. If there's some way I can help you while I'm here, I will."

Fallyne studied me a moment longer. At last she sighed and

stood up. "You can stay the night while I make up my mind."

I didn't have to fake my gratitude. "Thank you," I said.

Miranda was waiting as Fallyne and I stepped out of her office. We crossed paths without speaking. I wondered briefly what Fallyne would ask her, but such thoughts flew from my head when Fallyne opened the door to a cozy room with a bed and a glass of water on a nightstand.

As soon as Fallyne left me alone, I closed the door and took off my boots, grimacing as my feet slid free. My injured ankle was still swollen despite Miranda's healing, but I was too tired to take off my sock to inspect it before collapsing on the bed.

A knock on the door woke me the next morning. I sat up groggily as Fallyne entered the room holding a plate with two small cakes and an apple. "Good morning," she said. "Eat your breakfast, then come join me in the garden." She set the plate on the nightstand and left without further ceremony.

Well, at least one couldn't fault her for beating around the bush.

The cakes looked familiar, but it wasn't until I bit into one that I recognized it. Queen's cake. The taste was unmistakable, though these weren't as good as Father's. I swallowed around a sudden lump in my throat. I was still angry at him . . . but I hoped he was all right. Wherever he was.

I reached for the apple, trying to think of something else. Yesterday morning I'd had clarity. But Miranda's reappearance complicated things. She'd outright admitted that she had meant to sell me to Shale, the ruler of the Gather. I couldn't trust her after that.

But she'd been remorseful. And she'd confessed to having feelings for me.

All of that could have been an act as well. I had no way of knowing. Just as I had no way of knowing what Alaric was doing at this very moment. He'd said that he could not disobey a direct order from Katen. What if she found out what he had been doing? Where I was? Could I really trust him enough to wait for his return? Waiting only made me feel like a puppet in someone else's hands.

I swallowed the last of the cake and sat back from the empty plate. Lacking any new revelations, I made myself presentable and went out to find Fallyne.

When Fallyne had mentioned a garden, I'd expected that she meant something sprawling and wild, spreading into the Silence. So I was surprised to find neat stone walls that enclosed a garden planted in even rows behind the house. Fallyne was kneeling in one corner pulling weeds when I entered.

Given how many people she cared for, I was surprised that she had time for such a simple task. As I watched, she sat back on her heels and wiped one gloved hand across her forehead, leaving a smudge of dirt behind.

"So," she said. "What do you want to do?"

Her directness startled me. I knew she wasn't talking about kitchen tasks or weeding. I looked around to make sure we were alone before replying.

"You said yourself that you weren't certain you could treat me. But . . . as I am, I can do little more than kill or be killed."

"Hmm." Fallyne got to her feet and walked over to me, carrying a bundle of the weeds she'd just pulled. "Have you heard the story of the Hand of Mora?"

I shook my head. She sat down at the table and began sorting through the weeds. I understood that she meant to make use of what she could. Spindleweed was utterly useless—even poisonous in large doses—but dandelion could be eaten.

"Mora was a girl not so much older than yourself, but so powerful. She could have held the moon in her hands, if only she had taken a different path. But she was frightened. Some people are, when it comes to power. Eager to grasp for more, terrified that everyone else around them is scheming to take it away. So she cast a spell to protect her power, so that no one could ever steal it from her—because no one could ever touch her."

"Ah," I said.

"Indeed," Fallyne replied. "In doing so, she cut herself off. She was so frightened of her enemies that she denied herself friends and loved ones. Now, there are many versions of what happened next. She offended one of the great owls, or cheated the god of death, or crossed a powerful king. But they came for her, whoever they were. They buried her alive. And the only friend who came to help, when she was alone and unconscious—he died when he touched her. He died, and for nothing except her refusal to trust."

Fallyne finished sorting the plants and looked up at me. "Mora was brilliant. Do you think that anyone else could have come up with such a curse? That takes a certain amount of genius. She could have had anything she ever wanted. *Everything* she ever wanted. But instead she lost it all. So tell me, Edina. You hold power. But is holding on to it worth the price of pushing everyone away? Know this: in the end you will be powerless—magic or no—unless you can trust, and trust well."

Conniving witch. She treats you like a child. The voice was back, but I thrust it aside. Fallyne was a sea of calm after so many days of storms. I wanted to believe in her words, in a world where everything could be solved, if only I could decide who to trust—and to trust wisely.

I had trusted my parents, but they were my parents—I'd trusted them by default, and they had betrayed me.

I'd trusted Miranda, and she'd lied to me.

I'd trusted Alaric—I still trusted him, I realized. And I *wanted* to trust Miranda. But perhaps that was a mistake.

I looked down at the table. "How do you know *how* to trust? Who to trust?"

"Well," Fallyne said. "You trusted me, or you wouldn't have entered my house. How did you make that decision?" *Because Alaric had told me I could.* Fallyne must have read the troubled expression on my face, for she continued speaking.

"The Silence is a cruel place, and the Gather is even crueler. It doesn't surprise me that you find it difficult to trust. But the world is an impossible place when you are alone." She smiled softly. "I remember being your age, deciding to tell the first girl who loved me that I was a girl too—not the boy my parents thought I was. Even though I loved her, I was terrified of being so vulnerable in front of her. But I chose well. I can still remember the way the weight lifted off my shoulders when she took my hand . . ." Her expression sobered. "Trust requires a leap of faith, even in the best of circumstances. To truly trust someone, you must trust yourself first, to make the right decision."

Fallyne stood up with the spindleweed. "And I've made a decision about you. You can stay here, so long as you don't interfere with my work. But my house is not a place to hide forever. Soon enough you will need to choose your path. If you want to rid yourself of the blood magic, I can try to help you. But that is your choice."

"You really think it can be done?" I asked.

"I won't lie to you. With the amount of magic in your blood, it would take time. Weeks, perhaps. And ridding yourself of the magic would not rid you of the curse. But perhaps it would relieve your burden. Think on it."

She retreated inside, leaving me in the garden to stew on her words.

She was right. I was tired of being afraid. I wanted to believe that I could find people to trust. That I could build something different for myself than the prison of my curse.

I looked back at the house. *You must trust yourself first.*

Miranda looked surprised to see me when I knocked on her door. "Can I come in?" I asked.

She shrugged and stood back as I entered the room, feeling strangely nervous. Miranda shut the door, and I realized that I didn't know how to do this, whatever *this* was that I was doing. I'd been alone all my life, alone in all the ways that mattered. I didn't know how to stop that, even when I wanted to.

"I didn't trust you before," I said, tracing the grain of the wooden table with my finger.

"For good reason," Miranda admitted. She flopped down on her bed and stared up at the ceiling. "But we talked about that. I thought you didn't want anything more to do with me."

By most accounts I shouldn't have. She'd burned me once, and I'd gotten away. If I was burned again, it would be my own fault.

Despite the season, the room suddenly felt too hot.

Miranda rolled onto her side, propping herself up with an elbow. I smiled, remembering how she'd nearly taken my breath away when we'd first met. Now she looked sleepy and inviting, and we locked eyes for one long moment. I was suddenly overcome with the desire to kiss her—more than I'd ever wanted to touch anyone else. What had passed between Alaric and me had been fueled by a desire for connection, and the fear of dying without ever experiencing what most seemed to take for granted. This new desire—it was entirely for *her*.

"So why *are* you here?" Miranda said. "I've told you the truth— what more do you want from me?"

The question fell into the space between us and hung, glimmering in the air. She waited for my answer, the afternoon sun playing on her hair.

I want you, but I don't know if I can trust you.

Because to kiss you would be to relinquish my power over you.

Because to kiss you would be to give you power over me.

I wanted to say these things but found I couldn't. I'd been bold with Alaric—but that had been different. What I had done with him had been a claiming of myself, my own independence, my own choices.

But with Miranda . . . I felt shy, and soft.

I sat down on the bed beside her. To her credit, she did not flinch. There was a darkening in her eyes, a flush that rose in her cheeks that made my heart race.

"Trust," I said, finally answering her question.

Miranda leaned forward until I could feel her breath on my face. If she fell, brushed against me in any way—

I held myself still although every part of me ached to touch her. I could smell apple on her skin, the lotion that she'd used after she had washed.

"I trust you," she whispered, a hairsbreadth from my lips.

She sat back, and I swallowed, hard. My hands began to tremble—both from the effort I'd exerted in keeping still and from how frightened I was. Frightened of letting Miranda into my world again.

Why was this so difficult? Being with Alaric had not been this difficult. Being with Alaric also didn't come along with an inability to look anywhere else but at Miranda's mouth, smiling at me.

Alaric and I had been on equal footing, and we had come together for our own pleasure, out of our own self-interest.

But being with Miranda would require me to be more vulnerable, to give of myself as much as I took from her. If I trusted her, I would fall. I would be entirely undone.

"I'm frightened," I said, my voice a whisper.

"Lena," she said, her voice cracking on my name. "When Alaric came for you—I thought for certain that I had led you to your death by tempting you into the Silence. I vowed never to forgive myself. Still, when I closed my eyes at night, yours was the face I dreamed about. Your eyes, your lips—" She cursed. "I haven't been able to stop thinking about your lips since the moment we met, you could drive me mad with them—"

I broke.

"Katen," I said, diving across the bed toward her. "The witch who cursed me is Katen."

And then my lips were on hers, and my world exploded with light.

Kissing Alaric had been heady and unsettling, like tasting wine for the very first time. In kissing Miranda it was as though I'd opened a bottle of something rare and fine—every sip demanded to be savored.

I ripped off my gloves and sank my hands into the curls of her hair—something I realized I'd always wanted to do, from the moment I'd met her.

"Do you know how torturous it's been?" Miranda murmured between kisses. "How much I wanted to touch you, only to know I *couldn't*—"

If she was a liar, I was dead. But if she was a liar, she was the best I had ever seen. I couldn't think straight for want.

Time slowed to a languorous pace around us. Everything crystallized—each touch of her lips, her hand plying expertly underneath my shirt, roaming up my back. I trailed my fingers down her arms, pressed my lips to the curve of her neck before returning to her mouth, smiling against mine.

We broke apart only at the sound of the floorboards creaking loudly outside as someone walked down the hall. Miranda giggled at the sound, and even her laughter drew me toward her. Our fingers tangled together as we waited for the person to pass by.

Instead, the footsteps stopped. There was a knock on the door.

"Edina? Are you in there?" Fallyne called.

I groaned and fell back upon the bed.

"Go," Miranda whispered. She pressed my gloves into my hands. "I'm not going anywhere."

I drew on my gloves and dragged myself to my feet. I took a deep breath and smoothed my hair as best I could, though there was nothing to be done about the flush of my cheeks.

I opened the door.

And there, standing in the hallway beside Fallyne, was my father.

CHAPTER TWENTY

The warmth drained from my body, leaving me speechless.

"*Lena*. You're all right." Father stepped forward and wrapped his arms around me, squeezing so tightly I could barely breathe.

My mind flooded with confusion. *What—how—?*

"What are you doing here?" I asked, feeling faint. "How did you even find me?"

I caught sight of Fallyne. My spine stiffened, and I pushed away from my father.

"You brought him here?" I said. Fallyne's even gaze told me she had. "How do you even *know* him?" Suddenly everything she had said to me seemed suspect.

She glanced at my father. "Joren and I have known each other a long time. Your father stopped here a few days ago and asked me to watch out for you. When you arrived, I sent him a message."

"How did you know who I was?"

Fallyne's eyes softened. "You used your mother's name, child. And there aren't many girls matching your description who bear the Hand of Mora."

"So everything you told me—was that just stalling to keep me here?"

"Don't blame Fallyne," Father cut in. "She was only doing as I asked."

I backed away from him. My initial shock was giving way to anger as everything I had learned about him since entering the Silence came rushing back to me. "I want nothing to do with you."

He looked past me at Miranda, and his jaw tightened. "I was wrong to treat you like a child in Onwey, I know. But please, Lena. Just talk to me."

I stared up at him. Somehow since I'd seen him last, dark circles had appeared under his eyes. He looked haggard and gaunt—and old.

"All right," I said quietly. "Let's talk."

I turned back to Miranda. She was hugging her arms to her stomach, looking as though she would rather be anywhere but here. "I'll . . . I'll be right back," I said.

She nodded, but the uncertainty in her features sparked fresh anger within me. I fumed as I put on my cloak and I stepped into the hallway.

Father led the way out of Fallyne's house to the side path bordering the garden.

Once we were alone, he turned to me. "We need to leave at once. It's not safe here."

My heart sank. Of course it was too much to think he would see that I had navigated the Silence successfully—that I was capable of taking care of myself. "No," I said.

Father stilled. "No?"

"You heard me." My hands clenched. "I'm not going anywhere with you."

"Lena, I know you're angry, but there are things at play here that you don't understand."

"Oh really?" I crossed my arms. "Like the Hand of Mora? Like the fact that if Katen finds me, she'll kill me to reclaim her magic?"

Father's face was like stone.

"Tell me, Father," I said, pressing on. "Do you really think you kept me *safer* by withholding this from me for the last seventeen years?"

He threw his hands up in mock outrage. "You want me to admit it? *Fine.* We lied to you."

"You let me think I was a monster!" I cried.

He nodded. "You're right. We did. Everything you want to accuse us of, we did. And I apologize for none of it, because that was what it took to keep you *safe.*"

I'd thought hearing him admit it would bring me relief, but I just felt cold rage. I waited for him to argue further so that I could say something that would cut him to the bone.

Instead, his shoulders slumped. "We struggled, your mother and I. We felt it was our fault, what happened to you. When that first boy died, you were so young. And then you were so destroyed the day your mother left . . . I was afraid of hurting you more."

I bit my lip. I still felt the constant shadow of my mother's absence. But . . . but when I tried to think back to what my father was talking about, the memory was gone. As though it had never happened.

He paused, his gaze intent on me.

"What?" I said.

"You were so shaken by that," he said slowly. "For years. But something has changed."

I raised my chin. "*I've* changed."

He shook his head. "There's something else." He peered closer, searching my face. "What have you done?"

I felt at the corners of my memory, like a tongue probing the edge of a broken tooth. But there was nothing there. I tried to keep my expression impassive. "Does it matter?"

Father's face darkened. "You lost it somehow. Traded or sold it. Oh, Lena . . ."

"Perhaps I'm better off without it." I shrugged, thinking of the box in my cloak pocket.

"No. Oh no, Lena." A strangled, sorrowful sound emerged from his throat. "That memory, as awful as it was—it was part of *you*. And this place—these creatures will take and take from you until there is nothing left. This is why I didn't want you here. You're meddling with things you don't understand. You're going to get hurt. Killed."

"I was already hurt," I countered. "And I was always destined to be killed. You tried to keep it from me, but I know now. I think in a way, I've always known. So you don't get to tell me what I can or can't do, not anymore. It was my memory to bargain with, and I don't regret it."

He stepped back, stricken.

"This was always going to happen, Father," I continued. "We couldn't have run from Katen forever. And what I wish is—" Something snapped within me, and I was surprised by the vehemence with which my fury poured out. "I wish you had prepared me for this. You could have told me the truth. You could have helped me stand against her. *Anything*. And instead you simply chose to run."

"Yes, we ran," he said. "Because there was no safer alternative. The Gather is deadly, yes. As are Katen and her father. But that is not the only danger here."

"Then *tell me*," I said.

A muscle worked in his jaw. "I swore to your mother I would not," he said softly. "That I would never expose you to the darkness that took her."

"What do you mean, *took her?*" I said.

Father only looked at me, and there was such immense sadness in his eyes. "I am your father. If you ever trusted me, trust me on this now."

A memory flashed behind my eyes—*a tall, almost skeletal man holding my hand, bundled up against the cold.*

No—I blinked and the image shifted, hazed, flickered in and out.

A tall man holding my hand, bundled—my small hands mittened, though it wasn't even near winter.

He holds my hand as we reach a stream and lifts me over the water as we cross.

My father had saved me. More times than I understood or remembered, he had saved me.

But he couldn't save me from this. Worse, he hadn't even truly tried.

"No," I said. "I can't."

"Lena—"

"Go home!" I cried. "I don't need you any longer. I don't *want* you here."

Before he could respond, I turned and tore down the path into Fallyne's garden. My heart was racing, my body shaking. After *everything,* how could he still not be honest with me? I wanted to go back and scream at him until he told me what he had meant. But also, I couldn't bear to look at him.

I ran to the trees that stood in the corner of the garden and leaned against one of them, trying to lose myself in its solidity. The air was frosty, a reminder that winter was coming. Tree branches splayed from the Silence over the garden walls, creating a patchwork canopy. I pulled my cloak closer around myself and looked up at the sky.

What if I *had* made a mistake? I'd run from my father, declaring that I could take care of myself. But more and more, I felt as though I was losing my footing.

I turned around and sank down to the ground. What should I do? I couldn't trust my father—not after all the lies. Fallyne had said that in order to trust others, I had to trust myself. Of course, Fallyne had turned out to be just as deceitful as any of them. But still—I was afraid again.

I picked up a pebble and threw it, watching it skitter across the garden. *What was I afraid of?*

Death? Yes. But life was not worth living without freedom. I was not frightened to die in pursuit of it.

My thoughts turned back to the girl waiting for me upstairs. *Heartbreak.* The moment I thought it, I knew it to be true. I'd spent so long yearning to be able to touch, I'd forgotten that human connection was more than mere physical contact. Now, after what had passed between us, I realized that one word of rejection from Miranda might destroy me.

I tried to conjure up the feelings that had overwhelmed me only an hour ago. But my thoughts were still so unsettled. What if—no. I could not go on like this. I had to choose. And I chose her.

The thought brought a smile to my lips—a small one, but real. I got to my feet and brushed off my trousers, thinking of how she might greet me when I opened the door.

Something rustled in the distance, and my body tensed. I looked at the entrance to the garden. Was Father returning to argue with me again? I wasn't surprised, though I wasn't sure that there was anything I could do that would finally change his mind—or he mine.

There was another rustle—and then there was a crash, followed by a long, eerie howl. *Wolves.*

And Miranda was still inside.

I tugged the gloves from my hands and started forward—

STOP.

I hesitated. I had never heard the voice so strident. But I couldn't stand by while Miranda was in danger. I started forward again.

Vines erupted from the ground, blocking my way. They reached up and twined around my wrists, yanking me back, away from the gate.

Let me go! I thought urgently.

No.

More vines wound around me, enclosing me so tightly that I could barely move. I struggled, and my breathing came faster. What if the vines somehow dragged me below the earth? I tried to lift my arm, but could barely even open my fist.

Be still. You are well hidden now.

The growl of a Wolf reached my ears, and I froze. I held my

breath as prowling footsteps entered the garden. The footsteps stalked through the garden, then retreated.

Screams and crashes and the occasional howl came from the house. My jaw clenched in anger. My knees started to hurt, and my feet began to cramp from this unnatural position. I shuddered at the sounds of destruction and tried not to imagine what they might be doing to Miranda. She was all right. She had to be.

After what seemed like an eternity, the house quieted. On the other side of the garden wall I heard heavy footsteps, then all was silent again.

The vines recoiled, setting me free. I tore the stragglers off my arms and threw them aside. "If you *ever* do that to me again, I will end you. Make no mistake."

The voice was silent at that. Good. Because I was furious, my body aching for a fight, and I was terrified of what I might find when I entered Fallyne's house.

I put one of my gloves back on and held my other bare hand carefully at my side. Then I cautiously made my way toward the back door.

Inside, the house was in complete disarray. I skirted a few girls sweeping broken glass from the hallway and ran up the stairs. My heart pounding, I burst into Miranda's room.

She wasn't there. The room had been ransacked, the sheets twisted and the lamp smashed on the floor. *No.*

I backed out of the room and searched the house until I found Fallyne in her office. Books had been thrown to the floor, their pages ripped out. The smoky air suggested that someone had attempted to set them on fire.

"What happened? Where is Miranda?" I demanded.

Fallyne knelt on the floor and picked up a book, turning it over in her hands. "The Wolves have never troubled us before," she murmured, almost to herself. "I was unprepared."

"*Miranda*," I said sharply. "Where is she?"

Fallyne finally looked up at me. "They took her."

My chest tightened. The Wolves must have come to finish the job they'd started the night I met her.

"This is your fault," I said, my voice strangled.

Fallyne got to her feet, eyeing me warily. "Lena. You know that's not true."

"I should have been there," I spat back. "I could have protected her. If you hadn't called my father, I could have . . ." Wait—what had happened to him? In my panic over Miranda, I hadn't thought of him until now. "What about my father?" I asked.

"He left before the Wolves attacked," Fallyne said. "Whatever you said to him seems to have driven him away."

One shelf of books had gone undisturbed by the Wolves' attack. Now it infuriated me. I reached out and grabbed a book from the shelf and threw it down—then another, and another.

"A tantrum solves nothing," Fallyne said.

I paused and looked at her, allowing my fury to spill over my face. She was wrong. This inane act of destruction served one purpose, at least. It made me feel just the slightest bit better. And it made me want to destroy other things.

I stepped closer to Fallyne. "You had best hope that she is all right," I said coldly.

Then I turned and walked away—out of the room, down the hall, out of the house.

It was well into the afternoon now. I looked up and down the path. The Wolves were nowhere to be seen. They had probably taken Miranda back to the Gather to face Shale. She might not live the night—

Or she might cut a deal.

The thought crossed my mind like a traitor. She had sworn she was on my side, that she was done with double crosses. But that was before she had been taken by the Wolves. Who knew what might happen now? She could tell them about me in exchange for her freedom, and then what?

I should run.

My mind cartwheeled forward. I couldn't go back to the Mundane—I was never going back there. But on the other side of the Silence . . . there were better places than the Gather, I was certain. I could survive, now that I knew more about myself, and one day I might even enjoy my life—

But I'd already chosen people to trust. Alaric. And now Miranda.

What was my life worth, if I abandoned them?

Alaric would always be an unwilling servant.

And Miranda would probably be dead.

I exhaled, sorting through my options again. Alaric had never told me when he would return. Now I regretted mightily the fact that I had no way to contact him.

Except by using my curse, I realized. Then he could track me.

But if I used the curse, I would have to kill someone.

And in the meantime, Miranda was getting farther and farther away.

What should I do? How far should I go for the people I lov—

I wouldn't think it. I didn't even know what that meant, even after what I had shared with Alaric and Miranda.

I tried to refocus my racing thoughts. I assumed they'd take her to the palace. So all I had to do was sneak into the stronghold, find Miranda, and get out without being detected by Shale or Katen or, well . . . anyone. At least stealing a spelled box from a house of dragons and a water monster had prepared me for this moment.

Ah, who was I fooling? This was going to be a disaster.

CHAPTER TWENTY-ONE

I bathed before I left. If I was going to the palace, I could not look like an urchin. My cloak wouldn't help in that respect, but I didn't dare leave it behind.

I pilfered powders from another girl's room and covered the bruises and scratches of the last few days as best I could. Then I dressed, making certain that all of my things were in order. Boots, gloves, hat pulled down low over my forehead. Cloak neatly fastened, hood up. Other than that, I had only the contents of Miranda's and my bags: the net that Miranda had made, her wolf medallion, my knife, and the dragon scale.

And then there was the box with Alaric's wings.

If I'd told Alaric about the wings when I had the chance, maybe we would already be free. But then I wouldn't have met Miranda again. And maybe she would be dead.

You might very well meet the same fate, the voice cautioned. **This is a fool's errand.**

"Do you intend to stop me?" I asked. I had not forgotten the way the vines had overpowered me.

No. But this is not a safe road to travel.

"Nevertheless, I have made my choice."

Why? You owe them nothing. It didn't seem to be a malicious question. I got the sense that the Silence truly did not understand. That it was curious.

"Because they are mine. I choose them." I shrugged. "I can't explain better than that." But I paused. I was woefully unprepared for going into this alone. And if I had more power . . .

"Will you help me?"

I am at your call. Should you need aid, let three drops of your blood fall to the earth.

That was what the voice had offered back at the dragons' lair. "And what will that mean for me?" I asked.

Nothing that you can't change your mind about later.

"That's not a real answer."

This is not something that I can tell you. You must see for yourself.

That was not particularly comforting, but at least this time the voice wasn't trying to persuade me that its aid would come for free.

The Wolves had made no effort to cover their tracks. I picked up their trail outside the house, following them toward what I hoped would be the Gather.

The last time I had been alone in the Silence, I had felt it come to life around me. Now everything seemed sinister—a reflection of my own dark thoughts.

I arrived back at the Gather just as dusk spread across the sky. This was a different entrance from the one Alaric and I had used, but the black stones were identical, glowing faintly as people stepped upon them. I passed over them without incident and made my way into the city.

The Gather was vibrating with excitement over the revel—I overheard snippets of speculation about what marvels would be seen at the palace. Gone were the worried glances and unhappy faces. I supposed that even a tyrant could be looked upon with gratitude when he provided such an affair.

I kept to the side streets until it became impossible to do so any longer as the city's traffic funneled into a steady stream moving toward the palace. Together we approached the wall separating the high and low districts—the markets and tradespeople from the majority of blood mages.

The gate leading to the high district stood open. It was manned by bored-looking human guards who seemed to be there just for show—as Alaric said, the revel was the one occasion when all were welcome at the palace. I needn't have worried, as they waved everyone through without scrutiny.

In the high district, large estates rose on either side of a widening street, lit by hundreds of tiny lights that shimmered and danced as we passed. Groups of glamorously dressed people appeared on the streets, as did gleaming carriages drawn by horses. It was beautiful . . . but it lacked the vitality that had so enchanted me in the market. Everything here seemed cold.

The crowds from other gates across the city flowed together as we made our way toward the palace. A nervous shiver danced along my skin, and I touched the net in my pocket, reminding myself of Miranda. I had to do this for her.

Soon the palace itself came into view. First there was a large, ornate double gate protected by Wolves and human guards. Behind it rose towers with pointed black spires. I followed the crowd as it flattened into a line hugging the palace walls. I didn't speak to those around me, not trusting myself to say something unmemorable.

Just after night fell, there came an eager shout ahead of us. The gates were rising. Slowly the line began to move. My stomach jumped as someone jostled me from behind, and I set a hand on the wall to steady myself. I kept my gaze down as I approached the gate.

"Stop."

I froze as a Wolf put out an arm in front of me. I hadn't been so close to one of them since the cliff. This Wolf wore a cloak fastened with silver clasps engraved with the phases of the moon, but the clothing did nothing to hide the grotesque nature of her shape. She was unnaturally tall, standing like a human despite her Wolf form, fangs bared and ears twitching. She looked me up and down disdainfully. "You are not dressed in a manner befitting a revel," she said. "Out of line."

"But I thought everyone was welcome tonight," I blurted without thinking.

The Wolf growled. "Not wearing that, you're not. Show some respect." She looked past me. "Next!"

I gaped in disbelief as the line moved around me. I'd known I wasn't dressed *well*, but I'd done my best. And to be turned away *now*, when it mattered most?

I felt the urge to push my way through the gates, no matter the consequences. But that wouldn't save Miranda.

"Cheer up, girl. You have another chance tomorrow, after all."

I looked up. Leaning against a wall was a woman carrying a tray of gaudy baubles—brooches, bracelets, earrings that shimmered with starlight.

"What do you mean?" I asked.

She blinked at me owlishly. "Don't worry about missing petitioners' night. Everyone knows that revel night is better fun. So you still have a day to find something suitable to wear."

A man wearing an extraordinarily pink tunic picked a pocket fan off the tray, and the woman turned away to attend to him.

My thoughts raced. What was I going to do? I had no money. Perhaps I could figure out some way to do some work in exchange for a gown? But I didn't know anyone in the city. . . .

That wasn't true, I realized. I *did* know someone in the Gather.

This time Cyn was the one who opened the door. She stared at me suspiciously. "What do you want?"

"I need a gown," I said.

Her eyebrows shot up. "What for?"

I shook my head. "What I need from you is an outfit that will get me into the palace tomorrow night. That is all you need to know."

She glanced up and down the street. Finally she looked back at me. "And if I get you a gown—my debt will be paid?"

"Yes," I said, not caring that it wasn't my debt to forgive.

She thought this over, then nodded. "All right. You'd better come in."

Inside, the dog was sleeping by the fire, its paws twitching as it dreamed. My lips quirked up into a smile.

Cyn went upstairs and soon returned with a few gowns folded over her arm. She laid them out on the table and stepped back. "Well?"

These were certainly better than what I was wearing, but they were still everyday garb. They were not impressive enough to guarantee admittance to the palace. "No," I said, frowning. "I need something fit for the revel."

Cyn's eyes darted around the room, and I realized that she

believed Alaric was here. "The other dresses—the work is recognizable. They might know it came from this shop."

On another day, I might have been more sympathetic. Today, I had no time to spare.

I shrugged. "That is not my problem."

She pressed her lips together and nodded.

This time she ducked behind a curtain and brought out two gowns on dress forms.

"These are the only ones in the shop not spoken for," she said, as if daring me to object.

I did not. The first gown was a light periwinkle blue that shimmered as I trailed my hand over the fabric. High-waisted and short-sleeved, it looked like a gown fit for a princess. It was beautiful—but I could not risk exposing so much skin. Not when I would be so close to so many people.

I turned my attention to the other gown. This one was made of a green fabric so dark it was almost black. The neckline was cut low, but the sleeves were long. Tiny, glittering gems had been sewn into the skirt. As I looked at it, I had the disconcerting feeling that I was falling.

"That one," I said. "May I try it on?"

She nodded.

When I stepped out from behind the changing curtain, Cyn had uncovered a mirror set against the far wall.

It had been a long time since I had stared at myself in a mirror. I could see the weight of the last few days sitting on my shoulders. I looked . . . tired, I thought. And angry.

The sleeves were a little tight, and the bodice wasn't quite right, but overall it was a better fit than I had expected.

Cyn looked over my shoulder. "It's too long," she said.

Only by an inch or two, and that served to cover the fact that my boots were entirely inappropriate for the gown.

"It's fine," I said.

Cyn reached toward me to adjust something on the dress, and I jerked back, my heart skipping a beat.

At that moment, the door opened behind us. I whirled to see the same dark-haired woman who had been here last time. Her gaze darted from Cyn to me and back again.

"Cyn?" she said uncertainly.

"This will do," I said quickly. I picked up my skirt and went behind the curtain once more.

"What's going on?" asked the woman.

"Not here," Cyn said. She lowered her voice, and I couldn't make out what she said next.

I rushed to change back into my old clothes and stuffed the gown into my bag. When I emerged, they were gone.

I'd gotten what I'd come here for. I could have just walked out. But something made me pause and turn around. The door at the back of the room was closed. I crept toward it and put my ear to the wood, listening.

"This can't continue."

"He holds my life in his hands. Do you think I *want* this?"

"The raven isn't even here."

I couldn't hear Cyn's reply.

"Do you want your life back or not? She would reward this information," said the other woman.

"I can't go. The charm—"

"Then I will."

There was silence.

I pushed open the door and found Cyn standing alone in the kitchen. She jumped. "I thought you had left," she said. She glanced nervously about the room.

"Where did she go?" I said. There was another door at the back of the kitchen—she must have gone through it.

"Nowhere," said Cyn. But she was sweating.

"Tell me," I said, my pulse quickening.

Cyn's jaw tightened. "I'm not telling you anything. You have no power here—not without the raven."

I peeled off one of my gloves. "You have no idea what I can do to you. *Tell me.*"

Cyn glanced between me and the door. Then she yanked a drawer open and grabbed a knife. "You have gone too far, the both of you. I'm going to get my life back, and you cannot stop me."

The other woman must have gone to Katen. They must have decided to bargain with her—Alaric and me in exchange for a reprieve for Cyn. I couldn't let that happen.

Cyn lunged toward me, swiping at me with the knife. The blade caught in the fabric of my cloak, and I pinned her arm against my side with my own. As she tried to pull away, I grabbed her wrist with my bare hand.

At first she seemed almost confused—and then, as her skin began to melt and flame crackled up her arms, she began to scream. I backed away as her body fell, burning, to the floor.

This time I couldn't look away. This had been no accident. I'd killed her. Purposefully.

But this time I didn't feel nauseated. All I felt was the cold certainty that I'd done what I had to do, and that I would have done it again.

I wouldn't have had to in the first place if Cyn had just done what I'd asked. If she hadn't betrayed us, she wouldn't be dead. But she had. And she was.

The dog barked behind me, and I startled. *Katen.* She would sense that I'd used the curse. It wasn't safe to stay here. And what's more, there was a woman on her way to the palace right now, intent on giving me away.

I grabbed my bag and ran out into the night. The streets in the tailor's quarter were close to empty. I sprinted back out of the quarter and turned down the street that led to the high district.

Not too far ahead, I saw the other woman. She glanced back at me once—then she turned and started to run. I sprinted after her. If she reached the gate, she might alert the guards.

Even though it was late, this area of the city was busy—and rowdy. I dodged a group singing drunkenly and narrowly avoided what sounded like a lovers' quarrel between two young men.

Ahead of me the woman slowed, held up by the revelers.

There was no chance that I would be able to drag her away from the crowd. I would have to do it here, in the midst of everyone. I ducked my head and lengthened my stride, keeping my bare hand tucked inside my cloak.

She glanced over one shoulder again, and I darted to her other side, raising my hand and brushing my fingers against the back of her neck.

She jumped, as though she'd been stung. I kept walking past her, keeping my head down.

There was a horrified shriek behind me, and then a growing chorus of screams. I glanced back, my face arranged into an appropriate expression of confusion and fear as flames leapt into the air. Then I turned and arrowed straight for the gate.

Katen would know that I was in the city now, but she might not think to look for me in the high district. Neither would she suspect I was working with Alaric, or expect me to walk right into the palace.

I reached into my bag and ran my fingers over the gown. I would be hiding in plain sight. I just had to hope that Miranda was still alive when I got there tomorrow.

CHAPTER TWENTY-TWO

The problem I had not sufficiently thought through was that, unlike in the low district, the high district had only gated houses with nowhere for me to hide.

I held my head high and tried to walk as though I had a destination in mind, all the while sweeping my gaze over the street, scanning for alleyways or unlocked gates. Did I dare return to the low district? Someone would have recognized the woman, so it was likely Cyn's body had also been discovered by now.

Someone nearby was whistling a hauntingly familiar tune. I turned and saw Rin come around the corner. She wore a hat pulled low over her head and walked with an insouciant strut—the very picture of someone convinced of their own importance. What was she doing here?

Surprise crossed her face as she recognized me, but she didn't stop to speak. Instead she jerked her chin slightly. I fell into step with her, more than a little bewildered.

"Miranda's pet—what are you doing here?" she muttered.

So she wasn't going to let that go. "I might say the same to you," I replied.

She looked me up and down without breaking stride. "Well, you don't look much better than the last time I saw you."

Rin did look better. The last time I'd seen her, one arm had been in a cast. Now the cast was gone and she was dressed just as well as any of the blood mages I'd seen tonight. Which, since she was clearly trusted in Haven, meant that she was dressing the part for a reason.

"What's your game?" I said. "You can't be here just to enjoy a party."

Her lips quirked in a wry smile. "I don't trust anyone associated with Miranda. I have to go."

She turned and began to walk away, whistling once more. And suddenly it hit me—I knew where I'd heard that tune before. *Melor.*

"Wait!" I said, running to catch up with her. "What is that song you're whistling? I've heard it before."

Rin's eyes narrowed. "What do you mean?"

"*Down below the briars and the vines,*" I sang softly. "Isn't that it? What does it mean?"

She drew in a surprised breath. "You really don't know anything, do you?"

I could tell she was about to brush me off again. I couldn't let that happen.

"Look," I said. "I heard that song from a man who had been driven out of his mind by the Silence. He was killed in the Mundane. I don't know anything else about it. But it must mean something that you're singing it now."

Rin looked away from me, and then seemed to come a decision. "Come with me," she said. "And don't ask questions."

I had no better ideas or options. "All right."

We made our way farther into the depths of the high district, passing increasingly ostentatious estates, until suddenly Rin turned down a dark side alley. She withdrew a pin from her pocket and pricked the end of one finger, producing a drop of blood. Then she pursed her lips and blew. The droplet floated up into the air and spun, widening into a thin circular film. Through it I could see the inside of a room and the impression of several figures within.

"It's me," Rin said. "Let us in."

A door opened in the darkness ahead of us. Feeling increasingly apprehensive, I followed Rin through.

A tall man wearing a black mask over his face stood in the hall. He stepped aside as we walked past and closed the door behind us.

"What is this?" I asked.

Rin looked over her shoulder. "You'll see."

A door at the end of the hallway opened into what appeared to be a large receiving room, though someone had clearly been using it to store furniture. We were inside one of the high district estates, I realized.

Rin pulled a small bag out from underneath her coat. The waxed paper crinkled as she set it down on a large table at the center of the room.

At the sound, two small heads popped out from underneath a couch. The lid of a trunk flew up, and a third child looked out. When they saw Rin, they sprang out of hiding—a girl with brown hair tied into two braids and two boys who looked to be wearing more dirt than clothing. "Is that for us?" asked one of the boys.

Rin raised her eyebrow. "What is the first rule of being a blood mage?"

"To never cross the lines of our own power," the girl said quickly. A dark mark flickered faintly over her left cheek, then disappeared. I felt suddenly sick.

"Very well," Rin said. "Go see what it is."

The trio fell upon the bag, which turned out to contain several caramel candies. They were quickly devoured, sticking the children's teeth together as they giggled.

My heart twinged in my chest as I watched them. "You're helping them," I murmured to Rin. "Why didn't you just say that?"

Rin beckoned me to follow her into the next room.

"Why are they here?" I asked. "Who do they serve?" I was sure their master would not be happy to find them missing.

"The less you know, the better," Rin said, standing by the window and looking out onto the street.

"It's admirable," I said softly.

Rin shrugged. "We all make choices to bring good or ill into the world. Every day, each of us." She looked sternly at me. "Which brings me to you. What are you doing in the high district tonight?"

I could have lied, but I found I didn't want to. I believed Rin. I wanted to make an ally of her. "Miranda was captured by the Wolves. I intend to rescue her tomorrow night at the revel."

"Ah," she said. After a moment, she nodded. "And you were roaming about the high district because . . ."

Because I'd just killed two women in the low district. But I didn't trust Rin enough yet to admit it. "Poor planning," I said. "I didn't have a place to stay out of sight until the revel."

"I see." Rin pondered this for a moment. "Your poor planning didn't have anything to do with the disruption back at the gate, did it?"

I thought about the body I had left burning in the street. For the first time, the weight of what I'd just done settled on me. I looked away, but Rin stayed quiet. Expectant.

"Do you believe . . ." I swallowed. "Do you believe it's unforgiveable to do something wrong if you have no other choice?"

"There's always a choice," Rin said immediately. "But that doesn't mean there's always a good one. There is no shame in survival, no matter what it takes." Her voice turned gruff. "Would you hurt an innocent child?"

"Of course not!"

"Then you're a sight better than most of the ghouls who live in these houses. And trust me, *they* do not trouble themselves with questions of right and wrong." She straightened. "You can stay here today. It's an abandoned estate, and we work to keep it that way. You shouldn't be bothered."

"Really?" I couldn't hide my surprise at her generosity.

A sudden, bright smile crossed her face. "Well, as long as you stay out of those rooms back there." She straightened her coat and started toward the door.

"Wait," I said. "I have one more question."

"What?"

"The song. What is it? You never told me."

"It's an old song about the Silence, and the bonds that people used to have with it. Supposedly." Rin shrugged. "The words are nonsense, mostly. But it's . . . a reminder. That things were different once, and might be again someday."

"Would you ever try to wake the sleeping princess from the legend yourself?" I asked.

Rin laughed. "Those are fairy stories," she said. "Anyone who thinks it's possible has gone mage-drunk."

"I think it's true," I said softly. "I don't know if it's possible to wake her, but I think . . . I think that she would change things, if she woke."

"Really?" Rin raised an eyebrow at me. Then she dug into her pocket and pulled out a pebble. She set it down on the small table standing between us. "Then I'll tell you this. If you ever *do* get to the sleeping princess, feed this stone a drop of your blood. And I'll consider coming to see if you're telling the truth."

"Thank you." I reached out and pocketed the pebble. It was more than I had expected, truthfully. I didn't know that I would call on her—but knowing that there was someone else in the Gather who was trying to do good was heartening, if only just a little.

I found an empty bedchamber and spent most of the next day trying—without much success—to sleep. The house was ponderously quiet around me. I wondered what had happened to the previous holders of the estate. Punished by Shale, perhaps. I found that I didn't much care, if those people were the same sort who would use children to carry magic for them.

I changed into my gown as the sun set and used a cracked mirror while I brushed my hair. The powders I'd used yesterday had smudged and faded, but there was no helping it. This was the best I could do. I straightened the gown and secured the contents of my cloak pockets.

Rin was gone when I made my way back to the receiving room, as were the children. The only one left was the man in the mask, who nodded to me but did not speak as he opened the door to usher me back into the night.

This time the Wolf at the palace gate waved me through without a second glance. I followed the person in front of me underneath the suspended teeth of the gate and into the courtyard. There was no turning back now.

Sharp white stones crunched under my boots. I crossed my arms over my chest, trying to keep my nerves in check. I was surprised to find that not a single person broke from the line, which stretched straight as an arrow from the outer gates to the tall silver doors of the palace.

The others in line milled around anxiously, though I soon noticed a distinct divide between my companions. Some looked how I felt—ill at ease in their finery, their nerves and excitement showing on their faces. But there were others whose costumes were more elaborate than anything I could have dreamt up, even after last night. I assumed they were all blood mages, since they were surrounded by servants, many of whom had the black ink of the blood plague darting and dipping across their faces. Anger burned within me at the sight. To their mages they were simply disposable vessels, like the children I had met yesterday. Like me.

I could not look at the mages. I was afraid that if I did, my rage would shine through my eyes. That I would fly across the courtyard, hands raised to sap them of life.

But I couldn't do that. I was here on a mission—to find Miranda. I had to keep that in the front of my mind, to close my eyes and my heart to the injustice around me. There was no alternative, if I hoped to make it through the night.

As I approached the front of the line, I saw a Wolf in a silver-clasped cloak guarding the main palace door. Beside the Wolf was a tall spindle mounted on a large stone obelisk. Blood dripped down the spindle onto the stone as each person ahead of me walked up and pricked their fingers upon it.

My heart started to pound. This must be the price of entry. What would happen when my blood spilled onto that stone? In the forest a tree had sprung up when my blood touched the earth. And the Silence had indicated that *something* would happen if I did it again. . . .

I could leave the line, but that would only draw unwanted attention. I was trapped. The only thing I could do was hope nothing unusual happened when it was my turn.

The Wolf yawned, baring their fangs as the person in front of me passed over the threshold of the palace door. I stepped forward and stripped the glove from my right hand. Then I pressed my finger down upon the spindle.

I hissed in pain, but held myself in place until I saw a drop of blood drip down the shaft of the spindle. Then I drew my hand back and pushed forward into the court, resisting the urge to look back.

To my surprise and relief, there were no shouts that anything was amiss. And no trees sprouted up from the earth. I took a deep breath and pulled my glove back on, then continued down the long hall and into the heart of the Gather at last.

I'd read books that described kings and queens in palaces of opulence. But this went far beyond anything I'd ever imagined.

Gauzy fabric hung down from the high ceiling, creating the illusion that I walked below draping forest canopies. Music stirred the air, a dark melody that caught at heels and muddled thoughts. The walls were black jade, but the floor was opalescent and pale, the color of oyster shells.

Everywhere I looked there were people dressed for carousing, their ornaments glittering silver and gold. Their flowing garments seemed designed to catch the eye in rich saffron, deep purples, a blue as dark as midnight, as they whirled about the room. Raucous laughter rose from a group gathered near a fountain, a brown-haired girl beaming at its center. I took off my cloak, holding it over my arm.

The single source of light in the hall was a moonlike glow over the center of the floor. Standing there was a stone column, and upon that, a cage large enough for a human. Two, in fact.

I gasped, putting my hand to my mouth. There was blood running down the arms of the two people in the cage, but no one seemed to pay them any attention. Instruments stood before them, playing without being touched. Their faces were masks of pain. The sight made my skin crawl, but I worked hard to keep my expression neutral. They were clearly mages, able to use magic to play their instruments rather than using their hands. But surely this must be some kind of punishment? Who would willingly inflict this upon themselves?

A murmur went through the crowd, and I looked past the cage to see Alaric enter the ballroom, moving so smoothly he almost glided. Our eyes met across the room, and his face blanched in dismay—then his expression went blank, and he looked straight past me. There was an undisputable hush as he moved, pausing for greetings when flagged down. These people knew him, and they clearly feared him.

This hush, however, was nothing compared to the way the chatter ceased when the long doors opened next. Shale stood in the doorway, framed by a light as bright as several small suns. The effect was blinding in the darkened hall. When my eyes could focus again, I saw that he wore a wine-red shirt with long, flowing sleeves and a long knife buckled around sleek black trousers. He surveyed the room archly, and I had the feeling he noted every single person in attendance.

"This is a wonderful night," he said, projecting his voice. "Wouldn't you agree?"

The crowd around me responded with enthusiastic cries and applause, and I quickly joined them. This was clearly the only acceptable response.

Shale raised his hand, and there was immediate silence.

"We are a city made whole by blood, and every year we honor that by giving of ourselves to restore the bloodstones of the Gather. But this year, the hundredth anniversary of the founding of the Gather, it seemed fitting that our revels also honor that heritage." He paused to smile, his teeth gleaming white.

A shiver ran down my spine. Something bad was about to happen.

Shale snapped his fingers. Another set of doors to my left banged open, and three Wolves entered, escorting three people in chains. The crowd retreated, leaving more than enough space for me to see that the prisoners were two men and one woman . . . and that I recognized two of them. The woman was Miranda, her hair matted and standing up in tufts, and her face bruised and pale. . . .

And one of the men was my father.

My heart leapt up to my throat, then plummeted into my stomach. Miranda was alive! But how had my father gotten tangled up in this? Fallyne had said he'd left. My heart raced as I tried to reconstruct my plan. Even if I ran forward now, I didn't see how I could tear down all of the Wolves at once—or Shale.

I tore my eyes away from the unfolding scene and scanned the room for Alaric. He was no longer alone. Katen stood at his side, wearing a brown gown so dark it almost faded into the background. She might have disappeared entirely if not for her red-gold hair, which fell down her back in long, loose curls. As I watched, she put one hand to her forehead and the other on Alaric's arm. He turned toward her, murmuring in her ear. My throat tightened.

Seeing Katen through a magical conjuring or across a crowded street was different from seeing her here, so close—it was a blow that shocked the breath from my body. This was the woman who had altered the trajectory of my life, ripped through the very fabric of my being and remade it. And now I was close enough to finally tear myself free.

Shale's voice cut through the air again. "Tonight these traitors to the Gather will beg for their lives. *If* they are worthy, I may be merciful, for who among us has never practiced the fine art of deception?" His eyes flashed up. "Who among us has never acted with treachery in their hearts?"

He had to have a target for his words. These were not aimless rantings. I looked back at Katen, who stood pillar straight and still.

Shale raised his hand toward his lips. By the time the two met, there was a goblet in his hand. I gasped as a goblet appeared in mine, so surprised that I nearly dropped it. Others in the hall were doing the same with varying degrees of success—some had clearly experienced this magic before.

"A toast!" Shale called. "To the Gather!"

He took a long drink from his goblet. I hesitated before raising my own, but there seemed no way to avoid it. I sipped from my goblet, then spat it back out, wishing I could wash out my mouth. The liquid tasted chalky and bitter and dank all at once. I refused to think about what it might contain and settled for holding the goblet at my side.

Whatever it was, the beverage looked disturbingly like blood on Shale's lips when he finally raised his head from his own goblet. He snapped his fingers, and the chains yanked forward of their own accord, dragging the prisoners down to the floor.

Shale looked around the room, his lips spread in an anticipatory grin. "Let's begin."

CHAPTER TWENTY-THREE

S tand up," Shale commanded.

The man I did not recognize stood, his shoulders shaking. Shale proceeded to accuse him of cultivating plants from the Silence in the windowsill of his house, placing the entire Gather at risk. The man begged for mercy as Shale yawned in boredom.

At last, Shale raised his hand in the air. The man fell instantly silent. "My deepest regrets," Shale said, his voice echoing through the hall. "You have been found wanting."

He unsheathed the knife from his belt and grabbed the man's hair with one hand, wrenching back his head. Then he drew the knife across the man's throat with the other.

I screamed. Luckily, I was not the only one.

Shale looked up, his eyes narrowing. We were quiet once more. *Do not move*, I told myself, though I was woozy with the effort it took not to run. *You must not move.*

Blood spurted from the man's neck, and Shale cupped it in his hands, letting the body fall. Closing his eyes, Shale spread his fingers wide. Blood rose into the air like raindrops, then spun out across the hall. The floor shook beneath my feet—and then collapsed inward at the center of the hall, taking the pillar with the musicians' cage down with it. With another flick of Shale's fingers, the newly created pit filled with water.

As I watched, the ripples faded, the water stilled. Did he mean to drown them? I held my breath, waiting. Suddenly the cage reappeared, suspended in the air above the pit. The musicians had abandoned their instruments, clinging to each other instead. Now they collapsed to the floor of the cage, gasping for air. Aside from the water gurgling, there was utter silence in the room.

"Well?" Shale said.

We applauded. I felt sick for doing so.

Shale walked to the water's edge and knelt, letting the water wash over his hands. When he stood, his hands were clean, though his shirt was blood spattered beyond redemption. I wondered whether he intended to keep it that way.

"Now," he said. "A dance."

The man's body lay in a pool of his own blood. Father and Miranda were shoved down so that they knelt beside it, waiting. The floor had just fallen out of the hall, and Shale was calling for a dance? I shuddered. The death was a spectacle, and I had no doubt he meant to kill the others in just as spectacular a fashion. And I wasn't sure that I could save them.

Shale snapped his fingers. It took me a moment to realize that he was snapping at the musicians, who jerked themselves to attention. They sprang upright in their soaked clothes, cutting themselves anew to call enough power to play their instruments. Tears ran down their cheeks, but Shale didn't seem to notice. Instead he turned to the rest of the audience, spreading his arms in welcome. "Is this not a revel? Join me!" he cried.

The music resolved into a frenetic melody, and the hall burst into motion, everyone rushing not to be the last standing still. Goblets fell, cracking as they hit the floor. Whatever had been in them must have been mage-made—my head swam, and I had to fight to keep myself steady as I joined the fray. There were no rules, no steps. There was only the constant knowledge that however I moved, I must not stop. I took the hand of a short man in a gold tunic and turned with him twice before moving on to a young woman in a long shimmering dress. I spun with her long enough to read the fear in her eyes before dancing away on my own, trying to forget her too-tight grip and shaking hands.

With each turn I tried to make progress toward Miranda and my father—if I could only get to them, perhaps we could take advantage of the dancing to make our escape. I marked Shale's position on the floor, trying to stay far from him. Alaric and Katen as well, though their movements together seemed slow and stately compared to the frenzy of the rest of the crowd.

Until suddenly Shale snapped his fingers again, and the music cut out. "Enough!"

The world stopped. I gasped, stumbling to a halt.

"It is time for our next piece of entertainment. Katen?"

Katen stepped out of the crowd. "Yes, Father?"

"Bring forth your raven. I wish to show off his talents."

Katen chose her words with care. "Alaric is not a blood mage—I fear his display will be lacking compared to yours."

Shale waved a hand dismissively. "I will decide who is lacking."

Katen bowed her head. "Yes, Father. I only meant to help."

"Help?" Shale snorted. "Lend me the use of your raven—but you will not do that, will you? You *need* your pet. Without him you are weak."

"As you say," Katen said. "You know my small tricks are nothing compared to the power you wield."

Shale snorted. "Your raven can execute the next prisoner, and *you* will entertain our guests with it, my darling daughter. Unless there is some reason you hesitate to do my bidding."

Katen pressed her lips together. "Very well," she said. She lifted a hand. A shadow played over her fingers like a wisp of smoke and was gone.

She brought her hand down. Alaric exploded out of a cloud of night just behind Miranda. I held my breath—Alaric grabbed the back of her shirt, pulling her upright—

Miranda swore and spat blood on the ground—had she bitten her tongue for it? Where the blood hit the floor, it burst into flame.

Shale snarled, but it was too late. The fire spread across the floor as if it had been thrown, chasing people away from the center of the room. I searched through the smoky air—where was Miranda? But instead of Miranda's eyes, I met Alaric's.

Go, he seemed to be saying.

My eyes began to water but I refused to look away. I couldn't leave without them, not when I was so close.

Around me were the shouts of the revelers, each as desperate to escape the hall as they had been eager to enter only an hour earlier. Beside me, one mage reached for a servant, slicing a blade across his arm. The servant flinched, but water rained down from the ceiling, cutting a shallow window in the roiling smoke. And through it I caught a glimpse of the prisoners being hustled from the hall by the Wolves.

I followed, darting across the clear patches on the floor.

There was a scream behind me. I didn't look back but kept my eyes fixed firmly ahead. I put my fingers on the wolf medallion and hoped that its power still worked as I pulled open the door through which Miranda and my father had disappeared and walked quickly through.

The hallway I found myself in was narrow, short, and quiet. So quiet that even my heartbeat was loud in my ears.

Shadows moved at the end of the hallway. I donned my cloak and ran as quietly as I could to catch up. I turned the corner to see the Wolves start down a staircase, Miranda and my father chained between them.

After a moment of hesitation, I went after them, following at a safe distance as we descended into the depths below the palace. The black stone walls seemed to swallow the torchlight, leaving me inching forward as I listened for movement in the darkness ahead. Finally I reached the bottom and found myself at the entrance to a dungeon. The Wolves stood at the far end. I darted through the nearest open door as they pushed Father and Miranda into a cell without removing their chains.

The cell door clanged shut. I pressed myself back against the wall as the Wolves passed by and went back up the stairs. After their footsteps had faded, I ran for the cell.

"Miranda!" I whispered. "Father!"

Miranda looked up and blinked slowly, as though she couldn't quite believe what she was seeing. "Lena?"

"Lena, what are you *doing* here?" my father said hoarsely.

"What are *you* doing here?" I said. "I thought you left!"

"The Wolves. They picked me up on the path outside Fallyne's house. Bad luck on my part. I think they did it for the fun of it," he said grimly.

That must have been just after our argument—after I'd told him . . . I was ashamed of the way I'd spoken to him now.

"Lena . . . ," he started.

No. If he speaks, I might crumble. "There's no time. Where do the guards keep the keys?"

Father shook his head. "They're spelled shut. Lena—you need to get out of here now."

"What about magic? Can we break the locks that way?"

Miranda's shoulders slumped. "This dungeon is built to hold far more powerful blood mages than me."

I knelt down and put my hand through the bars of the cell. Miranda gripped it tightly. "I can't believe you came for me. But you have to go."

"No," I said, desperation creeping into my voice. I couldn't leave them. Not after what had happened to that man out there.

"Lena, you must!" Miranda insisted.

"I'm not leaving without you," I said fiercely.

"Listen to the girl, Lena," Father barked.

"Miranda," said a voice behind me. "You've made new friends, I see."

"Callie," Miranda said, shocked. She let go of my hand and pushed herself to her feet. I stood and turned around.

The girl I'd seen laughing at the revel—Miranda's best friend—was almost skeletally thin and of medium height. Her hair was short and brown, and her eyes were dark. In the court of the Gather she had shimmered, drawing the eye. Now, black marks swirled over her cheeks as she descended the last stairs into the dungeon, her steps slow and careful.

"Have you recruited more people to your fool's mission?" Callie said. "For your own sake, you must let this go. You are too late."

"It's not too late," Miranda said. "I can help you if you'd just *let me.*"

"You can't," Callie said, her eyes feverishly bright.

Miranda slumped back. "You don't need to die for them," she said. She sounded as though she was reciting lines from a familiar argument. "The mages care nothing for you."

Callie shook her head. "That's something you never understood. You were always special, always. And I was nothing—until I came here."

"You were never nothing," Miranda said, her voice strained with emotion.

Callie let out a bone-rattling cough. "I'm sorry that it's come to this," she said, looking between us. And then she opened her mouth and screamed.

"Lena, go!" my father cried.

"Run!" Miranda said, tears in her eyes as she looked past me at Callie.

It was too late to avoid notice now. I pushed past Callie and tore up the stairs, my heart racing.

I burst into the hallway, breathing hard. Running footsteps approached from the end of the hall on my right. I turned left and ran. I rounded one corner, then another—and stopped short at the sight of torchlight bobbing against the wall from around the next turn.

I dove through the nearest open door, but I had no way to lock it. I shut the door and ran to hide behind a desk that stood in the corner.

Once the footsteps had faded, I opened my eyes. What was I going to do? The dungeon was probably swarming with guards, and what was worse, Callie would be able to describe me to them. Perhaps I should have used the curse—but whatever Miranda had said about Callie, I couldn't have done that to her.

I had to move. There would be a search, and they would reach this room soon enough. I stood up and started toward the door, but before I reached it, the doorknob turned. There was no time to hide as the door swung open and Katen stepped into the room. I froze.

"What are you doing in here?" she said sharply. She looked me up and down in confusion—and then in surprised recognition.

"You're the child," she said, almost to herself.

Perhaps I could bluff my way out. "I don't know what you're talking about," I said. "I need to get back to my—"

Katen reached out and caught my wrist with her hand. The touch seared painfully through my skin, and I yanked away from her, stumbling back. What had she done to me? I glanced down and saw that the skin around my wrist had blistered.

"You're not going anywhere," she said.

I gritted my teeth and drew my knife.

She looked at it and laughed. "And what do you think you're going to do with that?"

I looked her straight in the eye. "I'm going to kill you," I said.

To my consternation, Katen smiled. A genuine, sympathetic smile. "I completely understand why you would try."

She leaned back against the door, cutting off my escape route. "Little Lena," she mused. "Though you're not so little anymore. I suppose I should have expected that. But I must say, I didn't expect you to come find *me*."

I shrugged. "I got tired of running."

"Perhaps. But I'm surprised that your father would ever allow you out of his sight long enough for you to enter the Silence."

As angry as I was with Father, I couldn't stand the thought that this woman had brought such pain to his life—or my mother's. "Don't talk about him," I said. "This is between me and you. No one else."

"Oh, child," Katen said. Now she sounded unexpectedly tired. "Don't you know by now? No one acts alone."

She raised her hand, and I rushed forward, knife raised—but she dodged me, and suddenly Alaric was standing in the room with us.

Katen addressed him as she nodded to me. "Tie her up. And afterward, we're going to have a talk about why it is that you couldn't find this girl yesterday, and yet here she is, serving herself up on a platter to me."

"Stay away from me," I warned, raising the knife again.

Alaric turned to me, his expression anguished—but that didn't stop him from plucking the knife from my grasp and pocketing it. His hands around my wrists were like steel clasps. He produced rope seemingly out of thin air and bound my wrists together behind my back. Then he pushed me down into a chair and proceeded to tie my legs as well. As he began to rise, I bent forward and whispered into his ear. "Your wings are in my pocket!"

His eyes widened in understanding—but he did not reach for them.

No.

Alaric stood and turned to Katen. "Anything else, mistress?"

"We'll bleed her now. The timing is unfortunate, but I don't see any way around it. I won't risk her escaping again."

I thrashed against the restraints, unable to conceal my growing panic. *Help!* I called. I would do anything the Silence wanted, if only it would save me now.

The voice ghosted through my mind, fainter than I had ever heard it. **Your blood must fall—**

But I'd lost my knife. There was no chance of that now, and I had no one to blame but myself. If only I had stayed with Fallyne—or better yet, given Alaric his wings when I'd had the chance. Instead I was going to die.

CHAPTER TWENTY-FOUR

istress, I suggest we wait until the palace is asleep,"
Alaric said.

A small flicker of hope sparked inside me as I
watched Katen consider his proposal.

After an agonizing few seconds, Katen nodded. "You're right.
Less chance of Shale sensing the transfer."

I let out my breath, my heart beginning to slow once more.
Across from me, Katen slumped into a chair and sighed. "Well," she
said. "Alaric's bought you a few hours yet."

Anger burned through me. I could think of nothing that would
save me now—and if I was to die soon, I wanted to tell this woman
just what I thought of her. "You've ruined my entire life."

She leaned forward, resting her elbows on her knees as she
looked at me. "Is that what your parents told you? That I tricked
them, that I ruined their lives and yours?"

"You know they had no choice. My mother was dying!"

She snorted in disdain. "Eighteen years ago I was sent to hunt
your mother down and kill her. I found your parents in the Mundane. But instead of facing their fate with honor, they begged me
for lenience. *Anything,* they said. They would do anything to be
spared. So I asked—*anything?* Even give up a child?"

Her eyes flashed to mine. "You should have been there to see how quickly they accepted. The tears of joy they shed. So you see—*I* am not the reason you're in this position today. Your parents were more than happy to participate."

That couldn't be true. "You're lying," I said faintly.

"Why would I lie to you about *that?*" Katen waved her hand dismissively. "It matters little to me one way or the other. Alaric was there, he can tell you."

Alaric? I met his anguished gaze. "Your mother was not ill," he said reluctantly. "It happened as my mistress says."

I suddenly felt as though I couldn't breathe.

"I suppose it *was* a life-and-death situation," Katen continued. "But the sort of life-and-death situation where I was going to kill *her*. And she chose you instead."

She raised an eyebrow at me, utterly remorseless.

They made the bargain to save your mother's life, I remembered numbly. And the worst part of it was—it was still *true*. "But—but why?"

"Humans have an incredible capacity for selfishness, child. Though I suppose they thought they might buy themselves time to weasel out of the bargain." She smiled, amused, perhaps, that two mere humans had thought they could thwart her.

"No," I said. "Why would you be sent to kill my mother in the first place?"

Something—surprise?—flickered behind Katen's eyes. "Your mother committed treason against my father. Did your parents tell you *nothing?*"

"They told me you were a monster," I said. "That's certainly true."

"You were at the revel, weren't you?" She smiled grimly at the revulsion that must have shown on my face. "Shale has been my father for over one hundred years. He is vain, jealous, paranoid—he always has been. I was afraid that he would kill me. So I did what I had to do, to survive. That doesn't make me a monster."

"I was an innocent child," I spat. "You don't know what your curse has cost me."

"You don't think it cost *me* anything?" Katen barked, sitting up straighter—adopting the demeanor of a princess of the Gather once more. "Imagine, if you will, having one talent. One thing that was an inextricable part of you. And then imagine having to cut it out of your body, one thread at a time. I've forced myself to release it in dribs and drabs for the last eighteen years, keeping myself weak."

She shuddered, remembering. "And all because my father would have me killed, if he ever discovered how much more powerful I am than him."

I watched Katen's shoulders sag as if under an invisible weight. Despite myself, I was tempted to empathize with her. After all, I too was well versed in being trapped by fathers.

"If you were truly so powerful, you could have broken from your father and left the Gather," I said.

"No, I couldn't," Katen said. "My father may have founded this city, but it is my birthright. I will not allow anyone to take that away from me."

She stood up. "I tire of this. Alaric—stay here and keep watch. On your life, do not allow her to escape."

Katen swept from the room, leaving Alaric and me alone at last.

He whirled on me immediately, clearly furious. "What are you *doing* here? Why didn't you wait for me?"

"Wolves abducted Miranda from Fallyne's house," I said. "She would have died!"

"Better her than you," he shot back.

I let that go. "Never mind, we're wasting time. Check my cloak pocket—I have your wings."

Alaric bowed his head. When he looked at me again, his expression was mutinous. "I *can't*," he said.

"What do you mean?"

"I mean that I cannot touch the box," he said. "Even if I could, the only way to open the box is with Katen's blood. And I cannot lift a finger against her."

He sprawled into a chair and buried his head in his hands. "And all of this I would have told you, *if you had told me you had it.*" He looked up at me. "You lied to me. Why?"

"Perhaps for the same reason you withheld this from *me*," I snapped. "I wasn't certain I could trust you. Clearly, you decided you couldn't trust me, either. Why else wouldn't you tell me the truth about my own mother?"

A muscle twitched in his cheek. "You had no right," he said softly. Dangerously.

"You are bound to Katen! You cannot claim there was no reason to have doubts about you."

"I claim nothing but what is mine," Alaric growled.

"Then it's too bad you didn't trust me enough to follow through."

He closed his eyes. "You're right," he said. "I am not blameless.

And I apologize . . . for not trusting you. And for laying the blame entirely at your feet."

My anger melted away, and my shoulders slumped. "I'm sorry too," I said softly. "But what do we do now?"

"Nothing," he said after a while. "Katen has ordered me not to allow you to escape. So this is the end."

The end. I'd entered the Silence to take my life into my own hands. Instead I'd only discovered that the cage I'd been born into stretched so much further than I'd imagined. I'd never had a chance.

I bowed my head and waited for the inevitable.

The door opened, and Katen entered, looking tired but resolute.

"I'm glad to see you haven't become entirely incompetent," she said to Alaric. "Give me the knife."

This was it. My entire life punctuated by this one moment, and I'd had only days to live on my own terms. I would never break the curse. Never visit the dragons and tell them my story. Never see Miranda again. My heart started to race as Katen bound up her hair. Alaric handed her a knife. She approached me, angling the blade down toward my arm. I watched as the knife met my cloak—but the fabric did not yield.

Katen frowned and grabbed the fabric, rubbing it between her fingers. "Magic," she muttered. "I should have known."

She nodded at Alaric. "Take off her cloak."

Alaric's hand came down on my shoulder, squeezing minutely. I looked past him to Katen, watching us intently, the shut door, the desk I'd hid behind, a delicate green glass goblet on the far end . . . *glass.*

Alaric knelt, freeing my legs. Then he pulled me out of the chair and cut the ropes binding my hands. I pushed him away, sending him stumbling back as I sprang across the room. I picked up the goblet and smashed it against the desk, then seized a glass shard and drew it across my palm, hissing in pain. *Help! Please!*

"Stop her!" Katen cried, but it was too late. My blood dripped onto the floor, running into the clay seams between the stones. . . .

Enormous vines tore up around me, lashing out at Alaric and Katen.

For a moment I was too flabbergasted to move.

Run! the voice shouted. My legs obeyed.

I sprinted out the door and down the hall. The walls seemed to be closing in around me as I fled, my sense of direction dissolved by panic. I was lost in the heart of the Gather, and there was a monster at my heels.

Suddenly a thick fog rolled through the hall, obscuring my vision. I stumbled to a halt.

"Who is running in my palace?" a soft voice crooned. My chest seized in terror as Shale emerged from the fog, a streak of blood smeared across his cheek.

"Who are you, pet?" he said.

I raised my hands carefully. I was close enough that perhaps I could catch him off guard.

"No one," I replied, my voice shaking.

"No one who has been badly frightened by *someone*," he said, his gaze falling to my bloodied hand. He was no fool—I could almost see the gears turning in his head. "You know, a surprising amount of blood magic passed through the gates tonight. But I wasn't able to put a face to the power . . . until now." His eyes narrowed. "Who is your master?"

Now. I darted forward, reaching for him. He sidestepped me with ease, moving faster than I thought a human could. Something hit me hard in the back, and I fell, sprawling across the floor. I cried out in pain as my injured hand hit the stone.

More vines burst forth—but Shale was better prepared than either Alaric or Katen. A funnel of flame shot out from his hands, burning the vines until they turned black and shriveled on the floor at my feet.

"Did you think I would not sense the Hand of Mora on you?" Shale said. "I would have thought my enemies would choose a more competent assassin."

Another blow from an invisible force hit my stomach and forced the breath from my lungs, leaving me gasping. I turned onto my side to see Shale pull a blade from the very air and level it at me. I would be dead in moments, unless—

"Wait!" I cried. "I have information—I can tell you—"

He paused. "Yes?"

I swallowed. "I am not your enemy," I said. "But someone in this palace is. If you grant my friends and me safe passage out of the Gather, I will tell you who placed the Hand of Mora upon me. I will give you their name."

Shale smiled. "I think you had better tell me *now*, and I'll decide if the information merits your freedom."

He raised the sword, preparing to strike. "Katen!" I gasped. "Your daughter, she did this to me. She is working against you."

Shale's amusement vanished, leaving behind a face like stone.

"Please," I said. "I'm not lying, I swear—"

The fog began to dissipate, and I could see the hallway once more. And there, coming around the corner behind Shale, was Katen.

"What is going on here?" she said, her face the perfect picture of concern.

Shale glanced at her, keeping the blade steady on me. "I've just had a very interesting conversation," he said. "This urchin"—he kicked my leg, and I winced—"claims that *you*, daughter, are plotting against me."

The blood drained from Katen's face. "That is not true. Please, Father, believe me."

"Silence!" he said. Katen was still, but when Shale turned to look down at me, her expression turned murderous. "It is an interesting story you tell," he said to me. "But there are inconsistencies."

Inconsistencies? But every word I'd said was true.

"My daughter lost the majority of her magic many years ago, but it was a formidable amount of power. If you were carrying *that* much magic, you would surely be dead from blood plague by now. But you are not."

My heart sank. Whether or not he believed Katen to be plotting against him, it was clear that he did not believe *me*.

"*However*," Shale continued. "You must be valuable to someone, since they have gone to the trouble of placing the Hand of Mora on you."

"Clearly she has been put up to it by a true enemy," Katen said quickly. "Whoever it is must be hoping to drive a wedge between us by telling the girl to repeat such a ridiculous lie."

"Perhaps," Shale replied. "And yet she is clearly in distress. And you are the first person to find us here."

Katen reached out her hand, palm up. "Take my hand and feel the truth for yourself. I would never lie to you. I would never turn on you."

Shale ignored her hand. Instead he withdrew the sword from my neck.

"What is your name, girl?"

I didn't know the scope of Shale's powers. What if he could tell a lie if it fell from my lips? "Lena," I said softly.

"You remind me of someone . . . ," he said, his eyes narrowing. I worried for a moment he might know of my parents. But then he shrugged. "Who are the friends for which you seek safe passage?"

"Miranda," I said quickly. "And a man named Joren. They were the two other prisoners at the revel tonight."

Katen stiffened. Had she recognized my father's name?

Shale raised his eyebrows. "Interesting," he said. "I don't remember Miranda having such . . . *dangerous* friends."

"She is a new acquaintance," I said hotly.

"Is she? Well then, I make you the same offer I made to her. You can win your safe passage . . . if you go to the castle of briars and kill the princess sleeping within."

Miranda had told me this quest was tantamount to a death sentence. Was Shale just trying to dispose of me, or did he really think I stood a chance of killing the princess? Or was this all a ploy to get Katen to react and give herself away?

I realized I didn't care. I would do anything to save our lives.

I took a deep breath. "If you will allow them to accompany me on this quest, then I accept."

"She is lying," Katen broke in. "They will not go to the castle. They will run."

"My daughter makes a good point," Shale agreed. "There is nothing holding you to this bargain but your word." After a moment, he snapped his fingers. "Miranda may go with you. But I'm keeping your other friend here. If you do not bring me proof of the princess's demise in five days' time, his life will be forfeit."

Katen nodded approvingly. "You should send someone along with them to make sure they don't lose their nerve. I offer Alaric's service as a sign of my enduring fealty to you."

"*Really*," Shale said, clearly delighted by Katen's offer. He turned back to me. "Very well. The raven will assist you on this quest. And I will grant you a compass that will point toward the castle no matter how the Silence tries to hide it. Let it not be said that the ruler of the Gather does not make fair bargains."

He sheathed his sword and called for the Wolves. When one appeared, he addressed him. "Go to the dungeon and fetch Miranda. Bring her here unharmed."

As there was no longer a sword pointed directly at me, I took the opportunity to stand. Shale snapped his fingers, and a silver compass appeared, floating in midair before me.

"Do not lose this," he said. "It will not go well for you if you do." I plucked it from the air and pocketed it, feeling uneasy.

Shale turned to Katen. "And where *is* your raven?"

Katen started. "I didn't think that you would send them off so quickly," she said. "Alaric is handling another matter."

Another lie. He was likely still battling the vines.

"On a revel night?" Shale said. "Summon him."

Katen frowned but did as her father demanded. After a moment Alaric appeared, a little disheveled but otherwise unharmed. His gaze flicked between the three of us, but he remained silent.

"You will accompany this girl and her companion to the castle of briars," Katen said. "Do not leave them under any circumstances."

The Wolf returned to the hallway with Miranda, still in chains. She gaped at me in surprise—I shook my head subtly, trying to tell her not to speak.

"The three of you are hereby ordered to storm the castle of briars," Shale declared. "Do not return to the Gather until you have slain the princess."

CHAPTER TWENTY-FIVE

No one spoke until we were well out of earshot of the city—and then Miranda flung herself at me, hugging me tightly. "You came for me," she said, her voice trembling with emotion.

I hugged her back. I felt a little faint—I couldn't quite believe that we were still alive. Over Miranda's shoulder, I saw Alaric looking away. I pulled back gently. "Are you all right?" I asked.

She nodded. Then she looked down and exclaimed in surprise, "You're hurt. Let me help you."

Miranda's fingers were gentle as they held my hand, palm up. She brushed her fingers over the cut on my palm, making me wince, and I watched as the skin knitted itself together. The blisters on my wrist proved less cooperative, though Miranda was able to soothe the burning sensation. Even after everything that I had seen in the Gather tonight, the way she healed still felt special. When she was done, I held up my hand, turning it back and forth to examine it.

"Thank you," I said.

"I don't believe this," Alaric muttered. "You told *her* about the Hand of Mora?"

My cheeks flushed with embarrassment as I pulled my hand out of Miranda's. "That is not your business."

He shook his head in disappointment. "Think of what she

could do with that information. She was going to sell you to Shale!"

"And earlier, you were about to help Katen bleed me to death!" I retorted hotly. "I don't think you're the best arbiter of who I can or can't trust right now."

"*Enough!*" Miranda said sharply. She looked between the two of us. "Far be it from me to interrupt a good argument, but we need to decide what to do."

"We go to the castle," Alaric said. "We have no choice."

"That's not true," Miranda said, looking at me. "We could still run."

And condemn my father to death? I couldn't. No matter how furious I was with him.

"No," I said. "I must go to the castle, or else he'll kill my father." I looked at Miranda. "I'll understand if you choose not to come."

She hesitated only a moment before shaking her head. "I'm staying with you."

Relief washed through me. "All right," I said. "What's first?"

"We need to start moving," Miranda said. "It won't be long before the Wolves will come after us."

I looked at Alaric. "Is that true? I didn't think they would interfere."

Alaric fell silent, frowning. Then he spoke carefully. "Historically speaking, those sentenced to the castle of briars either die upon said briars, or they are killed by the Wolves as they try to escape the sentence. We should not assume that we are safe simply because we appear to be alone, or because you struck a deal with the king."

It seemed Shale certainly intended for us to die on this quest one way or another—and Katen's magic along with me. Even if we succeeded against the odds, what then? The princess would be dead, and Shale's power over the forest cemented. What would that mean for me?

No. I shoved aside the doubts. I had entered the Silence with one mission: to rid myself of the curse. In order to do that, I had to see Katen dead. And the only way I was going to do that was to escape Shale's wrath long enough to do it. Alaric was right. Things would have been simpler if I'd stayed away from the Gather. But I didn't regret saving Miranda's life.

I was still determined to find a way to free us. But it was also the middle of the night, and after everything that I had been through in the palace, my body was beginning to shake with the effort of staying upright.

"I need to sleep," I said. "Do either of you know somewhere safe?"

"Haven is too far," Miranda said.

"There is my shelter," Alaric said grudgingly. "But I am not strong enough to carry more than one person at once."

"Then do it one person at a time," Miranda said, rolling her eyes.

Alaric glared at her.

"We're in this together," I reminded him. "Regardless of how we might feel about being stuck with one another."

With another dark look at Miranda, Alaric pulled me aside. "I do not trust her," he whispered in my ear.

"How shocking," I said.

Alaric's lips thinned with disapproval, but he didn't reply. He just grabbed hold of me, and the familiar rush of air hit as we flew. He let me go as soon as we reached the camp, but I touched his arm tentatively before he could take off again.

"I'm truly sorry," I said. "About your wings."

He shook his head. "Don't, Lena."

"But there must still be a chance, isn't there? You said that I just need Katen's blood to open the box. We can find a way."

"It's too late," Alaric said. "Don't speak of it again." He hesitated, then pulled my knife from his pocket. "Here. You'll need this." Before I could say anything else, he launched into the air once more.

I reached into my pocket and felt the comforting weight of the box. I *would* find a way to free him. I owed him that much.

Do not be afraid to come to the castle, said the Silence.

I looked at my palm, now healed over. That the Silence was encouraging me to do something that Shale had commanded was a little unnerving. But the forest had saved me when nothing else could.

"What happens when I spill blood for you?" I asked.

Our bond grows stronger. The closer we grow, the easier it will be.

"The easier *what* will be?" I said, but the voice fell quiet once more.

I was only alone for a few minutes before Alaric returned with Miranda. She grinned as they landed, looking windswept and eager.

"So this is your lair," she said. She whistled as she turned around, suitably impressed.

Alaric's expression was impatient, but he said merely, "We should sleep." He drew a circle of protection around the shelter, then stalked a few paces away and lay down unceremoniously, closing his eyes.

Miranda found a blanket and spread it out on the ground. She sat down on it and patted the spot beside her. "Come," she said.

My cheeks flushed as I remembered the last time we had spent together. Circumstances had changed—but my feelings had not. And yet . . . Alaric was only a few feet away. I glanced at him, surprised by a sudden twinge of discomfort. Then I pushed the feeling aside. We had agreed to that one afternoon, nothing more. I'd done nothing wrong, and I refused to feel bad about being with Miranda now.

I lay down, trying to find a comfortable position. I was acutely aware of Miranda beside me—the soft sounds of her breathing, the small movements she made as she settled. How did anyone ever accustom themselves to such sharp attunement to another? Every nerve in my body was singing.

Outside the circle of protection, a trio of ghost lights flared to life. I watched them dance. Miranda had told me that those entranced by the lights might see relatives who had passed on. But I'd never had anyone but my parents. For the first time, I wondered who I might see in those lights. If my mother was not only gone, but. . . .

Miranda moved, shifting so that her arm lay next to mine. Our fingers brushed together and awareness jolted through me. Slowly, I turned my palm up. After a moment she took my hand in her own, anchoring me in the sensation of our fingers intertwined, our bodies connected. Peace came to me, unexpected and precious.

When I looked again, the lights had disappeared.

Alaric was toasting some traveler's bread in a skillet over a fire when I woke—where did it all *come* from?

246

I extracted myself carefully from Miranda's arms and went behind a tree to relieve myself. Then I sat down next to Alaric. For a while we were quiet. Alaric poked at one of the pieces of bread, then flipped it out of the skillet and offered it to me. I chewed slowly, not sure what I should say. My discomfort from last night was gone, but I still felt I ought to say *something* to him. I decided to work my way up to it.

"It wasn't my intent to hurt you, by keeping your wings a secret," I said.

When he didn't say anything, I tentatively continued. "And I'm sorry if I—if Miranda and me last night . . . caused you any pain."

Alaric took a deep breath and held it before letting it out again. "What's done is done. We need to move on," he replied. I wasn't sure if he was talking about the wings, what we'd shared, or both. But at that moment Miranda materialized at my side, and the conversation was lost.

"Good morning," she said. Alaric passed her a piece of bread without speaking. She sniffed at it suspiciously before taking a bite. Alaric only looked away.

I sighed. "The first thing we need to do is get to the castle." I looked at Miranda. "Do you remember the way?"

She shook her head. "You don't understand. The castle . . . it moves. Like the trees of the Silence."

"Then I suppose we have no choice but to use this," I said, pulling the compass out of my pocket.

Miranda gasped. "He gave you the compass?"

Alaric's jaw twitched. "Shale does nothing out of the goodness of his heart. If we use the compass, there will be a price."

"What price?" Miranda asked.

"Most likely? He will know exactly where we are so long as we have it."

I looked down at it as though it were a venomous snake ready to strike.

"Do we have a choice?" I asked. "We only have five days. We can't afford to take a wrong turn."

"You're right," Alaric said. "We must accept the hand that has been dealt."

With Alaric's warning echoing in my ears, I opened the compass. The needle spun and settled on a point somewhat west of us. As I watched, the needle wavered—but I suspected this was as accurate a guide as we would get. "Let's go," I said.

It was difficult work. This part of the Silence was wild and overgrown, making our progress slow and sometimes painful. Even the cool autumn day didn't stop sweat from dripping down my back.

What do you propose to do once you reach the castle?

What do you mean?

You need not bow to the mage's demands. He is nothing more than a parasite.

A parasite who will kill my father—and me—if I don't see this through.

Blood magic may have carved out its place in this forest, but it is not the only power here, nor the most powerful. With me, you could have more—you could hold the Gather in your hand, and crush them.

I couldn't deny that I wouldn't mind crushing the Gather, at least in this moment. But still, the venom in the forest's voice chilled me. I had seen Shale's grip on the Gather—I had seen Katen's wiles and her justifications. Could the Silence, whatever it was, truly be worse than that?

In exchange for what? I asked. *What do you want from me?*

Vow yourself to the Silence. Bind your life to ours, the voice said seductively.

A shiver ran down my spine. *What does that mean?*

Leave your friends. Come to me and I will show you.

Leave Alaric and Miranda? *No,* I said. *I can't do that.*

Miranda abruptly stopped walking, and I almost ran into her. "We have a problem," she said.

I looked up. Ahead of us the ground sloped downward, ending in a rocky shore at the edge of a lake so large that I couldn't see the other side.

I looked down at the compass. Its arrow pointed straight across the lake, unwavering.

CHAPTER TWENTY-SIX

No matter which way I turned the compass, the arrow remained infuriatingly steady, pointing straight across the water.

"The Silence has shifted," Alaric said. "It has put the lake in our paths, though for what reason, I do not know. We must go around."

"What about flying?" Miranda suggested.

"Despite what you may think, my powers are not limitless," Alaric replied testily. "Every time I fly, it costs me. And I can't afford to be powerless when we reach the castle."

"Fine. Then which way?" I said.

"Left. That will take us farther away from the Gather."

"I'm surprised you still know what direction the Gather is."

Alaric looked away. "I always know. Because I always know where Katen is."

Katen. As we started along the shore, the memory of our encounter reared its head once more. My wrist still ached where she had touched me. Which reminded me . . .

I looked over at Miranda. "When you explained blood magic to me, you said that a mage's power depends on their knowledge of nonmagical trades. Do you know what Shale's and Katen's skills are?"

Miranda bit her lip, pondering. "They're both so old, I'm sure they have a wide breadth of skills. And I don't think either of them have needed to display their full strengths in a long time—their reputations carry a lot of weight. But Shale was known as a warrior once."

That made sense. I remembered the fluid way he had moved in the hallway, the way he had wielded his sword. "And Katen?"

Miranda shook her head. "I don't know."

"Poison, among other things," Alaric said quietly. "She studied botany for years."

Miranda turned to him. "And why are you telling us this? Aren't you her servant?"

"That is not your concern," he said, unblinking.

"Isn't it?" she said. "You're here to spy on us, to report back to your mistress, isn't that right? The only thing I don't understand is why you and Lena suddenly seem to be friends."

The memory of Alaric's and my first kiss, and everything that had come afterward, flashed through my mind. My cheeks flushed, and I looked away.

Miranda must have noticed my reaction, though. "Lena?" she asked, quieter. "What happened between you two?"

Before I could answer, the lake roiled behind us.

"What was that?" I said, turning around.

Alaric was already drawing his sword. "Get behind me."

But Miranda didn't move. She stayed anchored to the spot as the waters began to rise. In the distance I saw something break the surface. I drew my knife.

Ripples flowed toward us, marking the movements of something large underwater. I held my breath as they approached—then dissipated. The surface stilled until it was as smooth as glass. Then, at the center of the lake, a creature rose out of the water.

Its skin was green or perhaps blue—the color seemed to shift with the light—and rows of gills ran down the sides of its throat. Large, milky eyes were set above a wide mouth. It bared its fangs into something resembling a smile and raised long tentacles into the air. Feathery tendrils flowed like sleeves along the tentacles as it beckoned to us—and then a high, keening sound filled the air.

Sudden sorrow flooded through me, bringing tears to my eyes—and Miranda stepped into the water.

"Miranda!"

She did not react, only kept walking until the water was up to her thighs, her waist. Alaric sheathed his sword and ran after her. He grabbed her arm, pulling her back toward the shore—but beyond them, I saw another creature surface, and another. Soon there were twelve in total. Their keening multiplied, assaulting my ears. And slowly Alaric turned around to face them. And then he, too, began to walk out into the water.

My chest seized with panic. Miranda had told me of her encounter with mermaids that enticed humans with a song, but these creatures were unlike any mermaids I'd ever imagined. And for some reason I was the only one unaffected. I had to save them. But how?

This is Silence magic. "Help me!" I shouted.

But the voice was silent.

I had a knife, but what use would that be against such creatures?

I sheathed my knife and dug my hands into my pockets, rummaging around for something—anything—that would help. My fingers closed around the box with Alaric's wings, and I pushed that aside. There was lint, mostly, and the gloves I wasn't wearing.

The dragon scale, the net, Rin's pebble. And then I touched something else. The last acorn.

I ran after Alaric and Miranda, gasping as I splashed into the cold water. They were still ahead of me, the water now up to their chests. What would happen when they went all the way under?

In the distance, the creatures opened their mouths to reveal rows of sharp fangs. And then they began to close in.

I pushed my feet off the sandy bottom of the lake and swam. Alaric and Miranda were close to being submerged. As I approached, one of the creatures wrapped its tentacles around Miranda, dragging her under the surface.

I drew my knife and grabbed one of the tentacles, trying not to recoil from the feel of slime oozing between my fingers. The contact sent a searing jolt of pain through my body, and I screamed as we were pulled under.

I opened my eyes into white frothing water. I held fast to the tentacle as I flailed, stabbing at the creature with my knife. An enraged shriek pierced my skull, and tentacles wrapped around me from behind. They squeezed my torso, dragging me deeper. I was running out of air—water swirled around me as I felt fangs sink into my neck.

Blood stained the water red, and there was a sudden roiling as the creature recoiled from me. The pressure around my chest vanished—I was alone.

I kicked furiously to the surface and burst into the air, gasping. Water streamed down my face as I looked around. Where had the creatures gone?

Alaric was floating near me. I grabbed his arm and he blinked, shaking off his stupor. "What—?"

"No time," I said. "Where's Miranda?"

His face was a mask of confusion. I scanned the lake, my heart pounding. She wasn't there.

Taking a deep breath, I dove back under. The water was clearing, and the creatures had disappeared. Where *was* she?

I spun frantically. *There!* A dark figure floated just below the surface in front of me. I swam to Miranda and grabbed her arm, pulling her up to the surface of the water.

Her face was pale, and her body limp. I couldn't feel her breathing.

"Let me," Alaric said hoarsely. He hovered one hand over Miranda's throat, clenched his fingers, and then straightened them.

Miranda's eyes flew open, and she began to cough. I pressed my lips together to keep from crying out in relief. Instead I settled for holding her tightly, keeping her head safely above the water. She looked dazed, but at least she was conscious.

With my free hand I flicked the cap off the last acorn. "I need passage away from here now!"

Something in the water brushed my leg, and I fought the urge to scream.

In the distance, one of the creatures resurfaced. I felt another brush against my leg, and I flinched. I looked down to see an eel, its dark head angling up toward me.

I flicked the acorn cap into the water, and the eel darted away.

"We need to follow the eel! Miranda, can you hold your breath?"

She nodded vaguely. That would have to do.

"Help me," I said to Alaric. He grabbed Miranda's arm without argument.

I took her other arm, nodded to Alaric, and we dove.

Near the surface the water was clear, but as we descended, there came a point past which I couldn't see. I could only kick harder and hope that I wasn't dragging us all to our deaths. I could see nothing, feel nothing except Miranda's arm and the water moving around us, the heaviness in my limbs, the pressure in my lungs, demanding relief . . .

My every thought narrowed to one sharp point. *Swim.* The eel flashed light in the darkness ahead of us, the only indication that there was anything left in the world other than our bodies and this crushing black expanse of water.

Then something changed. The water seemed to level out somehow, as though our descent had stopped, as though the eel was now leading us up again.

And then, suddenly, there was air.

We surfaced, gasping, into darkness. Together Alaric and I dragged Miranda out of the water and onto cold stone. A light flared to life in Alaric's hand. He held it high, and the light dispersed around us.

Miranda's face was ashen, her hair plastered to her skull. But she was still breathing, still conscious.

"Are you all right?" I asked, taking her hands between my own. She was so *cold*.

She nodded, shivering. Her eyes darted first to me and Alaric, and then beyond. "Where are we?" she said, her voice frightened.

I looked around for the first time. We were in a large earthen cave—somewhere underground, judging by the roots that tangled across the ceiling and sank down through the walls.

"We should not be here," Alaric said, his face grim. "This place is evil."

Miranda was still shaking. I ignored Alaric's warning and put an arm around her shoulder. She had succumbed to the creatures so easily. Even Alaric had been spellbound. Why had I been spared?

They cannot harm you. You are mine. They know that now.

These creatures were of the Silence. The Silence had intervened for me . . . but not for Miranda and Alaric. Anger sparked to life within me. What if it was more than that? What if the Silence had *commanded* them, somehow?

Did you try to take them from me? I demanded.

You are essential. But you risked your life for them in the Gather. You almost died. Without them, you are stronger. Less vulnerable.

"No!" I shouted. "You cannot take them from me. If you think I am yours—*they* are mine."

There was a curious pause. **I understand,** the Silence said finally. **I . . . miscalculated.**

Alaric and Miranda looked at me incredulously. "What is going on?" Miranda said. "Who are you talking to, Lena?"

"Not here," I said shortly. Alaric's lights flared brighter, illuminating a path on the other side of the grotto. I helped Miranda to her feet. "We should move."

We walked in watchful silence. The tunnel sloped upward and after a while opened into another cave, this one glowing with dim blue light. While the cave into which we had surfaced had been empty, this one was occupied by an enormous tree rooted at its center. Blue veins ran up the trunk of the tree, pulsing intermittently. At the base of the tree sat a person.

Miranda clutched my arm. "She's dead!" she whispered.

She was right, I realized as I looked closer. And not just

dead—this was a person who had been dead a very, very long time. The corpse was completely desiccated—almost mummified. Tree roots snaked in and out between its ribs, and small tendrils of green growth stretched out of its eye sockets and mouth.

Suddenly the ground pitched below me, and I stumbled forward. I threw out my arms as I fell, landing hard at the base of the tree. Vines curled around my wrist, pulling me toward the body. I watched in horrified fascination as my fingers touched its hand—

A bright light flashed before my eyes, and I found myself standing alone in a sunlit glade. Feathery ferns brushed against my legs, and a fox scampered past. In the distance, a narrow road cut through the trees. I felt strangely languorous, almost dreamy. This was the Silence, I realized. But it was safer, brighter—a memory of a time before.

Watch.

A girl appeared beside me. She was about my age, her hair dark, eyes flashing. In the way of dreams, I recognized her. Someday she would be the corpse at the base of the tree.

She looked at me, and then back at the road. **Watch.**

Another girl came down the road—no, the same girl as the one next to me, but there was a lightness about her, an innocence that was absent from the girl at my side. Flames danced along her knuckles as she walked, and she laughed, delighted.

Watch.

Three women followed her down the road. They met in the center of the grove, and I watched the girl's expression turn from surprise to confusion to fear. They argued. The girl turned as though she might run.

One of the women pushed her down. The others held her arms

as she struggled, fire sparking from her fingers. The first woman drew a knife. She knelt down and drove it into the girl's stomach.

A strangled sound caught in my throat. I flinched, closed my eyes. **Watch.**

I couldn't bear to, but my eyes opened as if of their own accord. I watched as the woman stabbed the girl twice, a third time. Blood sprayed into the air and flames leapt high.

Red stains bloomed on the blouse of the girl standing next to me. The Silence began to burn, but she did not react. She watched her own execution impassively.

Why are they doing this? I asked.

I lived near here, once. They thought I was a witch. They feared my power.

The women left the girl's body in a jumbled heap and ran from the burning glade. Blood had covered their hands, soaked into their clothing.

Time tripped forward—the flames flourished, then faded. I watched day turn into night in the blink of an eye. A sprout, a tendril—a sapling shot up through the girl's chest. Her body moved and settled.

What are you? I asked. *What did you become?*

The girl's lips twisted. **They cut my throat and I died, but I didn't stay that way. The Silence found me. When I woke, we were as one. It *saved* me. I killed the women who cut me down. And you can do the same. Join us. All you have to do is say yes.**

If I do . . . we will be bound together forever?

The girl smiled a cruel, inhuman smile. **With the power of the forest at your fingertips, you can exact revenge on all those who have harmed you.**

Before I could reply, the ground trembled. My vision went dark, and the next thing I knew, I was back in the cave. Alaric was pulling me up, dragging me away from the tree—the body.

"Did it speak to you?" he was asking urgently.

How did he know? "I—"

"Do *not* listen."

He wants you powerless. But I will give you power. All you need to do is ally yourself with me. I will give you new life, as I gave the first girl. Just a prick of a finger and a vow. Imagine the merfolk obeying the slightest twitch of your finger. Imagine commanding the ravens, the water, the earth—all of the forest at your beck and call. Imagine burying the Wolves, Katen, and Shale beneath your feet.

Against my better judgment, I took a step forward. Because if that was true—if *I* could command those vines, if *I* could tear up the bloodstones . . .

The corpse seemed to move—perhaps it was a trick of the light, but for a moment I saw the face of the girl she had once been—sharp-featured, dark eyes, long black hair.

What vow? I asked.

I could sense movement behind me, but I ignored it as the Silence spoke.

A simple trade. We are already tied, you and I. While you live, the entirety of my power will be yours. And when you die, your life force will join mine. You will be part of the Silence forever.

A globe of flame spun across my vision and landed at the base of the tree.

I blinked, disoriented, as the fire spread, crackling up the trunk. Suddenly an avalanche of beetles erupted from the tree, racing for the fire. They quickly crowded over it, starving the flame.

"Wait—" I began.

"More!" Alaric cried.

I turned my head to see Miranda lobbing globes of fire faster than the beetles could cover them. Smoke began to fill the chamber. Alaric grabbed me by the arm and pulled me back.

"There's no way out!" Miranda cried, coughing.

Let us out! I cried.

They attacked me, growled the Silence. **They caused this.**

But we will all die if you don't let us free, I said. *All of us.*

It was getting harder to breathe. I lowered myself to my knees, searching for fresher air. Where could we go? There was no way out of this chamber but back to the grotto. . . .

Miranda grabbed my hand. "Look!"

My eyes were streaming with tears. I wiped them away with my sleeve and saw the wall of the chamber shift, roots stretching and parting to reveal a passageway. Water poured from its mouth, rushing to douse the fire.

"Come on!" Miranda charged forward, and Alaric took my other hand. We ran faster, faster, faster, sloshing through the muddy passage until at last we saw sunlight in the distance. We sprinted for it, bursting forth into open air.

CHAPTER TWENTY-SEVEN

W hat *was* that?" Miranda gasped, once we had stopped running. In this part of the forest the trees were half-bare. Leaves crackled under our feet.

I'd kept the Silence a secret until now, but I'd promised Miranda the truth. Besides, I was angry with it for toying with me. Now that I knew the forest wanted me alive, I wouldn't be stopped from speaking.

"That was the Silence," I said.

Miranda's eyes went wide. "You mean the forest itself?"

I nodded.

"What does it want with you?"

I bit my lip. Some things about the Silence still felt too close to reveal, I realized. In some ways, its desires felt like *mine*. "It . . . thinks that we can help each other."

Miranda shook her head. "I don't understand."

"I don't completely understand it myself either," I admitted.

Alaric shook his head, disappointed. He wanted nothing to do with the Silence. Was it only because he had been cast out by the ravens? Or was there more to his animosity?

Miranda looked between the two of us, her eyes narrowing. "I remember . . . the creatures. The lake. And . . . you went in after me?" she asked Alaric incredulously. "Why?"

I didn't think Alaric would respond—I had a feeling that he enjoyed being enigmatic, regardless of whether or not his oaths required it. So I was surprised when he answered without hesitation.

"Because it was the right thing to do," he said. "Because I am not exactly the creature you think I am. And because Lena would not have forgiven me if I'd let anything happen to you."

Miranda's shoulders slumped. "Oh," she said quietly.

She was exhausted, I realized. And no wonder, after what she'd endured over the last few days. Shale's dungeon, a near execution, the merfolk, the Silence . . . and much of that had been my fault.

"Can we talk?" I said hesitantly.

She shrugged.

"We'll be right back," I said to Alaric.

"Lena . . ."

"We won't go far," I promised.

Miranda and I walked in uncomfortable silence until Alaric was almost out of sight. Then she turned to me. "What is it?"

"I owe you an apology," I said, forcing the words out. "This quest, the Silence—it's my fault. If it weren't for me, the merfolk wouldn't have attacked you. And with what's to come . . . if you want to leave, I'll understand. I won't hold it against you." I held my breath, waiting. If she left—if she left me now, the Silence would leave her in peace. Shale might forget about her. However I felt wouldn't matter, as long as she was safe.

"Leave?" she said blankly. "You want me to leave?"

"No! I don't *want* you to leave. I just meant—it's dangerous to be around me right now, and I think it might only get worse. I don't want you to feel obligated to stay. I want you to be safe."

She looked at me strangely. "Is this because of Alaric?"

My brow furrowed in confusion. "I don't—what about Alaric?"

"You were with him, before we met in the canyons," Miranda said.

"Yes," I said, my confusion growing. "We came to an accord after you and I were separated."

"No—you were *with* him. I can tell by the way he looks at you."

I blushed. Was it so obvious? It wasn't that I was ashamed. I wasn't—not at all. But being intimate with another person—in all the ways one could be—was still so new to me. It bothered me, just a little, that she had been able to tell so easily. This was something I would have preferred to hold close to myself. "Does it matter?" I said cautiously.

"Of course it matters," Miranda cried in frustration. "If you're with him, why did you kiss me? Why did you bring me here with you only to send me away *now*? I thought you *wanted* me. Was that not true?"

"But I'm not—we're not—" I struggled to put the words together.

She looked at me, anguished. "Don't lie to me. Please."

I closed the distance between us, taking her hand in my own. "I won't. It's true that I . . . was intimate with him. That was when I thought I'd never see you again—when I thought I had days to live, if that. I'd gone my entire life without being able to touch another person besides my parents. From birth. Being with Alaric was . . ." I looked down, worried about saying something wrong. "I needed to know what it felt like, to finally be able to touch someone without fear. But when I saw you again, I realized that desire for its own sake is very different from desire for *someone* in particular. I kissed you because I wanted to kiss *you*. I wanted you for *you*."

A hint of a smile glimmered at the corners of Miranda's mouth. "I see," she said.

I bit my lip. "Alaric . . . I care for him a great deal. But not in the same way I care for you. I promise."

"Then why did you want me to leave, if not because of him?"

I threw up my hands. "I've said it already: I'm trying to give you an out! You almost died because of me."

A smile—a real smile—broke across her face. "Ah, but I *would* have died at Shale's hands if not for you. And it's not as though I have anywhere better to go. . . ."

Hope swelled in my chest. "So . . . you'll stay?"

She raised an eyebrow. "Do you *want* me to say?"

"Of *course* I do—"

Her laughter rang through me. "Come here," she said. She cupped a hand behind my neck and leaned toward me. Our lips met, sending a thrill down my spine. I drank her in, reveling in her warmth, her lips, her touch . . . when she let me go, I couldn't stop smiling.

"Are we all right?" I asked, a little breathless.

"All right," she said, grinning at me. "Now, we'd better get going. There's still a castle to storm, after all."

I grabbed her hand, and as we hurried back to Alaric, I couldn't help thinking that there was nothing sweeter in the world than holding hands with a girl and running with abandon through a sinister forest—and that I might be cursed, but that I was so, so lucky.

We used Shale's compass to reorient ourselves, and then we walked until we could walk no more. As the sun set, Alaric found a grove of trees for us to make camp. He drew another circle of protection, and this time we traded watch shifts, but thankfully nothing in the forest stirred throughout the night.

Still, Miranda was yawning as we swept away the traces of our camp and set off once more. I struggled to keep my eyes open, but there was nothing for it but to keep going, one foot in front of the other.

By midmorning, Alaric announced that we were getting close.

I didn't question him—I'd learned by now to trust what he said regarding the Silence and what lay inside it—and my heart began to beat faster. So far we had been single-mindedly occupied with the task of getting to the castle. But once we were there, how would we get inside? And could I truly bring myself to murder a defenseless, sleeping girl?

I had killed before, every death a new weight upon me. But I'd never used the curse on an innocent person on purpose. Even Cyn and her partner had meant to betray me.

"Who is she?" I asked. "The princess sleeping in the castle."

Alaric flinched, ever so slightly.

Miranda jumped in. "They say she's been asleep for one hundred years."

One hundred years. I turned to Alaric, newly suspicious. "You knew her. One hundred years, that can't just be a coincidence. You knew her before she was asleep."

"Yes," he said simply.

"Then doesn't it bother you, to think about killing her?"

He shrugged eloquently. "I've killed a lot of people. One more or less makes little difference."

But I knew there was more to it than that—I'd seen the way he'd flinched when I mentioned her.

"Then I can count on you not to interfere?" I said.

Alaric stared at me, his dark eyes fathomless. "You can count on me not to interfere with *anything* you choose to do once we arrive at the castle."

This must be yet another thing he was bound not to speak of. I looked over at Miranda. "What about you? If this princess is meant to liberate the forest . . . do you think we should be helping her instead?"

Miranda looked away. "I've lived in the Gather for years and seen nothing that proves to me that this princess can really make a difference. I did hope the legend was true, once. But if killing her means ensuring our survival and saving your father's life . . . then I'll support you in this as well."

"In that case . . . how does one kill a princess, anyway?"

"For you, it could be as easy as touching her hand. If she's sleeping, that will probably make it easier," Miranda said.

Alaric didn't say anything, just kept walking.

"But if it were that simple, wouldn't Shale have killed her long ago?"

"Remember, Shale has never been able to get *inside* the castle. So he's never had the chance to get close enough to her to try."

"I wonder if we'll have any better luck," I said wryly.

"We're about to find out," Alaric said. He raised a hand and pointed.

I looked in the direction he was pointing but saw nothing beyond the endless trees. The day was brilliant, sun layering through the branches to fall in patterns on the ground. For several more minutes we kept walking, and there was only forest—and then all at once there was a gap in the trees, and I couldn't imagine how I'd missed it before.

Before us lay a vast, thick wall of briars. The thorny branches were too dense to make out the castle wall beyond, but I could see the top of a tower reaching high into the sky. It had the unexpected appearance of a sandcastle made by giants, a misshapen, precarious affair threatening to fall.

Next to me, Miranda let out one long sigh. She wrapped her arm around my shoulder and squeezed. "We're here."

CHAPTER TWENTY-EIGHT

My skin crawled with nervous anticipation. "What now?" Miranda bit her lip. "This is as far as I got last time," she said. "The Wolves appeared and—well, you know the rest."

There were no Wolves here. Not yet, anyway.

We looked up, taking it in. The briars were more than twice my height, and moved seemingly at will, bending and curling toward us as though they were deciding whether to attack. As one cluster of briars shifted, I gasped. There were *people* in the thorns. Bodies that had been wrapped up in the briars and still hung there, a gruesome display of death. I swallowed down bile and tried to breathe shallowly.

Looking down, I saw that the ground in front of the briars was littered with human castoffs: scraps of fabric, the rusted blade of a knife, the occasional shoe. Something in the mess caught my attention. I knelt down and picked up a piece of cloth. No shimmering Gather silk—this was homespun wear, the sort that anyone in the Mundane might have woven for themselves. The sort that the people of Onwey had worn.

These were not all Shale's people. Some of them were those who had been called from the village. But why would the Silence call them here, to die?

"Have the briars ever parted?" I asked.

Miranda shook her head. "Not to my knowledge."

I looked at Alaric. "Is there another way into the castle? Could you fly over the walls?"

"No," he said wearily. "Katen ordered me to try, many years ago. The briars only grew taller."

"So we're stuck," I said.

Not so, whispered the Silence.

What are you offering?

You know my offer. The briars will part if you spill blood to the earth.

But that would mean taking yet another step down this path, binding myself closer to the forest.

"Lena?" Alaric said. "What are you doing?"

I blinked and found Alaric's hand on my arm. Without realizing it, I had taken a step toward the briars.

Wouldn't you like to wield the entirety of my power? Pay the price to enter my domain. Then make your vow once you are inside . . . and join me.

My head was suddenly spinning. Alaric caught me as my knees buckled. He carried me away from the wall and set me down out of its reach. Miranda followed, clearly worried.

"What does it want?" Alaric asked.

I stared at him. "The Silence will let us in if I offer it my blood."

He shook his head. "Don't take that bargain."

"Why does it matter? She pricks her finger, and the Silence allows us to pass. It's no worse than blood magic," said Miranda.

I grimaced. "It's more than that. Every time I spill blood, the Silence binds me tighter to it. And this is the seat of its power." I decided to leave out the part about *forever.*

Miranda's face turned grave. She crouched down, looking me in the eye. "Then I agree with Alaric—don't do it."

"But you just said—"

"Callie was lured in by the promise of power and look where she is now. I won't lose you, too," Miranda said, her voice cracking.

I put my hand over hers. "It's the only way. And it's no more than I've already done."

Alaric pressed his lips together. "Lena . . . you should run and not look back. But I know you will not."

He was right—I couldn't run. Not when I had come this far. Besides, I had tasted true power in the Silence. I'd held my own against the Wolves. I'd taken Cyn's life, and then her friend's. I'd called the vines of the forest and faced the merfolk. And none of it had destroyed me. I would not let the Silence—nor any human—be master over me ever again. I was stronger than that frightened girl I'd been, who'd always believed she was a monster. And I would do everything in my power never to feel that way again.

Miranda let go of my hand. "What are you going to do?"

Before I could answer, eerie howls broke through the air. We turned around to see a pack of Wolves, a dozen at least, stalking toward us through the trees. My breath caught in my throat.

"Lena?" Miranda said. Hearing the fear in her voice only strengthened my resolve.

"I'll do it," I said quickly. "Alaric—hold them off."

I pushed myself to my feet and ran back to the wall of thorns. I knelt in front of it and pulled out my knife. Before I lost my nerve, I sliced across the back of my arm, wincing in pain. Blood welled up from the wound.

I turned my arm and watched the blood fall to the earth.

The ground shuddered below me, rippling outward. My vision doubled, and my ears rang. There was a sudden cacophony of animal sound—and then the forest was still. It felt as though the Silence had somehow physically relaxed—as if it was *breathing* easier than before.

The wall of briars began to move. Behind me I heard a snarl, and then a whimper of pain, but I couldn't take my eyes off the briars. The smallest vines were as thick as my arm with thorns that looked needle sharp. They receded slowly, followed by larger briars peeling back to reveal a narrow pathway of pale stones.

I rose to my feet and turned around to see Alaric clench his fist. The Wolf nearest to him howled, falling to the ground in pain. Miranda was throwing globes of fire, but they were outnumbered—the Wolves still advanced.

"Let's go!" I cried. They raced toward me and we plunged into the briars, the Wolves hard on our heels.

Close, I thought. *Keep them out.*

The briars snapped shut much faster than they had parted, trapping several of the Wolves in the thorns. I heard their unearthly screams—and then moans—and then gurgles—as the briars shifted, devouring them.

Soon there was no trace of the world outside—or the Wolves. All was quiet.

Miranda looked almost ill. Alaric looked entirely unsurprised.

"Well," I said slowly. "I suppose there's only one way to go."

We proceeded nervously down the path, hemmed in by walls of briars. They shifted and swayed around us, tendrils reaching too close for my comfort. I was glad when the light ahead of us widened, and we were finally through.

Before us stood a freestanding gate covered in ivy. Beyond it was a dry moat, with a crumbling drawbridge drawn up on the other side. Even if we could cross the moat, there was a stone wall on the other side that we'd have to breach as well.

We passed through the gate and walked toward the moat, the stone path growing smoother under my feet. My heart sank as we reached the edge of the moat. It was too deep to climb up the other side. And there didn't seem to be a way to lower the bridge from here.

"Any ideas on how to cross?" I said.

Alaric grimaced. "I can't fly. My exertions over the last few days have cost me. I need time to recover."

I looked around. *Help?*

Build a bridge.

I rolled my eyes and tried again. *How?*

The presence of the Silence rushed through me, leaving me breathless and off balance. But now I knew what to do. I knelt down and brushed my hand over the cut on my arm. Then I pressed my bloodstained palm to the earth.

Something tickled in the back of my mind, like an itch I couldn't scratch. I looked up to see a few thorny vines hovering in the air before me.

Despite myself, I smiled. These same vines had just made quick work of a pack of Wolves, I knew. But now they looked tentative—and helpful.

Will you make me a bridge?

For a moment the vines hung in the air. Then they braided together and extended, floating out across the moat. As I watched, they anchored to the other side and waited, swaying in the breeze . . . but I was almost certain they were not strong enough to support my weight. I touched the vines tentatively, and they moved, wrapping around my hand.

Thorns ripped into my skin, but when I tried to pull away I found I was held fast. I hissed in pain as blood dripped down my wrist—and the vines grew, thickening and lengthening until the once-slender braid formed a sturdy, narrow bridge across the moat.

"Go!" I said tightly. "I don't know how long I can hold this."

Miranda stepped toward me, alarmed. "Hurry!" I said.

She cast me one agonized look. Then she squared her shoulders and stepped out onto the bridge.

The vines dipped as they took her weight, and my arm was pulled down with them. I staggered forward, tears springing to my eyes.

"You have to let go," Alaric said at my side.

The vines were beginning to crawl up my arm. They would swallow me, I realized, if given the chance.

"I can't," I said, panic coloring my voice.

He reached into the vines but recoiled, hissing, as they lashed out at him. He took my free hand instead. "Lena, look at me."

Blinking away tears, I met his eyes.

"You must force them off," he said.

"I don't know how!"

He squeezed my hand tightly. "The Silence's will is strong. Yours must be stronger."

I closed my eyes, trying to concentrate. I could feel my own body, the sharp pain where the thorns bit into me, Alaric's hand in mine . . . But I could feel the presence of the vines, too, their unadulterated joy as they twined around my wrist and arm, seeking more. And behind them, there was the dark anticipation of the Silence. I froze.

"Lena!" Alaric cried.

Warmth washed through me, pushing back the darkness. I anchored myself to the sensation of Alaric's hand in mine as I burned the vines out of my mind. They could not have me. I would not allow it.

The pain eased, but I dared not open my eyes for fear of what I might see.

"Good," Alaric said, his voice seeming to come from far away. "Keep going."

The vines were reluctant. I pushed harder, imagining scorching the stragglers to ash. My skin tore as the vines ripped angrily away—and then Alaric wrenched me back, and I was free.

"Come quickly," he said, pulling me toward the bridge.

My arm was on fire and my feet unsteady as I took the first step. Tendrils of vine raised up hopefully, brushing against my boot. I snatched up my foot and stumbled as fast as I could to the other side.

My panic didn't begin to subside until we reached solid ground once more. I fell to my hands and knees, gasping. The Silence hadn't warned me that using this power would be like *that*—like the very life was being leached out of me.

Flowers burst out of the ground around me, their petals sharp contrasts in white and red. Their chattering was different than I remembered—now it seemed as if they were speaking on the other side of a closed door, and if I could only concentrate hard enough, I would understand them. . . .

"Heal her," Alaric said to Miranda. "There will only be more of them as long as she is bleeding."

Miranda grabbed my hands, and I yelped in pain—but once her magic began working on my torn skin, the presence of the vines disappeared. The flowers' chatter cut off. I slumped back, my mind suddenly quiet.

Alaric took me by the arm and helped me to my feet.

"What *was* that?" Miranda said, her eyes wide.

"The power of the Silence," Alaric said grimly. "Let's move."

True power comes with a price . . . and I was beginning to understand what that price might entail.

But my misgivings were temporarily forgotten as I looked up and realized that we'd reached the inner wall. Before us was a small wooden door set in the stone. Alaric reached for it.

"Locked," he said.

"Allow me," Miranda said. She pressed her bloodied fingers to the lock. The air chilled, and I heard the crackling sound of ice forming. Miranda stepped back with a satisfied smile. "Alaric? If you would be so kind."

Alaric struck the door with an open palm. The lock shattered, and the door swung slowly open. We stepped through to the other side.

Years of decay had taken their toll, but still I could scarcely believe my eyes. We were standing inside a round courtyard, the castle rising tall before us. Tree roots had pushed their way up through the stones in the courtyard. Of the three buildings that made up the castle, one had collapsed into ruins, giving itself over to climbing ivy and wild roses. Another remained standing but was so covered in greenery it was difficult to tell that there was stone beneath. The third building was the largest, rising up into the tower we'd seen from outside the briars. It was clear that this building was almost as fragile as its counterparts. Parts of the roof had fallen in, and the wooden door looked mossy and rotted. And yet, while the forest had seized most of the castle, it seemed to have taken special care to keep the tower whole.

Something about this place made my breath catch in my chest, made my throat tighten. I felt like I'd been here before. Like I was moving through a half-remembered dream.

I led the way into the hall beneath the tower. The stairs were blanketed in years of dust and dirt, and our footsteps were muffled. My legs began to ache as we ascended, and my breath became short.

At the top of the tower was a landing. At the end of the landing stood an open doorway. Beyond the doorway was a room. I stepped over the threshold.

The room was perfectly round and empty, save for a stone statue standing at its center as though it had sprouted right out of the floor. The stone was of a flowering tree cleaved open as if by lightning. The figure of a woman reached up from within the split trunk. She was tall and dressed in traveling clothes, her long hair spilling out of a plait. One hand was flung outward as if caught in the middle of a gesture, while the other lay flat against her side.

We'd found the sleeping princess of the Silence.

Miranda stepped toward the statue, but I put out a hand to hold her back.

"What are you doing?" she said.

She was speaking loudly, too loudly. My body was beginning to shake, and my ears were ringing. I felt dizzy, almost sick. Miranda placed a hand on my arm, and I shook her off.

"No," I said.

"Lena, what is it? You're scaring me."

I turned to face her, my vision blurring with tears.

"That's my mother."

CHAPTER TWENTY-NINE

I don't understand," Miranda said.

I whirled around, looking for Alaric—but he had disappeared. He must have run—he must have *known*—and he'd brought me here, completely unsuspecting, to kill her?

From the stories, I had expected an innocent beauty too young to be trapped by such a spell. How wrong I'd been.

She *was* beautiful, though. It had been so long since I'd last seen her that her features had faded in my memories. Now they snapped back into focus—the lines at the corners of her mouth and eyes, the proud set of her jaw. In real life her hair would be dark, her skin the same light brown as mine, though at the moment it was the same pale stone as the rest of the statue.

"Lena, how could that be your *mother?*" Miranda asked. For a moment I'd forgotten she was even in the room.

"Get out," I said.

"What?"

"You have to leave." My voice was shrill and trembling. I pointed back toward the staircase. "Please, just go!"

I half expected her to fight me. After a moment she nodded. "I'm giving you five minutes," she said, backing out of the room.

I turned around to face down the statue.

How was this possible? My mind struggled to fit everything I'd learned into something resembling coherence. The sleeping princess had been in lore for generations, while my mother . . . Well, she'd been my *mother*. For seven years, anyway.

Then she'd abandoned us. Because she couldn't stand the curse that made me monstrous.

But things were different now. I knew the truth of the Hand of Mora. *And she did too.* She'd always known—but then why hadn't she told me?

For a moment I was incandescently elated.

Then memory hit. She'd sold me to save herself and then run when she discovered what I'd become.

She had left me.

A hot coal of hatred burned in my chest.

But she was still my mother. And one thing was certain: I couldn't kill her any more than I could let Father fall to Shale's wrath.

I raised my hand and carefully matched my fingertips to hers.

A chill crept up my fingers, then over my arms and across my chest. I opened my mouth and exhaled a cloud of cold mist, but somehow, I was not afraid. I let the ice roll through my body, and when the wave subsided, I closed my eyes and breathed back warmth. Warmth through my chest, down my arms and legs. Warmth to the tips of my fingers and toes. Warmth back into the stone.

I opened my eyes. The pallor melted, revealing flesh below. My mother's fingers twitched, and I watched the change spread, her hair turning dark and lustrous, her clothing becoming fabric once more. Slowly her body peeled away from the rest of the statue, and she fell forward.

I barely caught her, and we toppled together to the floor. She staggered quickly to her feet, drawing a knife as she found into a fighting stance. "Who are you?" she said, her voice hoarse from disuse.

I held up my hands, trying to show I meant no harm. "Mother, it's me. Lena," I said, my voice shaky.

Her dark eyes focused, then widened in recognition. She straightened abruptly, her arms falling to her sides. "Lena? Is that really you?" she said, bewildered.

Something cracked within me. I ran forward and wrapped my arms around her. Ten years ago she'd dwarfed me. She was still the taller of us, but now it was a matter of inches, not feet, and my chin just fit over her shoulder as I clung to her. After a moment's hesitation, she hugged me back tightly, and I melted, tears coming so quickly I couldn't see through them.

She released me too soon. "Lena, what are you doing here? You're in danger!"

I didn't know what to say. I had so many questions. I didn't know how to talk to this woman—my mother—

"Are you really a princess?" I said.

"There is no time for that now. Where is your father? We need to get you out of here."

I looked down. "He's not here."

She paused, holding me at arm's length. "How old are you?" she asked at last.

"Seventeen," I said.

"I've been gone for—" She covered her mouth with her hand and sank slowly to the floor, her legs folding beneath her. "Ten years?" she whispered, rocking back and forth. An anguished cry broke from her lips.

I didn't know what to do. Whatever words were appropriate for comforting the mother who'd disappeared more than half my life ago, I couldn't find them. I felt overcome by a combination of exhausted heaviness and the strangest sensation of weightlessness, as though my body might suddenly float away.

Eventually Mother stilled. She took a few deep breaths, regaining her composure, and finally looked up at me once more. "You've changed."

I shrugged uncomfortably. "I suppose I'm taller now."

She gave me a small, sad smile. "Of course. And how did you get here, if not with your father?"

The weight of the journey I'd taken crashed down upon me. How could I even begin to explain that I'd been ordered to kill the sleeping princess without first explaining Miranda and Alaric— and why I'd run away from Father and the Mundane in the first place? My entire life had been upended in a matter of days.

"It's too complicated a story," I said. "But Shale ordered me here to *kill* you—and if I don't succeed, they'll kill Father."

"They have Joren?" she said in dismay.

I heard a throat clear and turned to see Miranda in the doorway, her eyes wide. "You woke her," she said to me. "I wasn't sure you'd be able to."

Mother raised her knife. "And you are?"

"Miranda," she replied. "Is it true, what the story says? That you're going to liberate the forest from Shale and Katen and end the Gather?"

Mother lifted a hand. "Wait. One moment. So Shale and Katen still rule the Gather?"

Miranda nodded.

"And are they chasing you? Is there a reason to suspect an attack is imminent?"

"Wolves were after us, outside the castle. They saw us enter. So . . ."

"Soon," Miranda said, finishing my sentence. "When Shale learns we didn't die by the briars, or kill you, they will surely come."

Mother nodded, her face resolute. "And how *did* you both get past the briars?"

"I spilled blood before them," I said.

Her expression was stricken. "Oh no, Lena . . ." To my surprise, she began to cry. "You were never meant to come here. How did this happen?"

I stared at her, the painful sting of her abandonment and betrayal searing through me anew. Fury rose within me. "*You* made all of this happen!" I cried. "You and Father chose to save yourselves over me, and then you lied to me about what the curse even was. You made me believe I was a monster, and then you *left* me."

"What are you talking about, Lena? Father and I chose to save *you*. I—"

I cut her off. "I don't want any more tales. Tell me the truth. Tell me what really happened when Katen cursed me. Tell me why you left."

She exhaled slowly. Then she addressed Miranda. "Would you mind leaving us? I owe my daughter an explanation."

"Of course," Miranda replied, clearly more than a little awed by this turn of events. She glanced at me. "I'll be right downstairs."

Once she was gone, Mother looked at me. "Before I begin— please, please believe that I always meant to come back to you."

I rolled my eyes, and was gratified by the hurt on her face as she continued. "My family has served the forest—the Silence—for generations. One elder at a time carries the mantle, communicating with the forest spirit and channeling its magic. It's because of this bond that there is such power here. And that power is what drew Shale and Katen to this land.

"They were fleeing whatever crimes they'd committed in their own lands, searching for a refuge here. The forest wouldn't have them. So we wouldn't speak to them either, and neither would the creatures under the forest's protection. Save one." Mother's lips twisted into a scowl.

Alaric's words came back to me, fitting neatly into the tale I was hearing now. "The raven. Alaric," I said.

"You've met him?"

"We've been traveling together. He told me he made a mistake in helping Katen and Shale."

"*Mistake?* He betrayed the forest. My entire family. This castle was once protected—no one could find their way here unless their feet already knew the path. But that *traitor* fashioned a compass. And he gave it to them."

I drew in a sharp breath. Shale's compass—Alaric had built it?

"They wiped out my entire family in an attempt to choke the Silence's power. I only survived because the forest moved the castle and trapped me in this tower, encased in stone and briars before Shale and Katen could get to me too."

I remembered Father reading me a story long ago. *And the princess slumbered for one hundred years, waiting . . .*

"How did you get out?" I asked.

Her face softened, just a touch. "Your father," she said. "I sang in my dreams. I called out to anyone who could hear me. Most couldn't. And of those who could, most perished before getting anywhere near the castle. But your father . . . somehow he convinced the briars to let him through. He woke me."

Was Father somehow . . . magic? He couldn't be a blood mage—the Silence would never have let him enter the castle if that were true. Perhaps the forest had believed it would benefit somehow, though I struggled to see how.

"When I woke, I had nothing. I knew it would only be a matter of time until Shale and Katen found me, so Joren and I ran away. We found a place we thought would be safe, a place without magic." She smiled, lost in memory. "The voice of the Silence couldn't reach into the barren lands. I grew a garden. Joren wrote songs. We were *happy*. Then Shale sent Katen to kill me."

"Why?" I asked. "Why would they care about killing you all the way in the Mundane?" Katen had said my mother had committed treason, but now that I was here, I found that difficult to believe.

"Because I was the last of my family, the last to serve the forest. So if I died, the Silence would die as well."

She met my gaze, and I understood what she wasn't saying. That now she was no longer the last. *I* was here.

"What happened the day Katen came?" I asked.

"I thought she would kill us. Instead, she offered a trade."

"Me for your lives," I said bitterly, remembering what Katen had said.

"*Our* lives. You must understand," Mother said, taking my hands in her own. "We didn't know I was pregnant yet. And we didn't know whether Katen's spell would work in a land without magic—we took a chance. Sadly, it didn't pay off."

"And then you left me when things got too rough," I said, growing impatient.

"No. After what happened with that boy, I knew I had to come back. To find a way to break the Hand of Mora."

I snatched myself away from her, suddenly furious. "You let me believe my whole life that I was cursed!"

"You *were* cursed. And we thought we were doing the right thing."

"By leaving me?" I was starting to cry again, and I hated it.

She sighed. "I left to save you, Lena. I believed I'd be back within a season, that it would never matter that you'd been cursed, because by then the curse would be broken. I had no idea it would be ten years."

"What happened then?"

"I came into the Silence to kill Katen. But during our battle, the Silence took me prisoner. It sensed my presence the moment my blood hit the earth. It dragged me to the castle once more and forced me back to sleep. I've been calling for help ever since. But no one came. Until you."

She'd been calling since she'd been trapped . . . and for years before. . . . Realization hit me, and I gasped. "It was you!" All those people bewitched by the Silence, doomed to die by the briars or by the villagers' mercy—they'd all been answering her call. "Do you have any idea how many bodies hang in the briars? You lured innocent people to their deaths!"

"I did what I had to do. Much as I'm sure you did," she said pointedly.

I flushed, looking away.

"Now it's your turn to explain how you came here. But first, tell me—what bargain did you make with the Silence?"

"The Silence offered me power in exchange for blood, offered of my own free will. What is so wrong with that?"

She tilted her head as she studied me. "Nothing, except the price you pay," she said slowly. "Did you make a vow to serve it too?"

"No," I said, surprised she knew about the vow. "Not yet."

"Good. Now come. I will show you the price of such a vow."

I followed her reluctantly out of the tower, down the stairs, out into the light. She led me across the courtyard to the building covered in greenery and lifted a curtain of ivy, inviting me inside.

It was only one room, a cool open space that smelled of damp earth and wild roses. Ivy covered the windows, leaving everything in shadow. Mother stooped to remove her shoes, and I did the same, dropping my boots by the door. The floor was earthen, and my toes dug into the dirt as I walked, bringing to mind childhood days spent in our garden, lazing among the sweetheart buttons my mother had coaxed into bloom.

There was something else here too—a presence waking after a long, long slumber. I felt it stir as Mother led the way to a pit at the center of the room and started down a staircase that descended into the darkness. I followed her.

When my eyes adjusted, I saw that we had come to a vast underground chamber. Its ceiling was supported by enormous tree roots that glowed with blue pulsing veins. There were at least twenty of them spread about the cavern . . . and at the base of each one was a body. Many of these bodies appeared to belong to elders, people who had lived long and full lives. But a few were young— my mother's age, even mine.

"I've seen this before," I said, staring. "We encountered a cave like this on our way here."

Mother nodded. "Then you saw the first girl who served. There are many stories about the origin of the Silence. What we are certain of is that many generations ago, a girl traveled this way, back when it was simply a forest. She met with ill fortune on the road and died violently. When her blood soaked into the earth, the spirit of the Silence awoke. That was the body you saw."

She doesn't know, said the Silence. **She tried to reject me— she never saw what truly happened to that girl.**

I jumped, trying to keep my focus on my mother's words.

"I'm guessing the forest is speaking to you right now? Calling me a liar?" she said, watching me carefully.

"Yes," I said reluctantly.

"Then hear this now. The spirit of the Silence is malevolent and sly. Once it was awake it needed the sacrifice of human blood to keep its consciousness alive. My family—our family—struck a bargain with it. Service and sacrifice, in exchange for the powers of the forest." She waved a hand at the bodies around her. "Once you become the elder, you do not leave the forest. When you die, your life force goes into its service. Sometimes even that isn't enough. The forest is capricious and inhuman—at times it has even demanded an elder die before their time. So you see—you've been cursed by a blood mage, and that is a terrible burden. But do not make the mistake of thinking that a bargain with the Silence will save you."

The Silence had *killed* those people?

Some, yes. Their lives served the forest. They kept us *alive*.

I saw the fear in her eyes. "You didn't run just because of Shale and Katen, did you? When Father woke you all those years ago?"

She shook her head. "There is always a price to pay for power. *Always.*"

And sometimes, it is worth it. . . . The Silence said, tracing its way through my mind.

Mother continued. "The power of the Silence can be . . . overpowering." She looked across the cavern, her gaze resting on each body in turn. "All the elders of my family lie here now, their spirits feeding the forest." She turned to me. "I didn't want to serve, not like the rest of my family. When I was the only one left, I refused to take the vow. I wanted a better life than this. For myself *and* for you. That is why I ran. And in the end, it made little difference.

"I've spent the last ten years a prisoner as the Silence tried to force me to take the vow. It won." She looked down at her hands. "I am the elder of the Silence now. But I don't want that for you. I know the forest has spoken to you, done things for you. But over time, the weight of the spirit bearing down upon you—if you are unprepared—can crush you. The wisps of power you've been able to call so far are nothing compared to what the Silence can truly do."

"Then what would you have *me* do?"

"You are not yet irrevocably bound. Its voice will not follow you past the forest borders. You can still leave it behind. You should go now, while you can."

"But what about Father? If I run, Shale and Katen will kill him!"

"He would say the same thing," Mother said firmly. "We have given up everything to keep you away from here—from Shale and Katen *and* the Silence. Don't throw away our sacrifice."

I sat back. "What if that's not what I want?"

"You are young. You'll learn—freedom is worth so much more than power."

"But I'm *not* free," I said. "I never will be—not unless I can defeat Katen. Which I cannot do without power. You know them. Tell me I'm wrong. Tell me there's another way."

She said nothing. We both knew there was no other way to free myself from the curse, and still she would forbid it.

I stood up, unable to speak through my rage. Instead I left her alone in the chamber of my ancestors and ran back up toward the light of day.

CHAPTER THIRTY

Miranda was waiting outside, but I couldn't even look at her for fear of what might come spewing out of me if I did. I flew past her, as though if I ran fast enough, I could outrun this fury.

The castle grounds weren't large, but over the years vines and briars and trees had grown up, breaking stones and tearing walkways apart to create a veritable maze. I ran through it with no objective but to outrace the stabbing pain in my chest. Everything was too much, every lie my parents had told me, everything about my history that had been kept from me. The impossible choice that now lay before me.

I stumbled over tree roots and around vines and found myself eventually in a smaller courtyard hidden from the outer gardens. And there, standing with his hands clasped behind his back, was Alaric.

"You!"

He didn't retreat as I stormed up to him and pushed him hard in the chest. "You knew! You knew my mother was here the whole time, and you said *nothing!*"

"I'm sorry," he said. "I cannot speak on the secrets of the Silence with those who do not already know them. And you did not."

Hot tears spilled down my cheeks. "So you just *let* me walk in there completely unprepared, you—you monster! What were you going to do if I didn't recognize her—let me kill my own mother?"

I would have struck him had someone not caught my wrist from behind. Miranda wrapped her arms around me, and I began to sob, burying my face in her neck.

"I'm so angry," I whispered. "They knew what the curse really was, and they didn't tell me. No one told me about our family's ties to the Silence. Father fed me lies and let me think that my own mother had walked out on us, on *me*—"

"I know," said Miranda. "I know."

I dissolved into tears once more. It was an old wound, my mother's disappearance. I'd thought it was well healed over—most days, I didn't think of it at all. But seeing her now had torn it open all over again. She'd lied—she'd lied, and then she'd left me. In this moment, despite Shale and Katen bearing down on us and the horrible truth of the Silence's cruelty, nothing else seemed to matter as much as this.

Alaric's hand came down on my shoulder, and I flinched—but he left it there, a steady presence as I wept in Miranda's arms.

Gradually, the world knit itself back together. I slowly became aware of myself again, my body, my tears, my flushed cheeks. Then Miranda's arms around me, comforting and warm. Then Alaric's hand and the ground under my feet, the tree roots sprawling across the courtyard. The earth, the sky.

I pulled back from Miranda and wiped away my tears.

"I'm so sorry," Alaric said, a catch in his throat.

"You didn't tell me the whole truth of your history. You said only that you were tricked into service—not that you had betrayed the Silence. My mother's family."

He looked away. "I was ashamed. For one hundred years I have been made to live alongside the constant reminder of my worst act, the first thing I would take back, if only I were able. I never lied to you. I only sought to protect old wounds."

"You should have done better," Miranda snapped.

I took a deep breath, then another. The betrayal caused by Alaric's omissions stung. But I couldn't help but think of how he'd run into the lake to save Miranda. How he'd hidden me from Katen as long as he could. Did those acts merit a second chance? I thought of Miranda, too. I had been right to forgive her. So what did my instincts say about Alaric now?

I turned around to face him. "I understand why you made certain choices," I said slowly. "But don't do this to me again. *Please.*"

Alaric nodded soberly.

"You're just going to let him off?" Miranda said, indignant.

"*Everyone* makes mistakes, don't they?" I said. She sighed, but didn't protest.

Alaric smiled—and then winced.

"What's wrong?" I asked.

"Katen," he said through clenched teeth. "She's calling me."

"No!"

He looked at me in anguish. "I must go. I'm sorry."

My chest hurt. The next time we met, we would be on opposite sides, and there was nothing I could do to stop it.

He turned to walk away. I bit my lip and reached into my pocket. "Wait, Alaric!" I held out the box.

Alaric looked down, puzzled—then understanding dawned in his eyes. "Is this—"

"Yes," I said. "I wronged you, before. And I swear I will right it. I'll find a way to get close enough to Katen to free you."

He pulled me into a tight hug, releasing me before I could react. "Keep them safe," he said. Then he launched himself into the sky.

"That's what this was about?" Miranda said, once he had gone. "His freedom?"

"Both of ours," I said. After everything that had happened, keeping this secret from Miranda seemed impossible. "We made a bargain. I would get his wings and free him from Katen, and he would kill her for me." I looked down. "But it hasn't quite gone to plan."

"That's an understatement."

I let out a small, mirthless laugh. For a moment we stood in silence.

"Are you all right?" she said finally.

My shoulders slumped. "I don't know. I thought I knew what we were up against when we came here. Now . . . I don't know."

There was a bench in the corner of the courtyard. Miranda took my hand, leading me to sit down on the mossy stone. "Did you know anything about your family being connected to the Silence?"

I shook my head. "Before today, all I knew about my mother was that she left."

"What do you want to do?" she said softly.

"I can't kill my own mother for Shale. But I can't abandon my father to be killed either."

"Perhaps there's another option."

I looked at her blankly. "What?"

"The story about the sleeping princess and the Silence . . . and the fall of the Gather. You hold Katen's magic inside of you— perhaps there's a way to use it against her, now that you and the Silence are . . . working together."

Images of the chamber below the castle flashed through my mind. It was difficult to reconcile everything my mother had shown me. She had meant to impress upon me the grotesque nature of our family's service to the Silence—the horrific price they had all agreed to pay. And I had felt uneasy at the sight of those bodies, especially the ones who had died because the Silence had demanded their sacrifice. They were my mother's ancestors—*my* ancestors—even though I'd never known them. But they had agreed to all of this— to their service, to becoming the heartbeat and the engine of the Silence. Was that so high a price to pay for the power that came with it? And . . . there were only two of us left.

"If I vow to serve the Silence, I could forfeit my own life. It could overpower me."

Miranda nodded. "It might . . . but you also carry Katen's magic within you, and yet you do not have blood plague. Your family has ties to the forest—that must be what gives you the strength to withstand it. Surely that means you are strong enough to hold your own against the Silence."

Her confidence made me smile, and for the first time since arriving at the castle, since learning the truth about my mother, I felt hope.

Yes . . . listen to your wise friend.

When you offered your bargain, you left out the part about how you might one day decide to kill me.

We only have the two of you left, the Silence said plaintively. **We would not lose either of you if we could help it.**

That was not particularly comforting. *You only want me because you would die without me.*

We want to live, the Silence said. **Isn't that what you want as**

well? What you've always wanted? My power needs a vessel. You could be that vessel. You would not die by our hand.

I believed it now. That despite its inhuman nature, it knew how close it had come to the brink of death—whatever death meant to a forest made conscious. And Miranda was right—I was stronger than I'd ever dreamed of becoming. I'd entered the Silence to break my curse, and I would. I would not run. My mother only knew me as small and helpless. I would prove to her—to everyone—that I was strong enough to wield the Silence's power without being overpowered.

I found my mother sitting in a corner of the garden. It occurred to me, watching her now, that I didn't know her at all. She had always been prickly, while my father had always been the one to offer a kind word or a sweet, and I'd quickly learned to go to him for small comforts. Now, seeing her battle worn and weary, I wondered what I'd missed by virtue of being too young to see things for what they truly were.

Now I noticed the ways in which the forest was attuned to her. A tree root had risen out of the earth to form the seat upon which she perched, and the tree she leaned back against had burst into bloom—no matter that it was late autumn.

She looked up as Miranda and I approached. I couldn't read the expression on her face. "You two should leave tonight," she said. "I'll open the briars so you can get through, and I'll give you cover as long as I can. Once Shale and Katen realize I'm awake, they'll forget about you. The farther you are from this place, the safer you'll be until this is over."

"No," I said firmly. "I'm not going to run. I can't live like this anymore. I'm going to kill Katen and put an end to the Gather myself, whether or not you help me."

Mother threw her hands up. "I am trying to protect you!" She got to her feet, clenching her fists. "There may be fairy stories about heroics and battles and quests, but they say nothing about the true cost of victory," she said, her voice shaking. "Do you know why? Because in real life, the chosen one doesn't always win. Sometimes they end up in the dust, choking on their own blood. I can't promise you victory. Ten years ago I tried to be a hero and almost died."

I recoiled. "But—what about the Silence? What about Father?"

She shook her head. "The Silence takes more than it gives. I am not as powerful as Shale and Katen together. But I can hold them off long enough for you to get away. And your father would want you to run. He'd rather you live a long and happy life than sacrifice everything for him."

She pushed past me, but I caught her by the arm. "I don't care what you say, I'm *not* leaving. This is as much my fight as it is yours. Now, you can waste more time arguing, or you can help us."

Mother looked down at my hand, then up into my eyes. Whatever she saw there made her turn away. "All right," she said quietly. "In that case, there is something I need to teach you."

She addressed Miranda. "Could you see if you can find any weapons left in the castle?"

"I can do that," Miranda said, leaving the two of us standing together.

Mother held out her arms. "Now take my hands."

I did as she asked. She closed her eyes, and I cautiously followed suit. My breathing slowed to match hers, and I could feel my pulse growing calm. Energy gathered in the air around us, a swift current clamoring for release.

"The Silence responds to bloodletting, yes," I heard her say. "But if you are fully bonded to it, you can call its power without such crude tactics. Open your eyes."

I did so, and gasped. The world had gone black, as though I stared into a void. The Silence's presence here was so overwhelming, it pushed at the edges of my consciousness, pressing me toward the ground. I could feel that I was being observed, an insect on a pin. Somewhere in the darkness, my mother began to speak.

"My mother taught me how to protect myself against the storm of the Silence, and now I will teach you. The key is to choose three talismans to use as an anchor, to keep from being swept away. They needn't be precious—as long as they are precious to you," she said softly. "For the past ten years, mine were one of your father's shoes, the first flower that my great grandmother helped me grow . . . and the cloak I made for you. As long as I kept my mind focused entirely on those things, I would remember who I was.

"You choose now. You needn't tell me what they are."

I was suddenly struck by the fear of choosing wrong. I'd spent so much of my life plagued by uncertainty and doubt. What if I still didn't know who I was?

You do, I told myself firmly. *You are the girl who faced down the dragons. Who chose a girl with eyes like starlight and a mischievous grin. Who knows her heart. You can do this.*

My cloak. Strange that my mother and I shared this talisman, and that it was the first that came to my mind. My gloves—they

had protected me my whole life. And . . . Miranda's net. The promise of a better future.

"Have you chosen?"

"Yes."

"Now we grow."

We knelt to the ground. Hands on the earth, and I could *feel* its
life around me, the green potential of it. Mother hummed a little,
and I felt an eager surge of energy move through my body, seeking
release. It was too much—I couldn't catch my breath—

"Your anchors!"

Cloak. Gloves. Net. *Miranda.*

The energy ripped out of my chest and down my arms, out
through my fingers. A sprout emerged from the earth, glowing a
faint green. It pushed our hands apart, growing faster, taller. I fell
back as it became a shoot, a sapling, a tree.

"Anything the Silence grows, you can call into being. Anything
within the Silence's domain, you hold power over. If you must use
the forest, remember this."

My mother sagged to the ground, her hands falling from mine.

"Are you all right?" I asked.

She didn't respond as she pushed herself slowly back to her
knees. "Now you know something of what it feels like to be a con-
duit for the Silence's energy. It is immense power, but it can go
wrong so quickly." She set her palm against my chest, just below
the collarbone. "To wield the power of the Silence without losing
yourself, you must remain grounded. Anchors keep you rooted.
Without them, the Silence can twist you so easily." She rubbed her
arm absentmindedly.

"Did you . . . did you ever speak to the girl? The one who woke the Silence?" I asked, feeling almost silly for asking.

Mother looked at me sharply. "No," she said. "There is no girl to speak to. There is only the Silence—its power, and its corrupting spirit."

Tricks. Boundaries. Weakness, hissed the Silence.

She got to her feet and brushed dirt from her coat. "Now I've shown you power, and I've shown you the evil at its heart. Are you *certain* that you want to stay?"

"Yes," I said without hesitation.

She sighed. "Then promise me one thing. Do not take the vow. Not yet. Not while I can protect you."

I swallowed, hard. Then I nodded.

"Thank you," she said.

Miranda was sitting at the foot of the stairs to the tower, her head bent over her knees. A pile of rusty-looking weapons lay beside her. She looked up as we approached and jumped to her feet, her hands diving into her coat pockets.

Mother looked up at the sky. "You should get some rest."

"But isn't there more to do?" Miranda said.

"You need sleep in order to face Shale and Katen. We still have some time. The Silence will wake me if their arrival is imminent," Mother said.

"What about you?" I said.

She placed a tentative hand on my shoulder. "I've been sleeping for the last ten years. I don't need rest."

She started up the stairs.

"Wait!" I said.

She looked back at me, her face already distant. I didn't know how to put my emotions into words, so I said the first thing that popped into my head. "Do you think there's any fresh clothing here?"

She pointed to one of the halls leading off the entryway. "There are a few storerooms through there."

With that she turned and kept climbing, leaving Miranda and me alone.

The storeroom, while covered in thick layers of dust and cobwebs, still boasted a serviceable array of clothing in chests. We found trousers a little too long, and a shirt a little too large, as well as a number of sheets that we grabbed and lugged back through the hall and into a small bedchamber.

Miranda gravitated toward one corner of the room while I stripped off my gown, which was very much worse for the wear. The easy companionship we'd established during our journey to the castle had evaporated—indeed, this was the first time we had been alone together since Fallyne's house. Now Miranda sat stiffly on the low bed like she expected to be called to attention. I too found myself ill at ease. I sat down next to her. For a while we stared out at nothing in particular.

"How are you?" she said finally.

"Marvelous. Couldn't be better," I said sarcastically, drawing my knees up to my chest.

After a pause, she offered, "You look a little like her."

"My mother is a beauty fit for the legends written about her. I don't compare."

"Don't be silly," Miranda said. She placed a hand on my cheek, her gaze even. "You have the same face. Strong. And you are beautiful in your own right."

My heart warmed, just a little. "How are you? It's been so

overwhelming. I should have asked you before. I'm sorry."

"I didn't expect you to be some mysterious wielder of the Silence's powers, but overall, I think I'm doing quite well. Under the circumstances." Miranda winked at me.

I shuddered. "Let's not talk about that. Please?"

"All right. Then what?"

I reached for her hands, weaving our fingers together. *Anything.* "After," I said firmly. "What will you do, once Shale and Katen have fallen?"

Miranda's lips parted in surprise. "I—I hadn't really thought about it," she said sheepishly.

"Me either," I admitted. "Would you . . . go back? For Callie?"

"Maybe," she said, biting her lip. "Though after what we saw in the Gather . . . I don't think she can be saved anymore."

She squeezed my hand. "For a long time my dream was to be free of the Gather. Now I think I'm ready to dream something new."

Now I was the one to look away, for fear of betraying what passed behind my eyes.

"Don't do that," Miranda said. "Don't look away." She raised my chin with two fingers and pressed a careful kiss to the corner of my mouth.

I froze, my skin burning where she had touched me.

She kissed me again. My lips parted against hers, and my eyes fluttered shut. I felt raw and vulnerable. So much of what I knew about the world had been stripped away, and yet she made me feel safe amid the chaos. I reached under her shirt and settled one hand softly on her hip. My breathing hitched at the feel of her skin, the nearness of her.

I brought my free hand up to frame her face, then cupped the back of her neck. I pulled her closer, deepening the kiss.

The last time we'd kissed had been all eagerness and heat, and that passion was still there. But this time there was an undercurrent of darkness—the shadow of what was to come—and it made everything sharper. For so long I'd only wanted not to die. Now I wanted to live—with her. And it terrified me that I might not get that chance.

We melted clumsily into the sheets on the floor, her arms around me, my fingers tangled in her hair, her hands tracing my spine. We threw off our clothes and lay breast to breast, and I could feel her heart pounding almost as fast as mine.

I shivered and Miranda laughed, then raised herself up on one elbow. Her hair fell over her face, and I lifted a hand to tuck it back behind her ear, reveling in the sensation of such a simple, marvelous touch. She caressed my cheek, then leaned down and kissed me again. Her hand drifted to my collarbone, feathered over my breast before coming to rest low on my stomach.

She hesitated, pulling back and looking down at me. "Do you want—"

"Yes," I said instantly, reaching up to her face as her fingers dipped lower. *Yes. Yes. Yes.*

CHAPTER THIRTY-ONE

I woke with my back pressed against Miranda's breasts and stomach, our legs tangled up together. It was fully night now. For a moment I wasn't sure what had woken me. Miranda's breath tickled my ear, but that wasn't it. What had it been?

There—someone was speaking, their voice muffled by distance.

I slid carefully out from under Miranda's arm and picked through the darkness for my clothes, feeling dazed. My head was full to bursting with thoughts of Miranda—her hair, her lips, her hands. She was a fire that enveloped me until I happily burned. Of all the things I had dreamed up for myself, I had never imagined *this*. The way everything had felt not just pleasurable, but *right*. Like there was a secret that only we shared, like I wanted to spend today and tomorrow and the next day doing anything at all, as long as it was with her. I felt . . . clarity. And pure, unadulterated happiness.

After jumping haphazardly into my trousers and dragging my shirt over my head, I crept barefoot across the hall to the stairs. The muffled voice grew clearer as I climbed, resolving into the familiar dry tone of someone I knew. Alaric had returned.

I peeked around the open doorway of the tower to see him standing in a corner of the room, opposite my mother. "How dare you use my daughter for your own foolish plots," she snapped.

"I saw—"

"You saw *nothing*," she said. "You did *nothing*."

"And I've paid the price for over a hundred years," Alaric said wearily. His hair was bedraggled, and he had deep, dark circles under his eyes. He looked . . . haggard. What had happened while he was away? "Listen to me, Edina. I am not here to stand against you. I am here because I care about Lena. And I am here to tell you—they will be here in the morning. And they are bringing Joren."

Father?

Mother's shoulders hunched as she swore. I stepped into the room. "Is he all right?"

Mother looked up. "Lena, you startled me!"

"Sorry," I said. "Are you all right?" I asked Alaric.

He grimaced. "I've been better. She will call me back soon. When she forces me to attack . . . it will be impossible to go against her." He looked at me. "It would be prudent to finish what we started."

"I will try," I said, thinking of the box tucked safely in my cloak pocket.

"Then I must leave," he said. "We should not risk me overhearing what you plan."

He turned to Mother. "I am sorry for what is to come."

I suddenly realized that the next time I saw him would be on a battlefield—and that I might never speak to him again.

"Everything is going to be fine. You're going to be fine," I said, hoping it was the truth.

He smiled briefly. And then he stepped back, launched himself up into the air, and was gone.

My mother watched me, a sour look on her face. "If you think he is for you—"

"Don't," I said sharply. "You don't know what you're talking about."

"Fine," she said. She turned back to the window.

Was that it? "What about Father?" I said. "If they're bringing him here, they must mean to use him somehow. Do you have a plan? He will be in danger!"

She stiffened. "Lena, your father is not my priority."

"How can you say that?" I cried.

She whirled around, her eyes angry and bright. "It's likely they're bringing him because they hope to threaten me into bringing down the briar walls. But those walls are our best defense. They have kept the castle and its inhabitants safe for generations. I will not drop them."

"But can't you do something else? What about the Silence? Can you use its power to save him?"

She only looked at me. "What I am going to do is defend you. At the right time, I will attack Shale and Katen. But I can't risk everything to walk into an obvious trap."

"So you're just going to let him *die*?" I said, my voice cracking.

"The right path is not always the easiest."

"The right path is to save my father's life! I need you to tell me how we're going to do that."

Mother's shoulders slumped. "Oh, my girl. I'm sorry. I can't."

I turned around and fled down the stairs. I flung myself down on a bench in the courtyard, tears flooding my eyes. This was my fault. If I hadn't come into the Silence, we would still be in the Mundane. Father would be safe.

And now . . .

Why do you listen to her? You have the power to make change at your beck and call.

I couldn't help but picture the girl who'd been murdered as I heard the Silence speak. *But who are you, exactly?* I asked. *The girl, or the Silence?*

We were the girl. Now we are the forest. We are both—and so too can you be.

That was not reassuring. I tried not to dwell on it as I went back down to Miranda and gently shook her awake. She smiled at me sleepily, but her expression grew grave as she saw the look on my face. "What's wrong?"

"Shale and Katen are coming. They have my father with them. And my mother refuses to act."

"Why?"

I shrugged. "I don't know. Because she's afraid? She said that she won't open the briar walls. That it's a trap."

"I see," she said. "And what do you think?"

I scowled at the ground. "Of course it's a trap. But I don't know what else to do. They're going to kill him."

"Maybe we can rescue him. You and me."

Her words were unexpected—I clung to them like a lifeline. "Really?"

She grinned at me. "Your mother may be the sleeping princess of the Silence, but I came here for *you*. Hers aren't the orders I intend to follow."

I took her hand and threaded my fingers through hers. "It's going to be dangerous."

"My goodness," she said, blinking innocently at me. "I had no idea."

I laughed. "I might be able to convince the briars to let us out, but I don't know what will happen next. How can we possibly hope to defeat whoever we encounter out there?"

I pushed aside the thought of the Silence, for now. The idea of somehow being subsumed into the Silence's consciousness . . . it was one I didn't relish.

"My magic?" Miranda said. "Though I must confess I've been exhausted over the last few days. I don't know how much I'm good for."

"I wasn't watching earlier. Did you injure the Wolves with the fire you made?"

She nodded.

"And *I* have all of Katen's magic bound up in my blood," I said slowly. "What if . . . what if you used it?"

Her eyes lit up. "I'd love to." She sounded practically gleeful at the thought of stealing magic from Katen.

"I don't know what forces Shale and Katen will have with them. But there must be enough power for us to defeat some Wolves—or at least distract them, and get to my father. Then we'll deliver him somewhere safe . . . and go back for Katen."

"All right," Miranda said.

I looked at her for a long moment, memorizing her features. Then I leaned forward and pressed my forehead against hers. "Thank you for being with me through this."

She kissed me quickly—a hope for things to come. "Let's go. If they're already on their way, we don't want to be caught off guard."

The tower where I had left my mother was now dark. I stared up at the window, wondering if she was asleep—and if not, what she was thinking. She would stop me from doing this if I told her,

I was certain. She had objected so strongly to any suggestion of opening the briars.

Still, guilt twinged uncomfortably through me as I took Miranda's hand and crept through the courtyard back toward the moat.

The bridge of thorns that I'd made was still there, but I was reluctant to trust that it would behave if I set foot on it. Instead, Miranda and I found the ropes for the drawbridge.

The bridge creaked as we lowered it. I couldn't decide if I would rather go faster—and louder—or slower, prolonging the agony. By the time it was down, my heart was racing. We ran across it as though it might collapse underfoot, and it was only when we faced the wall of briars once more that my thoughts caught up with the situation at hand.

The briars had parted for me before. I was determined that they would do so again. For a moment I considered using the anchors that Mother had taught me—then I thought better. I'd never done it on my own, and I preferred not to take unnecessary risks. In the darkness, I took out my knife and drew it across the back of my other arm. The pain of this act had lessened—or I was becoming accustomed to it. I turned my arm and let the blood fall to the earth.

The vines reached toward me hopefully. I stepped back, out of their way. *Let us pass.*

Wind blew through the castle grounds, and the brambles slowly peeled away, revealing the stone pathway beneath.

"Here we go," Miranda said under her breath, holding her knife steady. She squeezed my hand, and we stepped onto the path.

It was still dark when we arrived on the outside of the briar wall, but I could hear the forest shifting in the night. Something was moving out there—the Silence, yes. But there was more.

If Miranda conjured a light, we risked drawing attention to ourselves. Suddenly every sound was sinister, every vague movement in the dark was an enemy rising up against us. How could I have thought that I could do this?

Use me.

This time I didn't hesitate. I dragged my knife over my skin, brushed my fingers against the wound, and pressed my hand to the earth.

The forest illuminated around me. I gasped. I could sense *everything*—the swaying trees, the vines thrashing. There was no path around us, only forest grown so thick it seemed almost impossible to traverse. But beyond that . . . I closed my eyes, feeling the roots vibrate under the weight of a large force moving in our direction.

I opened my eyes. "Shale," I whispered to Miranda. "He's here."

CHAPTER THIRTY-TWO

My consciousness bled into the Silence—through the roots, the earth, the very blades of grass crushed below the feet of the mages. I felt the paw prints of dozens of Wolves, a contingent of other humans, and . . . deep grooves in the earth that told of a cart carrying heavy cargo. What was Shale bringing through the Silence?

Whatever it was, it was too large to break through the thickets and underbrush closest to the castle walls. I could hear crashing sounds as the party fought against the trees.

I relayed what I'd learned to Miranda, who gripped my hand hard. "Lena . . . that sounds like an army. The cart probably holds blood carriers."

She was frightened, I realized. She didn't think that we could go up against such a force.

Perhaps she was right. Perhaps we *were* outnumbered, regardless of what power we could muster. It seemed the time had come for desperate measures. I dug Rin's pebble out of my pocket and pricked my finger, letting my blood coat the stone.

Nothing happened.

Feeling more than a little foolish, I whispered, "I woke the sleeping princess. And if you want the chance to kill Shale . . . the time is now."

Miranda looked down at the pebble. "What is that? Who are you calling?"

"Someone from Haven," I said. "But it's a long shot. I don't know if they'll come. We need to keep moving."

"Lena . . . I don't know if we have a chance of killing Shale."

I didn't know either, if I was being honest. I took a deep breath. "I don't think we have much of a choice at this point," I said.

She nodded. Then she grabbed the collar of my shirt and pulled me to her, kissing me fiercely. "For luck," she said.

"For luck," I repeated breathlessly. I took her hand, and we started to move.

Shale's party was carrying torches, making it easy to mark them as Miranda and I crept through the forest. They also seemed completely unconcerned about the noise they were making. And why should they be? They knew we were expecting them. Shale surely expected my mother to do what she had before and stay safely ensconced within the briar walls. Miranda and I hid behind a large boulder, close enough to observe the army Shale had amassed.

Wolves were at the head of the party, followed by Shale and Katen. After them came Alaric and a group of blood mages, some of whom I thought I recognized from the revel. Last came a cart pulled by horses with coats so dark, they blended into the night. The cart carried at least thirty humans chained together, and it was driven by . . .

"Callie," Miranda whispered. Callie, holding reins in one hand and a whip in the other.

Miranda gripped my hand tightly as the cart rolled past us, and I saw there was another person chained to the back of the cart. Father.

Shouts rose from the front of the party. It seemed that the forest was so thick here, they couldn't bring the cart any farther. As we watched, the cart slowed to a stop. Four Wolves stayed with the cart—the rest moved forward. I heard shouts and crashes as Shale's army cut through the forest and out of sight, toward the castle.

My pocket was suddenly uncomfortably warm. I reached in and pulled out the pebble, which scorched my fingers. I bit back a surprised yelp of pain and dropped it to the ground—and heard a soft voice whisper, "Lena?"

"Rin?" I knelt down next to the pebble.

"Tell me," she said without preamble.

"Shale, Katen, and a small army of blood mages have marched on the castle of briars," I said quickly. "The princess is awake. If you intend to take a stand against him, the time is now."

There was silence.

"Are you sure about this?" Miranda whispered.

I wasn't sure of anything anymore. I shook my head.

A small circle opened in the air before me. It whirled and widened until it was as tall as me. Through it I caught a glimpse of a pit of fire—and then I fell back as a small group stepped through.

Rin and Tadrik stood there before us, leading a band of five others. A wave of relief washed through me.

"You called *Rin?*" Miranda said, baffled. ". . . How?"

"There's no time," I whispered back. "Thank you for coming," I said to Rin.

"What's the plan?" Rin replied, ignoring Miranda.

"We don't have much of one yet," I confessed. "But they have my father captive. Miranda and I intend to rescue him."

"Without a plan?" Rin said, disbelieving.

"We have the princess," Miranda said defensively. "She will wield the power of the Silence."

Rin and Tadrik exchanged a look. Were they about to abandon us? My stomach clenched at the thought.

Finally Tadrik sighed. "We cannot attack outright—that's a fool's errand. We will have to wait for an opportune moment."

It didn't seem that an opportune moment would ever come, not given how powerful Shale's army was. And soon it would be dawn.

The Silence's pain flared through my mind, followed by its anger. What was happening? I peered around the boulder and saw flickers of light—torches?—in the distance.

Then the scent of smoke reached me, and I realized that the forest was burning.

Rin gestured with her hand, and a window opened up in her palm. Through it we saw that the front of Shale's force had reached the briar walls and set them alight—but the flames were being choked to death by vines. Noxious smoke drifted through the air.

"Do I not have the strongest blood mages in the Gather before me?" Shale cried. Even at a remove, his voice made my skin crawl. "How is it possible that you cannot bring down these briars?"

The mage standing before him muttered something inaudible.

"This is our one chance to finally put an end to the blight of the Silence," Shale hissed. "If you cannot wield your power to its fullest, then you are not worthy of wielding it at all."

Suddenly there was a sword in his hand. He stabbed the mage in the stomach, then jerked the blade up through the mage's chest.

Miranda moaned in fear. The mage collapsed to the ground,

and Shale stumbled back, off balance. When he stood up, I saw red bleeding across the whites of his eyes.

"That goes for the rest of you!" he shouted. "If you do not clear a path to this castle, I will do it myself."

He stalked out of view, and Rin closed her fist. The window disappeared. "He will come back this way," she whispered.

Tadrik held up a hand, gesturing in silence. His group backed away into the forest as Shale came into view, stalking toward the cart. Fury roiled off of him as he ripped open the door and grabbed hold of the chain, yanking the first prisoner to the ground.

No. Oh no.

But there was nothing I could do as he grabbed the person and slit their throat, drinking in the power they held.

Shale let the body fall to the ground. He raised his bloodied hands in the air as sparks gathered at his fingertips. Then he swept his arms down, and the world caught fire.

Flames flowed across the earth, scorching a path toward the castle.

Fire seared through my body, and I dropped to my knees, gasping in pain. The Silence was screaming.

Miranda grabbed my hand. "What is it?" she whispered.

I shook my head, unable to speak.

Shale swung himself up onto the cart next to Callie and snapped his fingers. The cart jerked forward.

"We need to act," the gatekeeper murmured once the cart was out of sight. "He'll kill them all, and once he absorbs all of that power . . ."

"He'll be unstoppable," Miranda said. "How will your mother be able to defeat him?"

Rin looked at her, considering. "Absorbing power is difficult. He will be distracted. Vulnerable."

Tadrik nodded. Then he looked at me. "You said you mean to rescue your father?"

"Yes," I said through clenched teeth. Mother had been right. The pain I felt belonged to the Silence, and the closer I was bound, the closer I would come to being overwhelmed.

Help me.

How?

Wake the vines. Help me put out the flames.

I pressed my palms to the earth. The fire in my bones subsided as vines burst into the air, rushing to smother the nearest flames.

"What *is* that?" said one of the Haven mages.

"The Silence," said Miranda. "It is waking."

Murmurs spread through the group. Miranda knelt at my side. "Can you keep going?"

The sounds of the forest were ringing in my ears, almost drowning out the rest of the world. I closed my eyes, trying to clear my head. "Yes," I whispered. I had to. There was no other way.

Rin looked at us. "We'll follow the cart and attempt to free the prisoners before it's too late."

"We're coming with you," I said, pushing myself to my feet. Whatever else was coming, I had to save Father first.

"All right," said the gatekeeper. He gestured to the Haven mages. Together, we started through the forest toward the castle.

Shale's tracks were not difficult to follow. The path he had burned still smoldered, despite the vines working to put out the fire. The air was smoky and almost unbreathable. As we approached the castle, it became clear that Shale had ordered his entire force to the front, to attack the briar walls directly. Oppressive heat permeated the air. Ahead of us, the forest was still burning.

Something moved on the path in front of us, and I jumped. Rin held up a hand, and we fell back into the trees just as a small figure came stumbling into view.

Miranda darted forward before any of us could move. "Callie!"

The girl still carried the whip that had set her apart from the rest of the blood carriers, but she was breathing hard, and there was a spatter of blood on her cheek. She looked at Miranda, dazed. "What are you doing here?"

"What are you doing with *them?*" Miranda replied.

Callie slid to the ground, coughing. Miranda helped her up and led her from the path into the safety of the trees. Her eyes widened as she took in our group.

I didn't let down my guard. She had betrayed us the last time we had seen her. I was certain she would do it again. "If you so much as breathe the wrong way, I will kill you," I said.

Callie looked back at Miranda, who shook her head.

"Please," Callie said. "He'll kill me if he finds me."

Rin made a disgusted sound. "You didn't seem to have a problem with it when it wasn't *your* neck on the line."

Callie was crying now. Tears spilled down her cheeks, leaving clean tracks through the ash on her face. "It wasn't supposed to be me. I was only meant to drive the cart. I was only doing what I was told—"

"You should never have let it come to this," Miranda said. "It isn't *right.* You know that as well as I do."

Rin leaned toward me. "She's in a bad way," she murmured. "She won't last much longer, no matter what."

Callie glared at us through her tears. "I know that," she said, a touch of arrogance creeping back into her voice. "Don't you think I know that? But—but this is not how it *should* be. I can't go back there to die like this. I *won't*."

"If you want to stay alive, then give us power," Tadrik said, his expression hard. "The magic you carry. Give it to us."

Callie nodded eagerly. "Yes."

Rin knelt at Callie's side. "Give me your hand."

Callie obeyed without protest. Rin dragged a knife across her skin, and Callie winced as blood welled up to the surface of her palm. Miranda took her other hand.

"It's going to be all right," Miranda whispered. Callie leaned toward her, resting her head on Miranda's shoulder.

I looked away. I had to believe that Callie had once been worthy of Miranda's love and loyalty. But I couldn't find it in myself to feel pity for her. She had knowingly transported innocent people to their deaths—it was only now, when she was facing the consequences herself, that she had changed her tune.

A vague wisp of silvery smoke rose into the air. Rin sat back, inhaling the smoke. When she spoke, her voice was hoarse. "Good," she said. "Let's go."

"Wait," I said. "My father was chained to the back of the cart. Do you have the key?"

Callie shook her head. "Not for him." She pulled something out of her pocket and dropped it to the ground. "This is for the rest of them. But he was chained separately."

The gatekeeper grabbed the key from the ground. "This is the best chance we will have to attack Shale and free his victims," he said. "After this, it may be too late."

"I'm ready," I said.

"Me too," Miranda said, surprising me. She looked back at Callie. "Will you be all right here?"

Callie nodded weakly, but as Miranda stood up, she fell back against the ground, gasping in pain.

"Callie!" Miranda was instantly at her side. "What's wrong? Are you injured?"

Black marks swirled across Callie's face as she lifted her hand. Miranda took it between her own, bowing her head.

I met Rin's gaze. "We need to move," she said.

Callie's breathing was becoming more labored as the marks of the plague grew upon her face. "I'm frightened," she whispered, almost too low for me to hear.

"It's all right," Miranda said. "I'm here." She squeezed Callie's hand, tears spilling down her cheeks. My heart ached at the sight. There was so much pain ahead of her. *Pain.*

"Here," I said gruffly, digging the dragon scale out of my cloak. "If you want . . . if you want to be rid of the pain, break this scale. Someone will come for you."

I wasn't sure I was making the right decision, offering her this relief. But she still meant something to Miranda, if not to anyone else.

Callie focused her gaze on me with difficulty. "Break it for me. Please," she rasped.

I looked at Miranda, who nodded jerkily. I snapped the scale in half.

We didn't wait long. A sudden gust of wind rushed through the forest, sending me stumbling forward. I caught myself against a tree trunk and looked up to see the young dragon standing in the center of the group, their nose in the air. Several of Rin's people gasped.

"What is that?" the dragon asked, peering at Callie with interest. "She smells *delicious*."

"She is—dying," I said. "Can you ease her passing? You may take as much of her sadness as you wish."

The dragon bared their fangs in what appeared to be a grin. They sauntered forward and curled their body around Callie's head. Their tail came to rest across her chest.

"What are you doing?" Miranda said, alarmed.

I put a hand on her shoulder. "The dragon is helping," I whispered. "I promise."

I watched as Callie closed her eyes. Her jaw unclenched, and her brow softened, even as her breathing grew more labored, as the marks of blood plague swirled over her face. The marks grew, engulfing her face and spreading down her neck. She coughed, and then choked—and then she lay still.

Miranda pressed her hand to her mouth, stifling a sob.

The dragon's tail recoiled, and they sprawled languorously back against the earth. "You didn't lie, human," they said. "Having an entire memory of painful death to myself . . ." They bared their teeth. "Exquisite."

I remembered the disorientation and confusion I'd felt after my own memory had been taken away. "What if I could offer you more?" I said.

The dragon was instantly alert. "More?"

"Yes," I said, the beginnings of a plan coming together in my mind. "All the memories you could want. Though I must confess that not all of the humans will be willing to give them to you. Some of them may bite."

The dragon flicked their tail, unconcerned. "Human bites are trivial."

"Even mages?" Rin broke in.

"Mages especially," came the reply. "Human magic barely even stings."

"Perfect," I said. "Then—if you don't mind, please don't feed off anyone in this group. We're going on an ambush. I'll fill you in on the way."

"An ambush!" the dragon said. "How delightful!"

The gatekeeper grunted as the dragon jumped to their feet, and shrugged as I looked his way. "The more the merrier, I suppose."

"Indeed," Rin said. "Now, have we finished dallying?"

The Haven mages grouped together once more, leaving the dragon, Miranda, and me standing apart.

"Miranda," I said quietly. "Are you ready?"

She rose to her feet, keeping a generous distance between the dragon and herself. "Yes," she said. "Let's go."

The air grew warmer the closer we got to Shale's army. Once we could hear the sounds of Shale's rampage clearly, the gatekeeper held up his hand, calling us to a halt a good distance from the briar walls.

"The mages and Wolves are up near the castle walls," Rin said, studying the window in her hand. "Shale is the only one near the cart."

"Do you see my father?" I whispered.

"There is a man on the back of the cart," Rin said. "But Shale has already dispatched half of the prisoners. We need to move quickly."

She looked at each of us in turn. "Strike fast, strike hard. Our aim is to free the prisoners and kill Shale. Take down anyone who stands in the way."

Rin and the gatekeeper took their mages and melted into the forest. Miranda gripped my hand tightly.

"Are you all right?" I asked.

"No."

Of course. "I'm sorry. That was a terrible thing to ask."

She nodded. "Later. We can talk . . . later."

"Stay with me?" I said, hoping that my voice didn't betray how afraid I was. This was it. The point of no return.

She looked at me, her expression resolute. "Always."

I kissed her quickly, then turned to the dragon. "There are prisoners chained to a cart out there. Don't touch any of them . . . or the raven wearing the form of a man. Feel free to choose any of the others."

The dragon nodded, their tail flicking.

I pushed up my sleeve and cut shallowly across the back of my arm. "Here," I said to Miranda. "Take as much as you need."

Blood fell to the earth, and I could feel the Silence drinking it down. Miranda touched her hand to my arm, and power rushed into her body. I shuddered as it drained from mine, leaving me feeling light-headed and weak.

Miranda recoiled. "It's so much," she said, her eyes unfocused. "I had no idea how powerful Katen's magic was."

And we were about to go face her. I had no doubt Katen was only pretending to be on her father's side. If she saw me, everything would change.

I put my palm to the ground. My consciousness dropped down into the earth, and I pushed it forward, feeling the wheels of the cart, the feet on the ground around it, the light footsteps of Rin's approach. Beyond them were the wall and the mages, but I tried to hold myself back. One task at a time.

Up ahead of us, there came a shout of anger.

"Let's go," I said. Vines erupted from the earth, wrapping themselves around my arms. I could feel them singing, their desire to grow and spread up my body. I tried to hold on to my anchors, tried to keep myself in one piece. Cloak. Gloves. Net. The vines tightened, and I forced them into the shape I wanted—elongated plant limbs that shielded us as we ran forward.

Chaos was well underway by the time we were close enough to see what was happening. Shale and the mages had managed to burn a wide clearing around the briars. It seemed now that most of the mages and Wolves were occupied with trying to bring down the walls. Shale was standing with the cart, which had stopped at a distance from the briars. I couldn't see Katen or Alaric anywhere.

As we approached, a barrage of clay hands—the gatekeeper's doing—flew through the air, buffeting Shale from all sides. Shale staggered and almost fell, but quickly recovered. He snatched one hand, then another out of the air and crushed them with his fists. The bodies of the blood carriers he'd killed were scattered at his feet.

A portal opened on the other side of the cart, and Rin ran through with the Haven mages. Together they raised their hands, chanting. Shale's body slammed to the ground, and he lay, stunned. Rin ran around to the front of the cart and unlocked the chain linking the remaining prisoners.

I grabbed Miranda's hand. "Let's go!"

We ran to the cart. My father was crouched behind it, trying his best to cover his head.

"Father!" I called.

He looked up. "Lena?" he said incredulously.

Miranda inspected the chain binding his hands to the cart, then shook her head. "I think Shale fused it directly to the cart."

Father coughed. "I don't believe the chain is magic. I'm not a mage—it wouldn't be necessary."

Miranda bit her lip, then nodded. "I'm going to try to break the chain," she said. "Cover for me."

I heard a growl and whirled to see a Wolf running toward me. I lunged forward and grabbed their fur, then pushed them away as they caught fire. My eyes were watering. The world was haze and smoke, the forest thick around us—and somewhere in that smoke and noise were blood mages who meant us only harm.

The dragon raced past me and leapt into the air, flapping their wings as they soared straight at a mage rising up out of the smoke. The mage screamed as the dragon collided with them, and the two disappeared from my view.

A moment later the dragon was up again—the mage stayed down.

I heard something clink behind me and turned to see that Miranda had managed to melt the chain holding my father to the cart. Father rose to his feet, rubbing his wrists. He looked at the scene of destruction around us, his face paling. "We need to run!" he said. "Now!"

"No," I said. I threw my arms around him and felt his surprise before he hugged me back. Then I closed my eyes and called the vines.

They wrapped around his chest before he could react. *Take him away*, I called. *Take him to safety.*

The vines eagerly obeyed.

"Lena, no!" my father cried.

But I couldn't be distracted by thoughts of his safety, not now. I turned to Miranda. "We need to—"

Miranda shoved me hard in the chest, and I fell back as a dark shape swooped low through the air between us. The shape circled, and suddenly Alaric was standing before us. I called the vines back to my arms, readying myself.

Alaric's expression was pained as he unsheathed his sword, his teeth gritted. "Stand aside!" he cried at Miranda.

"No!" Miranda shouted back.

He swung at me. I spun away, lashing at his arms with the vines. Miranda planted herself between us, globes of fire in her palms. "Attack him!" I whispered.

The vines darted forward just as a heavy force slammed into me, and I flew backward. Plants sprang from the earth beneath me, cushioning my landing, but the impact still jarred my hip and arms.

I pushed myself up. Alaric was grappling with the vines, but someone else was running toward me. *Katen.*

Help me, I called.

Thorny vines ripped up from the earth, catching at Katen's skirt and climbing her legs. She cried out, and I could feel the hunger in the vines for *more,* the thorns pricking into her skin, drawing blood—

"Lena!" Miranda grabbed my hand, and the connection was broken.

A Wolf charged at us, snarling—I grabbed their fur, bringing them down. Something flew at our heads and I ducked—Miranda turned, throwing fire. The dragon leapt past me, heading for Katen. . . .

Shouts and cries of agony reached my ears. Something was happening at the briar walls.

I turned to see the briars unknitting, peeling apart. Wolves and mages alike ran, but the briars fell upon them hungrily, coiling around them and squeezing tightly. Blood—there was so much blood—

And from within the briars walked my mother.

CHAPTER THIRTY-THREE

W hat was she doing?

Me, I realized, a shock going through my body. She must have come for me.

Shale screamed in fury, breaking my concentration. I turned to see him grab the last of Tadrik's hands and throw them down. The gatekeeper staggered back, blood trailing down the side of his face. He wiped it away and raised his staff, smearing the blood along its length. The staff glittered and split into a gossamer-like web, and he drew back his hand and threw it. The web flew to Shale and clung to his body, holding him in place.

I looked over at Alaric, who was still working at untangling himself from the vines. Katen was gone—she must have cut herself free. I didn't see the dragon.

Rin sprinted past us, a portal growing in her hands. There was nothing on the other side of it but black emptiness. She arrowed toward Shale, who lifted his foot and drove it down against the ground. The earth cracked and shook, throwing me off my feet—and the web holding him shattered.

He reached out and pulled one sword, then another, from the air.

Rin threw the portal at him—he sidestepped it and slashed straight through it with one sword. The portal collapsed on itself, vanishing as though it had never been. Two, three, four more hands darted at Shale's neck—he didn't even bother dodging them, only cut them down.

I couldn't use the curse against Shale—the only way I could help now was by using the Silence. But as I reached down to draw upon its power, Shale spun, his swords flashing silver—and the gatekeeper crumbled to the ground.

Rin's scream pierced the air. *No!* I looked frantically around the burning battlefield. Two of the Haven mages dragged Rin back, into the forest.

Miranda grabbed my arm, pulling me down behind the cart as Shale strode to the gatekeeper's body and pressed his hand against the bloody wound, drawing out his magic.

"Daughter!" he screamed.

Katen appeared as if out of nowhere, her clothing ripped and bloodied from her encounter with the vines. But she still walked confidently toward her father.

"Here," Shale called, holding out his bloody hand. "Take this magic and *kill* the forest-witch."

He pointed toward the castle—toward my mother, whose briars were devouring the mages around her. She stood in the burned clearing, her face grim.

Katen took her father's hand, drinking in the power he offered. Then she turned around. Shale and Katen strode together toward the castle.

Time slowed. The forest went silent. Katen flicked a finger, and the world caught fire, a blazing thread that snaked down the path and climbed my mother's coat, licking at her throat. My mother shed the coat in an instant and shouted one word. A brutal wind whipped through the air, knocking Katen to the ground and snuffing out the flames.

My mother strode forward through the ashes. "Is that the best you can do?" she shouted across the blackened clearing. She spread her arms wide, inviting attack.

Katen rose to her feet, wiping her sleeve across her cheek. Then she raised her hand. A shadow played over her fingers—and then there was a blur of darkness as a raven shot across the sky—Alaric in flight. With a raucous caw the bird sped toward Mother, trailing a curtain of needle-sharp ice.

Shale sheathed his swords and raised his hands. An acrid scent puckered the air as he let his hands fall open. A blinding bolt of lightning crackled off his palms and arrowed across the clearing. My mother fell to her knees.

I screamed. Katen glanced behind her, searching for me. Shale didn't move as my mother dragged herself to her feet.

Fog spread through the forest, obscuring my vision. And then an endless pour of water fell from the sky, as though someone had taken a lake and upended it on our heads.

It was impossible to see much beyond the tips of our noses as Miranda and I crept forward. A dark shape barreled toward us, knocking Miranda to the ground. She screamed as the Wolf swiped at her with a claw—I pressed my palm to the ground, yanking vines out of the earth. They swarmed the Wolf in an instant and wrestled them down. The earth opened, swallowing them whole.

Yes. More.

I grabbed Miranda's hand and pulled her up. The water was rising, first around our ankles, then our knees. I couldn't see much past the end of my own arm. Where was everyone? What was happening?

Something hit me from behind, and I flew through the air before landing hard. I pushed myself to my feet, coughing up water.

Alaric loomed out of the darkness, his face mournful. "I'm sorry," he said.

A ball of flame flew through the air—he batted it away without even looking. I reached for my knife—he stamped down, pinning my hand to the ground. I screamed, and the earth was alive beneath me—I reached down with my other hand and dug my fingers into the mud. The earth liquefied, and a hole began to open—

But suddenly I was airborne, cradled in Alaric's arms as he flew. "I'm sorry, I'm so sorry. I cannot disobey—I'm sorry—"

"Miranda!" I screamed.

But she was gone, and I was flying to my death.

Call the ravens! commanded the Silence.

I'd never called animals before except for guides. I barely knew what I was doing with the vines. But the Silence said to call them, and so I did—*Bekit! I need you! The Silence needs you!*

Suddenly the rain stopped, and I could see again. Water everywhere as I tried to catch my bearings. Nothing. The only hint of what lay beneath this sudden ocean was a spire that stood stark in the middle of the barren waterscape.

"The tower," Alaric said grimly. "Your mother was wounded—she retreated. They followed her in. Shale and Katen."

Fear washed through me. Was my mother dying? Was that why the Silence hadn't protected her?

We touched down on the tower balcony just as the stone statue toppled and crashed down.

Shale and my mother wrestled on the floor. The tyrant's arm wound around Mother's neck as she struck back with her dagger.

She curled her fingers, and vines burst through the stones to strike at Shale. The tower shook.

I stamped on Alaric's foot and pushed him away. I ran into the tower, ready to attack—and Katen barreled into me. We fell together, her full weight forcing the air from my lungs. I jabbed her with my elbow, catching her in the gut, but could not break free. Katen grabbed my wrist, and pain seared through me, blisters rising on my skin. Briars tore out of the walls, snaking around Katen's arm and yanking her back. I crawled forward, gasping for air.

There was a shadow in the doorway. I turned my head to see Miranda sprint into the tower and leap on Shale's back, flames glowing at her fingertips. Mother threw off Shale and rolled to her feet.

Katen whistled shrilly. Alaric burst in through the window in raven form, catching Miranda with his claws. Shale leapt forward, crashing into Mother—they fell, rolling across the room.

I picked up a stone and threw it, striking the raven in the head. Alaric fell to the floor. Miranda wiped blood from her cheek. I ran for my mother, but Shale lifted one hand and curled it into a fist. I screamed in agony, cradling my injured hand—it felt as though he'd taken a hammer and crushed it.

Mother faltered—Shale pushed her hard against the wall, and her head cracked upon the stone. Quick as a whip, Shale grabbed Mother by the neck, squeezing hard. With his other hand, he pulled his knife and plunged it into my mother's stomach.

She shuddered, then fell limply to the floor.

No. No, no, no, no, no!

Something rustled behind me—the briars peeling away, retreating. Katen pulled herself free and came for me, grabbing my wrists. The touch of her fingers burned as she bound me with rope that materialized out of thin air. I couldn't muster the will to bat her away. I stared at my mother's body, unable to process what I was seeing.

"No!" Miranda threw herself at Shale, one long dagger in her hand. He struck her aside without even glancing at her. She flew across the room, head striking against the far wall, and lay still.

Someone was weeping loudly—was it me?

Shale stood up, his breathing labored. "Well," he said.

Mother had been right. The story was wrong. There was only blood left now. Mother was dead. She was dead, and it was my fault.

"You've done it," Katen replied. She stood up and kicked me in the back. I fell hard to the floor.

Call on me!

What use was that now? My mother was dead, and nothing mattered.

"No," Shale said, frowning. His eyes were on me. "The girl— she's forest spawn too. We kill *her*, and sever the hold of this forest once and for all."

It felt like a giant was squeezing my head—hard, unrelenting pressure that brought tears to my eyes and ringing to my ears. I couldn't make sense of what was happening.

Katen's knife was loose in her grip, but she wasn't looking at me. One moment she was there, and then I blinked, and the next she was across the room, her hand on her father's arm.

Shale screamed, a high-pitched whine that burst through my grief-stricken haze. His skin was blistering before my eyes, peeling and blackening. And then Katen raised her knife and plunged it into his heart.

Shale collapsed to the floor. "Daughter?" he said, almost too faintly for me to hear.

"Yes," Katen said, though her voice shook. "For all those years you made me kneel before you. You would have killed me, had I not hidden my magic." Her hand slipped down the blade, coming to rest on Shale's chest. Blood seeped up through his shirt, and when Katen lifted her hand, her voice had changed timbre. "Your power is now mine—"

Katen laughed, and it was an eerie sound. Her pupils widened, black spilling over the whites of her eyes. It was too much power for her, I realized.

A bird burst through the tower window, swiping at Katen with its claws. *Alaric.* No, not Alaric. A different raven—and then a second, and a third—and more, and more—the ravens of the Silence.

Katen cursed. Lightning crackled over her hand. She flicked one finger, and the lightning tore through the air, the scent of burning flesh following. The ravens fell. Blood trickled down her cheek, and she wiped it away with the back of her hand.

Those screams—

The memories of those dead boys washed through me, but I couldn't find it in myself to feel guilt. Did it matter, how I felt about them now? I was about to join them in death.

Katen snapped her fingers, and a charge jolted through my body. I saw a raven's body twitch, and then Alaric stood there in human form, looking dazed. He stared at the fallen ravens on the floor. Katen approached me, fire playing across her skin.

"It's time to return my magic, little Lena," she crooned.

Katen knelt beside me, pressing a knife against my neck. I could feel its point against my skin, hard enough to hurt—and then the wet drip of blood down my skin. I was dizzy now, light-headed from cold or shock or grief. I was going to die.

When Miranda had used Katen's power, she'd drawn it out of me like thread from a spool. This felt like ripping teeth from my mouth as Katen dragged the power out of me. I curled in on myself, mewling in pain.

Miranda was on the floor, one hand reaching for me, or was it a trick of the light? Miranda would never have been here at all, but for me. My mother. My family.

Give me your vow!

There was roaring darkness welling up around me, a savageness altogether different from the blood that Katen spilled, a gaping maw that left me with only one clear thought: *The wings.*

I forced my bound hands into my pocket, cold fingers clasping the box. Then I shifted, my vision blurring. Katen was laughing, her fingers swimming before my eyes, and there was fire running through my veins—

Slowly, slowly, I reached up and closed my fingers around her hand.

She looked down, almost surprised, as I took away my hand—wet with her blood—and pressed my fingers down upon the box.

The box shattered, coming apart in my bloody hands. Katen screamed and struck me across the face. I tasted blood—my vision began to flicker.

Katen lunged for the wings, but she was too slow. They flew up and away from her. Alaric transformed, his human body blurring into that of a raven. He dove at Katen, striking out at her with his claws. My eyes fluttered shut. A darkness pressed down upon my consciousness, demanding entrance.

Let me in.

I knew it for what it was. The Silence had lost my mother, and it wanted me. I'd tasted its power before, but now its entire weight was upon me, and I knew my mother had been right. If I let it in, I would be crushed. And if I did not, I would die.

But there was nothing left in me to care. There was no happiness, no hope, no sadness, even. All I had left was ... rage.

Rage for the small things—the gloves I'd been made to wear before I could even walk properly, the garden gate shut to keep me penned in, the yearning I'd felt each night I walked outside by myself. And rage for the larger injustices that ate at my heart—the lies my parents had told me every day of my life, the boys who had died by my hand, the truth of the curse, the role I had been made to play by power-hungry mages in an arena I'd never wanted. My mother's blood, spilled today on this ground. My own life force bleeding out.

Yes. I vow myself to you. Use me.

The spirit of the forest rushed into my body, and a smile crossed my lips that was not mine. I rose to my feet. This was raw *power* coursing through my veins, crackling at the edges of my fingertips. I had a brief moment of understanding Shale's madness before it burned through me, demanding to consume. I opened my mouth. I screamed it out.

The tower tipped with a deafening crack. We—the Silence and I—raised our hands and tore brambles up through the floor and sent them to wrap around Katen's body. The vines tightened as she struggled, tearing ruthlessly into her skin. We bared our teeth in triumph, raised our arms to the clouds, brought down the sky.

The world broke apart. The water surged across the forest, and we felt it rush through riverbeds long dry, filling lakes to bursting, washing the roads down to nothing. City walls cracked and groaned, and we were the water creeping up the streets of the

Gather, driving out the mages who had sought to conquer us.

Katen spat fire at us in desperation, and we caught it in our hand before dropping it to the floor, crushing it under our foot. She was weak, hanging limply from the brambles that held her suspended against the tower wall. Such folly to pour her power into an unknowing vessel, to hide her raven's wings away and believe that she could steal an empire. The time had come for her to fall.

We were still bleeding where Katen had cut us. We touched the wound and laughed, and licked the blood from our fingers. We snapped the briars from the wall and drove them through the witch's heart.

Deep within us was a voice that wept. We closed our fist around it and drove it further down. We did not weep. We were vengeful darkness and infinite rage, and we did not weep. We consumed, we tore, we wrenched trees apart and flooded our domain. We burned our rage into the earth, scorching out the blight that had festered here for too long, and it was not enough.

A whirling storm gathered outside and brought lightning down, casting fire into the trees. Above us a raven flew, the sole interruption in this sky. It circled the tower twice as we watched, then dove toward us, landing on the balcony.

We knew this one, the raven that had abandoned his own for harsh fellows and a black heart, the raven that had turned his back on us. Yet he folded his wings and plummeted into frail human form, and stood tall on the stone before us. Why had he come? Why had he not fled?

The raven held out his hands to us. "Lena."

We faltered. We had no name, not anymore—

"Lena, come back," the raven said. He took our hands between his. Something sparked within us, a half-remembered dream of standing before him on a sunny path, the warmth of his skin, the *realness* of him—but we were fire and death, and we did not weep—

Tears ran down our cheeks. We had power jumping from our skin ready to strike, but he . . . had captured my hands—no, no, *our* hands . . . and we—*I* could not speak through my swollen, tearful throat.

The raven brushed his thumbs over my scraped knuckles. Someone else drew me against her from behind, putting her arms around me.

"Lena, come back to us," a girl's voice said, and it was as though she lit a candle in the night, casting a glow within my darkness.

Miranda.

It took all that I had to remain upright as Miranda's warmth swept through me, coaxing me back to my body. *Cloak. Gloves. Net.* The anchors swam through my mind and were gone again—they were not what anchored me here. It was *Miranda* who had called me back. Miranda and Alaric. The crash of the Silence retreated, and I was left trembling, my clothes still drenched, my body still bloodied, my mother still . . .

Miranda pressed her forehead against mine, and I closed my eyes. "What happened?" I whispered.

Alaric answered, bruised and pale but standing taller than I'd ever seen before. "You gave me my wings, my freedom," he said.

"You saved us all, Lena," Miranda murmured.

Had I? My memory was washed out and indistinct, fragments of images jumping in and out of my mind. I looked around the room. Shale dead, his heart ripped from his chest. Katen's body ravaged by thorns. My mother motionless, her eyes vacant.

I sank to the floor. I wept, and wept, and wept.

CHAPTER THIRTY-FOUR

L ena, I'm so sorry." Miranda's arm was around my shoulders. I raised my head, an act that required almost more strength than I had. The Silence was still there, its spirit curling sleepily at the edges of my mind. The tower room had been torn apart, first by the battle, and then by the havoc I had wreaked with the forest's power. I could not look behind me—that was where Mother lay. There had been so much death, here, and in the Gather—and the Silence had reveled in it. *I* had reveled in it.

I thought about the blood mages I had seen. And then I thought about the children I'd met in the Gather—children who'd done nothing wrong except be unlucky. Were they all right? I had no way of knowing, but I feared the answer was no. The Silence had not cared who it struck and who it spared—and I did not believe it had spared more than a few. It had been sated, but its hunger for blood and death would always be there. And now I was tied to it forever. Katen was dead, the Hand of Mora lifted—but perhaps I had only traded one curse for another.

Miranda squeezed my hand so hard it hurt. My other hand was swollen and purpling, certainly broken.

"You've done it," Alaric said quietly. He was sitting motionless against the opposite wall. He'd been injured—I could see the bloom of blood against his shirt. But his color was all right, and as

I watched him, he smiled at me crookedly. "The legend. The sleeping princess will end the Gather if she wakes. She woke. And you ended it."

Miranda's gaze swung to Alaric and then to Shale's and Katen's bodies. "You're certain?"

"I am over one hundred years old," Alaric snapped, though there was only a little bite to his words. "Believe me when I tell you that I doubt there's a building left standing. The Gather cannot go on—especially not as people learn what happened. And . . . I owe you a great debt."

I was too tired to do more than nod. I dragged myself to my knees. Miranda and Alaric were on either side of me in an instant, helping me to my feet.

"I can walk by myself," I said, though it was a pitiful rejoinder in the face of my stumbling steps.

Still, they let go, and I walked with one hand on the wall for support, my breathing shallow, until I stood in front of Katen's body.

Her body still hung from the brambles, the thorns that had ended her life protruding through her chest. I reached out and touched the vine. We'd been more alike than I wanted to admit. She had walked in her father's shadow and had done everything she could to break free from it. All I'd ever wanted was to break free from my curse. And now . . . I'd bound myself to a new horrible fate.

Would the Silence take her body too, and plant it below with the rest of them? What would it want, when it became hungry again?

I had tried so hard not to look at my mother's body. But now I couldn't help it. I went to her, dropping to my knees at her side.

I had done this. If only I had stayed away, if only I had left the Silence well enough alone—she would have been alive.

"*Lena.*"

I looked up to see Father standing in the tower door. He barely glanced at Alaric and Miranda—instead he limped across the room and sank down to the floor beside me. His arm went around my shoulders, holding me tightly against him.

And then he saw my mother's body.

Shock crossed his face, and then grief—and then resolve. He let go of me and leaned over her body, putting his ear just above her mouth. Then he sat back and looked around the room, his gaze zeroing in on the fallen statue. "The statue. Bring me the flowers."

There was movement behind me, and then Miranda appeared, pushing stone petals into my hands.

"I have them," I said, my voice shaking.

"When I tell you, place the petals over the wound."

I held my breath, waiting.

Father wrapped his fingers around the hilt of the knife and pulled it from her stomach. Blood welled up from the wound as he drew it out. "Now!" he said.

I spread the petals over her stomach. Blood pooled around them—and then, slowly, the petals sank into the wound, knitting together with her torn flesh. The wound shrank, then closed. A seam of dark stone ran along my mother's skin where the petals had lain—just where Shale had stabbed her.

I looked anxiously at her face. I didn't know what my father had done, but I hoped—I *hoped*—

Her eyelids fluttered.

I found my father's hand and held it as tightly as I could.

Her chest moved, just barely.

And then, after what seemed an eternity, she opened her eyes.

She looked at me . . . and then her gaze fell on Father, and she began to cry.

"Edina," Father said softly. He dropped my hand and gathered her in his arms so, so gently.

I rose to my feet and backed away as they embraced.

"Wait, Lena." Mother pushed herself up, her eyes wide as she took in the aftermath of the battle. "Oh, Lena," she whispered, as she saw the vines. "You promised you wouldn't."

But what else could I have done? "You were dead," I said, my voice cracking with emotion. "I had to."

She began to cry. "All I wanted was to spare you this."

"It was the only way," I insisted, even as anger spiked within me. I could feel the Silence still in my mind, a voice that didn't quite belong. But what other choice had there been? "Mother, it will be all right."

"No," she said. "No, you are going to leave this place." She pushed Father away, struggling to her feet. "As long as I live I will be here. The Silence needs only one elder. It cannot have us both, not yet."

"Edina, please—sit down," Father said.

She looked at him, her expression softening. "No. She is young. She has the entire world to see. She has to go."

I could feel the sorrow in her voice, and the anger. I knew how much it cost her to say that. I knew how much she had wanted to escape this place, this fate.

"Mother, leaving the Silence behind was your dream," I said. "It's not mine."

"You don't know what you're saying," she said weakly.

"I know that I have earned the right to make my own decisions," I replied.

I hadn't forgiven them. I knew that much. There was still a deep well of anger within me at the depth of the lies that my parents had told, the missteps they'd made. But at the same time, I understood why they had done it. And I knew that for my mother to offer this, to stay here in the place that had been her prison, cost her far more than she would admit. But she would do it—for me.

"I took on the Silence willingly," I said. "And—and I know you were alone with it for so long. But you aren't alone anymore."

Father caught her as she started to fall. He looked at me, tears shining in his eyes. "You have done well, child," he said, his voice gruff. He looked down at Mother. "Best leave us be, for now. She needs rest."

I bit my lip, unsure. I desperately wanted to reassure my mother, to tell her that the Silence was so much more than the evil she believed it to be. That I had not just traded one master for another. That I had chosen my own fate, and I did not regret it.

Mother gave me a weak smile. "There will be more time for us to talk," she whispered. "I promise."

Miranda touched my elbow gently. "Come," she said. She held out a hand. I couldn't remember what hands were meant to do. "Walk with me."

Alaric came to my other side as I turned around, endlessly weary.

And so I left my parents in the castle of briars and descended the stairway hand in hand with a raven and a mage.

The Silence hissed in my mind—it still hated Alaric. I took great pleasure in ignoring it.

We made our way down the stairs. I allowed Miranda to place my hand on her sleeve as we walked, stopping in the gardens. My fingers were cold—everything was cold. I couldn't stop shivering, but Miranda's face was warm.

There was a snuffling sound, and I looked down to find the dragon splayed contentedly on the ground in the corner.

"You're all right!" I cried. I was seized by the urge to hug them but held myself back.

The dragon rolled onto their belly, their lips spreading in a toothy grin. "I'm going to grow so *large*," they said. "This has been such a feast. Thank you for inviting me."

"I am glad," I said. I nodded to them politely, though their words sent a shiver down my spine. I knew I'd come away lucky, extending an unconditional invitation to such a being.

Miranda stared at me as Alaric led us to an emptier section of the gardens. "You never told me where you met a *dragon*," she said.

I laughed. "So you don't balk at the Hand of Mora, or merfolk attacking you, or the *Silence*, but dragons? *That* is what frightens you?"

She blushed. "I can't help it—they scare me."

After seeing this dragon in action, I couldn't blame her.

"I want to find Callie," she said after a moment. "If she's still there—her body."

I sighed. "We should seek out Rin, too, and see what's become of the Gather. And Haven. They will need our help. But after that . . . I don't know."

Alaric smiled. In his smile I could see the desire for clear sky, the rush of wind under wings, the satisfying fatigue of miles traveled. "You can do anything you want. The Silence will wait."

"But you saw what happened." I circled one hand in the air. "I made the vow."

Alaric tucked his hands into his pockets, looking up at the sky. "If you want to be free of the Silence, I will try to help you. I know its ways. I don't know where you plan to go, but there's nothing left for me here. My family cast me out long ago."

I nodded. I'd spent so long resisting this bargain. But now that I was here . . . Tendrils of new growth sprouted from the earth, opening into a flurry of small white flowers. I was ready for this, I thought. I *would* leave, as my mother wished. But eventually, I would return. The Silence belonged to me, just as much as I belonged to it.

"Will you come with me?" I asked Miranda.

She took my hand, interlacing her fingers with mine. I smiled, grateful for this touch. I would never take this for granted.

She raised an eyebrow at me. "Where to?"

I squeezed her hand and grinned. "I know you're scared of dragons, but . . . I did promise them a story. Still want to come?"

Miranda sighed and shook her head even as a smile broke out across her face. "Like I have a choice." She pulled me in close and kissed me.

I kissed her back, beaming against her lips. After everything that had happened, everything I had lost and gained, I was still here. I had spent so many years believing myself to be at the end of things. How thrilling it was to realize that this was only the beginning.

ACKNOWLEDGMENTS

I started writing *Briar Girls* in 2013 while enrolled in the Simmons College MFA Program in Writing for Children. Eight years later, it is impossible to thank everyone who has had a hand in shaping this book, but muddle through I must (with apologies to those I inevitably overlook).

A million thanks to the two superstars in this publishing journey with me—Rebecca Podos, who believed in *Briar Girls* for almost as long as I did; and Catherine Laudone, who helped make this book shine brighter than I ever dreamed it could.

Thank you to the entire Simon & Schuster BFYR team, including Brian Luster, Marinda Valenti, Hilary Zarycky, Emily Ritter, Morgan York, Sara Berko, Milena Giunco, and Emily Hutton. Special thanks to Sarah Creech and Leo Nickolls, who created the cover of my dreams.

Thank you to early readers of *Briar Girls*, including Clarissa Hadge, Greg Batcheler, Heather Goss, Kate Mikell, Mackenzi Lee, Kat Howard, Lindsay Eagar, and Keena Roberts. (Special thanks to Keena for naming Fallyne!)

Thank you, thank you, thank you to the booksellers who have read and championed my books, including (but by no means limited to) Abby Rice, April Poole, Nichole Cousins, Nicole Brinkley, Leila Meglio, Sinny Sam, Sami Thomason-Fyke, Paul Swydan, Casey Leidig, Chris Abouzeid, Tildy Lutts, Stephanie Heinz, Abby Rauscher, Katherine Nazzaro, and Mike Lasagna.

Thank you to the fellow authors who have been overwhelmingly kind and generous with their wisdom and time, including

Kate Elliott, Lindsay Eagar, Tessa Gratton, Dahlia Adler, and Maggie Tokuda-Hall.

Thank you to every reader who has picked up one of my books. I get to do this because of you, and I am so happy to do so.

Briar Girls was sold, drafted, revised, and completed during a pandemic year, one of the most difficult of my life. Thank you to the people who made this year better, including Darcy, Siân, Candace, Greg, Heather, Clarissa, Kate, Abby, Abby, Nichole, Nicole, and Stephanie.

Thank you as always to my family, without whom I would not be who I am. And to Martin, who was there from (almost) the beginning.